Praise for the Previous Mysteries of
Daryl Wood Gerber

On the Cookbook Nook Mystery series:

FINAL SENTENCE

"With a bodacious cast of characters, a wrenching murder, and a collection of cookbooks to die for, Daryl Wood Gerber's *Final Sentence* is a page-turning puzzler of a mystery that I could not put down."
—Jenn McKinlay, *New York Times* bestselling author of the Cupcake Mysteries and Library Lovers Mysteries

"In *Final Sentence*, the author smartly blends crime, recipes, and an array of cookbooks that all should covet in a witty, well-plotted whodunit."
—Kate Carlisle, *New York Times* bestselling author of the Bibliophile Mysteries

On the French Bistro Mystery series:

A SOUFFLE OF SUSPICION

"Gerber ticks all the boxes for a successful cozy: a capable protagonist, intelligent dialogue, a fine sense of place, eccentric yet plausible suspects, and clues galore."
—*Publishers Weekly*

"[Gerber] creates colorful, enjoyable characters. . . . One word of warning: her descriptions of the food and wine pairings are so very vivid and realistic that readers should not be hungry when they read this mystery."
—*Booklist*

"A sweet treat with dazzling characters, a sleuth full of charm, and blossoming romance."
—*Seattle Book Review*

"Just as delicious as the first . . . When it comes to the word 'appetizing' you automatically think of food. But when it comes to the literary scene, this series is well beyond appetizing. Not only are the foods incredible, but the characters and plot are equally superb."
—*Suspense Magazine*

A DEADLY ÉCLAIR

"*A Deadly Éclair* has everything a good cozy mystery needs: charming and off the wall characters, a unique setting, and a mystery in need of solving! Although this is my first novel by the author, it definitely won't be my last."
—*San Francisco Review of Books*

"*A Deadly Éclair* is like having dinner with old friends. It has the laughter, the stories, the fun, and the good food all in one cozy."
—BB Haywood, *New York Times* bestselling author of the Candy Holliday mysteries

A
Sprinkling
of Murder

Daryl Wood Gerber

KENSINGTON BOOKS
www.kensingtonbooks.com

KENSINGTON BOOKS are published by

Kensington Publishing Corp.
119 West 40th Street
New York, NY 10018

All Kensington titles, imprints, and distributed lines are available at special quantity discounts for bulk purchases for sales promotion, premiums, fundraising, educational, or institutional use.

Special book excerpts or customized printings can also be created to fit specific needs. For details, write or phone the office of the Kensington Sales Manager: Kensington Publishing Corp., 119 West 40th Street, New York, NY 10018. Attn. Sales Department. Phone: 1-800-221-2647.

Kensington and the K logo Reg. U.S. Pat. & TM Off.

ISBN-13: 978-1-4967-2635-3 (ebook)
ISBN-10: 1-4967-2635-9 (ebook)

ISBN-13: 978-1-4967-2634-6
ISBN-10: 1-4967-2634-0
First Kensington Trade Paperback Printing: July 2020

10 9 8 7 6 5 4 3 2 1

Printed in the United States of America

Thank you, Nancy Drew, for being such a wonderful protagonist. You made me love to read.

Acknowledgments

We shall not cease from exploration / And the end of all our exploring / Will be to arrive where we started / And know the place for the first time.
—T. S. Eliot

I have been truly blessed to have the support and input of so many as I pursue my creative journey.

Thank you to my family and friends for all your encouragement. Thank you to my talented author friends, Krista Davis and Hannah Dennison, for your words of wisdom. Thank you to my Plothatcher pals: Janet (Ginger Bolton), Kaye George, Marilyn Levinson (Allison Brook), Peg Cochran, and Janet Koch (Laura Alden), and Krista Davis. It's hard to keep all your aliases straight, but you are a wonderful pool of talent and a terrific wealth of ideas, jokes, stories, and fun! I adore you. Thanks to my blog mates on Mystery Lovers Kitchen: Cleo Coyle, Krista Davis, Leslie Budewitz, Roberta Isleib (Lucy Burdette), Peg Cochran, Linda Wiken (Essie Lang), Denise Swanson, and Sheila Connolly. I love your passion for food as well as for books. Thanks to my Cake and Dagger and Delicious Mystery author pals, Julie Hyzy, Jenn McKinlay, Roberta Isleib, Krista Davis, and Amanda Flower. I treasure your creative enthusiasm via social media.

Thank you to Facebook fan-based groups, Cake and Daggers and Delicious Mysteries. I love how willing you are to read advanced copies, post reviews, and help me as well as numerous other authors promote whenever possible. We need fans like you.

Thanks to those who have helped make this first book in the *Fairy Garden Mystery* series come to fruition: my publisher, Kensington; my editor, Wendy McCurdy; my copy editor, Debra Kane; my agent, John Talbot; my cover artist, Elsa Kerls; and my biggest supporter, Kimberley Greene. Thanks to Madeira James for maintaining constant quality on my website. Thanks to my virtual assistants, Sheridan Stancliff and Marie McNary, for your novel ideas. Honestly, without all of you, I don't know what I would do. Fly off to Neverland? You keep me grounded.

Thank you to Chief Paul Tomasi of the Carmel Police Department for answering all my questions. Any mistakes as to police department procedure are my own. Thank you to Beverly Turner, though we have yet to meet. Your book *Fairy Gardening* has been a true inspiration to me. Your instructional videos are amazing.

Last but not least, thank you, librarians, teachers, and readers, for sharing the delicious world of a fairy garden designer in Carmel-by-the-Sea with your friends. I hope you enjoy the first of what will become many stories.

CAST OF CHARACTERS
(listed alphabetically by first name)

Humans

Bianca, trail guide
Brady Cash, owner of Hideaway Café
Courtney Kelly, owner of Open Your Imagination
Dylan Summers, detective, Carmel Police Department
Emily Watkins, wife of Mick Watkins
Eudora Cash, romance author
Glinda Gill, owner of Glitz Jewelers
Gregory Darvell, dog trainer
Gus, a security guy working for Kipling Kelly
Hattie Hopewell, Happy Diggers garden club chair
Hedda Hopewell, loan officer
Holly Hopewell, cottage landlord and neighbor
Isabella Acosta, owner of Acosta Artworks
Joss Timberlake, assistant at Open Your Imagination
Kipling "Kip" Kelly, Courtney's father, landscaper
Lauren, a young customer
Logan Langford, landlord of Cypress and Ivy Courtyard
Meaghan Brownie, harpist, half owner of Flair Gallery
Mick Watkins, owner of Wizard of Paws grooming salon
Miranda Watkins, Mick's sister
Miss Reade, librarian
Oriana Gray, inn owner and councilwoman
Pastor Li, pastor at the congregational church
Petra Pauli, councilwoman
Rodriguez, female police officer, Carmel Police Department
Sonja Schmidt, assistant at Wizard of Paws

Tish Waterman, owner of A Peaceful Solution Spa
Ulani Kamaka, reporter for the *Carmel Pine Cone*
Victoria Judge, attorney
Wright Youngman, attorney
Yvanna Acebo, employee at Sweet Treats, weekend baker for
   Open Your Imagination

Fairies and Pets

Cocoa, Isabella's poodle
Fiona, a righteous fairy
Merryweather Rose of Song, guardian fairy
Paint, a trail horse
Pixie, Courtney's Ragdoll kitten
Shep, Mick and Emily Watkins's German shepherd
Zephyr, a nurturer fairy
Zeus, Petra's collie

Chapter 1

Do you believe in fairies? If you do, clap your hands!
—J. M. Barrie, *Peter Pan*

"Do you see her? Is she down there?" I tried not to let my five-year-old customer hear the panic in my voice. Of course Fiona was down there. She wouldn't have flown the coop. Okay, she was mad at me for telling her to make herself scarce, but honestly! "Look hard," I said.

After a breathless moment, the curly-haired girl—Lauren—who was peering into a huge strawberry terra-cotta planter, popped upright, and spun in a circle. "Yes, I do, Miss Kelly. I see her."

Once upon a time, when I was five, I'd danced among the flowers and twirled to my heart's content, too.

"Call me Courtney," I reminded her. Children who came into Open Your Imagination, my fairy garden and tea shop, didn't have to be formal. The more familiar, the more fun. "And keep your voice soft. You don't want to scare her."

"Courtney," she said. "I do see her. I really do."

"What does she look like?"

"She's . . . she's . . ." Lauren wiggled nervously as if I'd really put her on the spot.

I'd felt the same when I saw my first fairy. A week after my mother planted a fanciful garden filled with yarrow, lilac, and a host of herbs to attract butterflies, I met her. I had been dressed in something similar to what I was wearing now, denim overalls, a lacy shirt, and a gardening apron. She had been as pretty as the sunrise.

Lauren waved her arms. "She's green and silver and blue and . . . and . . ."

"Go on," I encouraged. I hadn't wanted to trust my eyes, either, but my mother had told me to *believe*. Meadows, rivers, and mountains, she said, were alive with spiritual beings who would give a helping hand to those who asked nicely. I stroked the silver locket that held my mother's portrait. She'd given me the locket that Christmas. An image of a fairy was etched into the lid. The word *Believe* was engraved on the underside.

"Mommy," Lauren called.

She and I were standing on the slate patio, a roofed outdoor garden space. Her mother was sitting at one of the many wrought-iron tables. She smiled indulgently and whisked her hand, encouraging her daughter to speak. Muted sunlight filtered through the skylight in the pyramid-shaped roof. The ornate fountain carved with fairies and gnomes burbled in the background. A number of customers browsed fairy figurines on the verdigris bakers' racks and spoke in hushed tones. A few others chatted about how pretty they thought the twinkling lights were that we'd woven through the vines and the potted ficus trees. A cluster of women was checking out the miniature Pink Splash hypoestes plants and golden Monterey cypress we had in stock.

"Tell me about her wings," I prompted.

"They're teensy," Lauren chimed.

I noticed a lot of activity inside the main showroom, the French doors and beveled casement windows of the L-shaped space providing a full view from where we stood. One woman was scrawling her name on the sign-up sheet for the upcoming tea. We didn't serve tea every day, only on Saturdays. So far, the response for this week's tea had been tremendous because we'd decided to pair it with a book club event. We were going to discuss *The Secret, Book and Scone Society*. Scones and tea . . . a perfect fit.

"And her dress?" I asked.

Lauren twirled in place, her tresses fanning out. "It's silver and looks like my ballet dress." She grabbed the seams of her pink tutu.

"So her dress is lacy?" I asked.

Lauren bobbed her head. "And she has blue hair and sparkly silver shoes, and she glows."

"That's Fiona," I said. Her *hair* was actually gossamer and caught the light, much like a prism or the lens of a camera. At certain angles, her hair could become a variety of other colors.

Lauren stopped moving and splayed her arms. "Why are her wings so small? She can't fly with those."

"She's able to fly but not long distances. She has to earn three sets of adult wings first, in addition to her current pair."

"How will she earn them?"

"By . . ." I tapped my chin. How could I explain it?

Fiona, for all intents and purposes, was a fairy-in-training. She should have been a full-fledged fairy by now, but imp that she was, she'd done one too many pranks in fairy school, so the queen fairy had booted her out and subjected her to probation, during which time Fiona had to get serious. By helping a human, she could earn her way back into the ranks.

"Courtney, yoo-hoo." Lauren touched my arm. "How will she do it?"

"By doing good deeds," I replied.

"Everyone should do good deeds," Lauren said matter-of-factly.

"Yes, they should." And not pranks like putting syrup in my tea as Fiona had done earlier. I'd warned her that the queen fairy would frown on her antics.

Months ago, when I'd pressed Fiona for details of her banishment, she had been vague. One major restriction was that she could not have fairy friends. Though more fairies existed in Carmel, she wasn't to socialize with them. Yet.

"How did you meet her?" Lauren asked.

"She came to me the day after I opened this shop."

"Like magic?"

"Yes, like magic."

After Fiona had told me about her predicament, I'd asked her if the queen fairy was a horrible, wicked fairy, and she'd blushed. *No,* she'd said. The queen was the most wonderful fairy in the whole world. When I grilled her for more information—like were other fairies on probation?—Fiona had dodged the question and instead educated me about her kind. In addition to types of fairies, like air fairies and water fairies, there were four classes of fairies: intuitive, righteous, guardian, and nurturer. Fiona was a righteous fairy, which meant she needed to bring resolution to embattled souls. Of course, there were rules in the fairy world. A righteous fairy couldn't intentionally put herself in harm's way.

"Have you always seen fairies?" Lauren asked.

"No."

At the tender age of ten, when my mother died, I had lost my ability to see them. No matter how hard I tried, no matter how much I rubbed the locket my mother had given me, I couldn't see another. In the ensuing years, I grew serious. In high school, I studied hard to make my father proud. In college, I turned my attention to chemistry and earth sciences. After graduation, I joined my father's thriving landscaping outfit in Carmel-by-the-Sea and dedicated myself to working the land: *dig, plant, don't have fun, repeat.*

Until a year ago when Fiona appeared. At first I saw a sparkle and heard a *tinkle* and a *ping.* And then delightful laughter. She had flitted from behind a pot and introduced herself with a curtsy. When I found my wits, I asked why she would reveal herself to me. She explained that although the sorrow over the loss of my mother had squelched my ability as a girl to see fairies, it was my nose-to-the-grindstone attitude toward life that had continued to suppress me. When I made the decision at the ripe old age of twenty-nine to spread my wings and start a fairy garden business, *voilà.* My heart opened, and Fiona swooped in. She hoped she could save me so I could save her.

"There she goes." Lauren pointed.

A flicker of light shot from a pocket of the strawberry planter and disappeared in the vines by one of the French doors. Fiona. Still miffed. Tough. If we were going to remain friends, she would have to follow my rules: *no shenanigans.* I wondered if the queen fairy had given her the same guidelines.

"Can she come to my house?" Lauren asked.

"Sorry. No."

Fairies had few boundaries, so Fiona could leave the shop and cruise around Carmel, but I didn't want every new believer thinking Fiona might drop in for a visit. Besides, as of this morning, Fiona had wanted to remain close to me. She'd told me she feared something extraordinary or tragic might happen. *To me?* I'd asked. She wasn't sure, but she wanted to remain *at the ready*. Needless to say, I'd been on pins and needles ever since her pronouncement. I didn't mind an extraordinary occurrence, like meeting a fairy, but a tragic one? Like my mother dying? No thanks.

Knowing she'd worried me, Fiona had played a trick to lighten the mood—the syrup. I'd snapped at her. She'd bolted.

Lauren pressed her face to the top of the planter, probably hoping Fiona would return, and said, "How old were you when you saw your first fairy?" Her words reverberated in the empty pot.

"Your age."

"Was it in the last week of April, like now?"

"It was the first week in June." I fingered the short-cropped hair at the nape of my neck as the memory came back to me full force.

"Was it here in Carmel?"

"Yes." I'd lived in Carmel-by-the-Sea all my life, except when I went away to college. How I loved living here. The town was charming and magical and bursting with positive energy.

Lauren stood up, her eyes wide. "Was it Fiona?"

"No, sweet pea. Another fairy. Her name was Aurora." Like my mother, Aurora had a cheery disposition and had loved the color yellow and the aroma of honey.

"Is Aurora the one who taught you how to make fairy gardens?" Lauren asked.

"No. I learned from a woman at the Renaissance Fair."

My best friend had encouraged me to step outside my comfort zone and attend a Renaissance Fair—in costume. While there, dressed as an enchantress, I had met a fairy garden designer. I was so enraptured with the whimsical creations, I begged the woman to teach me the art. As I learned to design gardens, the woman gave me tips on how to attract fairies. I remembered laughing at the notion. My childhood memories of playing with fairies were fanciful and foolish. And yet . . . how I'd wanted to believe again. Following my mentor's advice, I had planted a garden of flowers and herbs that would attract butterflies. I set up bird feeders, filled bird-baths with water, and hung crystals from the trees. As a feeling of spiritual wellness rose within me, I had realized I needed to change my life. I gave notice to my father and with a small fund my nana had left me—she had helped my father and me cope with our loss until she passed away at eighty—I had invested in Open Your Imagination.

Lauren's forehead pinched with concentration. "What's a Ren-sen Fair?"

"*Renaissance.*" I adjusted the strap of my floral-print garden apron. I'd added an extra pair of pruning shears in one of the multifunctional pockets, and the extra weight was pulling it down. "It's a fair where—"

"All right, Lauren. Time to go." The girl's mother clapped her hands.

Startled, Pixie, my creamy white Ragdoll kitten bounded from her perch on one of the wrought-iron chairs and dashed to me. She swiped me with her tail. I bent down and scratched her chin. "You're okay." She was nearly six months old. "Don't be a scaredy cat."

Pixie sat on her haunches and squinted, which made the flame markings on her forehead meld together.

I ran a finger across them. "You'd better get used to noise. There's going to be a lot of it whenever children visit us. Scoot." I nudged her, and she scurried off.

"C'mon, little lady," Lauren's mother said. She waggled the white basket in which they'd stowed their fairy garden choices. "Let's purchase the things we've picked out and head home."

At Open Your Imagination, I made fairy gardens and taught people how to build them. At the learning-the-craft corner of the patio, an area at the far right of the patio set with a modest-sized rectangular table fitted with benches, a couple of customers who had taken this morning's instructional class were still working on theirs. In addition to fairy figurines, I sold a variety of items that customers could use to create their own environments—waterwheels, gazebos, and the like. For a bit of whimsy, I'd stocked the main showroom with items for people, too, like tea sets and an assortment of garden knick-knacks, macramé hanging plant holders and wind chimes and bells—according to Fiona, fairies loved tinkling sounds. We also carried miniature plants, pots, tool sets, and aprons. Although Open Your Imagination was modest in size, we offered plenty of choices.

Lauren grabbed my hand. "Come with us, Courtney. I'll show you the fairy I picked out. She has my name."

Many of the miniature fairies, gnomes, or trolls that we sold had a name. If we didn't stock a particular name, we could special order it. And, honestly, anyone could change a fairy's name. They weren't written in stone.

"She has beautiful brown hair like mine, and a crown of flowers, and she's sitting like this." Lauren plopped onto the ground, crossed her legs, and rested her chin on her fist.

"I know, sweetheart," I said. "I helped you find her. Remember? Along with the swing set and the slide and the bunnies." Every fairy garden should have a theme. Lauren wanted hers to be about having fun, day and night.

Her mother bit back a smile and hoisted her daughter to her feet. "Upsy-daisy."

I followed them through the French doors into the shop.

"*Psst.*" Joss Timberlake, my elfin clerk and bookkeeper

who had a penchant for really colorful shirts, like the short-sleeved fuchsia Hawaiian one she was wearing, beckoned me to the sales counter. "He's here."

"He, who?" I was five feet five inches tall, but I towered over Joss. I had to crouch to hear her.

"Him." Joss caressed the ridge of her pointy ear and subtly hooked a thumb toward the front door.

Mick Watkins, who owned Wizard of Paws, the pet-grooming salon across the courtyard, was standing inside the Dutch door. There were additional businesses in the Cypress and Ivy Courtyard, including an art gallery, a bakery, a jeweler, a high-end clothing shop, and a collectibles store. If Carmel was known for one thing, it was its attractive courtyards and secret passageways. Our courtyard, which was multilevel and located between Lincoln Street and Dolores Street, with Open Your Imagination facing Lincoln, had been designed with a Cape Cod feel, its white clapboard buildings trimmed in baby blue and adorned with lots of plantings. The design was one of the main reasons I'd wanted to lease the property.

"What do you think he wants?" I asked Joss.

"Trouble."

I didn't know what I'd do without Joss. I was so thankful that on her fiftieth birthday she'd decided to seek a simpler life and had left her Silicon Valley accounting job. She was a whiz when it came to organizing the stockroom or balancing accounts and a decent person who cared about others, although occasionally, she could make snap decisions about a personality.

I said, "I've got this. Would you ring up this purchase for this sweet girl and her mom while I tend to Mick?"

"After I finish this sale." Joss was packing up an eight-inch pot, a small bag of soil, six two-inch containers of miniature plants, and a flute-playing, rose-colored fairy. Small-scale projects were often the first gardens that customers who were new to fairy gardening attempted.

I tapped Lauren on her freckled nose. "Good luck, young lady. Have fun making your garden, and, when you're done, encourage your friends to believe."

"I will."

Slapping on a winning smile, I crossed the parquet floor to greet Mick, a chunky man with a barrel chest, bulldog jowls, and thick brown hair.

"Hey, Mick." I jutted a hand. "Nice to see you."

Mick grunted, which made me bite back a smile. Over the past year, he had been vocally unhappy that I'd landed this particular lease. He'd hoped to expand across the courtyard, but our landlord had nixed the idea. One grooming establishment was enough, no matter how dog-friendly Carmel was.

Mick rubbed his jeans as though he were itching to respond to my offer of a handshake. I saw a flicker of light beyond him. Was Fiona toying with him? Had she given up being annoyed with me? Pixie, her whiskers twitching with curiosity, lingered behind Mick, too. She adored Fiona and often played chase with her.

"Can I help you find something, Mick?" I asked.

"Nope." He had a booming voice. I suspected his barrel chest had something to do with its tenor. "I came in to tell you that Logan Langford's on the warpath. He wants to renege on my lease."

"Did he say why?"

"Ha! A mute has a larger vocabulary. But watch out. Next thing you know, he'll be coming after you."

"Thanks for the heads up." I wasn't worried. Our landlord had completely embraced the concept of the shop. He intended to create a fairy garden for each of his eleven grandchildren because he had loved the novel *Peter Pan* as a child.

Seeing as he hadn't started the first garden, I was pretty certain I could count on a longer lease. "Anything else?"

"That's all." Mick stole to the right wing of the shop and peeked in. Was he looking for someone? Was that really why he'd come in? He checked his watch and, peeved, charged toward the exit.

The upper half of the Dutch door was ajar, allowing a cool breeze to enter the shop. Carmel was blessed with Mediterranean-style temperatures, although intermittently fog drifted in. Not today. Mick opened the door and closed it with a *thwump*.

I returned to the sales counter.

"Whewie," Joss said as she wiped the weathered white oak surface with a cloth. "He's sure not the guy you'd crown Mr. Personality, and here I believed he had a chance. Yesterday when he came in, he was all smiles."

"He came in yesterday?"

"With Petra Pauli."

"Councilwoman Pauli?"

During college, although I'd focused primarily on my landscape architecture degree, taking urban design, site construction, computer applications, and so many chemistry classes I could have become a chemist, I'd also enrolled in a load of history classes. California history, in particular. Over the years, I'd enjoyed reading up on Carmel and knew the sagas of many of the original families. Petra Pauli's father had been an Olympic pole-vaulter and went on to become a US congressman. Like her father, Petra had excelled at everything—cheerleading, debate team, academics. There wasn't a blot on her record. It was obvious that she aspired to greater things than simply remaining a councilwoman. My guess? Mayor of our fine town followed by governor of the state.

"The councilwoman is a piece of work." Joss brushed the underside of her nose.

"Yes, she can be a bit snooty."

The city council had enacted a number of quirky rules over the years. One of my favorites was not being allowed to wear high heels without a permit. To be fair, that rule was prudent because a person in heels could trip on the cobble-stoned walkways in town and suffer a sprained ankle. To make her voice known, Petra had added a few eccentric rules of her own, like banning silly string—that gooey stuff kids like to shoot at one another—in public.

"You were on an errand when they came in," Joss went on.

"How do they know each other?" I asked.

"Mick grooms Miss Pauli's collies. Hey, that rhymes. Fiona!" Joss called. "I made a rhyme." Fairies loved rhymes and all sorts of poetry. "Where is she?"

"Around."

Years ago, Joss had traveled to Ireland on a fairy tour to romp with fairies at dawn. In Kerry, she'd explored wood-lands. In Killarney, she'd walked the fairy trail. And in Dublin, she'd visited the leprechaun museum. But it wasn't until she encountered Fiona that she'd really experienced the magic.

"Back to Mick," I said.

"Supposedly, he wanted to show Miss Pauli the shop." Joss rolled her big brown eyes. Was she intimating that there was more to their relationship? "FYI, he raved about you and Open Your Imagination. He said we needed more creative thinkers in town."

"Well, I'll be darned."

Was Fiona working her magic on Mick? Any fairy, even a young righteous fairy, could influence a person. I searched for her but didn't see her in the main showroom. Out of the cor-ner of my eye, I spied Pixie on the patio dancing on her hind legs trying to bat a shimmering wisp with her forepaws—Fiona.

A few minutes later, as I was rearranging fairy-themed greeting cards on the revolving rack, the front door opened again and in strode Mick's wife, Emily.

"Where is he?" she demanded.

"Who?" I slotted the last grouping of cards in a bracket.

"My husband, who else? I saw him come in here."

Prior to today, Emily hadn't ever spoken to me. I'd tried starting up a conversation or two, but she'd snubbed me each time. She had never deigned to enter Open Your Imagination, either. With her long mane of hair, buckteeth, and flared nostrils, she reminded me of an angry bronco. Even her voice had a nasal quality. I bit back a snicker as I caught my unintentional pun—nasal/*neigh-sal*. A horse's whinny echoed in my mind. I blamed my father for my mental lack of decorum. He'd taught me how to pun. Perhaps I should add *no more puns* to my ways-to-improve-myself list, I mused. The list was getting long, but I could manage one or two more goals.

Emily sidled toward the left wing of the shop, running her finger along the shelving as she went as if she were inspecting whether we dusted or not. We did. Daily.

I strode to her, hand extended. "Emily, I'm so pleased to meet you finally. I'm Courtney."

"I know who you are."

"Mick has said nice things about you."

"He has?" Her mouth fell open, as though she couldn't believe it. Self-consciously, she buttoned her beige cardigan and adjusted the hem of the sweater over her tan trousers.

"Mm-hm," I murmured. Over the past year, in an effort to tamp down Mick's displeasure with my scoring the lease on this location, I'd escorted a few dog-owner customers into his shop to promote his business. "On a number of occasions, I've heard him tell his clients how good you are with your German shepherd."

"Shep."

"Yes, Shep."

"Is Mick here?"

"He was, but he left. Did you check Wizard of Paws?"

"Of course I did. Do you think I'm an idiot?"

No, but you are a tad caustic. I forced a smile. "Do you like tea, Emily? We're serving high tea on weekends now. Our chef is an expert with muffins and scones, and you've simply got to taste the Brie and strawberry tea sandwiches."

"I drink coffee."

"We serve coffee, too. A variety of blends. Have you seen the porcelain cups we sell? Coffee always tastes better in a beautiful cup, don't you think?" I gestured to the antique white oak hutch that displayed a host of cups and saucers. The Cape Cod exterior of the building had set the standard for the interior décor. White display tables. White shelving. A stylish splash of blue and slate gray for color. "If you have grandchildren, they might like the miniature red rose set—"

"No grandchildren. No children." A pained look crossed her face.

"I'm sorry."

An awkward moment passed between us.

I broke the silence by saying, "Your dog Shep sure is a beauty. Mick said you've trained him to do agility courses. Are you considering putting him in competition?"

"No. Not at this time. Mick is against it."

"Agility training is quite a challenge. You must be very talented."

"It's not hard if the dog is gifted." She folded her arms and set her jaw. Ice floes could be warmer.

Realizing I wouldn't be able to melt this one, I said, "Well, feel free to take a look around. If there's something I can help you with, let me—"

"Did he meet *her* here?" Emily hissed. The venom in her tone took me aback.

"Meet who . . . whom?" I stammered. Was it *who* or *whom*? English hadn't been my favorite subject.

"His lover," she said. "If he did, I'll . . . I'll . . ." Emily jammed a fist into her palm. She didn't have to say *kill him*. Her eyes said it all.

Chapter 2

Hand in hand, with fairy grace, will we sing, and bless this place.
—William Shakespeare, *A Midsummer Night's Dream*

Fiona darted into the shop and fluttered beyond Emily's shoulder. She threw her skinny arms wide, her young wings flapping like crazy to keep her aloft, and cried, "Trouble alert. Trouble alert. I told you to be worried."

Sparklers flashed in her wings. I knew she practiced photokinesis, doing tricks with light like humans did when aiming lasers and such. Was this sparkly-wing thing photokinesis or something new? Would the queen fairy approve or disapprove?

"Emily Watkins is danger," Fiona said.

"I'm on it," I whispered. "Don't worry." Emily couldn't hear Fiona, but I didn't want to speak at full volume and have her think I was nuts. "Emily—"

I reached out. She recoiled. Tears sprang to her eyes. She moaned, covered her mouth, and fled through the front door. It clacked with a vengeance. Did I need to warn Mick? No, I did not. Their marriage wasn't any of my business. Sure, I was curious to a fault, but I was not marriage counselor material.

Apparently, Fiona thought I was. She jammed her fists on her hips and stamped her foot in the air.

What? I mouthed.

She whizzed to my shoulder, planted her rump down, and folded her arms, which reminded me of a gesture a childhood friend used to make to get her way. I'd invariably caved.

Fiona sensed my weakness and smirked. "This will be on you if you don't go after her."

I hurried out the door and yelled, "Emily, wait."

She pivoted. Tears were streaming down her cheeks.

"Come back and have a cup of . . . *coffee*." We always had a pot of coffee as well as a pot of hot water at the ready for tea. "We're serving Kona coffee. It's delicious. Do you like cream?" I nabbed her elbow. "You're upset. Let's talk." I'd listened to numerous girlfriends spill their guts about boyfriend troubles. Why had I been their go-to person? Because I'd managed to end all my relationships amicably, as friends. I'd wished each and every boy or man I'd dated to go his separate way and live a happy life.

Okay, that was a lie. I'd cried my eyes out after each breakup, but I'd fooled my friends. After my fiancé called off our wedding, I'd resolved to never be a pushover again. I would say what was on my mind. I would put *me* first.

"Come on, Emily. Please."

"No." She jerked free. "I'm fine. Leave me alone." She hugged her cardigan and scurried away.

At the same time, our landlord Logan Langford swung his long legs out of his Lexus SUV. As he was getting out, he ducked, luckily missing the upper rim of the doorframe. It could have scraped skin from beneath his thinning salt-and-pepper hair. He stood to his full height and, with his chest puffed and chin jutting forward, marched toward me. Dressed

in his usual tight black T-shirt and black jeans, he reminded
me of a fighter eager for a brawl. I'd often wondered whether
he'd been a boxer back in the day. His nose was slightly
crooked.

Recalling what Mick had said about Logan's being on the
warpath, I cringed. Did he truly want to renege on my lease?
He didn't have any legal ground. Could he do so anyway? I
couldn't afford to pick up and move. Finding another space
this size in Carmel would be nearly impossible. If I had to, I
would make sure he knew of Fiona's existence to drive home
his love of Peter Pan.

"Where's Mick Watkins?" Logan growled.

Phew. He wasn't after me. On the other hand, I felt oblig-
ated to defend my fellow tenant. "Beats me, but you'd better
get in line. You're not the only one looking for him. His wife
has first dibs. What's the problem?"

Logan arched a bushy eyebrow. "I'm throwing him out.
Lock, stock, and barrel. Too many complaints. Too much
noise."

I'd never heard more than a few barks coming from inside
Wizard of Paws. Everything was indoors, including the air-
conditioned doggie play yard.

"Do you want to take over his lease?" Logan asked. "You
could expand your business."

"No, thank you," I said. "I'm perfectly fine with the size
of the business right now."

I would never admit to him—or to my father—that at
times I felt overwhelmed by the responsibility. I was paying
bills and wasn't in debt, but being a storeowner wasn't for the
faint of heart. Dealing with customers. Balancing books. Arguing with suppliers. Thinking of my father made me wonder
how he was doing. He had been upset when I'd gone out on
my own . . . to make fairy gardens, no less. *Fanciful*, he'd said.

Impractical. We talked often, but rarely at length, and not in the past few weeks.

A car honked. Mick and his gorgeous German shepherd, who were crossing the street, reared back and let a two-door coupe pass. Then they jaywalked toward us. Mick was carrying a to-go cup of something from Hideaway Café, the sole restaurant in the Village Shops across the street.

I waved. "Hey, Mick, Emily's looking for you. She came into my shop to find you, but you'd gone. She went that way." I pointed to the far end of the courtyard.

"I'll call her. Thanks."

Out of the corner of my eye, I spotted Petra Pauli, the councilwoman, leaving Hideaway Café. Coincidence? Or had she and Mick met for a tryst, as Joss had hinted? Was Emily right to be concerned that her husband was having an affair?

Not your business, I reminded myself.

Logan strode toward Mick, cutting him off before he could enter Wizard of Paws. "We need to talk."

"Why?" Mick gave Shep a hand cue. The dog sat straight, with his body over his hips.

"You're a nuisance."

"Says who?"

"The place is shabby."

What was Logan talking about? Mick had recently painted Wizard of Paws inside and out. There wasn't a nick or a scratch to be found. Even the front door with its etched glass panel was pristine. Not one smudge mark.

Logan wrinkled his nose. "The plants look withered."

"I do my best," Mick countered. "I change them out every six months."

Mick was telling the truth. He'd set out artificial turf pads so owners could curb their dogs before harming the plants. Some owners simply wouldn't comply. Even so, the Pretty in

Pink azaleas were young shrubs and the flowers that were in bloom looked wonderful against the building.

A gaunt middle-aged woman, talking on a cell phone, strutted out of Wizard of Paws and cut around Mick. The screen door closed with a bang. "Out of my way," she demanded.

"Sure thing." Mick edged to the right and rolled his eyes. I understood the gesture. The woman wasn't his favorite patron.

Passing me, the woman raised her nose haughtily as if I smelled. Why? What had I done? She paraded across the street and turned back. I shuddered. If looks could kill.

"Neighbors are complaining." Logan continued his rant. "There's dog hair everywhere. I hate dog hair."

"Which neighbors?" Mick glowered at me. "You?"

"Uh-uh." I swatted the air. "Not me." I hadn't carped about anything. "I like animals. All animals."

"Not her. Other neighbors," Logan said. Until now, I'd never noticed what a grating voice he had. "I want you out, Mick."

"Listen up, Logan, you got a complaint"—Mick aimed a finger at him—"talk to my lawyer. My lease is ironclad." He gave a tug to the leash, and Shep obediently followed him.

With a huff, Logan turned on his heel and stomped away.

In a moment of comically bad timing, as Mick reached for the screen door of his shop, the main door swung inward. The dark-haired man who was leaving pushed the screen door, which bumped into Mick. Shep scuttled backward and barked.

The man—Gregory Darvell, a renowned dog trainer—hurried outside and knelt on one knee. He put his hand under Shep's chin to let him sniff and then gently shifted his hand to the back of Shep's ears and started to pet him. "It's okay, fella. I didn't mean to spook you." Gregory said to Mick, "Sorry, man. You okay?"

"I'm fine, but you've got to slow down. You're always in a hurry."

Gregory chuckled and rubbed his neck. "Got to stay on schedule." He was a charmer with cobalt-blue eyes, thick dark eyelashes, and a dazzling smile. As a younger man, he'd probably broken a few hearts.

"No wonder you haven't won awards in a while," Mick said. "Your dogs are probably picking up on your tension. Chill."

Gregory bridled. "I am chill." But he wasn't. Even from this distance, I could see his cheek twitching. During his thirties, he'd won every dog contest in which he'd shown a dog. In his forties, he'd continued to dominate. I didn't know how he was doing in his fifties. I'd been too busy to watch the most recently televised dog show. Maybe the gild was off the lily.

He rose to his feet, standing a good six inches taller than Mick, and loosened his neck muscles with a quick rotation. "I dropped off Holly Hopewell's poms." Pomeranians. I understood the shorthand. Plus, Mrs. Hopewell owned the house I was leasing. Gregory showed the youngest Pomeranian in competitions. "Be good to them," he added icily.

"Always." Mick offered a wink and disappeared inside.

Feeling a bit tense, I strode into Open Your Imagination and retreated to the office. I needed a moment to *chill*, too. Angry energy seemed to be everywhere. Was a storm brewing? I thought of Fiona's warning and shivered.

As I was sifting through papers on my desk, Fiona appeared and hovered over my shoulder.

"Well?" she asked. "How did it go with Emily?"

I sighed and plopped onto the cream and blue Luisa settee, a piece of furniture I'd inherited from Nana. I rested my head against the wood rim. "She left in a tizzy. Seconds later our landlord showed up and had a row with Mick."

"I know. I watched you through the window. Why was Logan so upset?" she asked.

I gave her the details, adding that Mick had then argued with the dog trainer, and a woman I didn't even know had nearly accosted me. "But don't worry. Everything's copacetic." *Copacetic* had been one of my mother's favorite words, meaning everything was in order—no worries.

"Why don't I believe you?" Fiona asked.

The door to the office swung open.

"Hello, girlfriend," Meaghan Brownie crooned as she swept inside. Meaghan, my best friend and the harpist who played at our teas, was the person who had suggested I attend the Renaissance Fair. When I decided to start my own business, she was also the one who had alerted me to this shop's space being available for lease. She knew because, in addition to being a harpist, she was half-owner of Flair Gallery, located at the Dolores Street entrance to the courtyard.

"I need to discuss the song list for the book club tea," she said. "Is now a good time?" She sashayed behind the settee and kissed me on the top of my head, towering over me the way I towered over Joss. Her curly brown tresses graced her shoulders in stark contrast to the flowing white lace dress she was wearing. She didn't like anything clinging to her body. She said it interfered with her chakras. "I thought I'd start with—" She waggled a finger at my face. "Hmm. Now is *not* a good time. What is crinkling that pretty forehead of yours?"

"First Emily, then Logan and Mick, and . . ." I moaned.

"What are you talking about?"

"They're all hopped up and angry at one another. They're radiating bad energy." I laid a hand on my stomach. "It's got me wound as tightly as a top."

"Breathe." Meaghan perched on the settee's arm and inhaled deeply, encouraging me to do the same. We'd met in our sophomore year in college when we'd lived next door to each other in the dormitory. She had been drawn to spirituality and mythology; I had been interested in horticulture and facts. Opposites attracted. When she visited me one summer in Carmel, she fell in love with the place, gave up her pursuit of becoming a professor, and decided to devote herself to art and beauty. "Breathe," she repeated.

I obeyed. In a minute, I felt calmer.

"Is Fiona here?" Meaghan scanned the room. To my surprise, as spiritually attuned as my pal was, she had yet to see my fairy.

My mother would say it was one thing not to believe in fairies when you're in the city, and the lights and bustle take you away from believing, but when you're near the ocean, you can feel and hear them. You need to have the innocent heart of a child to believe. I wasn't sure what was holding Meaghan back.

"Yes, Fiona's here," I said, "and she's giving me guff."

"Good. Someone needs to keep you in line."

Fiona tittered.

Swell. Two against one.

"What is she giving you guff about?"

"She's worried about me. She has a feeling."

"I might not be able to see her, but I agree with her. I've been getting some weird vibes lately. Let's chat over a brownie." Meaghan reached into her snow-white crocheted backpack and pulled out a plate wrapped in foil. Given her surname, Brownie, she had felt compelled to learn how to make good brownies. Over the years, I'd tasted several dozen varieties: coffee brownies, chocolate brownies, mint brownies. Today she had brought peanut butter brownies—my favorite.

"Eat. Savor. Then talk to me." She unwrapped the goodies, set the plate on the oval glass table in front of the settee, and, after taking a brownie for herself, sat in the royal-blue Queen Anne chair facing me.

The light cutting through the window cast a glow on her face. Not the heavenly kind that might calm me. Something quite sinister.

Worry slithered down my spine. I scrambled to my feet and fetched a cup of tea. I always kept a pot of Earl Grey at the ready on a warming tray. I took a sip, but it didn't calm me. I told Meaghan about Fiona's prediction. "What if she's right? Could something dire be about to happen?"

"If so, you face it head on." Meaghan knew how to rebound after a challenge. "Courage is not the absence of fear, but the triumph over it. I think Nelson Mandela said that."

"I'll cross-stitch that on a pillow," I quipped.

"You should."

"If I knew how to cross-stitch."

I put aside my worry and concentrated on the song list. We settled on a few favorites including "Clair de Lune," "The Fairy Lullaby," and "My Bonnie Lies Over the Ocean." Meaghan wanted to try out a few Celtic tunes, as well, and of course "Greensleeves" was a given. How could I say no? She would play for forty-five minutes, and then the book club discussion would begin.

"Okay." Meaghan jumped to her feet. "Mission accomplished. I'm out of here. Feeling better?"

"At peace."

"Good." She blew me a kiss. "Share the brownies with your customers and then go home and get a decent sleep." She turned in a circle. "And tell Fiona, if she's real, not to do anything I wouldn't do."

Aha. The truth will out. My pal was a nonbeliever. One had to believe in fairies to see them.

Later, as I was closing up shop, Fiona announced that she was going to a seminar. When I questioned her, asking whether attending a seminar might violate the guidelines of her probation, she said that although she was barred from socializing with other fairies, she was allowed to learn from a fairy mentor in an off-the-record setting.

"So you can see other fairies," I said.

"Yes."

She added that fairies with different abilities often attended tutorials to learn how their counterparts operated. While all fairies could work with light, like Fiona, and most could manipulate chlorokinesis—making plants grow—some possessed the talent for telepathy, and a few had the ability to illusion cast, meaning they could make things seem more beautiful.

When I asked Fiona what she would be studying, she held a finger to her lips. "It's a secret."

"Nothing that will make the queen fairy mad, I hope."

"It involves books. She's in favor of books. All fairies are."

Just before six p.m., I nabbed Pixie and headed home. Joss would close up. I didn't need to drive to work. Carmel was a small community. A twenty-minute stroll was all it took to get to the one-bedroom cottage named Dream-by-the-Sea that I rented on Carmelo Street. Many of the homes in Carmel had been given names; it was a quaint tradition. A student of Ansel Adams's had built mine. He had loved the way sunlight graced the property.

I'd lucked out landing the place. Mrs. Hopewell owned five houses in Carmel, her own plus four others. A talented artist, she had taught my mother how to paint. During that time, she had grown quite fond of my mother and me. When Mrs. Hopewell was laid up with pneumonia a few years ago, I'd visited her often. She had mentioned Dream-by-the-Sea and said she had let it go to seed. She had described it in great detail. The English garden was overgrown, the flagstone walkways were covered with moss, and the clematis vines were climbing up the white-stone walls and choking the triple-edged moldings. No one wanted to rent it and deal with the mold and mildew. Would I like to take care of it? *Would I? Yes.* I promised her that I would fix it up to become the jewel it was intended to be. She rented it to me for a song.

As a gardener, I understood the property's potential. As an amateur photographer, I adored the light streaming through the trees. As a Carmelian . . . or was it Carmelite? *Hmm.* The latter was a religious order or type of nun. What did we call ourselves? It didn't matter. As a native of Carmel, I appreciated the history of this particular cottage. Ansel Adams was one of my heroes; his student had been nearly as talented.

When I first moved in, I tackled the front garden, trimming the geraniums and lavender to within an inch of their lives. The larkspur had been tricky, but it had grown back after a decent thinning. The catmint, although a dry weather plant, was rampant. How I loved the aroma. In addition, I planted more delphiniums and blue-themed plants to go with the cottage's periwinkle blue front door. I also decorated the front porch with a verdigris plant stand set with a variety of herbs, and I hung a few wind chimes—like fairies, I loved the sound of chimes and bells—plus I added a weather-resistant mission slat rocking chair. On occasion, I sat in it and watched neighbors pass by. I hadn't tackled the backyard yet, though I had trimmed all of the plants that were touching the patio and had cleaned away the moss and algae. It was a work in progress. So far, I'd set out three fairy gardens. I wanted to place one in every nook and cranny to create places where Fiona and her friends, when the queen fairy allowed her to have some, could gather. Not all fairies lived in gardens. Some built their nesting spots in trees and vines.

Tonight, however, I wasn't in the mood to tinker with

the front or rear garden, not with the fog creeping in and not with all I had to do. Neither was I in the mood to blog about fairy gardens, which I did at least twice a week. Instead, I focused on the series of how-to videos that I intended to air on YouTube. I believed that if I could virally engage a larger audience, I might grow the business. At some point, I could even offer online workshops. But I had yet to make my first video.

After feeding Pixie and eating a cup of homemade minestrone—I'd made a pot a few days ago that would last me a week—I sauntered into the living room to flesh out my ideas for the first video. I wanted to demonstrate, step-by-step, how to make a modest fairy garden.

I moved around the room reciting what I wanted to say and imagining the items I would need: soil, succulents, ferns, maybe a miniature white gazebo and picket fence. I would add one of my favorite fairies, the kneeling girl with pink-painted wings and an angelic face. I didn't want the presentation to be difficult beyond belief, but I wanted the fairy gardener to feel challenged.

Pixie, intrigued by the fact that I wasn't lazing in the reading chair drinking in one of the many books in my to-be-read pile, leaped from footstool to footstool to take in my spiel.

Rounding the ocean-blue love seat, I pondered whether I would need to hire a professional photographer when I was ready to go. A steady video camera wouldn't allow me to do close-ups, which my viewers would probably appreciate.

Making a mental note to explore that option, I settled at the antique desk beside the window and jotted down my script and a video setup to-do list, after which I networked on my laptop computer with a few other fairy garden builders in the *Fairy Garden Girls Dig It* chat room. We were a welcoming community and often discussed our designs.

Around two a.m., realizing I'd lost track of time, I exited the chat, slogged to the bathroom, did my ablutions, and wriggled into my footed cat-themed pajamas. Carmel could get cold at night.

Exhausted, I slipped under the sea-blue comforter, waited for Pixie to do her circle routine by my feet, then pounded my pillows until they were the way I liked them, and closed my eyes.

Hours later, though it seemed like minutes because I'd slept so deeply, I felt Pixie alternately dancing on her hind legs and crashing onto the bedspread.

"What the heck? Kitty, cut it out." I sat up, rubbed the sleep from my eyes, and read the time on the digital clock: five a.m. "Pixie, settle down. I mean it. I—"

"Courtney." Fiona appeared over the kitten's head. She sounded out of breath. Had she flown the whole way to my cottage without assistance? "I warned you." She alit on my forearm.

"About?"

"You have to see for yourself. At the shop." She threw her arms wide. "It's horrible."

Chapter 3

❦

Spread your wings and let the fairy in you fly.
—Anonymous

Fiona didn't stick around to explain. She darted out of the cottage. A streak of sparkling fairy dust trailed her.

Quickly, I dressed in jeans, aqua sweatshirt, and Keds. Even more rapidly, I threw on my cross-body purse, grabbed Pixie, and ran the distance to the shop despite the chill of fog seeping through my clothes and moistening my face and hair. On the way I called Joss on my cell phone. I apologized for waking her and told her something was up. I wasn't sure what. I begged her to meet me at the shop. She agreed.

When I arrived at Open Your Imagination, I screeched to a halt. The Dutch door was ajar. I didn't go inside. I'd seen enough scary movies in my lifetime to know I needed to gauge whether it would be dangerous or not. I peered through a window. The lights were switched off in the shop, but the hazy glow of a streetlamp provided enough illumination for me to see that nothing looked amiss. No shards of tea sets or fairy gardens lay on the floor, and I couldn't detect any strangers lurking in the shadows.

"Fiona?" I whispered.

She soared through the shop, her wings glimmering like silver, and hovered inside the front door. She signaled: *follow me.*

Adrenaline pumping, I pushed open the door. Fiona wouldn't lead me into danger. That would really tick off the queen fairy. I set Pixie on the floor. She stood stock-still and lifted her chin. Her nose twitched. Her tail coiled into a question mark. I switched on the main store lights, which lit up the frosted glass sconces on each wall. Everything appeared normal, as I'd deduced seconds before. I breathed a tad easier. Maybe Fiona had been overreacting when she'd said something horrible had happened. Perhaps Carmel had suffered a teensy earthquake tremor and items had fallen off the shelves on the patio.

Fiona zoomed toward me. "Don't dally. Come now."

I followed her. The moment I passed through the French doors to the patio, I realized I'd been mistaken. Not about the tremor or minor damage. But something was very wrong.

Mick Watkins lay in a heap beside the fountain, his head craned at an odd angle. Dark shadows made his face look ghastly. Pixie pounced to him and sniffed. She recoiled.

"Mick?" I tripped the switch on the wall. The twinkling lights woven into the trees and trellises flickered on. I tiptoed closer. "Hey, are you all right?"

Mick didn't budge. The carved gnomes on the fountain seemed to be gazing ghoulishly at him.

When I drew nearer, I gasped. Mick's head was gashed. Blood seeped from the wound. Red-brown goo—more blood—clung to the fountain's stone façade. I reached for Mick's wrist. He had no pulse.

I clapped a hand over my mouth. Pixie rubbed against my leg, curious to know if I was okay. I assured her I wasn't. Bile was rising up my esophagus. I raced around the patio and switched on all the lights. The floodlights in the corners blazed on. The reading lamps set by the tea tables shone brightly. Light did not make Mick look any better. Or any more alive.

I gagged and pulled my cell phone from my purse. I dialed 911 and waited through three rings. What would I say? I'd seen dead rats and roadkill. Every landscaper had. But I'd never come across a dead body. Heck, I'd never had to interact with the police for anything, not even jaywalking. Okay, yes, I'd had to answer to my father on occasion, back when he was a cop, before the incident that took out his knee and ended his career. He'd been a stickler about curfews.

A 911 operator answered. I alerted her to the problem, gave her the address, and was told to wait—like I'd go anywhere. She hung up.

"Did you see what happened?" I asked Fiona.

"No." Her cheeks turned crimson. "I was out. Remember?"

"At the seminar. Right. When did you get back?"

"A few minutes before I showed up at your place." She landed on my shoulder, plopped on her behind, and folded her legs. "Take pictures."

"What?"

"With your cell phone. Take photographs. Record everything."

I didn't want to go near Mick again, but she was right. Before the police came and messed up the crime scene, I needed to snap a few shots. Our insurance adjustor might need to know what had happened. Oh, no. Would Emily Watkins sue me for Mick's accidental death?

"See the straw and the dog hair and the—" Fiona motioned to a few cards lying next to Mick. "What are those?"

"Business cards." I checked them out but didn't touch them. One was for an attorney, another for Councilwoman Pauli, and a few others for local inns and restaurants.

"What's that around his neck?" Fiona asked.

"What are you talking about? He's not wearing a tie or a scarf."

"The brown mark. Look closer."

Stomach roiling, I crouched and inspected Mick's neck. The brown mark was striated with red bands on either side.

"He's been strangled," I whispered. "With rope." I'd worked with enough rope and cord over the course of my career to recognize ligature marks. Had the killer strangled Mick first and then shoved him, or shoved him and then strangled him? Did the sequence matter?

"Courtney!" Joss burst through the opened French doors leading from the shop to the patio, the flaps of her purple duster cardigan wafting. Her short hair lay flat on her head, making her look more elfin than ever. She drew to a halt and pressed a hand to her chest. The way she'd buttoned her purple-and-pink plaid shirt to her throat made her look uptight and tense. "What in the world? Is he all right?"

I shook my head. "He's dead. He was murdered."

"Murdered? Heavens to Betsy." Joss turned pale.

I hurried to her and steadied her. "Do you need to sit?"

"No, I'll be fine." She drank in a huge gulp of air. "What is he doing here?"

"I don't know."

"How did he get in?"

"The front door was open."

"No, no, no. I locked all the doors." She sliced the air with her hand. "You know I never leave without double-checking the locks." Having been a bookkeeper, Joss was meticulous about details.

"He must have had a key," I said.

"Why would he have a key? Uh-uh. No." She shook her head. "Did you check to see if the lock on the Dutch door was jimmied?"

I hadn't. Together we raced to the front door. Fiona trailed us.

Using the flashlight app on my cell phone, I peered at the doorknob and its lock. Pristine. Not a scratch. "Mick must have had a key," I repeated.

"Or he came in some other way, and the killer went out this way," Fiona suggested.

I gawked at her. "Some other way like via the pyramid skylight over the patio?" I raced to the patio and peered upward.

Fiona flitted to the skylight and inspected the locks. "Nope. These are secure. And the slatted air vents on either side are barely large enough for me to shimmy through."

I said to Joss, "I'm going to examine the other doors." There was an entrance on the patio and a door in our modest kitchen, both used for deliveries, plus a door near the office, which we never used. It was there for emergencies.

"I'll inspect the windows," Joss said. "Did you call the police?"

"They're on their way." Methodically, I studied each door. No scratch marks on any of the locks. Nothing picked or jimmied. Everything was secure.

"No mess-ups on my end," Joss yelled.

"For me, either." I returned to the patio and spied Fiona inspecting a clump of vines. "What are you doing?"

"I'll be right back." She zipped out of the shop.

"Wait. Where are you going?"

Joss hustled to my side. "Where is she off to?"

Fiona returned a minute later. A shimmer of fairy dust trailed her as she ducked behind the vines she'd previously been inspecting. She hummed. Loudly. Fairies, she'd told me, liked to hum, especially righteous fairies when they were working an issue.

A moment later, she reappeared and, wafting upward, gestured to the spot she'd just left. "There."

"What did you find?" I asked.

"See the vines? They're broken. They're covering a secret entrance."

"You're kidding." I tiptoed closer.

"No way," Joss murmured, trailing me.

"You can't see the entrance easily," Fiona went on. "It's on Eighth Avenue. But I had a gut feeling."

Did fairies have guts? Of course they did. They could live and die. They had to have organs. Fairy organs.

"Dig through the broken vines," Fiona ordered. "You'll see. That's how Mick got inside."

Sure enough, behind the vines was a two-foot by two-foot door, which was ajar. How had I missed it? Why hadn't my landlord warned me about it? It didn't have a lock.

As I stood up, a siren pierced the air. Then another.

"The police," Joss yelped.

With a whoop, the sirens ceased.

I hurried to the front of the shop and greeted a tanned male officer and a dark-haired female officer as they strode through the door, he in street clothes and she wearing the official Carmel Police Department blue uniform.

"Good morning," I said, even though the sun wasn't up. "No. Let me revise that. Not so good morning. What I mean is"—I massaged the locket with my mother's picture—"it's a very bad morning."

The male officer said, "I'm Detective Summers. Dylan Summers. My partner is Officer Rodriguez."

Rodriguez nodded. She had a tight ponytail and a tighter smile.

Summers flashed his CPD badge. "Where's the body?" In khaki trousers and white shirt with sleeves rolled up, he resembled any other local who spent hours at the beach or on the golf course. But he wasn't like any other local. I'd seen Summers once at a city council meeting. A seasoned detective, he had talked about community safety. After the meeting, a middle-aged woman told me he'd been married once but was a widower. His wife had died in a car accident a week after they said *I do*. If I hadn't gotten the scoop, I wouldn't have known he'd ever suffered sorrow. He had an easy smile and a commanding presence.

"Follow me," I said to Summers and Rodriguez as I led the way to the patio. "I'm the owner of the shop. Courtney Kelly. I . . ." I couldn't say my resident fairy had found Mick. I *could*, but would they believe me? No. *Lie number one, coming up.* "I came in early for work and found him like this. He's my neighbor, Mick Watkins. He owns Wizard of Paws, across the courtyard. I think he's been murdered."

"Please don't theorize, Miss Kelly. Leave the deductions to us." Summers smoothed his tawny hair and crouched beside Mick to get a better look. "Ligature marks," he said over his shoulder to Rodriguez. "Strangled. Head injury first, I suspect."

Fiona fluttered beside my ear. "You were right."

"Did you argue with him?" Summers asked me as he rose. I blanched. "No. He was like that. When I arrived. I didn't—"

"It's cold out here," Rodriguez said. "He could have been dead for hours."

"We close at six p.m.," I said.

Summers was tall. I had to tilt my head back to make eye contact. Given the crow's-feet around his eyes, I gauged him at about fifty to fifty-five, not far from my father's age. "Why was Mr. Watkins here?" He pulled an old-fashioned notebook fastened with a rubber band from his pocket, opened it, and removed the attached pen.

"I'm not sure."

"How did he get in?"

"The front door was open, but my assistant is conscientious about locking up. We . . . my assistant and I—" I indicated Joss, who was standing next to the French doors, arms wrapped around her teensy body. She waved her hand. "Her name is Joss Timberlake. She and I"—I still didn't mention Fiona—"think Mick stole in through a hidden door behind the vines." I pointed. "I didn't know about the hidden door. I had no idea it was there until—"

"Did you mess with those vines?" Summers asked.

My cheeks warmed. I pushed away my embarrassment and squared my shoulders. "While I was waiting for you to arrive, I did a bit of, um, investigating."

He grumbled. Rodriguez made a similar noise.

"By the way," I continued, "the killer might have followed Mick through the secret entrance and run out the front door, which would be why it was open when I arrived."

Summers scowled and made another note without making eye contact. "I repeat, don't theorize."

My shoulders stiffened. His tone reminded me of my father's whenever he would reprimand me.

"Rodriguez," Summers said. "Check the secret entrance from the outside."

"On it." She disappeared through the main store.

I said, "Detective, if you fingerprint the Dutch door's knob, you might—"

He shook his head. "We won't get anything. The killer was probably wearing gloves."

"What if he wasn't?" I countered.

"*He* could have been a *she*," Summers said.

Why had he or she strangled Mick? And when, exactly?

Summers brandished a hand. "Plenty of other people will have touched that knob."

"Not since then. When I came in, I used the exterior

knob. Won't prints layer over other prints? Won't the top-most be the most recent?"

Rodriguez returned and whispered something to Summers. He nodded, then directed her to examine the front door and jotted in his notebook.

I said, "I also noticed pet hair and some straw on the floor beside the business cards. My assistant cleans the place spotless every night before leaving. The floor should have been dust-free. Of course the pet hair could have come in with Mick since he works with animals, or the killer might have—"

"Stop," Summers said abruptly.

"I wasn't theorizing." My cheeks blazed with heat. Of course I was theorizing. I'd been a problem solver all my life.

Rodriguez returned and showed Summers a few pictures on her cell phone. "Don't pretend to be a lab tech, either," she said to me.

Was this their typical routine? Bad cop, worse cop?

"How many episodes of *CSI* have you watched, Miss Kelly?" Summers asked.

Far be it from me to admit that I'd binge-watched every episode after my breakup with my fiancé. I'd had a few murder-ous thoughts. Seeing professionals catch the bad guy every time had put me off the idea of killing him. Besides, I wouldn't look good in an orange jumpsuit.

"A few," I replied.

Summers smiled, trying to disarm me. It didn't work. When I had been a landscaper, one too many clients had dismissed me because I was young and female, another of the many reasons I'd set off on my own journey.

"By the way, have you considered that Mr. Watkins wasn't the intended victim?" he asked.

"I don't understand."

"It's your shop," Rodriguez said. "What if the killer meant to kill you, but Mr. Watkins just happened to appear?"

I gulped. "No way. I'm never here late at night."

"Maybe the murderer was lying in wait," Summers said.

"For me?" I shook my head. "I don't have any enemies."

"Everyone has enemies," Rodriguez chimed. "Even Dylan."

Summers chortled and turned a page of his notebook. "What can you tell me about Mr. Watkins?" He gazed at me somberly.

My mind was reeling, but I continued to answer as best I could. "Like I said, he owns . . . *owned* Wizard of Paws, the pet-grooming shop across the way." I jutted a hand. "He liked animals. He was married to—"

"What's going on?" a woman cried from the front of the shop. "Have you seen my husband?"

I whirled around. Emily Watkins, clad in a short-sleeved white blouse and khaki pull-on breeches fitted with a fashionable leather-and-rope belt and tucked into brown riding boots, was being detained by a third officer, a lanky redhead in his early thirties. Emily's right hand and forearm were wrapped in a wide elastic bandage with a Velcro-style fastener. When had she injured herself? She was carrying a brown leather jacket and a Michael Kors tote bag.

"Why are the police here?" Emily shrieked. "What happened? Mick, are you in there?" She pulled free from the officer and charged into the shop. "Courtney, I see you. What's going on? Where's Mick? Have you seen—" She drew to a halt beneath the arch of the French door and gasped. "Mick!"

She raced onto the patio, toward her husband.

In one swift move, Summers pocketed his notebook and grabbed her. He held her firmly at bay. "I'm sorry, ma'am. You shouldn't be out here."

"That's my husband. I'm Emily Watkins. Is he all right? Did he fall? What happened?"

"Red," Summers said to the red-haired officer, "secure

the crime scene and get officers down here ASAP to help tag evidence."

"Sir."

Summers addressed Emily. "Please, ma'am, exit the shop. Wait in the courtyard for me."

"Not until you tell me what happened."

"It appears your husband was murdered."

"Murdered?" Her jaw fell open. Tears sprang to her eyes.

"Please, ma'am, go to the courtyard."

"But Courtney's here," Emily snapped.

"She discovered the body, and it's her shop."

Emily's eyes fluttered. With stress or apprehension? I eyed the bandage on her arm. Yesterday, she'd been worried that her husband was having an affair. Had she followed Mick into my shop last night, shoved him, and then strangled him? In the struggle, had she injured herself?

Honestly, Courtney, your first instinct is to suspect the spouse? I *had* watched too many *CSI* episodes. On the other hand, I recalled how furious Emily had been with Mick.

"Mrs. Watkins," Summers said. "I'll speak with you outside. Officer Rodriguez, if you please."

Reluctantly, Emily shuffled toward Rodriguez, who was waiting to escort her out.

I glanced back at Mick. Why had he come into Open Your Imagination? How had he known about the secret entrance?

"Miss Kelly." Summers snapped fingers in front of my face. "I'm talking to you."

Fiona snickered. I shot her a dirty look. I was pretty sure Summers couldn't see her; otherwise, he would have mentioned her, right?

"Sorry," I muttered. "I was thinking."

"About?"

I was pondering Emily's injured hand and arm and wondering whether she would have had the strength to strangle her husband, but I didn't voice my thoughts. Summers didn't want to hear my opinion.

I cleared my throat. "Why don't my assistant and I make coffee and tea? Perhaps Mrs. Watkins would like a cup of something warm."

"That would be nice."

"Do you need to question me further?"

"Yes. Don't go far."

I picked up Pixie and traipsed into the main showroom. The aroma of fresh coffee wafted to me. Joss had beaten me to the punch. I was surprised Officer Rodriguez hadn't shooed her outside along with Emily, but Joss had a way with words. She must have convinced Rodriguez that she and her colleagues would be craving coffee in a bit. I asked Joss to go to the kitchen and see if we had any cookies or tarts lying around. The police were bound to be hungry, too.

After setting Pixie on the floor and pouring a stiff cup of coffee into a Villeroy & Boch Mariefleur mug, I went in search of Emily. I found her lingering outside the front door, rocking from foot to foot and stroking her long hair rhythmically.

The fog had lifted, and the sun was rising. Swirls of peach and orange clouds decorated the morning sky. On any other day, I'd have considered it a gorgeous sight.

"Coffee," I said, and offered Emily the mug. "I can add cream or sugar if you'd like."

She accepted it but didn't take a sip. "What a pretty pink flower," she said absently, admiring the china. After a long moment, she said, "Please tell me what happened."

"I don't know. We'll have to wait for the police to determine that." Like a model citizen, I was taking my cues from Summers.

"I can't believe it." Emily sucked back a sob. "Mick's dead. Just like that. Right when he was excited about writing again. It doesn't seem fair."

"Mick was a writer?"

She nodded. "He had dreams. He put his career on hold to start the business and support me. He was selfless that way. And then life . . ." She sighed. "He didn't dream of writing again until recently. He planned to write a thriller. He'd written notes to get started. An outline of sorts." Wistfully she added, "He'd hoped it would become a *New York Times* bestseller."

I studied her, trying to determine if she was lying about how much she admired him. She certainly hadn't felt this lovey-dovey about him yesterday.

"He got the bug to write as a kid when he realized how many fabulous authors had lived in Carmel," Emily went on. "Did you know the town became a haven for them after the 1906 earthquake hit San Francisco?"

"Yes," I replied. "It became a refuge for artists, too."

"Of course. That's why there are so many art galleries here." Emily smelled the coffee, but still didn't drink. "Mick was a realist. He knew writing didn't pay a lot, so he got a small business loan and invested in Wizard of Paws. He loved animals, and they loved him. The rest, as they say, is history." She finally took a sip of coffee and peered at me over the rim of the cup. "Who killed him, Courtney? Did you do it?"

My insides jolted. "What? Of course not. Why would you even think that?" Why had Summers asked me the same thing? Did I look guilty? What did a murderer look like?

"The nerve!" Fiona fluttered to my side. Anger was flowing from her in hot waves. My defender. My righteous fairy.

"Logan Langford wants to end our lease," Emily said. "With Mick out of the way, Logan probably expects you to expand your shop. That's a pretty good motive."

No, it wasn't. It was as weak as water.

"I don't want to expand." My voice cracked. "I'm perfectly fine with the size business I have."

"That's not what Isabella Acosta says."

"Who?"

"Isabella Acosta. She's one of our clients. She owns a miniature poodle."

"I don't care what she owns," I squawked.

"She told me she saw you arguing with Mick yesterday. Isabella can be a bit of a gossip. She asked me what the argument was about."

"She's lying. Through her teeth. I did not argue with Mick. Not yesterday. Not ever."

Undaunted, Emily handed back the cup of coffee and stared daggers at me. "Where were you when he died?"

"I don't even know what time it happened."

"Let's see." Emily tapped a finger on her chin. "I talked to him on the phone at ten last night, so sometime between then and now."

"That's a wide window."

"Even so"—Summers strode through the Dutch door into the courtyard, his notebook in hand—"give me a rundown of your whereabouts from the moment you left work until now, Miss Kelly."

My mouth went dry. Perspiration broke out on my upper lip, but I didn't wipe it off for fear of looking guilty. "I went h-home," I stammered. "I ate. Then I wrote a script for a how-to video I want to make. After that, I networked with an online group until nearly two a.m."

"Which group?"

"Fairy Garden Girls Dig It."

Summers wrote something in his notebook. I took a peek. *Isabella Acosta,* not the online group I'd mentioned. He'd overheard Emily mention the Acosta woman. Shoot. Who was she? Would Summers take her word over mine? Did he really believe I'd argued with Mick? Did he believe I had committed murder? Of course, he would question the Acosta woman. Any lead had to be followed up. But I was the one who'd called the police. Would a killer do that? Not to mention that my clothes were clean—not a drop of blood on them—and what would I have done with the rope?

I caught sight of a macramé plant holder with a potted succulent hanging inside the front door of my shop and gulped. The killer hadn't used one of the holders to strangle Mick, had he . . . she? If so, was it still on the premises, left there to frame me?

Fiona whizzed around Summers's head, stamping the air with frustration and uttering words in some ancient fairy language I'd never grasp. Righteous *and* furious. Not a good combination.

"Miss Kelly?" Summers said. "One more time. Your schedule last night."

I drew in a deep breath and recapped my evening, play by play: eating dinner, writing the script for the video, chatting online with fellow fairy garden builders.

"So you were alone," Emily cut in.

"I was online with friends until two a.m."

"That can't be proved," she muttered.

I shot her a look. "Where were you?" The words sounded venomous, but I'd never been accused of murder before. My pulse was pounding, and my cheeks were flaming with indignation.

"At an equestrian getaway."

"A what?"

Summers said, "I think she means a dude ranch."

"No, sir, I don't," Emily stated. "It's called the Equestrian Inn. It's new. Located in Carmel Valley, about twenty minutes from here. They offer plush accommodations and trail rides. There's nothing like a trail ride in the dark to help a person think. I've been into riding lately. It helps me problem solve."

"Problem solve what?" Summers asked. "Were you and your husband struggling?"

"No, that's not what I meant." Emily shook her head. "He . . . he—"

"Was having an affair." Joss crossed the threshold carrying a tray of floral paper cups of coffee along with a plate of sugar cookies.

"No," Emily squealed.

"Yes." Joss took Emily's cup from me and set it on the tray. "You had an argument with him about it, Emily. Sonja told me." Sonja Schmidt was the assistant at Wizard of Paws.

Emily blanched. Her cheek started to twitch. Her mouth began to move, but no words came out. Fiona swirled above her head and dashed her with fairy dust. The dust, she'd told me months ago, couldn't make anyone tell the truth; it just pacified them.

In an instant, Emily became calm. "Isabella Acosta saw me leave with my suitcase." She thrust an arm toward Wizard of Paws. "She came into the shop to pick up her poodle. Sonja had left for the night. Mick stayed late to personally see to Isabella's dog. Isabella can vouch for me."

"How did you hurt your hand, Emily?" I asked.

Summers shot me a look. I ignored it. I wasn't theorizing.

"I . . . stumbled getting onto the horse and wrenched my wrist."

Summers took a cup of coffee from the tray Joss was holding. "Thank you, Miss Timberlake. Much appreciated."

Joss nodded and returned inside.

"Miss Kelly," Summers said. "Give Mrs. Watkins and me some space, please."

"Yes, of course." I bobbed my head, acquiescent to the nth degree. Whatever the police asked me to do, I would comply. I was a model citizen. Not a murderer. I trudged into Open Your Imagination and asked Fiona if she could *sense* whether Emily was guilty of murder.

"Ha! When and *if* I ever get that good at my righteous duty, I'll become the queen fairy." Fiona was teasing, of course. The queen fairy was chosen through lineage. "Ahem." She aimed a finger at me. "I know you're fishing. You're trying to find out if we studied telepathy at last night's seminar."

"No, I'm not."

"Yes, you are, and no, we did not. But if you ask me, Emily is guilty of something."

Chapter 4

I think, at a child's birth, if a mother could ask a fairy godmother to endow it with the most useful gift, that gift would be curiosity.
—Eleanor Roosevelt

Hoping I could listen in on the detective and Emily, I remained close to the Dutch door and tweaked a display, but I couldn't hear them. Summers was being very discreet.

Joss swooped to me, still carrying the tray of coffees, and whispered, "How are you holding up?"

"My nerves are frayed."

"Finding Mick had to be harrowing."

"It was." I wrapped my arms around my torso but couldn't get warm. A chill had seeped into my bones.

"Take a coffee."

I hated drinking coffee out of a paper cup, but I grabbed one anyway and took a sip. The warmth streamed through me.

Joss took the tray to the coffee station and returned with a tin of her homemade oatmeal chocolate chip protein cookies.

"Just for you, not the cops." She opened the lid. "Nibble on one. For strength."

"Sugar doesn't provide strength."

"The protein will. The sugar is an added bonus. Remember what Mary Poppins said? 'A spoonful of sugar helps the medicine go down.' Eat."

I bit into a cookie and heard my stomach grumble a thank-you. I was starved. Hearing the worry in Fiona's voice, I'd run right over. No breakfast. No protein bar. No smoothie. My stomach was in knots, but I was coping far better than I thought I'd be. A suspect? A murderer? No way! Nobody in his right mind would believe that of me. I didn't even kill spiders. Granted, I might have whacked a few roaches in my lifetime, but who hadn't?

"You know the macramé plant holders we sell?" I asked softly between bites. I didn't want the detective to overhear us. Unlike me, I'd bet he had batlike supersonic hearing.

"What about them?" Joss asked.

"They're made of rope. Mick was strangled"—I swallowed hard—"with rope."

Joss's eyes widened. "All but the ones hanging in here are under lock and key in the cabinet with the soil." We kept our soil in a cupboard so it wouldn't dry out. We stored soil enhancers in there, as well, because we didn't want children to get their hands on them; hence, the lock.

Fiona alit on my shoulder. "What do you want me to do?"

I caught Summers looking in our direction. Had he heard her? Perhaps he'd seen me tilt my head to listen to her.

Instead of responding to my fairy, I said through the doorway, "Detective, is it all right for Joss—Miss Timberlake—and me to do our books? Or maybe straighten the shop? Or

catch up on a few preorders? Or—" I was babbling. I clamped
my lips together.

"You're fine as long as you keep away from the patio." It
had already been cordoned off.

"Yes, sir. Thank you, sir."

Moments later, after Summers released Emily, he ordered
the shop closed for the rest of the day. His team would require
a lot of hours to do what it needed to do: take photographs,
dust for prints, and inventory evidence. No doubt they would
find the macramé holders. I had to hope and pray they were
all accounted for and free of Mick's blood.

After the Monterey County coroner removed the body
and an outline was drawn where Mick had lain, a CPD officer
set tiny numbered cones on the patio beside the hair, straw,
and business cards. Summers oversaw each step of the investigation. Rodriguez had retreated outside, probably to help the
redheaded officer manage the crowds. I could see people gathering on the sidewalk and across the street, lookie-loos eager
for the scoop.

I put Pixie in the office—she was more than happy to
sleep on her cushy pillow—and Joss and I lingered by the sales
counter, reviewing yesterday's receipts and such. We peeked
at the patio occasionally to see what the police were up to, but
couldn't make heads or tails of the status. Fiona, on the other
hand, was a flurry of energy. She remained on the patio,
winging from container to trellis to fountain while the police
conducted their business. A flicker of light and a smattering of
fairy dust let me know where she was at any given time.
Once, I glimpsed a tech flapping his hand, as if feeling Fiona's
wing vibrations, but none of his colleagues seemed to sense or
see her.

Late morning, Summers strode into the main showroom. "Miss Kelly, a word."

"Please, call me Courtney."

He smiled, and I could see why all available women over forty might ogle him. Like my father, Summers possessed a forthrightness mixed with a hint of danger. "Do you know if Mr. Watkins had any enemies?"

"You mean other than me?" I quipped. My go-to response when pressed against a wall was sarcasm or humor.

"Other than you."

"No. Mick and I weren't close. We didn't share our personal stories."

"Okay." Summers flipped open his notebook.

I was beginning to despise the way he logged everything. "Do I need a lawyer?" I asked, a bite to my tone.

"It might be a good idea."

"Really?" My insides snagged. Had they found a macramé plant hanger with blood on it after all? Testing the waters, voice quavering, I said, "Simply because of the lease issue?"

Summers consulted his notes. "It's going to be difficult to corroborate your alibi."

I breathed easier. No macramé. No smoking gun. Yet. What a relief. I said, "The people I chatted with online know I was at home."

"Do they?" Summers raised an eyebrow. "Anyone could have been sitting in for you and typing those keystrokes. For all I know, you could have been here, working via this computer or your cell phone."

"But I wasn't. I was home. And in bed by two. What time did Mick die?"

"The coroner hasn't determined that yet."

"Will you tell me when he does?"

Joss drew near. "Detective Summers, the ISP address will confirm Courtney's home location." Given Joss's history in the tech industry, she knew more about computers than I did.

Summers swiveled to meet her gaze. "I suppose it could." That made me feel a tad better, but only a tad.

"Great," Joss added. "I'll pin that down for you."

"Boss," Rodriguez called from beyond the Dutch door. "You have a visitor. Councilwoman Pauli."

Summers growled, unable to hide his distaste. Were he and the councilwoman foes? Was there some history I needed to know? To me, he said, "Excuse me."

If Petra Pauli and Mick had been having an affair, as Joss claimed, this could be an impassioned exchange. I followed him.

The Dutch door was wide open. Summers stepped across the threshold. So did I. Even more people were clogging the street. A few were using their cell phones to record the event. I noticed an exotic, raven-haired woman trying to interview Red and getting nowhere. She held out a fancy recording device. The officer glowered at her and pushed the device aside. Rodriguez had returned to the street to handle a rowdy onlooker.

"Detective Summers." Petra Pauli strode toward him and forced a smile.

"Councilwoman."

Man, he could be icicle cool.

Petra was holding the leashes of two black-and-white collies, one with a white muzzle and the other with a brown muzzle. "What's going on?" With her big blue eyes, luscious lips, sweeping blond curls, and body-hugging black sheath, one might have thought the forty-year-old Swedish bombshell was primed for the runway or a cocktail party. "Why is the grooming shop closed?" she asked, her voice commanding. I'd heard her use the same tone at council meetings. She wanted everyone to believe she was a force to be reckoned with. "I had bath appointments for my dogs."

An hour ago, according to Joss who had left the shop for a breath of fresh air and a bit of eavesdropping, Rodriguez had questioned Mick's assistant, Sonja. The minute the inquiry ended, Sonja had closed the shop and gone home ill. She was not a suspect in his murder. She had a solid alibi. She had been with her grandmother at a nursing home. Five nurses had substantiated her every moment. If only a few nurses could attest to my alibi.

Petra saw me lingering and said, "Good morning, Courtney." She knew my name because I'd spoken up at a council meeting. A few misanthropes had wanted to end funding for the library. I'd opposed them.

"Not so good," I replied.

The brown-muzzled dog yipped.

"Sit." Petra tugged on both leashes. The black dog with the white muzzle sat dutifully. The peeved dog shimmied before obeying. Its hair wafted into the air. "Detective, if you will grant me a word. Wizard of Paws is closed. There's all this police activity. What in heaven's name is going on?"

Summers filled her in.

Petra didn't gasp when he revealed Mick Watkins had been murdered, but she fought hard to keep herself in check, which confirmed—at least as far as I was concerned—that she'd been involved with him. Had Mick told Emily he was leaving her for the councilwoman? Being jilted would strengthen Emily's motive and make mine look as insignificant as it was. Was Emily securing a defense attorney at this very moment to represent her?

"I demand to see where this happened," Petra said.

Fiona appeared and fluttered next to my ear. "Why does she want to do that? So she can trail dog hair everywhere? Maybe she killed him."

"No," I said.

Summers eyed me.

I batted the air to hush Fiona and offered a weak smile to the detective. "I meant, no, she shouldn't go in because you need to preserve the crime scene."

Summers suppressed a smile. "Exactly what I was going to say." He addressed Petra. "I'm sorry, Councilwoman, but I can't allow that."

"Surely you can make an exception for me. Mick was a dear friend." Petra raised her lovely but formidable chin. "I'll need to report the crime to the city council. If I inspect the crime scene, I'll be able to attest to the police force's commitment to solving the crime."

"Oh, we're committed. You can bet on that." The edge in Summers's voice was unmistakable.

"This is the first murder in how many years, Dylan?" Petra asked.

Summers didn't respond.

"Courtney, take my dogs." Petra thrust the dogs' leashes at me.

Automatically, I took hold of the handles, which matched the dogs' muzzles. The slip-style nooses pulled tight. I worked to loosen them on both dogs.

Summers shot out his arm, blocking Petra from entering the shop. "I'll be glad to attend the council meeting and answer questions, ma'am. You may not pass."

Petra growled under her breath.

"Officer Rodriguez," Summers called. "Please escort the councilwoman to her car."

Rodriguez, still dealing with the rowdy onlooker, gave Summers a thumbs-up gesture, acknowledging she'd heard him.

"I don't need an escort, Dylan." Petra's aquiline nose twitched. "I'm perfectly capable of navigating the crowd."

"I was worried about your high heels on the cobblestones," Summers noted. "Against the law, you know."

Petra clicked her tongue purposefully and seized the dogs' leashes from me. She commanded her dogs to heel. Onlookers cleared a path for her as she marched to a white Mercedes that she'd parked on the opposite side of the street. She threw open the rear door and encouraged the dogs to jump inside. With a final withering glance at Summers, she climbed into the driver's seat and sped away.

The lanky redheaded officer joined us.

Summers chuckled. "She's a charmer, don't you think, Red?"

"She's a handful, sir," he replied, his prominent Adam's apple bobbing.

"I can't wait until she runs for mayor. Mud will sling, and heads will fly."

"Let the fireworks begin," Red quipped.

Summers scratched the back of his neck. "Now, what were we discussing before we were interrupted, Miss Kelly?"

"Courtney," I stated. If he continued to use my formal name, I was going to feel as guilty as sin. And I wasn't, darn it.

A toot of a horn made me turn. Logan Langford hailed Summers as he parked and climbed out of his Lexus. He looked like he'd recently taken a serious meeting: blue power suit, blue tie. "Dylan."

It wasn't surprising that Logan, like the councilwoman, was on a first-name basis with the detective. Carmel didn't have a huge police force. People of import knew people in power.

Summers didn't budge. He waited for my landlord to join him. As with Petra Pauli, I sensed history between them.

"Do you know him?" I asked.

"His father and my father went to school together." Summers's jaw was ticking.

Meaning Summers and Logan were contemporaries? That surprised me. The detective looked much younger.

I said, "He owns this courtyard plus three others in Carmel, a couple of bed-and-breakfasts, and two tanning establishments."

"I know." Summers clucked his tongue. "In fact, I know just about everything there is to know about the Langfords."

In the 1920s, Logan Langford's family had settled in Pacific Grove and, thanks to real estate investments, soon became one of the wealthiest families around. Logan, his three boys, eleven grandchildren, and a couple of nephews were alive. His wife as well as his two siblings had passed away.

Given his long stride, Logan arrived in seconds. "Did I hear right, Dylan? Mick Watkins is dead? Where's Emily? Does she need anything?" He jerked his head to the right. "Is Wizard of Paws closed?"

"For the day."

"Man, I can't believe it. Mick was our age, fifty-something, right?"

"Younger."

"What did he die of? A heart attack?"

Summers studied Logan, not offering a thing.

Logan narrowed his gaze. "Is there something you're not telling me? All the police." He swept the air with his arm. "Was it a natural death? Or an accident? Why is your shop cordoned off, Courtney?"

I turned to Summers to supply the answer.

He broke his silence. "Mr. Watkins was murdered, Logan."

"Murdered?" Logan's mouth dropped open. "You're kidding. Who did it?"

"Let's be frank, sir," Summers said, not calling Logan by his first name. "The scuttlebutt is you had a beef with him about his lease."

Logan glanced at me.

I raised both hands, palms forward. "I didn't tell him a thing."

"His assistant as well as his wife were our sources," Summers went on. "A few others have heard you exchange words with Mr. Watkins over the past month."

"Yeah, okay, we argued. People with business arrangements argue." Logan smoothed the collar of his jacket. "My property. My rules. Mick broke them."

"Did you kill him?" Summers asked.

Logan glowered. "Being direct has always been your way, Dylan, but that's not the way to negotiate and get results. Your father knew how it was done. It takes wiles and wheedling. Didn't he teach you anything?" He snickered.

"Leave my father out of this," Summers said.

So I was right. Their fathers had more than going-to-school-together history. Logan was implying that Summers's father wasn't as aboveboard as his son. What had he done? Try to outbid Langford's father for a property? Vie for the same woman? Given as much as I knew about most of the families in Carmel, I knew nothing about this saga.

For a long minute, Summers worked his tongue inside his mouth. Then he clasped Logan's elbow and marched him toward Wizard of Paws, away from me. I watched as Summers talked and Logan listened, his mouth fixed in a thin, angry line. When Summers concluded, he thumped Logan on the shoulder. Logan jolted but didn't cede ground.

"I'll have my attorney contact you," Logan said loudly, and extended a hand. He smiled, but the smile didn't reach his eyes.

Summers didn't shake. Tersely, he said, "You do that."

I breathed easier. Emily and I weren't the only suspects. Good.

Chapter 5

How dreary a world would be without fairies.
—Anonymous

Just after noon, the police asked Joss and me to leave. Wishing we could stay but knowing we couldn't, I gave her the rest of the day off and then, after handing a duplicate set of shop keys over to the police, packed up Pixie, grabbed my purse, and headed out. I stopped on the sidewalk and glanced wistfully over my shoulder with thoughts running roughshod through my mind in no particular order: how long would the police need to gather evidence; what would they find; would this horrible mess ruin my business?

Last but not least, I thought *poor Mick.*

Fiona raced after me. "What are you going to do?" she cried. She was so distraught that her wings were working up a sweat. The beads of perspiration glistened in the sunlight. "That detective thinks you're guilty."

"He couldn't possibly," I said as confidently as I could

muster. All my life, I'd toed the line. Summers had to believe I was the epitome of innocence, didn't he?

"Didn't you hear him?" She paused midair and folded her arms. "I heard him. You need an attorney."

"What I need is a witness who saw me at home. The lights were on. Surely someone in the neighborhood caught sight of me." There were plenty of evening strollers and dog walkers in my neck of the woods. Like me, my neighbors enjoyed drinking in the night air, gazing at the stars, and listening to the surf crash against the sand.

"A witness." Fiona nestled on my shoulder. "Good idea. Or we could find someone to lie for you."

"To lie?"

"We could pay someone to say they saw you in your house."

"No, no, no." My father would have my head if I lied about something like that, let alone paid somebody to lie. Plus, I was pretty sure the queen fairy would banish Fiona to somewhere hot and ugly if she were to lie on my behalf.

"Courtney!" Meaghan, looking chic in a white angora cape and sweater dress, ducked past a female officer who was allowing customers to access other shops in the courtyard via a cordoned-off passageway. Meaghan grabbed me in a hug. Her cape tickled my chin. Pixie squirmed in my arms. Meaghan pulled back and scrubbed Pixie's chin. "I can't believe it," she said to me. "Mick Watkins is dead? Murdered? It's the talk of the courtyard. The talk of the town. I heard you're a suspect."

"I didn't kill him."

"Of course you didn't. No one in his or her right mind would believe that." She petted my arm. "How are you feeling?"

"In need of a brownie."

"I'm fresh out, but let me take you to Hideaway Café. It's under new ownership, did you hear? The prior owners retired to Florida. The current one has done a major renovation. I have yet to try it out. We'll get some tea, and hopefully they're still serving those caramel blondies they were famous for. I can't imagine they didn't keep those on the menu."

Driven by nervous energy, she was speaking a mile a minute, hands circling in the air. I got it. She was worried for me. So was I.

"We'll sit on the patio," she said, "and you can fill me in on everything." She jogged to the red-haired officer, said something, and waited for him to allow us to pass beyond his cordoned-off area.

Onlookers shouted questions at me as Meaghan and I strode across Lincoln Street. I didn't respond. Upset by the din, Pixie squirreled into my arms and buried her head in my armpit. I cooed sweet nothings to her. *Good girl. Sweet girl.* Fiona was still on my shoulder. She didn't say a word, but she was drumming her fingertips steadily as if preparing to audition for a rock band. Was she trying to come up with the name of someone she could find to lie for me?

Not happening.

As we neared Hideaway Café, I was struck by how lovely it had become. Like the other buildings in the Village Shops, it boasted a striking dark red wood and stone façade, but the owner had added bowers of flowers and a beautiful English garden. A half dozen small white iron tables and chairs decorated the entry patio. We stepped down the stairs into the café and waited by the hostess station. Exquisite photographs of Carmel hung on the walls. I peeked into the dining room. Warm-glowing resin candleholders decorated each white tablecloth. The strains of jazz guitar music filtered through a speaker system. The chatter of the patrons was low and comforting.

"Nice," Meaghan said. "I like it."

"Me too."

"May I help you?" a gentleman asked from behind.

I turned and grinned. "Well, I'll be. Brady Cash."

"Courtney Kelly."

I hadn't seen Brady in years, but he looked the same. Broad shoulders. Strong jaw. His skin was weathered in an athletic way. Back in the day, he'd played a mean game of basketball; we'd shot hoops often.

Brady petted Pixie on the head. "Hey, fella."

"This is Pixie," I said. "A girl."

"My mistake." Brady tickled Pixie's chin. "Hi, pretty lady."

Meaghan regarded me. "You two know each other?"

"Brady and I went to high school together. He was a senior when I was a freshman." I used my hand to make the introduction. "Brady, this is Meaghan Brownie."

Shamelessly, Meaghan gave him a once-over, appreciating his brawny looks. "I like the Pendleton shirt. You look like you'd be handy with an ax." Meaghan wasn't flirting. She was madly in love with a very talented, albeit temperamental, artist.

"I'm not bad with a saw, either, although hammers and I aren't friends," Brady joked. "I can't seem to miss my thumb. I'm better in the kitchen."

Fiona giggled.

"What are you doing here?" I asked Brady.

"After college, I became a chef." During high school, Brady had worked at his father's restaurant, the Cash Cow, located in Monterey, bussing tables and washing dishes. "Now, I own this joint."

"It's hardly a joint," I said. "In fact, it's enchanting."

"We serve burgers, so it's a joint." When he smiled, I remembered how appealing that deep dimple in his right cheek could be. "Though I'll admit they're gourmet burgers."

"I'll try one sometime," I said. "But right now, we're interested in a pot of Earl Grey tea and something sweet. Any tables available on the rear patio?"

"I've got one with your name on it." Brady grabbed two leather-bound menus and escorted us through the café. "You haven't changed a bit, by the way."

"Sure I have. I'm much, much older."

"You've got the same lovely face and curious nature." He hitched a thumb. "I saw you eyeing the photographs in the entry."

"Are they yours?"

"Mm-hm."

I said to Meaghan, "Brady and I were in photography club at school. That's how we met."

"I bet that was a pretty picture," Meaghan said sotto voce.

We stepped through a door and entered the rear patio, which was much larger than the front patio and teeming with flowers and vines. Strings of lights arced across the expanse.

"Here we are." Brady motioned to a white iron table with four chairs.

I sat in one and set Pixie on my lap. Birds chirping in the arbors caught her attention. She turned her head at every sound. Fiona flew to the branch of a vine. Flickers of light emanated from her. Was she practicing magic? Would the queen fairy need to rein her in? How would that work, exactly? Would the queen fairy send a minion to exact justice or would she appear herself?

"So, Brady"—Meaghan propped an elbow on the table and perched her chin on top—"if you get a lull in the action, why don't you join us so you and Courtney can catch up? How long has it been since you two chatted?" She wagged a finger between us.

"Years," I said. "He went off to Cal Poly—"

"I wasn't good enough to go to Berkeley, like Courtney," he replied.

"How did you know I went to Cal?"

"Your father is a regular at the Cash Cow. He and my dad talk. I happen to know you own the shop across the street, and you make fairy gardens."

"And yet you haven't come in?" I asked.

"I've been busy getting this baby off the ground." His eyes sparkled with charm. "How about I commission you to make a fairy garden for Hideaway Café?"

"Better yet," Meaghan said, "how about she teaches you? A one-on-one lesson."

"Sounds good." Brady smacked his thigh. "Whoa. Wait a sec. I'm as dense as fog. Something went down at Open Your Imagination this morning, didn't it? What's with all the police?"

"Mick Watkins—" His name caught in my throat. "Mick owned Wizard of Paws. He died inside my shop late last night."

"Aw, heck. What happened?"

I told him briefly.

Brady swept a thatch of hair off his forehead. "Wow. I knew Mick. Not well. He came in here a few times. With his dog. Have you met Shep? A real beauty." He gazed at me with concern. "Do the police have any suspects? Any leads? How are you holding up?"

"I'm managing. Tea will help."

"Whatever you want is on me." Brady aimed a finger at my opened menu. "My favorite sweet treat is the caramel blondie."

Meaghan thumped the table. "Hooray! You kept them. A man after my own heart. I could kiss you."

"Ahem"—I cleared my throat—"don't let your boyfriend hear you say that."

"*Pooh.*" Meaghan swatted the air.

"Speaking of boyfriends," Brady said, "did you and Chris get married? I don't see a ring on your hand."

Christopher Cox and I had met in high school right after he and his family relocated to Carmel. All four years, we were joined at the hip. When we went to college—he to Stanford and I to Berkeley—we remained faithful. After we graduated, we became engaged. And then, the day after we had a co-ed bridal shower, Chris had announced he didn't want to be married. Ever.

I brought Brady up to speed and added, "Chris was intent on becoming a judge, which would require all his focus. To my surprise, I wasn't bitter. If he hadn't bailed on us, I might have ended up with three kids, a minivan, and a man who didn't love me; not to mention, I might not have pursued my dream." I closed my menu. "Want to know the best thing about not marrying him? I haven't had to go through my adult life explaining that I was not named after Courtney Cox, the actress."

"Whew." Brady chuckled. "A narrow escape."

We all laughed.

"Did Chris become a judge?" Brady asked.

"He's on his way, last I heard. One more hurdle. Plus he did get married and has three kids."

After Meaghan and I ordered our tea and desserts, Brady left to inform our waitress.

"Talk," Meaghan said. "Mick. Dead. Spill everything. In detail. Not a quick recap like you gave Brady."

I told her about Fiona's finding Mick at five a.m. and alerting me, and then I filled Meaghan in about the crime scene, the evidence, the ligature marks, and testing Mick's pulse. The memory gave me the willies. "I don't know why Mick came into the shop. I wouldn't peg him for a thief. I think he hoped to meet someone."

"You mean like a tryst?"

I told her about the possibility that Mick had been having an affair with Petra Pauli.

"He was." Brady, not our waitress, returned with our order. He set a pretty white china pot on the table, plus two cups and saucers, a pairing of cream and sugar, and a plate holding two blondies.

"With Councilwoman Pauli?" I asked.

"Yep."

So much for that being a secret.

"Mind if I join you for a moment?" Brady asked. "I could use a break, and I'd like to get the lowdown. My clientele are bound to ask questions."

"Be our guest," I said. "Want to fetch another cup for tea?"

"Nah. I'm tea'd out."

I poured cups of Earl Grey for Meaghan and myself and added a cube of raw sugar to each.

Meaghan bit into a blondie and hummed her appreciation. "Just like I remember. Bless you."

"So, Brady," I said, "you're sure about the affair?" When I'd seen Mick leaving Hideaway Café yesterday and Petra Pauli exiting minutes later, I hadn't wanted to rush to a conclusion, although Petra's response to the police earlier this morning bolstered by Joss's claim did seem to cement the theory.

"They met once a week for lunch"—Brady slung an arm over the back of his chair—"and always requested the booth tucked in the corner of the bar."

"Whewie," Meaghan whistled. "Can you imagine being so indiscreet about it? Meeting right across the street from where he worked?" She leaned forward. "Did his wife know?"

"She suspected," I said and then revised. "*More* than suspected. The assistant at Wizard of Paws heard Mick and Emily argue about it."

"Oho." Meaghan lifted her teacup with both hands and leaned forward on her elbows. "Girlfriend, dish the dirt."

"That's all I know. I don't have a clue if the affair was serious."

"How did Mick break into the shop?" Brady asked.

"He stole in through a secret entrance, which Fiona—" I balked.

"Who's Fiona?" Brady asked.

Meaghan set down her cup and coyly said, "Do you believe in fairies, Brady?"

He raised a skeptical eyebrow. "What's the right answer?"

"You'd like to," Meaghan said.

"Okay, then." He gazed at me, clearly trying to assess whether this was a joke. "I'd like to."

Fiona flew to Brady and circled his head, giggling. Apparently, he wasn't immune to her advances. He raised his chin, as if sensing her. As fast as lightning, Fiona zipped to a tree across the patio and alit on a branch. I shot her an annoyed look. She doubled over in laughter, the imp.

If only I had a direct line to the queen fairy so I could get a clear understanding of fairy-on-probation *do*s and *don't*s. On the other hand, the queen, being omniscient, could probably see everything at all times and would lower the boom—*wand*—if necessary.

Fiona placed a hand across her heart and, intoning loudly enough for the world to hear, announced, "One day, everyone in the world will believe. We will win one heart at a time." I'd heard her utter the saying before. It was a fairy mantra.

Meaghan twirled a finger. "Go on about the secret entrance, Courtney."

"There are lots of secret entrances in Carmel," Brady stated.

I raised an eyebrow. "Are you sure?"

"Positive. My mother is a historical romance novelist. She knows about all the nooks and crannies in Carmel. She's told me lots of stories."

"She's an author?" Meaghan asked. "Have we heard of her?"

"If you read that kind of thing. She's sort of a big deal. She's written twelve novels so far. Eudora Cash."

"Are you kidding?" I exclaimed. "I had no idea. I've read all of her books. Golly. I never put two and two together." I liked to read across genres: mysteries, romance, and historical novels. Reading was a great way to let my mind roam free. "Back in high school, everyone called her Dory." I turned to Meaghan. "Dory ran the PTA. She threw the best parties." To Brady I said, "Was your mom writing then?"

"Nope. She was a late bloomer."

"Your father must be proud of her success," I said.

"He is."

"Guys," Meaghan said, "we'll get caught up on our reading lists later. Back to the secret entrance." She tapped a fingertip on the table. "Why did Mick go in that way and not through the front door?"

I said, "Because he didn't have a key."

"I'll bet he was meeting Councilwoman Pauli," Meaghan said.

"In my shop? Why? That doesn't make sense." I added that Emily seemed the likelier suspect. Believing Mick was having an affair, she followed him and slipped in after him. They fought. He fell and struck his head.

"Why strangle him?" Meaghan asked.

"I'm not sure. Utter rage?" I wondered if vestiges of her clothing could be found on the edges of the secret doorway.

Brady said, "Who do the police suspect?"

"Me."

"You're kidding."

"Emily Watkins claims that I wanted Mick out of the way so I could take over his lease and expand my business." I took a sip of tea. "She's wrong. I don't want to. But my alibi is iffy. I was home alone interacting with some people via the computer."

"Were you checking out online dating?" Meaghan asked hopefully.

"No."

My cheeks warmed. I would never look for a date on the Internet. I didn't judge anyone else for doing so, but that wasn't my style. Besides, I wasn't in the market for a relationship, no matter how hard my best friend pushed me to *try, try, try again*. For the past two years, she had been attempting to fix me up with someone. Anyone. She was furious that Christopher Cox had broken my heart. It didn't matter how many times I assured her that I was happy being single.

I said, "I was networking with fairy garden aficionados."

"That's got to be verifiable," Brady said.

"Not necessarily, but Joss, my assistant, is a computer wizard and is looking into it."

"So Brady"—Meaghan curled a lock of her hair coyly—"what's your story? Are you married?"

"I was," Brady said. "Not any longer."

Meaghan threw me a smug, Cupid-on-the-hunt look. Overhead, Fiona tittered. I ignored them both and took a bite of one of the blondies. Heaven.

"Tell me more," Meaghan cooed.

"She left me for an actor. A much older and wealthier actor." Brady cocked his head. "I understood why she did. She was born in Los Angeles and raised around the movie business. Against her will, she moved here with her mother when her grandmother got sick. She'd hated every minute of it. Truthfully, I lucked out when she left. I don't think we were ever in love." He refreshed my tea. "You know, if you need an attorney, I've got the name of a good one."

I swallowed hard. "I sure hope I don't."

Chapter 6

Every time a seed is planted, a fairy flower is born.
—Hans Christian Andersen

Still unable to return to my shop until the police relinquished control—Summers and I had exchanged telephone numbers; he or one of his staff would call me—I said good-bye to Brady and Meaghan and headed off with Pixie and Fiona. My sweet fairy was determined to stay by my side. After our visit to the café, I'd given her permission to return to the shop, but she was afraid of the police. The way they'd barked orders had given her the jitters.

When I stepped outside the café and drank in the fresh air, I realized how shallowly I'd been breathing since finding Mick.

Fiona said, "Aren't you curious to see where the secret entrance to your shop is?"

I nodded. "But we can't."

"Sure we can. Follow me." Fiona flew ahead.

Observing the margin created by the police tape that required onlookers to steer clear of the area, I trotted after her along Lincoln Street. At the corner of 8th Avenue, I halted and peered up the street. Fiona was correct. It was impossible to see the secret entrance. We moved closer. Even when I was facing it, it wasn't obvious, either. There was no handle, and the wood slats matched the rest of the courtyard's exterior. Mick would have needed to *know* the entrance existed. I didn't see any evidence cones marking items the police might have collected from the ground. I wondered if they had decided it was fruitless, given the amount of natural debris like pine needles and leaves in the area.

Strolling home, appreciating the waning sunlight, I wondered how Mick might have learned of the secret entrance. Had Logan told him? Had Mick asked for the floor plans for each of the courtyard buildings when he was deciding whether or not to lease? Did it matter how he'd figured it out? That was how he'd entered. Period. Had the killer been lying in wait inside Open Your Imagination for me—as Summers had suggested—or had the killer followed Mick? Who was the intended victim?

Minutes later, when we arrived home, Pixie bounded from my arms. She was ready to explore. And why not? There were birds and bugs and critters to chase. We had them in abundance.

"What should we do?" I asked Fiona as I made my way up the flagstone walkway and slipped into the house. "How about something to eat?"

Fairies preferred foods that were prepared with savory spices. They also liked sweet butter and teacakes. Fiona was partial to mallow fruits and hibiscus flowers.

"Not hungry," she murmured. She flitted to my computer. Round and round it she traveled, disappearing at the back of it for long moments. Did she think she could magically make it provide my alibi?

"I think I'll have a glass of fresh-pressed orange juice," I called out, hoping she would give up the hunt and join me.

I moseyed across the modest foyer to the kitchen, which was one of my favorite rooms in the cottage. It always smelled good, thanks to the herbs I'd planted. Each was in an odd-lot white mug that I'd painted with the herb's name. All were sitting on the tiered glass shelves by the window over the sink. A trio of vanilla candles as well as a vanilla diffuser adorned the teensy white table in the nook. Well-used cookbooks filled the shelves of my rustic white hutch and buffet, faux antiqued to match the kitchen cabinets.

Fiona reappeared.

"Where did you go?" I asked.

"On a quest."

"Find anything?"

"No."

"How about a taste of honey?" I asked.

She shook her head, furrowed her forehead as if she were thinking, and then zipped out of the room. In a matter of seconds, she returned. "All clear."

"What do you mean?"

"There's no one hiding anywhere."

I smiled, indulging her. Who did she think would invade my place? I had no valuables other than my precious plants and my computer. Then I stiffened, grasping her meaning. She was worried that the killer might have come here. Why take that risk? Would the killer, believing I knew more than I did, seeing as I had been first on the scene, want me out of the way? Or worse, was Detective Summers correct? Had I been the intended target? Would the murderer strike again?

I shrugged off the notion. No. Uh-uh. I would not rise to the urgency of Fiona's concern. I would not be afraid. When my mother became sick, she'd made me promise to be brave for the rest of my life, and I'd done my best to live up to that promise. However, I would not be stupid or caught off guard, either. I would be prepared. I set a baseball bat by the kitchen door and propped a shovel by the front door. Ready and armed for anything. I was pretty good at basketball, but I was a terror with a garden tool. Years as a landscaper had built up my arm, thigh, and core strength. My father would approve.

My father. I should call him and fill him in. And I would. Tomorrow.

"Juice," I said. "And then something fun." I needed to keep busy and not dwell on *what ifs* like the possibility of going to jail or the probability of being harmed. "I think I'll make a new fairy garden tonight for the eastern corner of the backyard. What do you think?"

Fiona didn't object.

I pulled out my professional grade press, and, using two oranges, quickly made a cup's worth of juice, straining it a second time into a Royal Doulton Pacific Splash cup—very nouveau with blue and white colors. According to my nana, vitamin C was always good for what ailed you.

While sipping the juice, I considered which pot I would use for my new project. Something bold and big enough to stand out.

After washing the cup and setting it to dry in the counter-top rack, I strolled to the backyard. Sunlight filtered through the cypress trees, and I reveled at my good fortune to live in Dream-by-the-Sea. When I finished creating, I would spend some time photographing the yard. I had documented every step of the front garden's transformation; I wanted to do the same for the rear garden.

The one large item I'd invested in for the backyard was a six-by-eight, polycarbonate walk-in greenhouse. Growing plants required steady temperatures. I kept all the tools I needed in the greenhouse: a rake for loosening soil, a trowel, a variety of spades, and an assortment of good shears. I also stowed a choice of durable aprons. My favorite was the floral one with deep pockets.

Stepping inside, I felt instantly at home. How I enjoyed the cozy aroma of the various seedlings and plants as well as the damp wood shelving. The metal counter and sink were spotless. *A messy desk indicates a messy mind*, my father would say. His attention to detail and his orderly approach to creating a new site was why he'd become one of the premier landscapers in the area. He'd taught me to be as observant. And I was. On a much smaller scale.

Pixie scampered to me, swiped my ankles with her tail, and meowed.

"Yes," I said. "Mama's going to make something. I'll use a clay pot, I think." Filling a clay pot with soil anchored me to the earth.

Pixie leaped onto her cat tree, made of oak with jute columns for scratching, and sprinted to the top. I'd set a duplicate tree in my bedroom. Curious by nature, my sweet kitten sat down, keen to observe my every move.

"How about a house-themed garden?" I cooed to Pixie. She tilted her head, not understanding.

The most important thing when creating a fairy garden was telling a story. Which pot and which fairies and environments I used mattered. I wanted this one to tell the story of my move into Dream-by-the-Sea. I lugged a large strawberry clay pot with eight pockets to the center of the greenhouse, packed it with dirt, and set a thatch-roofed house with a blue door in the center to represent my cottage. I adored the green vines trailing up the house's cobblestoned facing. The scale of it vis-à-vis the strawberry pot was just right.

Then I selected the plants. I trimmed off the lower half-inch of soil and roots from a four-inch pot of cryptomeria and planted the little *tree* behind the house. Around the sides of the house, I inserted two-inch pots of elfin thyme and ferns, and then added clumps of baby tears for grass. I drizzled a winding trail of pea-sized gravel to the front door to represent the flagstone path leading to my house. Once I'd watered the plants and tamped down the soil, making sure there were no pockets of air beneath the plants, which could make them heat up in summer—heat could cause root damage—I collected an assortment of three-inch polymer clay fairies, both boys and girls, each with different colored hair. The figurines had broader faces and chubbier cheeks than most other figurines. I aligned them on the metal counter, out of Pixie's immediate reach so she wouldn't be tempted to toy with them. They weren't fragile, but they could chip. I wanted them to look pristine until they were ready for their moment to shine in their new world.

As I gazed at the fairies, trying to decide which one would represent me, a memory of playing with my mother flashed in my mind. When she was a girl, her grandfather had built her a three-story dollhouse—blue with white trim. She'd entertained herself daily. When I turned four, she allowed me to enjoy it with her. She and I had played for hours, using that house to create so many stories. Oh, how we'd made each other laugh using cartoonish voices and saying silly things. After each encounter, we had shared a *spot of tea.* Imaginary tea, of course. The dollhouse now stood in my bedroom by the window, each piece of handmade furniture perfectly arranged to my mother's liking. I'd vowed that if I ever had a daughter, she and I would make it come alive again. I bit back a tear, the memory sharp.

"Are you okay?" Fiona flew to my side.

I nodded. "Fine."

"I miss my mother, too," she whispered.

I didn't know anything about her mother other than that she dwelled in the queen fairy's realm. Had she suffered because of her daughter's mischievous behavior? I caressed Fiona's wings gently. "I know you do."

When unsure about a fairy garden's story, I always started by positioning two figurines facing each other. Conversations didn't happen when one was turned away. I decided on a fairy with her arms wide open to represent me. She was welcoming and full of hope. I inserted a posing wire up her spine and positioned her beside the front door.

Meaghan and her boyfriend had been the first to visit my house. She'd brought a zither as a housewarming gift; I couldn't play a harp, but I could strum a zither. I didn't see a brown-haired fairy in my choices, so until I could find exactly the right fairy at the shop to represent Meaghan, as a placeholder, I selected a white-haired fairy with cheery cheeks, who was holding a guitar. I set her on the gravel path facing the fairy with outstretched arms. Then I stood a green-haired boy fairy opposite her—green, because Meaghan's artist boyfriend could act a tad jealous.

Fiona settled atop the girl's white hair and crossed her arms and legs. "This one reminds me of the councilwoman."

"She does not."

"Does, too."

"How so?" I lifted a blue-haired boy fairy from the shelf and wiggled him as if he were asking the questions. "Is it the hair?" I said in a low-pitched voice.

"She's too certain of herself. She's . . ." Fiona flicked her fingers, searching for the word. "Smug."

"Imperious."

"Bossy. Why did she demand to see the crime scene?" Fiona jammed a fist against her hip. "Tell me that."

I winked. "You're full of pluck tonight."

"You're too closed off."

Ha! She didn't have a clue how much my insides were churning. I was doing my best not to let all of my emotions burst out of me.

Fiona leaped off her perch and rammed into the green-haired fairy. He toppled.

I glowered at her. "What did you do that for?"

"He's pompous. He reminds me of Mick Watkins. And I knocked him over because Mick is dead."

Whoa. That wasn't the story I was going for.

"We need to find out who killed him and clear your name." Fiona lingered over the green-haired fairy.

I set the green-haired fairy on his feet opposite the white-haired fairy and wiggled him. Using a booming voice like Mick's, I said, "The police will find my killer."

Fiona crossed her arms. "If the councilwoman was having an affair with Mick, she might have killed him."

I picked up the white-haired fairy and, imitating Petra's commanding voice, said, "Don't be ridiculous. I'd kill Emily before I'd ever touch a hair on my beloved's head." I set her down and addressed the blue-haired boy fairy. "Don't you agree?" On his behalf, I said, "Yes, ma'am."

"Ooh." Fiona met him at eye level and batted her eyelashes. "Does the blue one represent the handsome detective?"

I frowned. "Summers isn't handsome."

"He's not?" Fiona's mouth screwed into a knot. "He looks like the actors on the covers of those magazines you skim at the grocery store."

I laughed. "Okay, he is easy on the eyes, but he's nearly as old as my father."

"Brady looks like those actors, too," she crooned in a singsong voice. "He's cute. Do you like him?"

I felt my cheeks warm. Seeing Brady had brought back so many lovely memories. Basketball one-on-ones. Photography class. Developing photos in the lab late at night. The day we met, I had acquired a crazy wild crush on him, but I was a realist and knew nothing would come of it because he was a senior and I was a freshman. And then a week later I had met Christopher, and, *poof*, all thoughts of Brady had flown out the window.

Christopher. What a waste of time. How had I missed the signs?

I returned the blue-haired fairy to the metal counter and lifted a long-limbed boy fairy with silver hair. I whisked him along the path toward the green-haired fairy and said, "You are bad. I want you out. No more lease." I made him jump up and down. "Do you hear me? Out, out, out!"

I paused when I realized that, yes, I was ad-libbing the argument between Logan Langford and Mick Watkins. I lifted the long-limbed fairy and twisted him to face me. I peered sternly at him. "Did you kill Mick?"

"Is ending a lease that important?" Fiona asked, picking up on my line of questioning.

"I'm not sure." I returned the long-limbed fairy to the scene.

"What if Emily wants to keep the lease?"

I grinned. "You're asking good questions."

Fiona planted her fists on her hips. "A righteous fairy has to be a thinker. So . . . ?"

"Emily doesn't work at Wizard of Paws, so I doubt she wants the lease, although she probably owns the business now."

"And she loves Shep."

"Of course she likes Shep," I said. "He's her dog. What owner doesn't cherish his or her own dog?"

Fiona adored Shep, too. Often, she darted outside when he was around. She appreciated his grace and warm nature. Emily couldn't see Fiona, but Shep certainly could. Whenever Fiona made an appearance, he barked merrily.

"Does Emily like the other dogs?" I asked. "That's the real question."

Scanning the figurines on the shelves, I selected a fairy to represent Emily—a six-inch tall, Schleich fairy; Schleich made a variety of gorgeous fairies and elves, this one with long hair and golden wings. She was riding horseback. Granted, she was out of scale to the other fairies, but she looked fearsome, so, for the moment, she was perfect. I wiggled the Emily fairy and cried, "I love to ride." I jiggled the silver-haired fairy in response and, mimicking Logan, said, "I hate dog hair."

Fiona froze midair and started humming. I knew why.

"Dog hair," I murmured.

Loose pet hair had been on the floor at the crime scene. I'd wondered earlier whether pet hair from Mick's work had piggybacked on him into my shop. What if Emily had transported Shep's hair inside? Had fur literally flown when she killed Mick? Had the police diligently processed the crime scene?

My doorbell rang.

I peered at the Ring app on my cell phone and spied my father standing on the front porch. He didn't look pleased, which meant he'd heard about the murder. Oops. I should have called him sooner rather than later.

Quickly, I raced from the backyard and through the house, raking my hair with my fingertips. Before touching the doorknob, I worked a kink out of my neck and slapped on a smile. *Here goes nothing.*

Swinging open the door, I said, "Dad, what a nice surprise. I'm going to eat dinner soon. Want to join me? Salmon with dill sauce, your favorite."

"You can drop the phony welcome, young lady." He marched into the foyer. "A client told me what happened to Mick Watkins."

My father and I looked nothing alike. He had cocoa-brown eyes. Mine were green. He had dark, gray-streaked hair. I was a summer blonde. Sunblock and sunhats had helped me protect my pale Irish skin. Dad had refused. He was tan and rugged, like a man who worked the land all day should be. And his scowl? I couldn't scowl like that if I tried. He'd learned how when he was a cop.

He shot a hand at me. "Why didn't you call me? Or send a text message? Something."

"It was a busy day."

He continued to scowl. "I want you to move home."

"No."

"You're not safe here."

"What you do mean? Mick was killed at my shop. Not here."

"You haven't been trained to defend yourself. What if—"

"I have been trained. By you."

Working in the outdoors was good for my father, but after ending his career as a policeman, to keep his mind mentally sharp, he'd spent every free moment teaching me the tricks of the trade. I was quite good at martial arts and not bad at a firing range.

He eyed the shovel by the door. "Plan to go digging?"

I didn't respond.

"You're not safe here," he said. "Alone."

"I'm fine, Dad." I tried not to think about Fiona's first instinct to search for an intruder when we'd arrived home.

"What if the killer was after you and not Mick?" my father asked.

I inhaled sharply. Had he spoken to Summers? They must have met while on the force. Had Summers put that notion in my father's head? Sure, the murder had happened in my shop. On my patio. But I wasn't the intended victim. *No way. No freaking way.* I paid all my bills on time. I followed through on promises. I had ended all of my relationships amicably. Okay, I was not a Girl Scout, but as I had said to the police, I did not have enemies. As far as I knew.

"Dad, I'm a suspect."

"Because the police think Mick was the target, but what if he wasn't?"

"Then the killer is dumber than a rock," I said. "I'm never in the shop past closing."

"Do you leave so your fairy can have playtime?" he chided.

I glowered at him. He didn't believe in fairies. I wished he would. An ounce of belief might soften the edges.

"If the killer wanted to get me," I said, "he or she should have come here."

"That's my point! They very well might," my father warned. "I've spoken with Detective Summers."

As I'd suspected. "Did you work together when—"

"No. He joined after I left. But we've played golf on occasion. Good man. Dedicated cop. I'll get him to back off."

Swell. Don't worry, sweetie. Daddy will handle this.

"If you come home with me, I can protect you," my father went on, not reading my body language.

"I don't need protection."

"Until you come to your senses, I'll have my guy act as your bodyguard."

"No."

"Yes." His *guy*, also a former cop, was now the security guard who oversaw the property where my father stored hundreds of thousands of dollars of landscaping equipment. My father petted my cheek. "You're looking thin."

I recoiled. "Dad. Stop. I'm not a little girl."

"You're *my* little girl."

I made a *pfft* sound.

He lasered me with a steely gaze. "I'm telling you, this business is trouble."

"This business meaning murder?"

"This business you're in. The nonsense about seeing fairies. It's fanciful. Not based in reality. There are people in town who don't like it one bit. You and your mother—"

"Stop." I shot a finger at him. "Do not bring Mom into this. She was the best mother in the world. She was creative. Colorful. She made me four cakes for my birthday every year so I'd have a choice. She"—I battled tears—"believed. She saw. She knew. Why don't you?"

"Now, listen, Courtney—"

"I'm done. I am not going to argue with you."

"Good. Let's go." He held out a hand, prepared for me to grab it.

"No, I mean, I'm not going to argue with you, *period*, Kipling Kelly."

He bridled. He hated when I used his full name, the one given to him because Nana—his mother—had loved reading the classics. Like I did. Like he did. We had a few things in common.

"Fairies are real," I continued. "My business is not fanciful. And I can handle myself. Alone. I'm staying put. I do not need your security guy, got me? End of discussion."

"Stubborn."

I grinned. "Darned tootin'."

Stubbornness. Now, that was the one thing I *had* inherited from him.

Chapter 7

Oh! Where do fairies hide their heads, when snow lies on the hills,
when frost has spoiled their mossy beds, and crystallized their rills?
—Thomas Haynes Bayly

To shake off my father's visit, I took refuge in the greenhouse
and finished making my house-themed fairy garden. I added a
porcelain kitten, a welcome sign, and a miniature mailbox
into which I inserted a light to represent Fiona. Pleased with
the result, other than the stand-in fairy for Meaghan, I set my
garden in the far eastern corner and spent a half hour taking
photographs.

Around nine p.m., my stomach grumbled. I retreated inside and threw together a simple omelet made with avocados,
cheddar cheese, and fresh chives. I'd lied about the salmon to
my father; I knew he wouldn't stay.

While eating, I reviewed the photos on my cell phone.
Overshooting the first in the batch, I caught sight of the evi-
dence photos I'd taken at the crime scene. I paused. Why had
Mick carried so many business cards? Why had he come into

my shop? Where had the killer found the rope used to strangle him?

Unable to answer any of the questions, I washed my dishes and crashed into bed.

I slept fitfully and woke Friday morning with a worry headache. I'd suffered them before, but this was worse than the others. The pain felt like a steel band was squeezing my head. Quickly, I chowed down two halves of a homemade English muffin slathered with blueberry jam; for some reason, against all known dietary facts, sugar helped me get rid of these kinds of headaches.

As I was washing dishes, Officer Rodriguez called and said I was free to open my business. I asked her if I needed official clearance from Detective Summers. She assured me I didn't. I wanted to ask if I was still a person of interest but refrained. To stave off the lingering worry headache, it was better to assume that I wasn't a suspect. Hope sprang eternal. Officer Rodriguez said one of her colleagues would drop off the extra set of keys and added that she hoped they hadn't made too much of a mess. I didn't care if they had. I was eager to resume my life.

Before ending the conversation, I asked Rodriguez the one question that had been plaguing me. Had the coroner established a time of death? She hemmed and hawed and finally admitted that Mr. Watkins had died between eleven p.m. and two a.m. Why was it so hard for her to tell me that? Did she think that if I could prove I was online during that time, I was off the hook? Did she hope I was guilty?

Don't be silly, Courtney. Rodriguez had no skin in the game. She wanted whoever was guilty to be brought to justice.

I thanked her and, to shake off the noxious sensation swirling in my stomach, dressed in a buttercup-yellow floral romper, a lightweight yellow sweater, and my favorite clogs. Then I fetched Pixie and headed to work. Fiona caught up to us at the front door and nested on my shoulder. She yawned and stretched.

"Good morning, sleepyhead," I said.

"Good morning to you. Happy May Day."

I stepped outside. "Happy first day of May to—*eek!*"

A husky man in jeans and a heavy overcoat was sitting on the rocking chair on my porch, a hat covering his face. He was sound asleep and snoring.

"Hey!" I stamped my foot.

The man startled. When the hat slipped off his face, I breathed easier. "Gus!"

"You know him?" Fiona asked.

I nodded. Gus was my father's security guy. Dad had followed through with his threat and sent Gus to protect me. I exhaled with frustration. *Honestly?*

"On your feet," I ordered.

Gus lumbered to a stand and ducked out of habit. He was enormously tall, so tall that he might have hit his head on the porch ceiling had I not warned him. "Sorry I scared you, Courtney."

"No worries, Gus, but you don't need to be here. I'm fine."

"Your father said—"

"Tell him I'm over twenty-one. I get to make my own decisions."

Gus snorted out a laugh. "Uh-uh. You tell him."

"For a big man, you sure are a chicken."

He cackled like a hen, waggled the shaka sign at me, and hustled down the path to the street.

As I walked to work with Fiona doing ballerina-style twirls overhead and birds chirping merrily as if they didn't have a care in the world, I wondered what I was going to do about my father. Ever since I'd left his employ, he'd worried about me. No, that wasn't entirely true. He'd been concerned when Christopher had dumped me, and he'd fretted about me after my mother died because I'd cocooned myself in my bedroom for three months, only coming out for food and school. I needed to cut him some slack. He was a good man. He loved me, and I loved him.

I called Joss and informed her we were open for business. She hooted with glee and promised to appear before ten.

As I strolled up to Open Your Imagination, I noticed Emily Watkins standing outside of Wizard of Paws, wagging her finger at Sonja, the shop's assistant. Emily's pale skin was washed out next to the beige blouse and neutral trousers and shoes she was wearing. Even her tan Michael Kors tote looked drab. I noticed her hand and forearm were no longer bandaged. Had she made a miraculous recovery, or had the injury been a ruse to make her look incapable of murder?

"Yes, yes," Sonja said, bobbing her head. She was a round-faced Danish woman with warm eyes, shaggy hair, and the patience of Job. Often I'd seen her walking a passel of dogs without ever letting an unruly one get the better of her, and I'd seen her handle rude clients without losing her temper. She didn't need my help managing Emily, whatever the source of their problem.

I strode into my shop and surveyed the situation. The police had done their best to straighten up, but things were out of order. In the main showroom, all of the display tables that had blocked the path from the patio to the front door had been shoved to one side or the other. On the patio, everything had been rearranged: pots, figurines, and plantings. *No stone unturned*, I mused. What could they possibly have been looking for amongst the four-inch pots of flowers, seedlings, and succulents? *Rope*, I concluded. The murder weapon.

Glancing at the fountain where Mick had lain made my

stomach do a flip-flop. I tried to push the memory from my mind, but it was difficult with Fiona zipping from vine to fountain to individual fairy gardens. When I asked what she was doing, she said she was *investigating*.

I let her do her thing and toured the rest of the patio. The Yale lock on the cabinet containing soil and macramé plant hangers was loose. I whisked the cabinet open and peeked inside. Everything looked in order. I counted a dozen hangers—the same number as we'd had the day before yesterday. I breathed easier. One hadn't been used as a murder weapon.

"Hallo-o-o," Joss crooned.

"On the patio," I shouted.

I met her at the French doors. She hugged me with sumo wrestler-worthy strength. *Oof.* For a teensy person, she sure was strong.

When she released me, I moved inside to the sales counter.

"How are you doing?" she asked, trailing me.

"Fine, given the circumstances."

"Look what I brought." She waved a ream of paper.

"What is it?"

"A printout of your online chat."

I took hold of it. "How did you—"

"My tech friend tracked down the conversation and transcribed it."

"You can do that?" I asked.

"He can." She grinned. "I can't."

I high-fived her. "You're a genius."

"I'm not sure it proves much," she said. "We'll have to see what Detective Summers thinks."

I sighed. "Supposedly his techs are reviewing everything."

Joss snorted. "*Supposedly*. That's why we needed a hard copy. Your lawyer—"

"If I need a lawyer."

"Your lawyer will want to see it. In the meantime, you

need sustenance. I picked up some lemon muffins from Sweet Treats." She unbuttoned the top button of her Jackson Pollock splatter blouse. "Is it warm in here or am I hot-flashing?"

"It's actually quite cool." The temperature outside was hovering in the sixties.

"Then I need water and a wardrobe change. Good thing I like to layer." She removed her blouse, revealing a T-shirt that read: *If you want your children to be intelligent, read them fairy tales.*

Fiona flitted to Joss, who held out a finger. Fiona alit on it. "Good morning," Joss said.

"May the day come up to greet you," Fiona replied and flew off.

At the sales counter, I fanned through the printout and reviewed the exchange. Yes, it was the right one. We'd discussed my video as well as promotional ideas. The discussion spanned the course of three hours, but there were gaps when I'd left my chair and had focused on my video script and hadn't engaged with my online counterparts. Uh-oh.

"What's wrong?" Fiona appeared over my shoulder.

"Nothing."

"You gulped."

Joss opened the Sweet Treats bag, fished out a muffin, and offered it to me. "So what do you think?"

I set the muffin to one side. "I'm certain the printout will help."

"You do? Swell." Smiling, Joss picked up a feather duster and set off across the shop. She liked to start at the far end. Routine, she said, mattered.

"Liar," Fiona said to me, sotto voce.

I shot her the stink eye, knowing she was right. I had lied. Given the holes in time, I didn't think the printout would sway a jury, let alone the police. I set the printout aside, trying to decide whether or not to give the account to the police.

Maybe I wouldn't have to. Perhaps they'd already arrested a suspect. On the other hand, Emily was free, and she was at the top of my list.

"Did you discover anything new during your, um, investigation?" I asked Fiona.

"Don't make fun. I'm quite meticulous. All fairies are."

"And?" I asked leadingly.

"The police picked up every scrap of pet hair and straw. The floor is spotless."

"Well, at least they got that done properly," I said. "Tidying up the rest will take a wee bit of time."

Fiona scratched the side of her pretty face. "The straw puzzles me."

"Mick must have tracked it in."

After unhinging the upper portion of the Dutch door to let in fresh air, I stepped outside and moved the trio of wrought-iron tables and the accompanying chairs into position. Passersby using the sidewalk had no trouble navigating around the tables; they were nestled in a slight recess. We didn't serve tea there, but we allowed customers to sit a spell and take in the view across the street of the Village Shops and the Vista Inn, which consisted of a dozen cottages.

I noted the redwood planters in front of the shop needed tending soon. Weeds were overrunning the pansies and basil. A good first impression was vital to encouraging new customers to enter the shop. I made a mental note, and then I tested the soil's moisture with my finger. Fine for now.

"How are you doing?" Joss asked as I returned inside. She'd stowed the feather duster and was waving a lotus-shadowed hand fan.

"You asked me that already."

"Yes, I know. Hot-flashing makes me repeat myself. But let's talk. Frankly. The police don't really think you're guilty, do they? They can't, of course. You're *you*. And they allowed you back in the shop, so that's got to count for something, right? But do they?" Her questions came in rapid succession. She didn't allow me to reply to any of them.

When she drew in a big slurp of air, intending to continue her cross-examination, I gripped her shoulders. "Breathe. Please. I need you to remain calm so I can be calm. No more questions. I have no answers."

"Okay."

"The police will do their duty," I went on. "They will find the killer, who is not me, and all will be right with the world."

"Is that what Fiona believes?" Joss scanned the room. "Where did she go?"

"Out there." I pointed to the patio. Pixie was on her hind legs doing a jig. Fiona was overhead doing cartwheels. "Listen, we have a lot to do today. We'll have to work on enhancing our public relations, given the fact that a death—a *murder*—occurred here. We're bound to get some blowback. We need people to know Open Your Imagination is a safe haven. I'm thinking that instead of charging for our upcoming seminars, we should offer free ones."

Joss said, "We could have a raffle for one lucky winner to pick a figurine of his or her choice, too."

"Great idea." I patted her on the shoulder. "Come up with more like those. Put on your thinking cap."

"Will do."

"Excuse me." A woman called from outside.

I turned and spied an attractive female with almond-shaped eyes and mocha-colored skin. Raven-black hair framed her face, and her exquisite silk dress hugged her lithe frame. She looked familiar, but I couldn't place her.

"May I speak with Courtney Kelly?" she asked.

"I'm Courtney."

She pushed the Dutch door open, stepped inside, and offered me her business card. "I'm Ulani Kamaka, a reporter for *The Carmel Pine Cone*."

A reporter. Uh-oh. What did she want?

"I'd like to do a story on your business."

Since 1915, the newspaper had been a superb source for news. I particularly liked the reader's picks for the best local shops, restaurants, wineries, and more.

"We think it will be of great interest to our following," Ms. Kamaka added.

I narrowed my gaze, suddenly realizing where I'd seen her. "You're the woman who was trying to get information out of the police officer yesterday."

Ms. Kamaka stood taller but had the decency to blush. "You've caught me out."

"He shut you down."

"Yes, he did."

I jutted a hip. "So why shouldn't I?"

Ms. Kamaka worked her tongue along the inside of her cheek.

"Be honest, Ms. Kamaka—"

"Call me Ulani."

I cut her off with a hand gesture. "What you're really after is the story about the murder."

"No." She hesitated. "I mean, yes, of course, but I really want to write a story about your business, too." She peeked past me. "I heard there is a fairy living here. Is it true? A real fairy?"

Judging by her eager gaze, she wanted to believe. I wouldn't deny her from having that moment.

"Follow me." I curled a finger. "I've got work to do. The police left this place in disarray. We can chat while I get caught up."

Ulani lingered in the main showroom, eyeing the tea sets and other gift items. She pulled her cell phone from her pocket and snapped a few pictures. "Is it okay if I document?" she asked after the fact.

"Be my guest." I'd bet she was hoping to capture the image of my fairy on film. She wouldn't be able to. Like the Cheshire Cat, Fiona morphed from view whenever a camera was around. She told me no fairies allowed photographs of themselves, although they would pose for an artist. That was why there were so many depictions of them over the ages. Fairies had a smidgen of vanity. "Joss, is the water hot for tea?" I asked.

"Sure is, boss."

"Ulani, fetch yourself a cup of tea from the tea cart. We have a variety of choices in the caddy. Then have a seat at one of the tables outside."

As she ambled to the two-tiered cart and studied the tea selections, I strode to the patio. Dealing with the rearrangement of the plants was foremost on my list. I set the four-inch pots to the left and the two-inch seedlings to the right. Using a moist rag, I wiped up the bits of handmade potting soil—a mixture of peat, moss, bark, perlite, and not too much sand or the soil would be too porous—and dumped whatever I gathered into a trough at the far corner of the patio. *Waste not, want not*, my father would say. How many axioms had he recited over the years? My mother and Nana had liked spouting them, too. I'd been a sponge and recalled them all.

Ulani joined me on the patio and set her teacup on one of the tables, but she didn't sit. Slowly, deliberately, she perused the area. She must have gleaned from someone that Mick had died in this area. She took photographs but was careful not to take too many of the fountain lest she give herself away.

I allowed it. There was nothing to see—no blood, no body outline. At least the police had cleaned that up completely.

Next, I moved to the shelving holding the fairy garden

environmental pieces: a variety of houses, porch swings, water features, trees, and boulders. So many choices. Was it only two days ago that young Lauren had selected her brown-haired fairy with the crown of flowers? She'd begged her mother for a porcelain mushroom and a butterfly. Her mother had drawn the line after the swing set and bunnies.

Ulani stopped in front of the shelves featuring individual fairies. "These are beautiful. May I touch?"

I'd hung a few signs around the garden. Most were inspirational like: *Take home a garden and open your world to the unbelievable,* or *Imagine. Create. Believe.* One sign was necessary to keep younger customers at bay: *You break it; you own it.* Parents understood that sign instantly.

"Of course." I figured she'd be careful.

Ulani lifted a peach-colored flower fairy with cascading ebony hair, the petals of her flower turned upside down to form her skirt. "You put these in gardens?"

"Yes. Look around the patio. You'll see a few gardens that aren't for sale. I made them for inspiration."

Ulani returned the fairy figurine to her spot on the shelf and toured the patio.

"Some people collect the fairies and hang them like ornaments," I said.

"Tell me about real fairies." Ulani's lips parted ever so slightly. She wasn't mocking me.

"Fairies—real fairies—like to visit gardens. They are nurturers of the earth."

"Hm-mm," Ulani murmured as she inspected other figurines. "How big are they?"

"Fairies come in all sizes. Large and small, male and female. Sometimes they'll surprise you and take human form."

She arched an eyebrow.

I grinned. "You can never be sure when a needy person might be a fairy in disguise."

"Ah, you mean like in the movie *Beauty and the Beast*, when the witch came to the castle and the prince shunned her."

"Yes, you understand. A beggar woman or a gypsy could be a fairy. My mother advised me to be kind to all."

Ulani lifted a one-inch-tall squirrel carrying a stack of books. "How cute is this."

"When making a fairy garden, it's fun to include creatures that enhance the world," I said. "For example, that particular squirrel would be good in a garden dedicated to reading."

She replaced the squirrel and eyed me, her mouth quirking up on one side. "What got you into this line of business?" She pressed the recording app on her cell phone. "Is it okay if I . . ." She jiggled her phone. Where was the fancy one she'd used on the policeman yesterday? Tucked away so as not to intimidate me?

"It's fine." I sidled past her and reset the squirrel in profile, which was the best way to view the little guy. "My mother planted whimsical gardens. I liked hanging out in them."

"When did you see your first fairy?" She eyed me warily.

"When I was a girl." I felt a stir in the air and looked around. Fiona wasn't in sight. I shook off the sensation and continued. "But then I lost the ability. Until a year ago."

"What changed?"

I explained, as I had to Lauren, that I'd opened my mind to possibilities. "To see a fairy, one has to . . . believe."

Ulani clicked off the recording app and resumed touring the patio, checking out every pot and figurine. Aloud, she admired the twinkling lights in the vines and the variety of plants. She gushed over the *Alice in Wonderland* fairy garden pot. It consisted of three pots, one set atop the other, each looking ready to topple. The Queen of Hearts was chasing Alice down a deep furrow of baby tears.

"'Off with her head,'" Ulani recited and chuckled. "I loved reading about Alice."

"Me too."

Finally, Ulani alit at the table holding her teacup and took a sip. "Were you scared?"

"To see a fairy?"

"No, to find Mick Watkins dead. Right here."

And there you have it, I thought. Not many people could keep curiosity in check.

I licked my lips. "Ulani—"

"I get it." She held up a hand. "You don't want to talk about it, but the story will come out. Why not tell it in your voice?"

"Because the police wouldn't want me to."

"The police." Ulani made an unladylike raspberry sound.

Out of nowhere, Fiona came to a skidding halt on my shoulder. She thumped her teensy foot. "Tell her no," she ordered. "We have to keep what we learn to ourselves. Not to mention, if I personally solve the crime, I get points with the queen fairy, and my wings"—she fluffed her baby wings—"need all the help they can get."

"I understand."

"You do?" Ulani's eyes lit up. "Does that mean you'll tell me everything?"

"No. I mean . . ." I sputtered. "That is to say, I *appreciate* what you need, but I can't help. I am adamant about that. I cannot share a whit about the crime. My fairy is advising me to keep mum, and I agree with her."

Ulani leaped to her feet and peered into the air. "She's here? Where?" She pivoted right and left.

Fiona hopped off my shoulder and stuck her thumbs in her ears. She wiggled her fingers. I silently willed her to stop—the queen fairy would not be amused—but she couldn't seem to help herself.

"She's not a true believer," Fiona grumbled.

I said to Ulani, "You'll need to speak with the police if you want to learn more."

Ulani let out a hiss. "They've already shut me out. They don't take me seriously." She whipped her long hair over her shoulder. "If you change your mind, please contact me."

I nodded politely, knowing I wouldn't . . . change my mind.

"In the meantime, I will put an article in the *Pine Cone* about your shop. It is truly magical."

Relieved to be let off the hook, I ushered Ulani to the front of the shop. "Thanks for understanding."

"Just doing my job." She started out the door and pivoted. "One last question. Is it true? Are you a suspect in the murder?"

I gulped. Heat scudded up my neck. My insides roiled with indignation. An impulse to shove Ulani out the door shot through me.

Luckily Joss raced to my side and grabbed one of my hands. "Courtney Kelly wouldn't hurt a fly. How dare you blindside her like that. Please leave."

Chapter 8

Buttercups in the sunshine look like little cups of gold.
Perhaps the Faeries come to drink the raindrops that they hold.
—Elizabeth T. Dillingham, "A Faery Song"

I stood by the door and watched Ulani until she drove away in her two-toned Mini Cooper. As she disappeared around the corner, a sea gull squawked overhead, as if mocking my edgy mood. To work off the tension, I fetched a trowel and pruning shears and tended to the front planters, tweaking the basil and removing a few faded flowers from the pansies.

Mid-snip, I paused because the screen door of Wizard of Paws opened and Gregory Darvell stepped out looking energized, cheeks flushed and eyes gleaming. Emily followed him and closed the screen door.

Gregory offered his hand to Emily and said something. I couldn't catch the conversation. As if sealing a deal, they shook formally and quite firmly. Again I wondered whether Emily had really injured her hand or had lied to make herself appear weaker and, therefore, incapable of murder.

What was the deal she was making with Gregory? Did he want to take over the business? Become a partner? Maybe a strong handshake was his way of offering condolences. They chatted for a minute or two, and then he turned and strode down the sidewalk.

Seconds later, the screech of brakes caught my attention. A blowsy woman, wearing a loud floral dress that clashed with her orange-dyed hair, lumbered out of a black Honda Accord and marched to Wizard of Paws. "Emily Watkins," the woman bellowed. "Stop. Right. Now."

Emily, who was holding the screen door open, jolted and released the handle. The door slammed with a *clack*. She clutched the collar of her blouse and backed up until her shoulders pressed against the screen door.

The blowsy woman's jowls jiggled as she approached Emily. If she'd been a cartoon character, steam would have been spewing out of her nostrils.

"Miranda," Emily said. "You heard."

"Of course I heard. What do you think I am, deaf? The whole town is talking. Who killed my brother?" Aha. Miranda was Mick's sister. Apparently, she was just as much of a bulldog as he'd been. "Are you putting the business up for sale? What's going on with his estate?" she asked, her questions coming out rat-a-tat. So much for nuance. Had she loved him? Was she sad about his passing? "What are the police doing about finding his killer?"

"Gee, thanks for asking how I am," Emily said passive-aggressively.

Miranda blanched and, sufficiently chastised, lowered her chin. "I apologize." After a moment, she met Emily's gaze. "How are you?"

"Distraught. Heartbroken. How are you?"

"Obviously, I'm stunned." Miranda clapped a hand to her chest. "And as brokenhearted as you." She shot a meaty finger at Open Your Imagination. "I heard he was killed in there. Is it true?"

Emily nodded.

Mesmerized by Miranda Watkins's abrasiveness and amazed by the amount of information she had already gleaned, I plunked onto one of the wrought-iron chairs. Where had she come from? Was she a local or an out-of-towner? She'd never ventured into my shop.

"Why was Mick in there?" Miranda asked. "What possible reason could he have to go into a garden shop in the middle of the night? He hated flowers. They made him sneeze." She drew a bead on me. Even though she didn't know me, I re-coiled. My pulse started doing a jig. "It makes no sense."

Emily said, "He stole in to search for fairies."

I gaped. Had I heard that right?

"Don't be absurd," Miranda said. "There are no such things, and Mick of all people knew that."

"He left me a note, Miranda," Emily said patiently, as if addressing a slow-witted child. "I've shown it to the police."

Miranda cocked her head. "Which means you were the only one who knew where he'd gone."

Good point, I thought. When exactly had Emily read the note? Why hadn't she mentioned it when the police questioned her yesterday? Maybe she had.

"Don't attack me." Emily wrapped her arms around torso, protecting herself from her sister-in-law's wrath. "I did not kill my husband. I was away. At a retreat. I found his note when I returned home, after he was dead."

Had "looking for fairies" been Mick's defense should he get caught having a tryst in my shop with the councilwoman? Or had he really been serious about encountering a fairy? According to lore, seeing your first one brought good luck. Had Mick hoped that seeing a fairy would change the course of his business woes or perhaps his *affaire d'amour*?

"The police will find out what happened," Emily said. "There will be justice for your brother."

I questioned that logic. If the murderer got away with it, there would be no justice.

"What's the business worth?" Miranda demanded, changing tactics. "If you sell it, I want my portion. I'm in his will." So much for loving her brother and being stunned. Money talked.

"I wouldn't know if you're in it. I mean, yes, Mick has written a will, but I'm not privy to the details." Emily raised her chin.

"Of course I'm in it. I'm his sister."

If Miranda was in the will, did that make her a person of interest in Mick's death? I imagined a list of possible suspects: Emily because of jealousy, Miranda because of greed, and Logan because he'd wanted Mick and his business out, but Mick had refused. Which motive was strongest?

"Listening in on a conversation is a bad habit," a man said from behind me.

I swung around and felt my insides snag. Detective Summers approached and towered over me, casting a shadow across my face. A chill ran through me. I lowered my shears lest he think I was dangerous.

He jerked his head in the direction of the two women. "What have you learned so far? If you're going to be a snoop, you might as well be a snitch."

I bridled at both words. "I wasn't prying. I was tending to my plants. On my own property. Open Your Imagination prides itself on keeping an attractive entry. Is that a crime?"

"According to CVC 21955, it might be."

I frowned. "CVC 21955 is the code for jaywalking, if I'm not mistaken."

Summers's smile broadened. "So you're up to date on your codes. Good for you."

"I'm a responsible citizen. I attend city council meetings. I like to know what's going on in my hometown. Plus, I care for my fellow man. Including Mick Watkins."

Summers sat in the chair opposite me. Were the white shirt and khaki trousers his uniform? His skin was glistening and his eyes were sharp, as if he'd recently worked out. "How are you doing?"

"Honestly?"

"I prefer honesty," he said. Dead serious, eyes narrowed.

"I don't like being a suspect. I hate that someone died on my premises. I've never seen a dead body. I'm having nightmares. But you probably don't care about that."

"Actually, I do." He folded his hands on the table. "FYI, I got a call from your father."

Good old Dad followed through. Swell. "What about?"

Summers grinned. "You, of course. He'd like me to back off. I can't. But I appreciate that he vouched for your integrity."

So my father wasn't as almighty powerful as he thought when it came to working with the police. That had to be a blow to his ego.

Summers leaned back in his chair. "How's business?"

"We just opened," I said, "but I'm hoping the incident won't affect us for long." I placed my tools on the tabletop. "By the way, that's Mick Watkins's sister, Miranda."

"I know."

"Miranda wants her share of the estate. Is it possible—"

"Stop. Miranda is not guilty. She was in New York the day of the murder, scouting out antiques." He smirked. "Yes, we're doing our due diligence. The woman has a solid alibi with plenty of witnesses. She flew in to San Francisco airport about two hours ago."

"She lives here?"

"Yes."

The fact that Summers was verifying alibis should have made me feel better. It didn't.

Summers said, "If I were you, I'd worry about your own situation."

Worry and *situation* didn't sound good. I put on a brave face. "You said your tech crew would determine whether my alibi about being online in a chat room was credible. Have they?"

"We've done some legwork. There are time stamps for your conversation, but as I said before, you're not out of the woods. No lawyer can prove, even by a time stamp, that you, yourself, were at that computer."

"I have a physical printout of the chat if you'd like to see it. One of Joss's friends worked it up."

Summers held up a hand. "Not necessary."

I shifted in my chair. "Maybe somebody saw me sitting at my desk in the living room."

"Like a Peeping Tom?"

"I don't close the drapes. A neighbor could have seen me."

"You should close the drapes."

I leveled him with a glare. "You sound like my father."

He chuckled. "Are you suggesting all cops, even former cops, sound alike?"

Fiona soared to me and hovered by my ear. "Tell him who you think did it."

I flicked my fingers to make her stop.

Undaunted, she flew to my other ear. "I can't do it for you. He's not a believer. He can't see me or hear me. Do it."

"How much is Mick Watkins's estate worth?" I asked.

"That's being evaluated."

I drummed the table with my fingertips. "You know, if Emily inherits everything—"

"Got it. Follow the money. Don't worry. I took Investigating 101." Summers bit back a grin, realizing his sarcastic response had irked me.

"Emily told her sister-in-law that Mick left a note saying he wanted to go into my shop to look for fairies."

"I read it."

"When did she find that note?"

"When she got home."

"If she knew Mick had come here—"

"Whoa." Summers held up a hand. "We've checked out of her alibi. She went to the Equestrian Inn as she stated."

"Are you positive?"

Fiona cried, "The straw! From horses."

I thumped the table with my fingertips. "There was straw on the patio floor by the fountain. What if it came from horses? What if Emily—"

"According to sources, Mrs. Watkins was at the inn all night and didn't leave until morning."

"Which sources? Did you speak to them personally or—"

Summers stared daggers at me. I sighed. If only I had a badge.

I said, "Logan Langford and Mick really went at it on Wednesday outside Wizard of Paws. Logan threatened Mick."

"I know."

Of course Summers knew. That was why Logan had said he'd have his attorney contact the detective.

Summers propped both elbows on the table. "Look, Miss—" He stopped himself. "Look, Courtney, you have good instincts. You have your father's grit. But like I said before, I don't want you to theorize. That's what I'm here for. It's my job." He stood up. "I'm good at what I do."

"I'm sure you are, Detective, but when did you last solve a murder in Carmel? You skirted that answer with Councilwoman Pauli."

He pursed his lips and his eyes wavered, making him look, dare I say it, vulnerable. I felt horrible for being so blunt, but worry and fear and a whole host of other emotions were roiling inside me.

"I can solve it and I will," he said evenly. "I'm seasoned. I've gotten to the bottom of plenty of art heists and home break-ins."

"But not murder."

"Carmel is a sleepy town when it comes to crime. People are kind to one another. They're decent."

"Sir"—I scrambled to my feet and raised my chin to meet his gaze—"someone knocked my neighbor out and strangled him. Someone *decent* didn't do that. Look"—I shot out a hand—"I theorize because I'm a suspect for no reason whatsoever other than location."

"You know what they say in the real estate business: *location, location, location.*" Summers splayed his hands in an effort to soften the message.

It didn't work.

Chapter 9

A rustle in the wind reminds us a fairy is near.
—Anonymous

Close to eleven in the morning, a confident woman in a simple ecru dress approached the sales counter. "Courtney Kelly?" Her kind eyes and the way she wore her hair in a loose chignon reminded me of my mother.

Breathing easier, certain she hadn't been sent by Summers to arrest me and take me to jail, I abandoned the paperwork that I'd been attacking—I'd been trying to decide whether to purchase an entire closeout selection of garden fairy replicas—and said, "I'm Courtney."

"Victoria Judge. I'm a defense attorney. Your father hired me."

A moan escaped my lips. Quickly, I apologized. "Miss Judge, there's been a misunderstanding."

"I don't think so," she said. "You're a person of interest to the police. We need to get on top of this. Where can we talk?"

Joss sidled up to me and whispered, "Are you okay?"

"I would be if I could knock off my father and get away with it."

"Ha! Don't we all wish we could? Fathers. What a pain."

I introduced Joss to the attorney and said, "We'll be in the office."

A half hour later, I had agreed to allow Miss Judge to oversee my case. I didn't alienate her. I didn't demean my father. If I really needed her to defend me, I wanted her to think I was the best and most compliant client ever. To clear my name, I gave her the printout that Joss's tech had provided, and to seal the deal, I sent her off with a fairy figurine, one with a deep purple petal skirt. Miss Judge was honored. Purple, she told me, represented justice. I actually knew that. My superstitious ex-fiancé had worn purple ties when he'd taken the bar.

After she left, I returned to the main showroom craving something sweet.

As if fate were smiling on me, Lauren skipped into the shop and offered me a bag with the Sweet Treats logo. "Courtney," she chimed. "We're back. Are you hungry? Mommy and me—"

Her mother, who was right behind her, cleared her throat.

Lauren blushed and began again. "Mommy and I"—she stressed the *I*; someone was getting grammar lessons—"just went to the bakery, and we brought you cookies as a thank-you."

I accepted the gift and peeked inside. "Sugar cookies. Yum. My favorite."

Lauren picked up a white shopping basket. "We're also here to pick out a couple more things for my garden."

Her mother said, "Lauren has the itch."

"I warned you," I said. "Many of our clientele get it." I remembered making my first fairy garden. It had taken me hours to pick out all the pieces.

"If it makes her feel creative," her mother said, "I'm all for it."

"Mommy says you can't use up creativity," Lauren chirped. "The more you use, the more you have."

Her mother smiled. "Actually Maya Angelou said that."

Lauren scrunched her nose. "I thought you said it."

"Darling"—her mother waved a hand, as if she were a fairy godmother—"tell Miss Courtney what you want."

How I loved doting parents. They were the bread-and-butter of a craft industry.

"Is Fiona here?" Lauren dashed to the patio to seek for her. "Follow me, Courtney."

Truth be told, I wasn't sure where my fairy had gone. Pixie was sound asleep on the white oak bureau behind the sales counter.

"Mommy, remember this?" Lauren sprinted to a demo fairy garden, the one I'd made a month ago featuring a girl standing on a park bench holding a kite. "See the cat figurine?" Beneath the bench, a teensy white porcelain cat lay sleeping. Twinkle Toes, the cat I'd had as a girl, had looked just the same. "This is the one I was telling you about, Mommy. She'll have fun in my fairy garden, don't you think?"

"There's a cat just like that one on the shelf," I said.

"And we need books. Any fun day in a fairy garden should include books." Lauren whizzed to one of the display racks and selected the squirrel toting the stack of books. "Isn't he adorable?" She twisted him in front of her mother's face.

"Adorable."

Lauren added it to her basket and gathered the mushroom and the butterfly she'd had her heart set on the other day, too. With her selections complete, she drew near and whispered, "I don't see Fiona anywhere. Is she all right?"

I crouched to her level. "She must be investigating something."

"Investigating?" Lauren didn't understand the word.

"Looking for answers," her mother explained.

"Answers about what?" Lauren asked.

"Life," her mother replied.

Or death, I thought glumly as I followed them into the shop to complete their purchase.

As Joss attended to them, more customers entered. A steady flow of them. A few regulars came to check on me. A couple wanted gory details of the murder, which I refused to provide, claiming the police would frown on my discussing the case. One woman, an elderly shop owner who, thanks to making a fairy garden, had found the childlike spirit she thought she'd lost, brought me a tuna fish sandwich. She was concerned that I might starve myself with worry. Each and every do-gooder's support gave me hope that although a murder had occurred on the premises, once it was solved and I was cleared of the crime, business would thrive.

After lunch—the tuna fish hit the spot and the sugar cookie was the perfect dessert—I decided to do what Joss and I had drummed up. I made a sign, set it outside, and a half hour later, held an impromptu *free* demonstration in the learning-the-craft corner of the patio.

Six adults and two redheaded children—a boy and a girl—sat on the benches. Everyone but the boy was eagerly watching as I gathered items for a brand new fairy garden. No script. No plan.

"I need a theme," I explained to my eager audience. "Yoo-hoo." I crooked a finger at the boy who looked to be about seven. "Want to help me?"

He shook his head. "Fairy gardens are girlie."

"Let's make one that will appeal to you." I walked to the shelves of figurines and opened my hand. "Do you like cars or bicycles or boats?"

"I like spaceships."

I grinned. "Terrific. Let's make a moonscape fairy garden."

"There aren't plants on the moon," he said, still resistant.

"But there are rocks," Fiona said, flying into view. Pausing midair, she stretched her arms and yawned. "Sorry, Courtney. I needed a nap. Did I miss anything?"

"We're making a moonscape." Being the teacher, I could repeat myself without upsetting those who couldn't see or hear Fiona.

"On it. C'mon." Fiona circled the boy's head. "Let's see what we can find."

The boy glanced upward and leaped to his feet, his interest piqued. Without question, he could see her.

"We need to create rocks and rivers and caverns," Fiona said.

"I want it to be blue," the boy cried.

"Good choice," I said. "Deep blue is perfect for outer space."

Over the next few minutes, with my guidance, he selected a handful of different sized rocks, a bag of blue crystal for a river, and a boy fairy with blue wings and blue hair. A miniature fishbowl, my young helper said, would serve as his space helmet, but then he changed his mind.

"Do you have a cowboy hat?" he asked. "I want my fairy to be a cowboy astronaut so he can lasso those aliens with a rope when they show up." He swung an imaginary lariat overhead. "Yee-haw."

The crowd chuckled at his enthusiasm.

Me? I flinched as the memory of the murder scene scudded through my mind. Had the killer strangled Mick with rope as a metaphor for capturing him and hauling him to justice? Had Mick done something illegal? Had Emily deemed his affair with Petra Pauli against the law?

"Which plants should we add?" Fiona asked the boy.

He huffed. "Nothing grows on the moon."

"Are you sure?" I asked. "Have you been there?"

He frowned.

Fiona tittered.

"Let's use a few dark-colored succulents to be moon plants," I suggested. "How does that sound?"

Grudgingly, he agreed.

Last but not least, he chose a miniature blue rocket. About a month ago, I'd added teensy cars, trucks, and space vehicles to our environment collection. Not all children, or adults for that matter, wanted their gardens to be fairy tale-like. Some wanted their displays to be rooted in reality. Whatever stirred their creative juices was fine with me.

An hour later, the boy and his grandmother left with a ten-inch-round moonscape fairy garden, free of charge. The other attendees each made a purchase and vowed to spread the word. Some said they'd had a *supersonic blast*. Others said fairy gardening was *out of this world*.

As I bid the last member of the class good-bye, I caught sight of Petra Pauli speaking to a customer near the entrance of the shop. Dressed in a tight-fitting jacket over a matching pencil skirt, she looked as though she'd just come from a power meeting, even though she had her collies in tow.

The dog with the brown muzzle began to strain at his leash. "Zeus, stop," Petra begged.

Zeus could use a few training sessions with Gregory Darvell, I mused. I hoped the dog's head wouldn't butt against any of the displays and unsettle our wares. We allowed customers to bring in pets, but we expected them to be obedient.

Petra ended her conversation with the other customer and allowed the dog to drag her forward. The dog with the white muzzle tagged along. Halfway into the shop, Petra stopped by a display table and yanked on Zeus's leash. This time he obeyed. One by one, she lifted the various tea sets. After checking the prices of each, she held a few of the individual teacups up to the light.

I joined her. "The finer the bone china, the better the light shines through."

"They're all so pretty." She thrust her dogs' leashes at me. "Here."

I gladly took hold. With a gentle tug and a tap to his rump, I made Zeus sit. He looked at me as if expecting a treat. I made a mental note to stock some in the future.

"Which is your favorite?" Petra asked.

"The Royal Albert bouquet." I pointed to the teacup sporting a bouquet of roses with the modern yellow edge and rich gold trim.

"Do you think they'd work in a teacup chandelier?"

"A what?" I'd never heard of such a thing.

"I saw it on TV the other day. Martha Stewart said I'll need at least five to seven cups and saucers to create it. You drill holes in them and insert the wires. It's quite complicated, but I'll hire an electrician."

I chuckled. Martha Stewart was a hoot. What couldn't she bake or make? "You might consider going to Goodwill or a discount store to buy teacups. These are probably too expensive for the kind of project you have in mind. If you drill holes in china, there will be breakage, I imagine."

Petra fanned her hand. "Don't worry. I can afford these. Martha said to use only the best."

Of course Martha would suggest that. She had an extraordinary budget.

Petra called Joss over, indicated seven individual teacups and saucers, and gave her a credit card. "Better make that eight," she said, choosing one more, "in case, like Courtney said, there's breakage. And sign my name while I tour the patio." She took the dogs from me.

Joss raised an eyebrow. Privately, I made a goofy face meaning Petra was used to getting her way. Joss bit back a smile and proceeded to ring up the purchase.

"I want to make a fairy garden," Petra said as she steered her dogs through the French doors to the patio.

I didn't believe her because, instead of perusing the fairy garden items on the shelves, she made a beeline to the fountain. Right where Mick had been murdered. Did Petra know the location because, as Fiona had speculated, she was the killer? Or had the police leaked the information? What would Petra's motive have been? Would she have killed Mick if he'd called off their affair? Wouldn't she have murdered Emily instead, as I'd theorized, and tried to win Mick back? Oh, my. The travails of a broken heart.

As Petra toured the fountain murmuring how unique it was, Gregory Darvell strode onto the patio like a man on a mission. Had I psychically summoned him when I'd mused about Petra's headstrong dog?

I approached him, stopping short of a wrought-iron table. "Good afternoon."

"Your girl said you could help me," he said.

"My girl? Do you mean Joss?" I snickered. "She's hardly a girl. She's your age."

"She's teeny."

Since when did people determine age by size? "Don't tell me you want to build a fairy garden."

"No." He held up two tins of tea: chamomile and plum flower ginger. "I was reading online that there might be teas that could calm my bichons. I've read that alternative medicines might be a good thing to try."

"Both of those teas are good for calming humans, and I've heard that giving a dog a treat soaked in chamomile will help calm its tummy, but I'm not a vet and I have a cat. I've never owned a dog." I jutted a finger at Pixie, who'd sauntered to the patio, intrigued by the collies. "Aren't you the expert?"

"Sure, when it comes to getting them to sit, heel, and jump through hoops." Gregory sighed. "But my two babies are quite quixotic. I've tried everything. Long walks. Going to the beach. I think their age is getting to them. They're eighteen."

"Wow, that's old for dogs, isn't it?"

"Not for smaller breeds." He swung his head left and right, scoping out the patio. "By the way, this is a nice place. It's got a good spirit." He leaned in and whispered, "I hear there is a fairy living here. Is it true?"

"Indeed, it is."

"Yeah, right." He snorted. "Nice fountain." He strode to it and dipped his hand in the water.

A shiver shimmied down my spine. An image of Mick lying at the base of the fountain flashed before me. I felt faint and gripped the back of a chair.

Fiona whooshed to my side. "Are you okay?"

I nodded, but I wasn't. Why had Gregory touched the water? Was I being overly sensitive to the environment?

Petra's dogs yipped and tugged her to Gregory. "I'm sorry," she said.

"No worries." Gregory set the containers of tea on the nearby table and extended a hand toward the dogs so they could smell him. When they were content, he knelt and rubbed them warmly behind the ears. "Hey, fellas, what are you up to?" Zeus nudged the pocket on Gregory's red plaid shirt. "You want a treat?" He gazed up at Petra. "Is it okay to give them a treat? No corn or wheat fillers."

I knew I'd guessed right earlier. The dog was a good little beggar.

"Sure," Petra said. "That's fine."

Gregory obliged and continued to stroke the dogs as they chomped. "Yes, yes, I love you, too."

"Would you care to take them off my hands?" Petra joked. "I'll sell them for a song."

Gregory rose to his feet. "Sorry. I have two dogs of my own. That's about all I can manage."

"Aren't you a trainer?" she asked.

"Yes, but I'm not like one of those cat ladies with twenty cats, and I don't board any of my show dogs."

Petra swiveled and peered at the fountain again. "Isn't it eerie standing near where Mick Watkins died?"

Gregory jolted and took two steps backward. "He died here? On the patio?"

"Courtney found him. Isn't that so, Courtney?" Petra gazed at me, her eyes glazed with moisture. Was she keeping her tears in check? Did tears exonerate her? "I heard a customer talking about it inside." Petra aimed a finger toward the main showroom.

How had that person learned the truth? If only I could stop everyone from spreading the word, but that was a pipe dream.

"It must have been ghastly, Courtney," Gregory said. "Is it true you're a suspect? I know you and Mick didn't get along, but I don't think you did it."

Petra gasped. "You're a suspect, Courtney? What nonsense."

My cheeks warmed. "Thanks for that vote of confidence, you two, but, for the record, Mick and I got along fine." I flapped a hand. "Yes, he could be crusty at times, but only because he thought I wanted to lease his shop's space."

"Do you?" Gregory asked.

"No. This is ample for me." The better question was what did Gregory want? What had he and Emily been discussing when Joss and I had shooed Ulani Kamaka from the shop?

Petra placed a hand on my shoulder. "Where were you at the time, Courtney, if you don't mind my asking?"

I did mind, but I had no qualms about sharing my alibi. "I was at home, chatting online with some fairy garden aficionados until two a.m."

Petra frowned. "Oh, dear. You were alone? That's such a weak alibi."

"No, it's not. I—"

"I wish I'd seen you there," Gregory said.

"I wish you had, too." I offered a thankful smile. "But that would have been a fluke. You don't know where I live."

"Sure I do. I have a client a few doors down from you. Tish Waterman."

"Tish." Petra sniffed. "That woman is as tart as a lemon."

On that point, Petra and I agreed. Tish was a spa owner who vocally espoused that fairies weren't real and that somehow my business—she was never clear on that point—was stealing clients from hers.

Petra's eyes widened. "What if she killed Mick? I've heard her rail about Open Your Imagination. Maybe she sneaked in here hoping to come upon you, but she ran into him instead and, believing a murder on the premises would ruin the reputation of your shop, she—" Petra sliced her throat.

I gagged. Could the theory be true? Tish Waterman had stolen in hoping to clobber me and encountered Mick instead?

Petra bobbed her head, convincing herself. "At every opportunity Tish posts notices around town urging her neighbors to boycott your store."

Perhaps Tish associated me with whatever accident had befallen her and marred her face.

"Nah, not Tish," Gregory said. "She's a lot of hot air, but she wouldn't hurt a flea. She dotes on her dogs."

"Dog owners have killed people," Petra countered.

Gregory said, "Courtney, you should canvass your neighbors. Get the word out that you need help. You never know who might have seen something."

"If we had a phone tree in town, I'd get right on it," Petra said.

"A phone tree. Great idea." Gregory aimed a finger at her. "We should have something like that anyway, in case of emergencies. Why don't you bring that up at Monday's city council meeting, Petra?" He glanced at his watch. "Gee whiz. Sorry. I've got to go. Duty calls." He collected the tins of tea and headed toward the archway.

Petra caught up to him and handed him the leashes to her dogs. They responded to him as if they'd been his responsibility for years.

As the group paraded into the main showroom, Fiona flew to me, her face flushed. "I don't like him."

"Why not? He seems quite nice, and he adores animals."

She scowled.

"I, on the other hand, don't trust Petra Pauli," I said, watching the councilwoman through the windows glad-handing customers in the shop. "Why was she circling the fountain? Was she looking for a bit of evidence she'd left behind?"

"Oho." Fiona folded her arms triumphantly. "Last night when we were playacting, you dismissed the possibility that she could have done the deed."

"Well, I'm allowed to change my mind. I'm human."

"Fairies change their minds, too. All the time."

"Good to know."

Fiona alit on my shoulder and toyed with a lock of my hair. "Petra mentioned Tish Waterman. What do we know about her?"

"Not much."

"You should make sure Detective Summers puts her on his radar."

Chapter 10

The longing of my heart is a fairy portrait of myself: I want to be pretty; I want to eliminate facts and fill up the gap with charms.
—Mark Twain

Later that afternoon, after leaving Detective Summers a message to touch base with me—I didn't mention Tish Waterman; the theory about her sneaking into my shop to sabotage it was iffy at best—I bid good night to Joss and headed out with Pixie in tow. I heard voices and turned to see Yvanna Acebo standing outside Sweet Treats with Logan Langford.

When not working at the bakery, Yvanna made goodies for our high teas. I don't think she ever took a day off. She had endless energy and a family of six to feed—two cousins, her grandparents, her younger sister, and herself. How she had muscled through after losing both parents in a car crash when she was twelve, I would never know.

As Logan spoke, Yvanna removed her pink apron and baker's hat and folded them neatly over her arm. Then she removed the scrunchie that was holding her dark hair in a knot and let her hair tumble to her shoulders. She nodded at something Logan said, added, "Thank you," and turned to lock the front door of the bakery.

With my kitten in my arms, I strolled through the courtyard, taking the stairs two at a time while glancing at Logan's retreating figure. "Hey, Yvanna. How are you?"

She spun around and smiled. Bright white teeth, beautiful mouth, caramel brown eyes. "*Hola*, Courtney. The better question is how are you?" She tickled Pixie's chin and cooed to her. "*Hola, gata.* You are *muy hermosa.*"

Pixie leaned into the love.

"You must be devastated," Yvanna said to me. "Poor Mick. Dead. In your store." She caressed the silver cross she wore around her neck. "How horrible."

"It's tragic."

"Do you want a cookie?"

"No, thanks."

"I made a new chocolate chip cookie using chiles for tomorrow's tea. *Mi abuela* says sugar eases the sorrows of the heart." Yvanna was known for her Latin-based flavors. My favorite was her spicy coriander sugar cookie. "I also made lemon cupcakes sprinkled with lavender petals."

"Those sound scrumptious, but I'm not hungry."

"How about a cup of homemade custard?"

She knew I adored her custard. It was so creamy and paired perfectly with fresh berries, when in season.

"No, thanks." I hitched my chin. "What did Logan want?"

"He asked to speak to my boss. I told him she's not here. She's on vacation in San Diego." Yvanna lowered her voice. "Do you think it's true that a developer wants to buy the courtyard?"

"What?" I blurted. "No way. I haven't heard that."

"Rumor has it that Mr. Langford intends to kick out all the tenants so the developer can raise the rents."

"Are you sure?"

She nodded.

Inwardly, I groaned. I did not want to move, nor could I afford to do so.

"I heard Mr. Langford threatened Mr. Watkins," Yvanna said.

"He did. I witnessed it. But I thought he just wanted the grooming business to be gone."

"Do you think Mr. Langford killed Mr. Watkins?"

"I don't know. I can't imagine he did, but Logan was miffed with Mick from the get-go. When Mick wouldn't give up his lease, Logan got angry. At the time, I thought Logan was carping for no apparent reason. Looking back, maybe it was because he was in negotiations with an interested developer." I recalled my roleplaying with the fairy figurines last night, when "Logan" had been over-the-top angry. Did I honestly believe he was guilty of murder? I stroked Pixie's foot to calm myself. "Who told you Logan wanted to kick us all out?"

"My boss. That's why she went on vacation. She heard from Glinda." Glinda owned Glitz, the jewelry store in the courtyard. Yvanna lowered her voice to a basso pitch. "My boss wanted to avoid Mr. Langford while considering her options."

"Are you sure she's not overreacting? Logan hasn't said a word to me, and Meaghan hasn't mentioned anything." Flair Gallery was the third largest physical space in the courtyard. Wouldn't Logan oust the biggest first? "I still can't imagine why he would want us vacating. I'd think a developer would appreciate full tenancy."

"Like I said, rumor has it the developer wants to hike up the rents."

Yes, that made sense.

"My boss thinks Mr. Langford is in debt and that's why

he's selling. She said he used to leave big tips in the tip jar, but lately not so much."

"Interesting."

"And Sonja told me—" Yvanna looked right and left. "You know Sonja. She doesn't talk much, but she listens. She said Emily Watkins has already discussed ending the lease with Mr. Langford."

"Really?"

"*Sí.* She said Emily hates the business and wants to sell everything, including hair dryers and dog crates."

I thought again of Emily and Gregory's handshake. Was he interested in getting out of dog training and buying Wizard of Paws? If so, would he be able to talk Logan or the new developer into extending the lease?

"Emily is passionate about riding horses nowadays," Yvanna went on.

"So I heard."

"Selling the business would give her the financial freedom to do everything she wants." Yvanna did a head slide, right and left, like an Egyptian dancer. "Even finding a new husband." She covered her mouth. "*Dios mío.* That was horrible of me. Don't repeat that." She glanced at her watch. "I've got to run. My grandparents like to eat at the same time every night, and my sister is the worst cook." She clasped my arm and said, "If you need anything, let me know. See you tomorrow for the tea."

As I watched Yvanna scurry away, I couldn't help thinking Emily's motive for murder might be becoming stronger by the second.

Walking home at night always brought me comfort. I loved when the sun started to wane and soft light filtered through the trees. I enjoyed listening to the birds as they sang their last songs before settling down to sleep. I appreciated being able to take in the various houses, one by one, each designed with a different flair. A Cape Cod, a gingerbread with thatched roof, a wooded retreat. My favorite, other than my own, was a yellow storybook cottage, teensy in scale, its trellises dripping with lush wisteria and its flowerboxes and garden rife with white and purple impatiens. I hadn't met the owner yet, but I hoped to. Neighbors said she owned one of the by-invitation-only antique galleries in town. I didn't own antiques other than what Nana had left me, so I hadn't tried to solicit an invitation. According to gossip, the woman was quite private.

As I was passing the storybook house, I paused, captivated by the silhouette of a woman dancing freely around what I presumed to be the living room. Sheer curtains prevented a more distinct view. I'd seen enough *Dancing with the Stars* to know the rise and fall of a waltz, although I didn't hear music.

Two blocks away surf boomed on the beach, waking me from my reverie.

"Whew!" Fiona zipped in front of me. "There you are. I thought I'd lost you."

"How could you? I'm on my way home."

"I didn't know which way you'd gone." Her wings were flapping double time. "You do like to roam."

She was right. I took different routes each night, sometimes turning down 7th Avenue, sometimes turning down 8th, and often walking along Lincoln before turning toward the ocean on 11th. Occasionally, I made a loop of a section packed with stores so I could window-shop.

"Where did you go this afternoon?" I asked. "I expected you to whiz in at any time and ask whether I'd talked to the detective about Tish Waterman, but you didn't."

"I was busy."

"Doing?"

"Lessons."

"For . . . ?"

"For when the queen fairy will allow me to own a fairy horse." She mimicked hopping astride a steed and tearing off. Making a U-turn midair, she flitted to me. "They're not easy to ride, but my mentor says I'm almost ready. I had to ride behind her on her horse, my arms wrapped around her waist, and she's sort of thick, so it made it hard to see where we were going."

Flying on a fairy horse would explain why her gossamer hair was disheveled.

"So . . . ?" she asked leadingly. "Did you speak to the detective about Tish?"

"No, but I left him a message. He hasn't returned my call. Tell me more about your lesson."

Fiona waxed rhapsodic about learning every detail about a fairy horse. It was *incredible, magical, extraordinary*. Their wings were beautiful and packed with enchanting energy. At times, their tails worked like sails on a boat.

While Fiona chattered on, I thought of Emily and her love of horses, and I wondered whether she had lied about going to the Equestrian Inn. Detective Summers claimed *sources* had confirmed her alibi. Why had she gone on a vacation so near to Carmel? Why not travel to another state? Had she visited the inn so the drive to town would be short, giving her ample time to kill her husband and return to the inn to establish her alibi? Though I'd pressed him, Summers hadn't revealed whether he'd personally talked to those *sources*.

As I was musing about whether I should take a mini vacation at the Equestrian Inn or at the very least a trail ride to get the skinny myself, Fiona cried, "Stop!"

I halted at the corner of Carmelo and 11th Avenue.

"It's her!" Fiona pointed.

My breath caught in my chest as I spied Tish Waterman, a whip-thin woman with carbon-black hair, passing the teensy congregational church two doors up. She was heading my way with her identical black Shih Tzus. Tish and both of the dogs were wearing matching argyle vests. If Tish weren't so bitter and if Petra hadn't planted the seed that Tish might have killed Mick to sabotage my business, I'd have found the owner-looking-like-its-dog thing sort of charming.

There were other people on the street, so I drew in a deep breath and kept walking. I was not in danger.

As Tish neared, I said, "Nice night, isn't it?" The weather was balmy for springtime. No fog. No drizzle. I hadn't needed to don my sweater over my romper.

Tish lasered me with a look. Was it murderous or merely contemptuous? I couldn't tell.

"Enjoy the evening," I crooned.

She sniffed. If I hadn't felt sorry for her because of the scar down her cheek, I might have snubbed her, too. My mother taught me bad behavior did not warrant reciprocal bad behavior, but there were times Tish simply pushed me to the limit. What had I done to her? Was it the notion that I could see fairies? If that were the case, she needed to get over herself. It wasn't as if I was asserting the existence of evil witches or bloodsucking vampires. Sheesh. If she didn't believe in fairies, so be it. Let it go.

Fiona said, "She walks stiffly."

"I'm not sure if that's her demeanor or because of the accident."

"She's very sad. She never goes into her garden, and it's so beautiful. There are twelve hybrid tea roses, all perfectly suited to the climate and beautifully tended by her gardener."

Suddenly, I felt a tinge of sorrow for Tish. She never went into her garden? She didn't enjoy the flowers and the aromas? What horrible fate had turned her so sour? I didn't honestly believe she was a murderer, but she might be dead inside.

"Hello, Courtney dear." Mrs. Hopewell, my next-door

neighbor, the woman who owned Dream-by-the-Sea, rose from behind her white picket fence, a sunhat taming her gray-streaked curly brown hair, the hem of her smock dress stained with dirt. Her house, which hadn't been dubbed with a clever name like mine, was another I enjoyed. It was a white gem with peaked roofs and dormer windows and a wraparound porch. She was trying to come up with a name for it, but as yet hadn't landed on one that she adored. "I'm weeding." She waved a handful of them.

"I can see that."

Her cream-colored Pomeranians started chasing each other through the overgrowth and barking.

"Hush, you two," Mrs. Hopewell said.

I drew near and noticed her sleek black cat sleeping on a nearby stone bench, oblivious to the yipping dogs. "You have a ways to go."

"Tell me about it." She chuckled. Her garden needed a lot of love, which always surprised me because she was so talented with a paintbrush. She captured elegant gardens in nearly all her work. "How I wish I could make my plants grow. I seem to kill them no matter what I try." Her smile made her aging eyes sparkle. "Perhaps a fairy garden would bring good luck. My older sister swears by them. She thinks they're magical." Mrs. Hopewell had two sisters. The older was a regular at Open Your Imagination.

"It's worth a try. My mother said wherever plants thrived, fairies thrived, and where fairies thrived, good luck was sure to follow."

"Why don't I commission you to create a fairy garden for me?" Mrs. Hopewell said.

"I'd love to make you one, but you don't have to pay me. Consider it my way to give back to you after all you've done for me. I love my home. I wouldn't have it without your goodwill."

"Oh, no, dear, I couldn't accept one of your creations for free. If I gave away my art, I'd be broke. We artists must stick together and charge what we're worth."

I smiled. "Wasn't one of the founding principles of Carmel that artists came from far and wide to promote fellowship between artists and the public?"

"Yes, of course, but not for free. Artists need to eat."

"Amen," Fiona said.

Mrs. Hopewell's cat lifted its head and looked to where Fiona was flying and, unimpressed, went back to sleep. At the same time, Mrs. Hopewell peered upward. Had she heard Fiona or simply picked up that her cat had sensed something? Fiona teased her, darting right and left. Mrs. Hopewell blinked repeatedly, as if detecting some kind of activity. A fairy garden might be just the ticket for her.

Out of nowhere, Mrs. Hopewell hiccupped as if startled. "Oh, dear, I'm an insensitive fool." She tossed her weeds into a nearby basket. "Mick Watkins. I heard all about it. I meant to stop by yesterday to console you, but my son and his adorable boy showed up. They just left. My grandson was teaching me about new emojis I could use while texting."

"You text?"

"Texting is the way I connect with all my grandchildren."

"You have more than one?" It pained me to think I knew so little about my landlord. I added *being more interested* to my ways-to-improve-myself list.

"Three. All boys." She beamed with pride. "The fourteen-year-old is the best at texting. He has his own phone. The other two have to beg their parents for the chance. A simple sassy word will lose them privileges for a week. Anyway, please forgive me. My son can be quite needy." I hadn't met her son, so I didn't know what she meant by needy, but I didn't pry. "How are you?"

"Coping."

"I have some stew warming on the stove if you're hungry."

"No thank you." My stomach was too raw. Eating didn't appeal to me.

"Did Mick deserve it?" Mrs. Hopewell asked.

The question drew me up short. Did anyone deserve to be murdered? What sins might fall into that category, and wouldn't an old-fashioned stoning have been enough punishment? I bit my tongue. What a horrid thought.

Fiona wiggled her fingers in front of my face. "Yoo-hoo. Are you wondering if the detective is going to arrest you?"

"No," I blurted.

"No *what,* dear?" Mrs. Hopewell asked.

I flicked the air to make Fiona back off. "No . . . he didn't deserve it," I said, answering Mrs. Hopewell's question. "No one does. Ever."

"Of course. I didn't mean . . ." She placed a hand on her chest. "I hope I didn't upset you."

"No, ma'am, you didn't. I'm on edge because I'm a suspect."

"You? Nonsense. You wouldn't hurt a fairy." She giggled at her turn of phrase.

"You're right. I wouldn't." If only Detective Summers would agree with us on that point. "In the meantime," I went on, "I need to canvass the neighborhood and see if anyone saw me sitting at my desk Wednesday night. Mick died between eleven p.m. and two a.m."

"What were you doing at your desk at that late hour, an online chat?"

"How did you—"

"I've seen you there on many occasions, fingers flying across the keyboard. You young people spend so much time on social media." She fanned the air. "Me? I prefer a good book."

"So do I, but sometimes work comes first. Did you happen to see me there that night?"

"No, dear. I'm sorry. I'd had a long day. Another gallery asked to hang my work. I was spent. After I walked the pups, I retired at ten."

Chapter 11

*For what is a fairy whisperer? She speaks to the fairies,
and then listens.*
—Daryl Wood Gerber

Even though I had no appetite, I threw together a small salad
of lettuce, tomatoes, cucumber, and goat cheese, and added
fresh basil and parsley to spruce it up. Then I moved to my
computer and ate while I visited the *Fairy Garden Girls Dig It*
chat room. Some of the same handle names from last Wednesday's exchange cropped up: Peter Pan's Girlfriend, Green
Angel, and Fly by Night. My handle was Fairy Whisperer.

I typed in: *You won't believe it. A man was murdered in my
shop and I'm a suspect.*

I added the sad-faced emoji and paused. My father hated
emojis and chastised me whenever I used one in a text. He
also loathed when I used text shorthand like *BTW, IMHO,*
and *THX.* Sometimes I did it on purpose to irk him.

Peter Pan's Girlfriend responded: *Oh, no. How awful.*

I continued my entry: *Some of u saw me here, but the police
say that's not enuf. Sigh.* I added a goggle-eyed emoji.

Fiona sat on the upper rim of the computer, her elbow perched on one leg. She wasn't glowing. She was glowering. At me.

"What?" I asked her.

"You're not taking care of yourself. You need to eat more."

"Don't mother me."

"If I don't, who will?"

I blew a raspberry at her. She blew one back. Hers sounded cuter than mine, more like a bee buzzing.

"Don't torture yourself by doing this." She jutted her hand at the computer screen. "They can't solve the problem."

"They can commiserate."

"You don't want their pity. You have to work through the clues yourself."

"What clues?" I hissed. "We don't have any clues."

"Don't snap at me." She flew out of the room.

I stewed, then realized she was right. I typed to my friends: *C U* and switched off the computer. I lurched to my feet, took my plate to the sink, and walked to the backyard.

When mulling things through, my mother liked to bake. I, on the other hand, needed to get my hands dirty. Rather than make another fairy garden for the rear yard, I decided to build the one I'd promised Mrs. Hopewell. I fetched a round sixteen-inch clay pot and a lantern and went to the greenhouse.

"What're you doing?" Fiona flew beside me.

"I'm making Mrs. Hopewell's fairy garden. I'm thinking of creating something that looks like Monet's *Water Lilies*. Mrs. Hopewell's artistic style is like Monet's."

"Excellent."

"I'm glad you approve."

After filling the pot with soil, I fetched an arched bridge and painted it green. Every fairy garden should have a focal point, something that drew one's eye. Often, it was the largest part of the scene, but not always. In Monet's *Water Lilies*, the observer was drawn to the bridge, but the water lilies themselves were the real focal point. I sealed the bridge with a coat of lacquer and set it aside to dry. At the rear of the pot, I added a miniature fake willow tree and bolstered it with live ferns to establish the backdrop of Monet's famous painting.

Next, I dug a trench to create the pond and filled it with white gravel. When creating the image of water with chips of blue glass, I liked to start with a base below the glass so the soil wouldn't seep up and mar the watery expanse. After fashioning the pond, I installed smatterings of green moss interspersed with yellow lichen on top, which gave the effect of lily pads.

Fiona settled onto the rim of the pot and began to hum a fairy song I'd heard her hum before. I didn't know the name of it. It reminded me of a melody from my youth, one Aurora had sung. The tune comforted me, so I hummed with her.

An hour later, after centering the bridge atop the water and adding a sweet bronze fairy who was reaching toward the water while balancing on a mushroom next to the pond, I watered the garden well and stood back to drink in my creation. It looked just right. Mrs. Hopewell wanted good luck for her garden. This one might do the trick, representing the bond between fairies and nature in all its glory.

"Feeling better?" Fiona asked.

"Yes. I'm ready to take on the world. After a good night's sleep."

"Me too." She yawned and stretched and zoomed out of the greenhouse. "See you tomorrow," she trilled, vanishing into the night.

I took a few photographs of the new garden and headed to bed.

★　★　★

Saturday morning arrived in a flash. While sipping a cup of honey lavender stress relief tea and nibbling on a poppy seed muffin slathered in butter, I quickly flipped through the mystery we would be discussing at the book club. I'd finished it weeks ago and had reviewed the reading guide the author shared on her website. Making mental notes about the victims and the suspects' motives helped cement the story in my mind. I wasn't going to lead the book club, but I wanted to have my facts straight in the event the book club moderator asked me a question.

Before heading to work, I carried the fairy garden I'd made, along with instructions for how to tend it, to Mrs. Hopewell's house. She didn't answer her doorbell, so I left the garden on the porch. Then I sent her a text message.

When I arrived at the shop with Pixie, the Dutch door was open, and the aroma of coffee wafted to me.

"You're early," I said to Joss as I strode past the display tables and into the office. I set Pixie on her pillow, stowed my purse in the lower drawer of the desk, hung my denim jacket on the oak coat rack, and returned to the main showroom.

"You know the old saying," Joss said. "The early bird gets the worm. The eager beaver builds the dam. Idle minds are the devil's workshop." She chortled. "All the clichés work today. I couldn't sleep, so here I am. We have twenty people coming to the tea. I have a list of attendees. Want to see?"

"No. You've got this."

She brandished a hand. "Nice coveralls."

"Thanks." I wasn't very good at throwing out clothes. If I really liked something and it brought me joy, I hung on to it. I'd purchased the stonewashed coveralls I was wearing in college. I particularly liked the bouquet of flowers embroidered on the left thigh. I'd donned a red T-shirt under them. Wearing red made me feel stronger and more confident.

"Have you seen Fiona?" I asked.

"Not yet. She's not with you?"

I shook my head, wondering where she might have gone last night. I hoped she wasn't doing something that would upset the queen fairy.

Joss and I spent the next hour dusting and reorganizing shelves. I was amazed by how quickly things could get out of order: a teacup turned so the handle was facing forward instead of sideways; a fairy figurine rotated so its back was the first thing a patron would view instead of its face. Customers might not care about these minor details, but I did.

Around noon, I took a breather to sit outside and caught sight of Detective Summers and Officer Rodriguez roving through the courtyard. Summers had his cell phone out. Was he taking evidentiary photos? Wouldn't the area be tainted by now, seeing as throngs of people had passed through since the murder? It dawned on me that maybe they were planning to stop in and discuss my call to the detective about Tish Waterman. On the other hand, they weren't walking in my direction.

I was considering running after them to bring them up to speed when they turned into Sweet Treats, and it occurred to me that they might be in the vicinity because they were hungry. Duh! So much for my sleuthing skills.

Rather than interrupt them—the theory about Tish was mostly likely just that, a theory, and weak at best—I returned inside to prepare for the book club. I wanted it to go off without a hitch and to be a carefree experience for our guests.

At ten minutes to two, a cluster of book club attendees arrived. All were in a chatty mood, even the two men. I loved how friendly people in Carmel were. If only something horrible like murder hadn't intruded.

Joss directed them to the patio. We'd draped the tables

with pretty linens and had placed miniature six-inch fairy gardens as well as cups and saucers, silverware, and tea caddies filled with choices of tea on each. Meaghan had set her harp—a beautiful Celtic lever harp made with rosewood—near the learning-the-craft corner. Yvanna was in our modest kitchen putting together trays of delectable goodies. Earlier, I'd tasted one of her chocolate chip cookies with chiles and nearly swooned. In addition to the lemon lavender cupcakes, she had prepared a delicious rosemary scone and a variety of tea sandwiches.

When Meaghan started playing "Greensleeves," memories of my mother filled my mind. She had loved that particular song. She would have been so proud of my decision to open the shop.

Fiona landed on my shoulder.

"Where have you been?" I asked.

"Studying."

"Studying what?"

"Magic. Don't worry. It's the good kind. Queen fairy approved." She cocked her head. "Why are you frowning?"

"I'm sort of nervous. I'm worried people will gossip about, you know . . ."

"The murder."

"And my part in it."

"Tosh," she said—a favorite fairy word. "These people know you."

"Not all of them."

"You are innocent," Fiona said. "Believe in yourself."

I glimpsed Meaghan in her element, playing her harp, her face euphoric and eyes closed. The vision helped me take a deep, restorative breath.

Until a dog yipped.

A gaunt woman in an exquisite silk sheath, today's book selection tucked under one arm, strode onto the patio with her chocolate miniature poodle. She was talking on her cell phone. I'd seen her before, exiting Wizard of Paws when Mick and Logan had been going at it. She'd been beautifully dressed then, too, and had moved with the same imperious air. Like her poodle, she sported a curly Mohawk.

A largish woman in lavender, who was sitting at one of the tables with her well-behaved Weimaraner and two other women with pooches, waved to the gaunt woman. "Isabella, join us."

The gaunt woman ended her phone call, took a seat at a table, and commanded her poodle to sit. When I overheard the woman in lavender introduce the woman to the table-mates as Isabella Acosta, I nearly choked. Isabella Acosta was the person who had falsely accused me of arguing with Mick. Why had she done so? She didn't know me. How could she have thought I was the one having an altercation with Mick that afternoon? Summers must have talked to her by now and dissuaded her of the notion. Otherwise, how could she have the gall to show her face here?

Holly Hopewell, dressed in a floral-print maxi dress, arrived next. Her leashed Pomeranians walked dutifully by her side. "Courtney, don't you look cute."

"You too." I smiled.

She shook a copy of the book we were reading. "Loved this. Did not guess who did it until the end. I'm so happy we're reading a mystery. I get tired of reading all those best-sellers about a woman's journey. I do not need to cry and feel angst-y." She bussed my cheek. "Thank you, by the way, for the beautiful fairy garden. It's simply lovely."

"Oh, good, you received my text."

"Of course I did. I check them every few hours." She scanned the patio. "Hmm. I'm feeling very confident about the vibes here. Perhaps today will be the day I spy a fairy. What do you think?"

"You have to believe."

"Ha! A prudent point, my sister would say." She patted my cheek. "By the by, I'm canvassing our neighborhood for you. I haven't found anyone yet who saw you at your desk Wednesday night, but I'll keep looking. Many of our neighbors live elsewhere and merely come in for a few days here and there. I've written a half dozen emails and left voice messages, too. Have faith." She guided her dogs to a knot of women who were standing near Meaghan.

The librarian, Miss Reade, a spry woman in her early seventies who was wearing a sparkly silver jacket over gray cigarette trousers, strode onto the patio. "Courtney, love, I'm here. Where do you want me?" She flourished a glittery fairy wand and winked. "I'm ready to let your fairy guide us to new heights."

I giggled. "Don't make fun."

"I would never. My grandmother was a visionary. My mother? Not so much. Me?" She laughed a full-throated laugh. "I am a true believer."

I enjoyed visiting our beautiful library. The water-wise garden was exquisite with plenty of natural fairy habitats. The interior was filled with books to enjoy. Miss Reade, who had been a school librarian as well as a weekend journalist before taking on her current position, considered it her mission in life to help people discover new authors. She often joked that, given her surname, she had been destined to become a book lover.

I guided her to an acrylic podium set near Meaghan and told her we would begin in about twenty minutes.

As I moseyed back to the entrance to the patio, I caught snippets of various conversations. One between Isabella Acosta and the other dog owners gave me pause.

"If you ask me, Gregory Darvell has lost his mojo," Isabella said. Even her voice had a haughty edge to it. "He's lost seven competitions in a row. He couldn't do a thing with my sweet Cocoa."

"Don't be ridiculous," said Hattie Hopewell, a flamboyant redhead in her sixties and older sister to my landlord. She and her brindled Scottie had slipped in without my noticing. I wondered if she'd spotted her sister. "Gregory merely needs to find the right dog." Hattie was the president of the Happy Diggers garden club; unlike her sister, she did have a green thumb. She loved making eight-inch fairy gardens. To my knowledge, she hadn't encountered any fairies yet, but I had hopes for her. "Ten years ago, he was brilliant with this one's mama." She caressed the Scottie's ears. "May she rest in peace."

The woman in lavender leaned toward her tablemates as if to whisper but didn't mute her voice. "I hear he's a suspect in Mick Watkins's murder."

"Gregory?" Hattie said. "Impossible."

The woman in lavender tapped the table with her fingernails. "Supposedly, Mick and he were at each other's throats last week."

That was news to me. How many people had Mick riled lately?

"Mick warned Gregory not to step foot near his shepherd, or else."

"What did Gregory do?" Isabella asked.

"Told Mick to heel, of course," the woman in lavender joked. "What he actually said was Mick's dog wasn't worth the trouble. That set Mick off even more."

"Don't listen to gossip," Hattie said. "Gregory is not a suspect. Besides he would be one hundred percent in the clear. He has an alibi. Wednesday night he went to San Jose to consult with a friend of my family's about her Dachshund. Oh, there's my sister. She knows who I'm talking about." Hattie rose from the table and bid the dog owners good-bye.

When she was out of earshot, the woman in lavender clucked her tongue. "Gregory being on the road doesn't prove anything. From here to San Jose and back is only a matter of hours. Mick was killed in the dead of night."

Isabella gasped at the word *dead*. So did I.

"Hello, everyone," a woman crowed.

All heads turned.

Petra Pauli strode through the French doors with her collies, which were yet again straining at their leashes. They dragged her toward the dog-friendly table. As Petra was wont to do, she handed off her dogs. This time to Isabella. Then she tossed a copy of the book club selection on the table and orbited the patio to hand out flyers. "Don't miss this coming week's council meeting," she said to our patrons. "We want to hear from all of you. Have complaints? Voice them at city hall. We're here to listen."

I noticed a number of women on the patio eyeing Petra's getup, a snug-fitting olive green sweater over ultra-tight camouflage-style jeans, which she'd tucked into brown boots. The boots matched her briefcase. Each item looked expensive and hip. Definitely not a mourning outfit. Maybe she hadn't been in love with Mick Watkins after all, or she didn't buy into the *mourners should wear black* tradition.

To each and every person, Petra offered a winning smile, whether that person was receptive to her pitch or not. How politicians continually maintained a public face amazed me.

After making one pass around the patio, Petra strode into the main showroom to offer flyers to more customers. Through the windows, I spied her talking to an attractive woman—a friend, judging by the way they hugged. The woman handed Petra a tissue. Petra lowered her chin and discreetly blotted her eyes.

Joss was standing nearby, one hand cupped around her ear. Was she listening in?

I caught her eye and beckoned her to join me. A minute later, she scurried through the French doors and drew me away from the crowd.

"We're waiting on two more people, and then we can start," she said. "I called each and verified that they're coming."

I glanced at Miss Reade, who was organizing her notes at the podium. "Perfect. Let's have Yvanna bring out the teapots of hot water and the treats. That'll take a few minutes. If the last two attendees aren't here by then, we'll start without them."

"Got it." Joss turned to go.

"Hold on." I clasped her wrist. "Not so fast. You were eavesdropping on Petra and her friend, weren't you?"

Her cheeks turned crimson. "You noticed?"

"I'm not blind."

"I heard Emily Watkins's name mentioned and decided to tune in."

"And . . ."

Joss lowered her voice. "Petra was complaining that Emily wouldn't let her into their house."

I raised an eyebrow. "Why would Petra want to go inside the Watkins's house?"

"Apparently to fetch a few of things that she'd, um, given to Mick."

"Like what?"

Joss batted her eyelashes. "Lingerie."

I nearly choked. "Are you kidding me? She admitted to Emily that she was having an affair with him?"

"Sounded like it to me."

"How brazen."

Joss bobbed her head. "Needless to say, Petra said Emily called her all sorts of colorful names."

"I'd have clocked Petra. The nerve." I shook my head. "Whether or not Mick was a cheater, Emily is mourning him. She deserves—"

"*Shh.*" Joss pinched my arm. "The councilwoman's heading this way. I'm out of here. Treats coming right up." She rushed into the shop.

As Petra neared me, I said, "Nice to see you."

She gazed at me warily and glanced over her shoulder. When she returned her gaze, she said, "What did your clerk tell you? Did she hear me and my friend talking about my set-to with Emily?"

I didn't respond.

"I can tell by your face that she did." Petra tugged the strap of her briefcase higher on her shoulder and moved a wadded up tissue from one hand to the other. "Did she tell you the gist?"

"I heard undergarments were mentioned." Even using the euphemism for lingerie made my cheeks warm.

"Excuse me, ladies," Yvanna said from the doorway. "We need to pass through." She wheeled a teacart carrying three-tiered trays of treats onto the patio. Her sister, a younger version of Yvanna, followed carrying white teapots.

Due to the interruption, Petra started to walk away.

I hurried after her. Now who was brazen? On the other hand, the murder had happened on my property, and I was a suspect. I deserved some answers. "Did you hope Mick would leave Emily for you?"

"It's none of your business, Courtney," Petra said icily.

So much for acting all buddy-buddy with me the other day and offering to head up a phone tree on my behalf. She peered down her aquiline nose at me and held the stare for a moment, and then suddenly she blinked and moisture filled her eyes.

"He . . . He . . ."

I grabbed a napkin off a table and offered it to her.

Petra fought for control but lost the battle. "He was going to leave Emily except he died before he got the chance." She dabbed her eyes with the napkin. "But he promised he was going to do so by the end of summer."

I licked my lips recalling our conversation the other day when she'd questioned my alibi. "Petra, if you don't mind my asking—"

"I do," she said, faster at the rejoinder than I had been. "But I'll tell you anyway, because I know what you're going to ask. Where was I when he was murdered? If you must know—" Tears dripped down her cheek; she swiped them angrily. "If you must know, I was at a secret meeting, political in nature. No one will be able to verify it, not if they want to keep their job. We abide no leaks."

That sounded cryptic. What kind of political meeting couldn't be disclosed? Who were the *we* she was referring to? Did Petra fear revealing her plan to me would jeopardize her future?

"Have you informed the police?" I asked.

"Why would I need to?"

"Because Mick is dead."

"I had no reason to kill him. I loved him. And *he* loved me."

I recalled my playtime with the fairy figurines when the Petra fairy had said she'd rather see Emily dead than Mick. That still rang true. On the other hand, Petra's alibi was weak. I mean, c'mon. She had attended a secret meeting that no one could verify?

I murmured, "I'm sorry for your loss."

Petra mumbled her thanks and strode to the dog-friendly table. She retrieved the leashes for her pets, settled onto a chair, and poured hot water into her teacup. Isabella said something to her. Petra laughed, which jolted me. Had the tears been fake? Were the two women talking about having duped me? Was I developing a bad case of paranoia? According to John Lennon, paranoia was just a heightened sense of awareness.

I sought out Joss and whispered, "Do you know the woman with the chocolate poodle?"

"Yep. She owns Acosta Artworks. Right across the street."

Of course. The gallery next to Hideaway Café in the Village Shops. I'd passed it and peered in the plate glass windows but had never paid attention to the name.

"I've wandered in on my lunch hour," Joss said. "Isabella has good taste. The artwork is very expensive. I'd need a year's salary to purchase something there. She just took on two of Holly Hopewell's pieces. Why?"

"Because she's the one who—"

"Courtney," Miss Reade called. "We're ready."

"Hold that thought," I said to Joss.

"Don't leave me hanging."

I crossed the patio to Meaghan. When she finished playing "Three Coins in the Fountain," I told her to take a breather.

She rose and bowed. The audience offered polite applause.

After Meaghan pushed her chair closer to the harp, she whispered, "Good turnout."

"It is. I hope everyone likes the event. I'd like to make this a monthly feature."

Meaghan looped her hand around my elbow. "If it's okay,

I'm going to head back to the gallery. A wealthy local is coming in to check out some seascapes. I'll come back later to pick up my harp."

"When you do, I want to discuss Isabella Acosta."

Meaghan wrinkled her nose. "If we must. Not my favorite person." She bussed my cheek and slipped out.

"Ladies and gentlemen." Miss Reade tapped her fairy wand on the edge of the podium. "Welcome one and all." She introduced herself. "Let's get started. Pour your tea, pass the scones, and may the fairies open our imaginations."

A few in the audience giggled and fixed their eyes upward, as if expecting a flock of fairies to magically materialize. At the same time, Petra shot me a withering look. Why? Was she upset that she'd revealed herself to me? Perhaps she was plotting how she would murder me because I'd put her on the spot and asked for her alibi. Not welcoming the creepy-crawly sensation slithering up my spine, I retreated to a table on the other side of the fountain where she couldn't ogle me.

Miss Reade said, "Before we launch into a hearty discussion, let's thank our hostess Courtney Kelly and her crew for putting on this festive event."

More polite applause. The married couple occupying the other two chairs at my table offered their thanks. The wife loved the tea sandwiches and the lemon lavender cupcakes. The husband patted his stomach and said he was partial to the savory rosemary scones. I nabbed one of those and bit into it. Heaven.

"Now, then," Miss Reade continued, "how many of you finished the book?"

Hands went up, but not all.

"That's all right. We won't share any spoilers." She held up the assigned book, *The Secret, Book and Scone Society*. "As you all know, the name of the town featured in this series is Miracle Springs. What type of miracles does the town offer?"

A person I couldn't see spouted an answer. The husband at my table did the same.

Miss Reade continued. "There are many literary references in the book. Did any resonate with you?"

Recognizing the questions the author had shared on her website, I waved a hand. "I liked the choice of *Dracula* and the character Renfield. *Dracula* is one of my favorite books."

Joss chimed in from the doorway, "Mine, too."

"So did I," another attendee said.

And on it went for thirty minutes . . . book lovers eager to exchange views.

At half past three, when Miss Reade was wrapping up the discussion, I peeked around the fountain. Isabella Acosta was standing near the exit hugging the woman in lavender. Petra Pauli had left.

As if knowing who I was looking for, Fiona flew to my shoulder and whispered, "I heard the councilwoman say to the poodle owner that she doesn't like you."

"Did she say why?"

"Because you're too curious for words."

"Curious as in *odd* or curious as in *prying*?"

Fiona scrunched her nose. "How would I know?"

"What was the poodle owner's reply?"

"Nothing, why?"

Suspicion gnawed my insides. I peered at Isabella again. She was standing by herself, her cell phone pressed to her ear. Was she spreading more lies about me? Before I could approach her, she sprinted through the shop as if she were on her way to a fire.

Fiona fluffed her wings. "The lady with the Weimaraner hopes they find Mick's killer soon. She said the murder was casting a pall over Carmel-by-the-Sea." Fiona cocked her head. "What's a pall?"

"A gloomy cloud."

As if the weather god had a sense of humor, suddenly the patio went dark. A huge cloud blocked the sun's rays from entering through the pyramid skylight overhead. I shivered.

Chapter 12

❧

Leave room in your garden for the fairies to dance.
—Anonymous

"Good-bye, thanks for coming," I said as customers left the shop. To a person, each told me how much they had enjoyed the tea as well as the book club. A few wished they'd seen a fairy. I suggested they sign up for a learning-the-craft seminar to make a fairy garden; it would help them open their hearts.

As the last attendee walked out, I breathed a sigh of relief. All in all, the event had been a hit. I strode outside to stretch and caught sight of Brady sweeping the sidewalk in front of Hideaway Café. He was whistling and seemingly at peace with himself. I envied his calm.

A screen door squeaked open. I spotted Emily Watkins and a lean man in a three-piece suit exiting Wizard of Paws. Shep, off leash, sauntered behind them and sat obediently beside the man, who automatically scratched Shep's head.

"You have no idea how much I needed you to do that," Emily gushed, toying with the bolo-tie necklace hanging around the collar of her wrangler shirt. "You were so gentle. You said all the right words." She kissed the man on the cheek, but when she glimpsed me, she reared back as if I'd startled her . . . or caught her in the act. "Oh, it's you," she cried.

Unsavory thoughts caromed in my head. Was she, like her husband, having an affair? Was this man her lover? Had she killed Mick to make room for someone new in her life?

"Courtney"—Emily beckoned me closer—"come say hello to Wright Youngman."

Wright? As in Mr. Right and Mick was Mr. Wrong? I silently chided myself and sobered my thoughts. Eager to learn more, I strolled across the courtyard.

"Wright Youngman, attorney at law." The man pulled a business card from his jacket pocket.

I scanned the card, which included his name, followed by specialties—estate planning, trusts, wills—all in bold. I recalled a similar card lying next to Mick's corpse.

Emily said, "When Mick's sister Miranda arrived and demanded her portion of Mick's will, I realized it was time to contact his lawyer and find out what Mick might have arranged. Mick was very private about these things."

Youngman started to speak when the screen door to Wizard of Paws flew open. Miranda Watkins tramped out and nearly rammed into Shep. The dog hopped out of the way and skirted to the other side of Emily for protection.

Miranda stared daggers at Emily. "Well, you must be happy." With her orange hair and dressed in black sweater and trousers, the woman reminded me of a scorched pumpkin. "You got your way."

Emily sighed. "Not my way, Miranda. Mick's way. He wrote the will."

"You niggled and taunted until he caved to your wishes, didn't you?"

"No, I didn't. I told you, not one word of his last will and testament is mine. I had no clue what he'd done. He and I managed the business together, and we talked about caring for animals, but we didn't discuss the future." Emily's eyes welled up. "He had secrets, Miranda. Lots of secrets."

I imagined Emily was referring to his affair with Petra. Were there more secrets? Had Mick done something illegal?

Miranda sniffed.

"I don't even know if he wanted to be buried or cremated." Emily splayed her hands. "We hadn't discussed—"

"Cremated," Miranda snapped. "Everyone in our family has been cremated. Our great-grandfather didn't believe in spending money for a plot when all we were going to do was turn into ashes." She knotted the hem of her sweater in her fist and released it. "According to him, a burial plot was a waste of money."

"I'd agree," Emily said weakly.

"Mick shouldn't have died." Miranda sucked back a sob. "Who wanted him dead? Who, who, who?" She spanked one hand against the other.

"I don't know." Emily chewed on her lower lip. "Honestly, Miranda, I don't."

Given her overly emotive state, I wondered whether Miranda was trying to hide the fact that she'd killed her brother to get her hands on his money, until I recalled Detective Summers clearing her. She had a verifiable alibi. In New York.

A long silence fell between the women.

Youngman cleared his throat. "Once again, Miss Watkins, as I said inside, I'm very sorry for your loss."

"Don't." Miranda held up a hand. "Don't. Say. It." She clipped off each word. "My sister-in-law will get the business and the house. And you'll get your fee. But me? I'm left out in the cold with nothing to remind me of my brother."

Emily said, "If you want his car—"

"It's electric."

"How about his golf clubs?" Emily offered. "I know you love golf."

"They're men's clubs," Miranda hissed.

Emily sighed. "I didn't think—"

"You never think, Emily. That's just it!" Miranda glanced at me and blinked. Hadn't she realized I was there? Was she suffering such a fit of pique that she was blind to her surroundings? Wedging her black clutch higher under her arm, she muttered, "I don't know what he saw in you, Emily. I really don't."

Emily said, "I believed in his dreams."

Youngman put a hand on her arm. "He told me as much."

Miranda rolled her eyes. "Dreams, *schmeams*. Are you telling me it was his dream to take care of everyone else's curs?"

"No. That's not what I said. I meant—"

"Good-bye, Emily." Miranda marched to the curb and turned back. "Don't bother to contact me again. Ever. If you see me walking down the street, make a U-turn. Got me?"

After Miranda turned the corner, Emily smiled at Youngman in the way she had when they'd first exited the shop, and I realized I'd misread everything. Youngman must have been *gentle* with Miranda when he'd told her how Mick had planned his estate. Youngman had used *all the right words* to soothe the raging beast—Miranda. Emily had been wise to leave the matter to him. If she had given the news to her sister-in-law on her own, who knew what havoc Miranda might have wreaked?

Youngman shook Emily's hand and said, "Whatever you need, call me. We'll take this one step at a time."

"The funeral first," she said. "The police told me I could proceed after next Wednesday."

The attorney nodded sympathetically and headed in the same direction that Miranda had gone.

Emily stared at me, her horsey face pale, her jaw twitching. "Well, that wasn't pretty."

"I take it you and she were never close." I offered a friendly smile.

"At the wedding, for her toast, she said Mick had married beneath him."

I coughed out a laugh. "She didn't."

"She did." Emily sniffed. "Nobody knew what on earth she was talking about. I went to college; he didn't. But I let it slide. Mick and I were in love. His ridiculous sister wasn't going to break us apart."

"Where did you and Mick meet?"

"At an animal shelter. We were working summer jobs. I was in charge of the small dogs. He was in charge of the pit bulls. Ours was a match made in heaven." She wrapped her arms around her torso and stood frozen, as if she were unable to move. "Or so I thought."

"What do you mean?"

Emily faltered. "I saw lots of people going into your shop earlier," she said, changing the subject. "Were you having a special event?"

"We had a book club tea."

"I've never joined a book club."

"It was our first," I admitted. "It went very well."

Fiona darted into view and circled over Emily's head. She uttered a fairy incantation. Shimmering lavender fairy dust drizzled down.

Emily shimmied her shoulders and lifted her chin. "I don't like Petra Pauli."

Oho. What kind of fairy dust had Fiona sprinkled on her, a candor formula? If only there were a potion that could make the guilty confess, but I knew there wasn't. Fairy magic had limitations.

"Mick was seeing her whenever I went away," Emily went on.

I blinked. She hadn't guessed about the affair; she had known about it. I said, "I heard you and Petra had a—" I didn't go on. Being brazen was one thing. I wasn't cruel.

"A fight?" Emily finished. "About her wanting to fetch her lingerie from my house?"

I kept mum. If Emily was willing to chat about it, I wouldn't stop her.

"We didn't fight. I told her I'd find whatever was in my house and I'd send it to her. I was very civil."

What some people viewed as a fight could be considered a civil conversation by others. I wouldn't quibble.

Emily squared her shoulders. "To answer your unasked question, yes, I knew for certain about the affair. Like I said, I went to college. I'm not a babe in the woods. I didn't press my husband about it because I thought the fling would fizzle." She combed her hair with her fingers. "I know I'm not pretty. I know I won't win awards for being the warmest person on the planet, either, but I loved him, and he loved me. I believed in him. I expected us to spend the rest of our lives together." She lowered her chin and gazed at me from beneath her long lashes. "Did Petra say something to you?"

"To me?"

"About our exchange?"

I gulped. I wasn't good when put on the spot. One more thing to fix on my ways-to-improve-myself list. I needed quick comebacks and pithy answers. "She intimated that Mick was in love with her."

"It was a dalliance, nothing more. Nothing!" Emily slapped her thigh. Startled, Shep keened. Emily bent to pet his head and peered up at me. "I know you didn't kill him, Courtney. I'm sorry I implied that the other day. I was shaken. Do you think Petra did?"

"Why would she have?"

"Because, like I said, Mick wasn't going to leave me. That had to make her mad. And she has a temper."

"You sound as if you know her well."

Emily screwed up her mouth.

"She has an alibi," I said. "She was at a secret political meeting."

"Ha! I bet if you call Oriana Gray, she'll know if that's a crock."

Oriana Gray, also a councilwoman, owned a sophisticated inn on Junipero Avenue. She could be quite vocal about street noise and the number of unsponsored events in Carmel-by-the-Sea.

"Oh"—Emily bit her lip and sucked back a sob—"if only I'd been there that night, I could have talked Mick out of going to your place to search for fairies."

Fiona zoomed to my shoulder. "He did what? Did you know about this?"

I nodded.

"Why didn't I know about this?" She flitted to and fro. "What else are you keeping from me?"

I couldn't answer her. Not here. I trained my focus on Emily. "Are you sure that's why Mick stole into my shop?"

"That's what his note said. You don't think"—she inhaled sharply—"he went there to meet her, do you?" The way she said *her* sent chills through me. "He didn't. He wouldn't. I mean, you don't understand. He and Petra did not go to clandestine places. Their affair was out in the open. They met at her house, our house, and well-known inns, too. It was like Mick wanted me to catch him."

My mouth dropped open.

"You're wondering how I know where they met," Emily continued. "You're wondering if I was spying on them. No." She waggled a finger. "I know because Mick had a habit of keeping business cards from every place he went. He was a sucker for them." She let out a scornful laugh. "Long ago, a mentor told him that having a business card readily available was the best way to promote Wizard of Paws." She mimed removing a card from a pocket and handing it to me. "As a result, Mick collected hordes of them, too."

I flashed on the business cards lying on the patio next to Mick's body. Why had he carried one for his attorney? Wouldn't Mick have entered Youngman's contact number on his cell phone? Maybe Mick had recently visited Youngman and, out of habit, had taken another card. If he'd visited Youngman, had he discussed changing his will by cutting out Emily and including someone else, say Mick's sister or Petra? Did Emily kill him before he could finalize the change? Had Summers questioned the attorney?

Shep nudged Emily's hand and growled.

She tugged his ears fondly. "I know, boy. I know." To me she said, "The poor fool has been acting strangely ever since Mick died. He does this growl thing all the time. Especially at two in the morning." She lowered her voice. "Between us, I wonder if Mick's spirit might be visiting me. I suppose that might sound silly to you, or perhaps it doesn't, seeing as you believe in fairies." She peered at me. "You do, don't you?"

I nodded. I didn't care if Emily thought I was crazy. Fiona was real. She flew in front of Emily's face and stared into her eyes as if trying to assess the woman's truthfulness.

"You know, my great-grandfather swore he saw ghosts at Point Pinos Lighthouse," Emily went on. "He told my brother and me stories that would make your hair stand on end about wraiths flying around and blowing in his face to taunt him. I've never seen a ghost, but I'm a believer."

Fiona blew air at Emily; she didn't react.

Shep butted Emily's leg.

She cooed to him. "Yes, I know, boy. Time to get going."

She met my gaze. "I think S-H-E-P might need special training to work through the trauma. Gregory Darvell has offered
to work with him. He said"—she nodded in Shep's direction—"he might be suffering PTSD. Can dogs get that?"

"I would assume any living, breathing creature can," I
said. "However, I thought Mick didn't want Shep to go into
competition."

"Gregory won't be training him. He'll only be helping
him psychologically, like a dog whisperer."

I wondered whether I should tell her the theory I'd heard
at the tea, that Gregory Darvell should be a suspect in Mick's
death. Did Detective Summers consider Gregory a person of
interest? The police weren't keeping me apprised of their investigation. I doubted they were looping in Emily, either.

"It'll cost a lot of money, of course," Emily went on, "but
Shep is all I have, aren't you, boy?" She tickled him under his
neck. "Yes, you are." She tilted her head. "What do you
think I should do?"

"About?"

"The D-O-G?"

I bit back a smile. Not because Fiona was sitting on Shep's
head but because Emily's spelling D-O-G so the *dog* wouldn't
understand was endearing.

"Whatever it takes," I said. "You want him to be happy,
don't you?"

"More than anything. He's my world now. Thanks,
Courtney. I appreciate your advice. Let's go, boy." Emily returned inside Wizard of Paws. Shep followed at her heels.

As Emily disappeared, I couldn't help wondering about
her motive to kill her husband. She had obviously loved
Mick, but he'd duped her, and, with him gone, as long as she
wasn't proven guilty, she would inherit everything. Money
could heal a whole heap of regrets.

Thinking about Emily's likely inheritance made me reflect on Logan and his possible money problems. Had debt driven him to murder? He and I banked at Carmel Bank, a locally owned business. Would a chat with my loan officer deliver answers? *As if.* No loan officer, not even mine who had a heart of gold, would give me the time of day about someone else's finances.

"What's got your face in a pucker?" Joss asked as I returned inside the shop.

"Nothing."

Fiona said, "She chatted with Emily Watkins. That woman is crisp."

Joss rested a hand on my shoulder. "Why don't you take a walk? You've been going strong all day."

"I need to make a phone call first."

I retreated to my office. Fiona accompanied me. Putting the phone on speaker, I dialed the Orchid, Oriana Gray's inn, and asked the clerk to put me through.

"Miss Kelly, what can I help you with?" Oriana had a firm, crisp tone. I'd never stayed at her inn or referred anyone to it. Were the beds at the place as hard and unwelcoming as she was? "I'm about to consult with a client. Spit it out."

"I want to ask you about"—my mouth went dry—"a meeting."

"I'm sorry," she said. "Did you say you want to set up a meeting?"

"No. I want to ask you *about* a meeting. With Petra Pauli. She . . ." I begged my courage to find its voice. "She said she had a secret political meeting last Wednesday night. I assume you were in attendance."

"Heaven's no. It started way too late for me. I go to bed religiously at ten every night. I need my beauty sleep."

Fiona yawned and flitted out the door without saying good-bye. Where was she going?

"I think Petra planned the meeting on purpose to keep me at bay," Oriana added. "Did she tell you that I was there?"

"No. I—"

"Then I don't know what the issue is." Oriana cleared her throat. "Look, Miss Kelly, I know what happened at your shop. You must be devastated. Petra said you're a suspect. That's a shame, but if there isn't anything else, I've got to go."

I thanked her for her time. When I hung up, I realized my hands were sweating and I was breathing high in my chest. Asking people point-blank for information did not come easily to me.

Needing air, I took Joss's suggestion and went for a walk. I would pick up my mail at the post office while I was out.

None of the homes in Carmel had mailboxes. It was a city ordinance. Within the post office, there were a number of rooms filled with keyed boxes of varying sizes. My box was located in the second room. As I was removing mostly mailer advertisements from it, Tish Waterman and her two Shih Tzus traipsed into the room. I'd never realized Tish's post office box was in the same grouping as mine. Once again the trio was dressed alike: her dogs in striped sweater vests and Tish in a black-striped dress that made her look licorice-thin.

"Good morning," I said, using a friendly tone.

Tish startled. The dogs yipped. She shushed them.

"How's your day going?" I asked.

Tish didn't respond.

"I love our quaint post office, don't you?" I continued, not acknowledging her silent snub.

She grunted.

"Look, Tish, I don't know what I did to deserve your

wrath, but if you'd explain what I have done wrong, maybe we could bury the hatchet."

"Bury the . . ." She stammered. "There's no hatchet to be buried."

"You're mad at me. Please tell me why. To my face."

She clicked her tongue.

"I passed by your spa yesterday, and it was filled to the max," I said. "Congrats on owning such a thriving business."

"It's not thriving, but it should be."

Okay, perhaps I didn't understand the difference between doing well and thriving. Apples and oranges.

Tish strode past me and opened her box, withdrew a slug of envelopes, and closed it.

"Why do you hate me?" I asked.

"I don't—"

"You do."

"Quiet." She wasn't talking to the dogs.

I refused to back down. "I hear your garden is beautiful."

She frowned and fiddled with the top button on her spring coat. "How would you know about my garden?"

"My fai—" I jammed my lips together.

"Did your fairy tell you?" She dragged the word *fairy* out, making it sound dirty.

I forced a smile. "I hear you have at least a dozen hybrid tea roses. Maybe I could photograph them sometime, and we could go to tea afterward and get to know each other better. Sound good?"

Tish's cheeks tinged pink, but she didn't say anything.

Insincerely convincing myself that we had taken a step forward in our relationship, I said, "Okay then." I closed my mailbox and locked it and stuffed my mail into my purse. "Good talk."

When I reached the sidewalk, my heart was pounding, but

in a fun, excited way. I noticed Carmel Bank was just down
the street. Was it Kismet or had I unconsciously steered myself
to turn in that direction so I could ask my loan officer about
Logan's finances? I gave in and headed to it.

As I reached the front door, I realized my folly. The bank
was closed. Of course it would be; it was late Saturday afternoon. I turned to head home and heard a woman call my
name.

"Courtney." Hedda Hopewell, Holly and Hattie's younger
sister, was walking toward me carrying a to-go cup from Perco-
late. I knew the café well. Ever since Hedda had set up the loan
for my business, we had gotten together for the occasional
latte. "What brings you to my neck of the woods?" She raised
her cup and tapped the paperback peeking out of her tote bag.
"After the day I had, I deserved some *me* time with a double
espresso." Hedda was nothing like her sisters. While Holly enjoyed painting and donning arty clothing and Hattie liked to
garden and dye her hair red, Hedda preferred numbers and
tailored attire. Her one fashion statement was her glasses. She
had numerous pairs in a variety of colors. Today's were aqua-
green. "How are you—" She clapped a hand to her chest.
"I'm sorry. How insensitive of me. I was going to ask how
you were doing, but not good, I presume. Finding Mick
Watkins. Dead in your shop. Want to talk? Let me buy you a
cup of coffee."

"No, I'm fine."

"Are you? Really?"

My heart did a jig. Was now the time to ask if she would
reveal Logan's financial status to me?

"Courtney?" Hedda tilted her head.

"The truth, Hedda? I'm a suspect."

"Heavens. Not possible." She patted my shoulder. "You're
as innocent as the day is long."

"Thanks for the vote of confidence."

"By the way, I heard you made a fairy garden for Holly. She adores it. She should have made it herself, of course, but she's not good with growing things."

"When will you make one?" I asked, my heart returning to a normal rhythm.

"Soon. Thanks to Hattie, I've visited your shop's website numerous times. I'm quite partial to the *Alice in Wonderland* garden you made. *Alice* was my favorite book as a child."

"We have a number of upcoming events. Why don't you sign up for one?"

"I will. I promise." Lowering her voice, she said, "Between you and me, I'm a tad nervous about making one. I know you think I'm buttoned-down, but I treasure a moment of whimsy. I do want to meet a fairy. However, I'm afraid if I mess up my garden, I'll squelch any possibility."

I smiled. She wasn't the only customer who felt this way. "Maybe you should make something with an *Alice in Wonderland* theme," I suggested. "Tuning into a childhood memory might open your heart."

"'Curiouser and curiouser!'" she said, quoting Alice. "All right, I will. And you, listen up. Come to me if you need anything, even a loan for attorney's fees."

"What?" I squawked. "No. I'm good. Thanks." I could cover any fees it might take for my attorney to exonerate me. *Exonerate. Oof.* I let out a sigh. "However, I was hoping to ask you . . ." I paused. Okay, I had one more thing to add to my ways-to-improve-myself list. Be forthright. Don't beat around the darned bush. "I was wondering . . ." I shifted feet.

Nope. I couldn't do it. I could not ask her to reveal whether Logan Langford was in debt. I would not put her in that awkward position. I flashed both palms. "I was hoping you might spread the word about my business." I pulled some business cards from my purse and handed them to her. "Would you do that? People trust you."

"Of course."

Heat rushed up my neck and into my cheeks. "Thank you."

Hedda clasped my hand. "Courtney, you need to find peace."

"Exonerating myself of murder will do that."

"I'm talking about finding inner peace, dear." She kept hold of my hand and pointed to my heart. "Realize what is missing, and you might discover a whole new world." She smiled. "Don't gape at me like that. I might be a numbers person, but I'm also quite philosophical."

As she strode toward San Carlos Street, a man called out, "Courtney, hold up."

Brady jogged toward me, a leather satchel over his shoulder, an envelope in hand.

"Were you just at the post office?" I asked.

"How'd you guess?" He sighed. "How I wish we could get mail delivered."

"I like the exercise."

"You would," he joked. "Hey, everything okay?" He gazed at me warmly.

If everyone was asking me the same question, perhaps I needed to take a look in the mirror. Did I look frazzled? Off my game? An emotional wreck? "Everything's fine. I'm heading back to work."

"Let's walk together." He offered me his elbow.

We turned onto Dolores Street and strolled at a leisurely pace, taking in the various paintings in the gallery windows.

Brady laughed at one point and said, "How can so many art galleries sustain themselves, especially given their odd hours?"

Some galleries were open mornings while others were open weekends only.

"Tourism," I chimed. "It's the heart and soul of our fair town."

"Speaking of art, how's your photography coming?" he asked.

"I'm not doing as much as I'd like."

"Me either. Remember that exhibition we had in high school? The one to raise money for art programs? I'd never seen you so nervous."

"It was the first time my father had ever taken an interest."

"That's right. I remember now. You'd kept your hobby a secret for years."

Fifty students had participated. The auditorium had been packed with viewers. When my father had appeared, I'd been shocked. He eyed my photograph of Pebble Beach at sunset, but didn't say a word. Later that night, he came into my room and said he thought I had talent, but he never wanted me to break the law again. I went to sleep smiling. Sneaking illegally onto the famous golf course had been worth the risk.

To this day, as much as I loved my father, I feared his judgment regarding my talent. He and I had finally found equal footing when I'd joined his landscaping staff. I understood how things grew, and I excelled at large-scale plans for houses and hotels. If only he'd accept that I had an eye for small-scale gardens, as well.

"You won first place that night," Brady said.

"And you came in second."

"I always hated you for that." He bumped my shoulder. "Not *hate* hate. I never stopped liking you."

He smiled, his dimple deep. I remembered Fiona crooning about how cute Brady was, but he was more than cute; he was downright handsome. The admission made heat rush up my neck and into my cheeks. If Brady noticed, he didn't mention it.

We cut down 7th Avenue and stopped at the corner of Lincoln Street.

I released his elbow and smiled. "Here we are."

"Maybe we could get together and talk shop sometime," he said.

"If I don't go to jail—"

He put a finger to my lips. "Don't even think it. You're innocent. Keep focusing on that."

Chapter 13

Wind chimes in your yard will serenade garden creatures—
squirrels, fairies, and angels.
—Anonymous

At a quarter past five, as Joss and I were straightening shelves in the main showroom, Meaghan raced in to retrieve her harp.

"I can't stick around," she said, sliding the harp into its travel bag. "My client who bought two seascapes asked me to dinner."

I rolled my eyes and asked if he was cute.

Meaghan thwacked me. "I already have a boyfriend, goofball. Plus this *he* is a *she*, and she's very wealthy. She wants to buy more art, and I have a business to run. Rent isn't free." She bussed my cheek, wheeled her harp to the exit, and was gone in a flash.

Moments after she left, I moaned. "Shoot. I was going to ask her about Isabella Acosta. When I brought up Isabella's name at the book club tea, Meaghan wasn't enthralled with her, but she didn't have time to discuss. There's something about that woman I don't trust. Not just because she pointed a finger at me."

"She's different," Joss said judiciously.

"You said Holly Hopewell's art is hanging in Acosta Artworks."

"Yep. Two beautiful pieces, both eight-foot-square seascapes. Holly must have had to stand on a ladder to complete them."

Maybe I'd ask Mrs. Hopewell about Isabella. Perhaps she could shed light on why the woman had borne false testimony against me.

Fifteen minutes later, when I was ready to tackle organizing items on the patio, Joss asked if she could head out a tad early. She wanted to see her aging mother, a former organist at the Presbyterian Church who was suffering from dementia.

"Of course." I never refused Joss time with her mom. How I wished I'd had more with my own.

"We had one of our best sales days ever," Joss added as she shrugged on her overcoat. "We should come up with more themed Saturdays to promote business."

"Love it. Tomorrow, let's put a plan together."

After Joss left and the last customer departed, I turned over the *Closed* sign and strode to the patio. Yvanna and her sister had tidied up. Every vestige of tea and treats was gone. However, the shelves, as I'd expected, were in disarray.

Pixie joined me and nudged my ankle with her nose.

I knelt and scratched her chin. "A few more minutes. That's all. Promise. Why don't you play with Fiona?"

Pixie meowed and swished the air with her tail, signaling Fiona still hadn't returned. I did my best not to worry. As long as she was keeping her nose to the grindstone and not pranking someone or socializing with other fairies, the queen fairy would be happy and let Fiona associate with me, right?

I said, "Fiona will catch up to us later."

For the next few minutes, I moved from shelf to shelf reorienting the figurines to face front. Then I reorganized the larger decorative items, including the water wheels, gazebos, slides, and silos, moving them to the lower shelves and repositioning the smaller items, like fencing, lighting, and ladders, to the shelves above. Customers needed clarity when viewing these items. The tendency for many eager newbies was to buy everything, but using too many big items could overpower a garden and using too many small ones created clutter.

Next, I tackled the learning-the-craft corner and potting supplies. First, I wiped down the table and benches, and then I folded the clean towels and tossed the dirty ones into a laundry bin that resembled a miniature log cabin. I checked the seals on the opened bags of soil and moss. If air seeped into them, they would dry out. After freeing the hose of kinks and coiling it into its embossed steel hose pot, I stood with my fists planted on my hips and surveyed the scene.

Satisfied that my work was done, I scooped my Ragdoll kitten into my arms, fetched my purse and denim jacket, locked the front door, and said, "All set. Let's go."

As we were walking past Wizard of Paws, it dawned on me that I hadn't turned off the coffee urn in the shop. I'd forgotten because when Joss left and I went to the patio, I'd lost track of my routine.

Grumbling, I made a U-turn and hurried back. I didn't switch on the lights as I slipped inside. Waning sunlight offered enough illumination so I wouldn't trip. I skirted around two center display tables and eased my way to the coffee and tea service. I paused when I heard a *thud* on the patio.

Fiona didn't make thud-like sounds.

In a flash, my sweet fairy materialized and flew to my shoulder. *"Psst. Did you hear that?"*

"Where have you been?"

"Focus. Someone's sneaking in through the secret door."

"You're kidding."

"I'm dead serious." She flapped her wings hard to keep herself hovering in one place.

Pulse racing, I peered through the interior shop window toward the corner of the patio where the secret door had been discovered, but I couldn't make out much. The twinkling lights were set to switch on at eight a.m. and off at six p.m. "I don't see—"

I heard a squeak and then something scraping and the faint sound of leaves fluttering.

"Aha!" Fiona cried. "It's our landlord."

Enough light filtered through the pyramid skylight that I could make out a head with thinning salt-and-pepper hair emerging through the foliage. It was, indeed, Logan Langford. How did he learn about the hidden entry? I supposed he could have known if he had master plans to every rental space in the courtyard.

Fiona tickled my ear. "Want to have some fun?"

"No, pranks. I want to alert the police."

"It's not a prank. Watch." Using magic, she raised a small set of wind chimes fitted with a graceful green-winged fairy on its handle. With great effort, she transported it to me. "When you see me sprinkle fairy dust, clang this."

Before I could respond, she darted through a vent and reappeared over the patio. She glimpsed right and left and swooped to the learning-the-craft corner. What was she up to? She hefted one of the towels I'd folded and whizzed to Logan, who had finished wriggling onto the patio and was lumbering to his feet. As he brushed off his knees, she showered him with gold fairy dust.

Even though my nerves were jangling, I clanged the wind chimes on cue.

Fiona tossed the towel in the air, flew beneath it, and started moaning so loudly I could hear her in the shop.

Logan caught sight of her and shrieked. "Ghost!" he cried. Crazed, he threw his hands into the air and raced toward the main showroom.

So he wouldn't spot me, I ducked down and peeked out the lower corner of the window. He whipped open the French door, sprinted through the shop to the Dutch door, and flew out the exit.

Fiona dumped her towel disguise and sped to me. Her laughter had turned to hiccups. Mine, too.

When I caught my breath, I said, "That was a prank."

"Wrong. It was subterfuge."

"He heard you because you sprinkled him with fairy dust, right?"

"Yep." She floated midair and smirked.

"Did you learn to do that at fairy school?"

"No. My mother taught me. It's sort of like transmogrification, but not."

She rarely mentioned her mother and then only briefly.

"Why do you think he was here?" she asked.

"Maybe, like Mick, he'd hoped to encounter a fairy when no other humans were around. Or he wanted to get an idea of which items to use to make his first fairy garden without the typical store distractions."

"Get real," Fiona said like a sassy teenager.

"Yeah, you're right. If I believe that, I have some swampland in Arizona to sell myself." I chuckled.

"What if he killed Mick and wanted to gloat?"

Her words gave me pause. What if Logan had hoped to kill me the first time and had come back for a second shot? I shuddered at the notion. No, I was not the target.

As I took the white towel that had served as our resident ghost back to the craft corner, I considered contacting Detective Summers about the break-in, but decided calling him when nothing untoward had happened seemed unnecessary. And how would I explain the *ghost* sighting to him if he confronted Logan and Logan admitted to having seen one?

I fetched Pixie, locked up the shop, and headed home. Fiona kept pace.

"So, where did you go earlier when I was cleaning up?" I asked. "More studying?"

"No, I went to take a nap. I've been tired lately."

"Why?"

"Because . . ." Beaming, she turned sideways to me and lifted her young wings. Teensy corners of new silver wings budded beneath.

"Are those the beginnings of your adult wings?" I asked.

"Yes!" She clapped her hands gleefully. "My first set. With all that's been going on, I hadn't noticed, but by helping you solve a crime, my sleuthing skills are being utilized, and because they're being utilized—"

"I'm not solving a crime."

"Of course you are. You're trying to prove yourself innocent while at the same time figuring out who did kill Mick, and I, being your assistant, am growing my wings."

"Don't you think it has something to do with your staying within boundaries, as the queen fairy ordered?"

"Whatever is causing it is great. I'm making progress. Wahoo." She threw her arms wide and did a loop-de-loop in the air. "Thank you."

"Uh, sure, anytime. I'll do my best to stumble across more crimes so you get more opportunities."

The cheerful sound of her giggles tickled me.

Even though the scary moment with Logan was over, the near encounter made it hard to sleep. I brewed myself a cup of chamomile tea and tried writing in my diary—a task I'd started after opening the shop to give me a record of how far

I'd come—but the effort was fruitless. *Guilty, guilty, guilty* was
ringing out in my head and making my notations nearly illeg-
ible. Reading was futile, too. It didn't matter which book I
picked up; I couldn't absorb one word. My nana would have
been appalled. To her, reading soothed the soul.

But my soul could not be soothed. Had Logan learned that
I'd met with Hedda Hopewell outside the bank and, fearing I'd
uncovered his secret, come to the shop to harm me? Would he
try again? Maybe I was overreacting to his intrusion. If he didn't
kill Mick to set his finances straight, who did?

Emily had the most to gain. Summers said his people had
confirmed her alibi, yet he'd stalemated me when I'd asked if
he personally had seen to the questioning. If my father were
on the case, he'd have wanted to be personally sure.

Taking the horse by the reins, I sat at my computer and
pulled up the website for the Equestrian Inn in Carmel Valley.
I was blown away by the scope of the place. Built in Mediter-
ranean style, it boasted one hundred and eighty hotel rooms and
suites. The prices of the rooms were steep, but, with each room,
one guest was offered a chance to enjoy a trail ride or take
jumping or rodeo stunt lessons. Boarding was offered for guests
who brought their own horses. In addition, according to the
inn's rave reviews, food was a draw. Twenty of the inn's acres
were dedicated to organically farmed and fresh-picked heirloom
vegetables, which enhanced the inn's four-star Forbes rating.

As I browsed the various drop-down menus, I landed on
how I might entice an inn employee to talk to me. I didn't
have to be at the shop until eleven on Sunday, and, as it just so
happened, the Equestrian Inn offered sunrise rides to guests as
well as non-guests—the inn's way of enticing new customers.

As my fingers tripped across the keys to set my reservation,
Fiona flitted to my side. "What are you doing?"

"Sleuthing."

★   ★   ★

At five a.m., I ate a quick bite and fed Pixie. At five thirty, Fiona and I arrived at the Equestrian Inn. Its staff was perky and accommodating. The trail guide, a pretty young woman named Bianca, complimented my riding outfit, a thrown-together mash-up of jeans, T-shirt, asymmetric sheepskin jacket, straw cowboy hat, and my favorite Western-style boots made of full-quill ostrich. I hoped they wouldn't get ruined. The itinerary didn't mention whether we'd have to get off the horses and walk through any grassy areas.

"How many of us are there?" I asked, matching Bianca's perkiness.

"Six." She swapped out my sunhat with a helmet. "For protection," she said, and then fitted me with a pinto horse named Paint.

"Paint is a good boy," Bianca said. "He won't give you any trouble. You're a newbie, right?"

My boot selection must have given me away. "I've done some riding," I said. I wasn't lying. I had. As a girl. At a stable. Around a rink. Within a month, I was bored with doing circles, so I quit.

Using a mounting block, I climbed onto Paint and slotted my boots into the stirrups. He snorted and crooked his head to peer at me. I patted his neck, assuring him I'd follow his lead. Fiona fluttered in front of his eyes and blew him a kiss. Paint raised his chin in greeting.

"Do you lead the night rides?" I asked Bianca.

"Some of them," she said.

"How about last Wednesday?"

"Yep. That was my gig."

"Then you met my friend Emily Watkins."

Bianca pursed her lips. "Possibly."

"You don't remember? She's about yea high." I held up a hand. "Long hair." I almost blurted that she had prominent buck-teeth but stopped. That wouldn't sound nice. "Toothy smile."

"Sounds familiar, but I can't be sure. We had over twenty on that ride, and honestly I don't memorize the names and faces of all my riders." Bianca tapped the side of her head. "I'm not a facts and figures gal. I don't keep much unneeded data in here. It interferes with my ability to recall what's on the trails and keep the horses in line. Okay, let's go." She took hold of Paint's reins and led me to where other riders were already seated on their horses. She climbed onto a beautiful black steed and, for a brief while, gave us a refresher course on stopping and steering our horses.

Minutes later, we were off. Bianca kicked her horse to get started. The other horses followed.

A few yards ahead, Bianca twisted on her saddle. "The trail ride will last an hour and a half. During that time, I'll give you all sorts of details about the flora and fauna of the area, and I'll answer questions."

We rode for a few minutes longer, and Bianca twisted on her saddle again. "If you're new to the area, you might not know this, but Carmel Valley and the surrounding areas are not known for sunrises. We're known for our sunsets."

As we rode, I drank in the sounds of the sea gulls and caught the fresh scent of morning. Incredible. Fiona was having the time of her life riding on top of a real live horse. Occasionally she reminded me that she would have a better time on a fairy horse because it would move faster. I chuckled and bent over to whisper. "I'll promise you a fast ride on a horse at a future date." When I was a girl, although I hadn't enjoyed riding in the rink, whenever we had broken into a cantor or a gallop, I had laughed gleefully, the same kind of laugh I'd let out when I'd taken a ride in a souped-up Corvette around Laguna Seca, a nearby speedway. I liked to go fast.

For a half hour, Bianca told us about the history of Carmel Valley, which had been shaped by the Esselen tribe and fostered and nurtured by the Spaniards, particularly Father Junípero

Serra. He had been interested in planting a reliable vegetable garden to supply goods to ships. Because vegetation required proper irrigation, work on a dam had begun around the Carmel River in the late 1700s.

Over the course of the morning, I didn't get another chance to talk to Bianca one-on-one. She was in the lead. My horse and I were two back, directly behind a chatty middle-aged woman with pigtails who kept Bianca answering question after question. If only I'd nailed that spot maybe I would have been able to jog Bianca's memory about Emily. On the other hand, perhaps she hadn't remembered Emily because Emily had lied about having taken the ride.

My favorite part of the ride was the last leg along the coast. The sky was a brilliant blue, and the ocean was roiling from the tide. Huge foamy sprays crashed the seawall. Heaven. However, by the time the ride ended, my rump was sore, and I was frustrated because I hadn't learned a thing.

When we were wiping down our horses—guests had to do a few chores—I looked for Bianca again, but she was across the yard talking to a man in a dark sedan. Detective Summers.

In a flash, I swapped out the helmet for my straw hat, pulled it down over my forehead, and ducked out of sight.

I hurried home, showered, and changed into a peach-colored sundress and matching sweater as well as gold sandals and a gold cross-body purse. On Sundays I liked to dress up for work.

As Pixie, Fiona, and I passed Church of the Wayfarer on Lincoln Street, the oldest Protestant church in Carmel-by-the-Sea, chimes rang out.

"Listen." Fiona danced in the air like a bell swinging to and fro.

I smiled. Like her, I loved the sound of bells.

Dozens of patrons were filing into the simple white building with its pitched, green-tile roof for Sunday's earliest service. I enjoyed meandering through the church's Master's Garden, which featured plants that were described in the Bible. It was so peaceful and a favorite for weddings.

Pixie wriggled in the front-of-the-chest pet carrier I'd strapped on. This morning she'd been so skittish for some reason that I was afraid she would dash out of my arms if I carried her, never to be seen again. I cooed to calm her and then retrieved my cell phone and tapped in the phone number Summers had given me.

"Who are you calling?" Fiona asked.

"The detective, to tell him about the break-in."

Around three a.m. this morning, I had awoken and decided I should loop in the detective after all, convinced that my sneaky landlord wouldn't bring up the ghost sighting.

The call went to voice mail. I left a brief message about the event.

Drinking in the morning air, I took the long route to the store so I could window shop. I didn't need any clothes, and I didn't need items for the cottage, but there was something about looking at window displays and dreaming of what I *might* want that fed my soul. New candles? New art? A piece of jewelry? I thought of Meaghan. She and I needed a girls' night out. Maybe we could do a bit of shopping therapy.

By the time I arrived at the shop, I'd blown my imaginary wad on a unique coffee table, a landscape of Carmel, and a slinky blue dress. I set Pixie on the floor and performed all the usual tasks. I tallied the register, plugged in the water for tea, made an urn of coffee, and opened windows to let in fresh air.

When I was done, I returned to the main showroom and pirouetted in the middle of the floor. How lucky was I to have my own business? I was in the middle of the second spin when I remembered that I was a person of interest in a murder. Talk about a blow to the solar plexus. So far, my attorney must have been successful at pleading my innocence because I wasn't locked up. When would she give me an update?

I glared at my cell phone. Would Summers call me back? Would he consider my landlord a suspect in the murder because he'd trespassed using the secret door? Did Summers have Gregory Darvell or Petra Pauli in his sights? Despite sources corroborating Emily Watkins's alibi, was she still a suspect? If not, why had Summers shown up at the Equestrian Inn earlier? To me, Emily's motive was the strongest: kill her husband, inherit his money, and then train her dog to be a fabulous, blue-ribbon-winning show dog—something her husband had refused to let happen.

My stomach grumbled. A piece of fruit for breakfast hadn't done the trick. I ambled to the kitchen beyond the office hoping to score a savory scone left over from yesterday's tea. There were two. A minute later, after a quick reheat in the microwave on low, *voilà*, I had a snack. I went to the patio to enjoy them, but seeing the fountain where Mick died squelched my appetite. Shoot. I tried not to think about all the book club attendees who must have been curious. Had Petra told the dog-friendly table where the murder had happened?

"Halloo-o-o." Glinda Gill, owner of Glitz, the jewelry store in the Cypress and Ivy Courtyard, popped into the shop. Glinda always popped or bounced. She was a tennis buff and light on her feet. I heard she particularly liked playing the net. She primped her bobbed blond hair. "How're things?"

"Things are good." My voice cracked.

"Methinks ye are a liar," Glinda said, employing language I'd often heard her use. She claimed her ancestors had been pirates who had terrorized the California coast. She even maintained that a pirate had built our courtyard. Was that why a secret passage had been constructed in my building, so pirates could come and go with their loot and not alert their enemies? Like Glinda, I could concoct farfetched histories.

"Fess up," Glinda said. "Spill the beans. Talk to me." Like a pirate wench, Glinda liked to dress flashily. She wore a formfitting red dress and an armful of bracelets. When I'd first met her, the lyrics from a Grateful Dead song had cycled through my mind: "Rings on her fingers and bells on her shoes."

"Truly, things are good," I repeated. "I took a trail ride on the beach this morning, which was awesome. And we had an amazing book club tea yesterday. Sorry you couldn't make it."

"Me too." Glinda poured herself a cup of coffee. "By the by, I heard through the grapevine that our landlord slipped in here last night."

"Which grapevine?"

"You know."

No, I didn't, but Glinda didn't elaborate. Had Summers or someone from the precinct clued her in?

She raised her coffee cup in a *cheers* position before taking a sip. "So . . . did Logan trespass?"

"Yes."

"Well, then you ought to know"—she crooked a finger to beckon me—"good old Logan wished Mick gone."

I gaped. "He said that to you out loud?"

"Not to me. To his attorney."

"Wright Youngman?"

"I don't know who that is. I'm talking about the attorney who negotiates all of Logan's leases on his properties. He's my current beau." Glinda tucked a hair behind her ear. "We've been dating about three weeks."

I swallowed hard. "Are you saying that Logan's attorney confided to you—"

"My beau confided to me."

"That Logan wanted to kill Mick?"

"Heavens, no. Logan said Mick was impossible and noisy and a pain in the neck, by which I inferred he wanted him *gone*. Not *dead*." Glinda let loose with a snort-like laugh. "Would anyone actually admit they wanted someone *dead*?" She picked up an Open Your Imagination business card and perused it front and back. "Nicely done. Did you design these yourself?"

"Joss did." The card featured ivy and a pretty blue fairy in the upper right corner, as well as a photo of a finished fairy garden in the lower left corner.

"May I?" she asked, and without waiting for a response slipped a card into the pocket of her dress. "One more thing. I also learned Logan wants to sell the courtyard. To a developer."

"I heard. Yvanna said she's worried that all the tenants' leases might be at issue."

"That's what I think, too."

"She believes Logan is in debt."

"Can you imagine what being in debt might do to the family name? 'Langfords don't quit. Langfords don't fail,'" she intoned while miming quotation marks. "That's their motto, you know. Langfords have a long history around these parts. Lo-ong." She dragged out the word. "If Logan knows what's good for him, he had better not besmirch the name." Glinda took another sip of her coffee. "Gee, this is good. What kind is it?"

"Kona coffee."

"Love it. So mellow."

I couldn't help thinking about Logan Langford and what he'd been up to last night. What if he'd broken into the shop to sabotage it, hoping that destruction of property would frighten me enough to quit my lease?

Glinda clicked her fingernails on the counter. "Listen up. I saw that cute police detective questioning Logan."

"Which cute police detective?"

"Summers."

"He's not—" I paused.

Yes, she would find him attractive. They were about the same age.

"He and Logan were standing by the fountain in the courtyard," Glinda went on.

The fountain, featuring a floating bronze sphere atop a twisted bronze base, was located directly between Glitz and Sweet Treats. One of Flair's artists had created it. People regularly strolled through the courtyard to view it.

"Detective Summers point-blank asked for Logan's alibi," Glinda said.

Hallelujah. The police and I were on the same track. Granted, if my landlord was a murderer, that could put a crimp in my lease situation, but I'd address that matter if it arose.

"Logan said he was at Church of the Wayfarer singing in the choir," Glinda added. "That has to rule him out as a suspect, I suppose. Choir members will vouch for him, and they wouldn't lie."

I sighed. There went that theory.

Joss hustled into the shop and threw her oversized tote bag behind the counter. "Sorry I'm late. My mom . . ." She sighed. "Now, who were you saying wouldn't lie?"

"Members of the choir," Glinda chimed.

"Ha! I've known a few pious liars in my day." Joss removed her sweater coat and smoothed the front of her neon aqua blouse. Fiona whizzed past Joss's face, making Joss gasp. Joss signaled to me. "Go on. Who wouldn't lie about what?"

I told her about Logan's stealing into the shop last night through the hidden door. Joss couldn't believe it. She asked if I was okay. I assured her I was.

"As for the lie," I said, "supposedly he was at choir rehearsal at the time of the murder. He has an alibi."

"No, he doesn't," Joss said curtly. "Choir practice does not last until two a.m." She poured herself a cup of hot water and dunked a bag of chamomile tea into it.

"Maybe he went out with choir members afterward," Glinda suggested. "I might have missed hearing that part of his account."

"I'm sure Summers will follow up," I said.

The door flew open. "Coffee! Must. Have. Coffee." Meaghan rushed in, the ends of her ocean-themed scarf fluttering. "Our machine quit. I'm in desperate need." She held out an empty mug with Picasso art on it. "Please. I'll promise you my firstborn child."

Glinda patted my arm. "I'll see you around. Let me know what you find out." She added sotto voce, "FYI, your cat is acting a bit nuts."

As she left, I glanced toward the patio. Pixie was dancing on her hind legs and batting the air. Fiona was taunting her.

"Find out about what?" Meaghan asked as she filled her mug and added a dollop of cream.

I gazed at my pal, a gleam in my eye. "You play harp at Church of the Wayfarer, right?"

Chapter 14

I'll seek a four-leaved shamrock in all the fairy dells, and if I find the charmed leaves, oh, how I'll weave my spells.
—Samuel Lover, "The Four-Leaved Shamrock"

As Joss rearranged greeting cards in the revolving rack, I explained the situation to Meaghan about Logan's alibi. When I finished, she agreed to do recon; however, she wasn't sure she could do it any time soon. Her day was packed. She had half a dozen appointments. Sunday was always a busy day at the gallery. And Monday wasn't going to prove much better. But she promised she would follow through.

"Meaghan, before you go, talk to me about Isabella Acosta. You're not a fan. Why?"

She wrinkled her nose. "The woman stole one of our artists."

"Stole?"

"Okay, enticed her with a better split, less commission."

"Is that ethical?"

"It's not illegal, but in Carmel, most of us gallery owners

have a pact to honor one another's agreements with artists. We don't poach." Meaghan scrunched up her mouth before adding, "It speaks to her character."

"No kidding."

"To add insult to injury, the woman never smiles, as if she's above us all. It's like she lost her joie de vivre years ago."

I didn't like or dislike someone who frowned, but a smile did work wonders.

"Gotta go." Meaghan blew me a kiss and flew out the Dutch door.

As she exited, Detective Summers sauntered into the shop dressed in his usual white shirt and tan khakis, but his easy smile was gone and a no-nonsense scowl had taken its place. Office Rodriguez followed him, dressed like Summers, her hair secured in a silver-tooled hair clip. She didn't look any happier than he did.

Summers said, "Did I see you at the Equestrian Inn earlier?"

I blanched. How I'd hoped he hadn't spotted me.

Fiona flew into the shop from the patio and skidded to a hover. "Uh-oh." Her presence felt good, like I wasn't alone and floundering.

Raising my chin, I said cheerily, "Yes, Detective, as a matter of fact you did."

"What were you doing there?" he asked, his voice gruff.

"Taking a sunrise trail ride."

His eyebrows drew together. "I repeat, what where you doing there?"

Joss joined us. "Everything cool?"

"I was just telling the police that I was following a hunch. Bianca, the trail guide for my ride, led the night ride on Wednesday, the one Emily Watkins said she took."

Summers grunted. "I told you my people had questioned the staff."

"Why did you show up, then?" I countered. "Checking it out for yourself, I assume. To be certain."

Rodriguez stifled a snort, which ending up sounding like a sneeze. Summers cut her a harsh look. In defense, she whisked a tissue from her pocket and blew her nose. "Allergies," she whispered.

I said, "Bianca didn't remember Emily, but she said her mind didn't work that way."

Summers clicked his tongue. "I know."

"Did you talk to anyone else?" I asked.

"The manager as well as the assistant manager. Emily Watkins had checked into the hotel, but . . ." He worked his tongue inside his cheek.

"But?" I said.

"But no one could specifically say whether she left and returned."

I pumped my fist.

"Don't get cocky, Miss Kelly."

"Courtney," I said firmly.

"I'm giving you a pass on this," Summers said. "But from now on, stay out of our way."

Rodriguez said, "Let's hear about the break-in."

"Yes, ma'am." I gestured to Joss. "Would you pour Detective Summers and Officer Rodriguez a cup of coffee?"

"None for me," Summers said.

"Black," Rodriguez said. "One sugar."

Joss set off to complete the request.

"My landlord stole in last night," I said. "Follow me." I strode to the patio.

Summers pulled his notebook from his pocket, removed the rubber band, and trailed me. Fiona flitted beside him, peering at him intently.

Rodriguez kept pace. Joss caught up to the officer and handed her a mug of coffee.

Standing near the fountain, I pointed out the foliage in front of the secret door. "He entered through there, which means he knew about it."

"Are you sure?" Summers asked.

"As sure as rain. After closing, I came back because I'd forgotten to turn off the coffee pot. I didn't switch on the lights because it was a quick trip from the door to the urn. I was in the main showroom when I heard a thud on the patio. I froze for a second and hid over there." I motioned to the window where I'd ducked down and went on to explain how the moonlight had provided enough illumination to see Logan.

"What did he do once he stole inside?" Rodriguez asked.

"He scrambled to his feet and turned right and left. I'm not sure what he was looking for. Suddenly, he screamed and ran out."

"Ghost!" Fiona cried.

Neither Summers nor Rodriguez seemed to detect her outburst.

Summers studied me as if he knew I was keeping something from him. My insides grumbled. Obfuscating the truth wasn't good for my digestion.

"Let me guess." Summers drew a long breath and exhaled. "He saw a fairy."

"It's possible." I didn't add that it was a *ghost* fairy. If the detective didn't believe in fairies, he certainly wouldn't believe fairies could don costumes.

Summers pursed his lips, pen poised over his notebook. "Did you feel threatened by Mr. Langford?"

"At first, I didn't know what to think. Was he the murderer, making a return visit?"

"Why would you think that?" Rodriguez sipped her coffee.

"Because Detective Summers suggested that I was initially the intended target, not Mick Watkins."

Summers nodded. "Go on."

"When I saw Logan Langford emerge through the foliage, I couldn't for the life of me figure out why he'd come in through the secret passageway. He's the landlord. By right, he has a key to the front door and may enter at any time."

"How did he know about that entrance?" Rodriguez asked pointing at the foliage. "We haven't leaked that information."

"I assume he has layout plans for each property," I said. "A door like that could be notated somewhere."

Rodriguez and Summers conferred.

"Don't you think it's odd that he sneaked in?" I asked.

"Perhaps he, like others we know, is trying to solve the murder," Summers said.

Rodriguez smirked. "Amateurs like to theorize."

The two of them exchanged a snide look.

Fiona placed her hands beside her head, as if she intended to blow a raspberry and wiggle her fingers. I shot her a look. She backed off.

Calmly, I said, "I theorize because I'm trying to clear my name. How are you doing on that front?"

"Your attorney has been in touch," Rodriguez said. "She's prepared to post bail should we choose to arrest you."

"I'm not guilty."

"Miss Judge agrees with you. She has repeatedly touted the evidence about your ISP being in use at the time of the murder."

Good to know.

"Your father has weighed in again, too," Summers added. "He'd like to see notes on the case. I told him I couldn't accommodate him."

"Still no suspect?" I asked.

"Oh, we have plenty of suspects." Summers pocketed his notebook and, using his cell phone, snapped a couple of photographs of the patio. "If Langford didn't take anything, there's nothing more we can do."

"Aren't they going to question him?" Fiona asked.

I reiterated her question.

"What will he say? 'Yes, I trespassed?'" Summers scratched his chin. "Look, if I were you, I'd put in a security system."

"That's expensive, and I'm not sure my landlord will let me. It would require installing wires and messing with the walls."

"Negotiate with him," Rodriguez suggested.

"And tell him what? That I want a security system because he sneaked in?"

"No. Don't say that." Summers frowned. "Tell him that your shop was broken into a second time. Tell him once word gets out about the second break-in, the rest of the courtyard will become a prime target for robbers, and all of the businesses may suffer, thus hurting his bottom line."

Far be it from me to tell the detective that, since the first break-in and subsequent murder, business was on the rise. We'd had to order more of everything in the shop, and learning-the-craft sessions were booked for a month. Curiosity was definitely the driving force.

Summers pocketed his cell phone. "By the way, I hear Ever Alert Security is pretty good."

"I've heard that, too," Rodriguez said.

Fiona flew to my shoulder. "What's their story?"

I had been wondering the same thing. Summers and Rodriguez seemed in sync. Were they a couple or had they been partners for so long that they dressed the same and spoke with a similar cadence?

"If there's nothing further . . ." Summers strode into the main showroom.

Rodriguez trailed him and handed her mug to Joss.

I followed. "Detective, did you find matches to the rope fiber on Mick's neck?"

He whirled around. "Here we go again."

Rodriguez coughed out a laugh. "What don't you under-stand about the words *don't theorize*, Miss Kelly? You don't want to be arrested for obstructing justice, do you?"

"Theorizing isn't obstructing," I countered. "Asking ques-tions isn't obstructing, either. To obstruct justice, you need to block prosecutors, investigators, or other government officials from doing their jobs, hence perverting the course of justice." Not only had I memorized city ordinances over the years, but, growing up with a policeman as a father and then being en-gaged to a lawyer and future judge, I'd also soaked up inane legal jargon. "All I want to know"—I flicked a loose hair off my cheek in frustration—"is about the rope."

"Matching DNA or rope fibers does not happen as fast as you think," Summers said.

Given my knowledge of chemistry and my fascination with mysteries, I actually knew how fast technicians worked, but I kept mum.

"Therefore"—Summers held up three fingers—"we're going the traditional route here: motive, means, and opportu-nity."

Fiona said, "Tell them about Logan's money issue."

I cleared my throat. "Logan Langford might be in debt. Sup-posedly, he wants all the tenants out so he can sell the place to a developer. What if Mick Watkins refused?"

"Who else are you willing to throw under the bus?" Sum-mers arched an eyebrow.

"That's not what I'm doing."

"You're spreading a rumor that Langford is in financial trouble."

"I'm not spreading it. I—"

"I don't buy it." Summers shook his head. "The Langford wealth is ages old. Even a spendthrift couldn't run through it.

Look for some other angle. No"—he held up a hand—"hold on. Retract that last statement. I did not mean that you, specifically, should look for another angle."

I gave him a thumbs-up gesture. "Got it."

How I wished I knew more about Logan Langford. Was he in debt? To the tune of how much? Why? Was he a gambler? Was one of his children or grandchildren or a dear friend in trouble? I would go into debt for family or friends.

Summers and Rodriguez headed to the door.

"For now, I'd check out installing a security device. Good day, Miss—" He glanced over his shoulder and grinned. "Courtney."

"Emily Watkins," I blurted as I ran after them. I wanted them to know about the inheritance and the attorney. Out of nowhere, I flashed on Emily's purse. If I recalled correctly, her Michael Kors tote bag had rope handles. Could she have used the handles to strangle her husband? No. Not a chance. Too short. How about the leather-and-rope belt she'd been wearing over her riding pants when she'd arrived on the scene? She could've unhooked it, strangled Mick, and re-hooked it in less than a minute. "Emily—"

"You don't quit, do you?" Rodriguez jeered. "You have to stop. You—"

Summers silenced her with a glance. "What about Mrs. Watkins?"

I felt my cheeks warm. "Nothing."

"Tell them," Fiona urged.

No. They wouldn't listen to anything I said. Rodriguez had shut me down. *Mine to know; yours to find out,* I thought and said, "Good day."

As Summers and Rodriguez left, I couldn't help thinking of my father. Summers reminded me of him. Direct. Plainspoken. When on the job, all business. I'd often felt nervous around my father, as if he'd discounted my opinion because I hadn't had enough life experience to warrant speaking up. That ended now. One more thing to add to my ways-to-improve-myself list. I was thirty. I'd traveled to China alone. I'd hitchhiked through Europe with Meaghan without repercussions. I'd opened my own business. My voice deserved to be heard.

Emboldened, I texted Dad and asked him to meet me for tea one day soon. I wanted to apologize for defying him about the security guard and thank him for the attorney, even if in the long run she wasn't able to help me, although I didn't write any of that in the text. Given the chance, my father would make a gigantic banner of my apology and hang it on the side of his house. Okay, he wouldn't make a banner, but he'd tease me for days.

Chapter 15

*Faeries, come take me out of this dull world, for I would ride
with you upon the wind . . .*
—William Butler Yeats, *The Land of Heart's Desire*

Joss gripped my arm and said, "Spill. What didn't you tell the
police?"

I detailed my theory about Emily and her rope-style belt
and the fact that the staff at the Equestrian Inn couldn't corroborate her alibi. I said, "She could've driven back, killed
Mick, and returned to the inn for the night. The trail guide
wasn't the sharpest tool in the tool kit."

"Ha!" Fiona said.

"Emily could've duped her and made her think she was on
the ride. In fact, what if Emily has taken the ride before and
knows the spiel, so if she's questioned, she could retell each
aspect of it?"

Joss said, "The police need to know this."

"I agree," Fiona chimed.

"The police told me to butt out."

Joss brandished a hand. "Maybe if you looped in your father—"

"You heard the police. Dad has been off the force for years. They don't want his opinion."

I hugged Joss and thanked her and Fiona for their support, and then set about business. First, I called my realtor to inquire about my lease. It turned out we could negotiate a renewal every year. However, if Logan wanted to throw me out for *cause,* I had no say in the matter. Next, I called my attorney to check in. It was Sunday. I didn't expect her to return the call.

And then, for an hour, Joss and I discussed the various ideas we'd had about new programs for the shop. I wanted to do a children's fairy tale reading hour. We would share fairy tales and other fairy-related writing like Shakespeare's poems. Joss suggested we offer a workshop during which customers could make fairy *homes,* easily accomplished by inserting battery-operated twinkling lights into mason jars.

Giddy with inspiration, I coasted through the rest of the morning. Late in the afternoon, I supervised a craft session with a pair of teenaged girls who wanted to make matching fairy gardens. They weren't twins, they told me, giggling, but they had been joined at the hip since preschool. Over the course of our two-hour-long session, I tried to dissuade them from the notion of making identical gardens. Each fairy garden should reflect its maker, I advised. I didn't add that teens invariably found better friends after high school, like Meaghan and I had. One girl with whom I'd gone to elementary school had turned into a major diva—aka *mean girl*—in high school. But my students were adamant. By the end of the session, they had built duplicate gardens and were thrilled with the result. Who was I to quibble?

After work, Fiona accompanied Pixie and me home. Fiona

and I didn't talk much. Both of us were lost in thought. Pixie was cuddlier than ever. I was pretty certain she was concerned about me. I snuggled her to reassure her.

I ate a grilled cheese sandwich and a cup of minestrone soup, and, rather than do anything related to work, settled into a chair to read a new mystery.

Around midnight, unable to sleep—the book was so good I could barely put it down—I fetched the aqua-blue afghan my mother had crocheted for me when I was eight, grabbed the shovel standing by the front door, and slipped onto the porch. I sat in the mission slat rocker, snuggled under the afghan, the shovel across my lap, and allowed the steady sound of the surf to lull me to sleep. Fiona joined me and circled overhead.

Around two a.m., I awoke with a start. I'd heard a crackle. And footsteps.

I threw off the afghan, lumbered to my feet, and readied the shovel. I peered into the darkness but couldn't see a thing.

"Fiona?" I whispered. She didn't respond. "Who's there?" I called stupidly, as if believing an intruder would answer.

Mrs. Hopewell's Pomeranians started yipping. They'd heard something, too.

What if Logan was creeping about? Did he mean to scare me or hurt me? I supposed it could be Emily. Perhaps she'd learned I'd gone to the Equestrian Inn and made inquiries. What if Petra Pauli had found out I'd talked to Oriana Gray?

"I'm not scared," I shouted, and jabbed the tip of the shovel on the porch to make a point.

However, I was also not an idiot. I retreated inside, switched on all the lights, and locked the doors. Feeling safer, I stole to a window and peered out. I didn't see any movement. No shadows. No darting figures. No flashlight being doused. No cigarette being extinguished. Maybe I had imagined the sounds, and possibly, when I'd startled, I'd alarmed the Pomeranians. I stared into the dark for another fifteen minutes. Nothing.

Around three a.m., I slipped into bed . . . with the shovel by my side.

Monday morning, I awoke feeling surprisingly restored. While I was eating a hearty breakfast of scrambled eggs with herbs and cheese, Fiona whizzed into the kitchen and began flitting from my plantings of basil to parsley to chives. She was humming.

"Did you dose me with fairy dust last night?" I asked.

"Whatever are you talking about?" Her voice was high-pitched and flirty. After a year of knowing her, I was savvy enough to recognize when she was lying to me.

"You did. I haven't slept that heavily since . . ." I couldn't remember when. "I faintly recall hearing an incantation."

She giggled and flew to face me. "It was a harmless potion, created with lavender, chamomile, licorice, and valerian root." Fairies could make all sorts of botanical potions simply by summoning the essence of plants. They never had to crush or destroy anything. "Don't be mad."

"I'm not, but next time ask me. I awoke and thought I heard someone in the yard, and you weren't there."

"What?" She covered her mouth, fingers spread. "Like a trespasser?"

"I'm not sure. I was deep in sleep. Maybe I dreamed it."

"I'm so sorry. You should never be without your edge. I won't do it again."

"Where did you go afterward?" I asked.

"Out."

I ogled her. *Out?* When I was a girl, my father had become quickly exasperated by that kind of vague response; now

I understood why. A cop, even a retired one, liked his child to tell the truth and nothing but the truth.

"Out where?" I asked.

"If you must know, I went to the library."

I breathed a sigh of relief. No harm could come from communing with books.

"Are you mad at me?" she asked.

"No."

Relieved, she spiraled up to the ceiling, hovered for a moment, and then, screwing up her face with wicked delight, dive-bombed Pixie, who was sound asleep on her pillow. The kitten startled and snarled. She lashed out with a paw. Fiona plunked on the top of Pixie's head and hugged her ribs to keep from laughing too hard.

Pixie rolled over and tried to crush her.

Fiona escaped in the nick of time.

Although Monday was my only day off each week, I often came in to the shop to do catch-up tasks. After arriving this morning, I contacted Logan Langford and told him about the break-in. I did not let on that I knew he was the culprit. To my surprise, he approved the installation of a security system. He wouldn't pay for it, of course, but he said it would add value to the site.

Getting a security company to come out and give a bid wasn't easy. Many of the companies were closed on Mondays, like we were. I finally cajoled two representatives to appear before the end of the day.

To bide the time until they arrived, I decided to respond to emails and such. Invariably customers who had taken their materials home to build their own fairy gardens had additional questions.

Midmorning, I settled at the chalked chestnut desk in the office to flesh out the ideas for more how-to videos, using ideas that I'd received from my online chat friends. Most of them said I'd need at least five videos to drive traffic to my YouTube channel. Using a fresh notepad, I jotted down: how to arrange foliage; how to position environmental features; which sized fairies went with which pots; how big a pot; and color scheme.

The landline phone jangled. I answered, "Open Your Imagination."

"Courtney Kelly, please," a woman with a crackly voice said.

"Speaking."

"Big Valley Nursery." The wholesale company that supplied many of our planting mixes and potted plants. "I'm sorry to tell you this, but we've put a flag on your credit."

"What's wrong?" I'd never had any problem with making payments. All the company's credit cards were at zero balance, and all its bank loans were up to date and paid.

"It seems you have broken a loan covenant. We'll have to hold shipment on your next delivery until this matter is cleared up."

"But I haven't broken any covenant. Who claims I have?"

"As I said, there's a flag on your account," the woman said. "Once you clear it up, please send us the proper paperwork."

"There's got to be a mistake," I cried.

The woman hung up. No room for debate.

I grumbled under my breath. How many of these phone calls did she make a day?

As I pulled up the Big Valley Nursery file on the computer, I wondered whether someone had deliberately messed with my standing at the bank. A loan covenant usually required that the borrower could not break the law or engage in immoral activity. I'd done neither.

Out of the blue, I thought of Logan Langford. Had he had a hand in the issue? Had he figured out that I'd spoken to Hedda Hopewell? Even though I hadn't pressed her for his information, was he retaliating because I'd considered poking my nose into his business?

I sent an email to Joss outlining the problem. She would have to look into the matter; she was a tiger when it came to negotiations. In an instant, she wrote back saying she would come in and handle it. I reminded her it was her day off. She replied that work would be more fun than doing laundry.

My cell phone hummed. I lifted it off the desk blotter and scanned the readout. Victoria Judge had sent a text. Plain and simple: *The wheels of bureaucracy move slowly. You are still a person of interest. Working to resolve this. Keep your spirits up.*

I set the phone down, and it hummed again. I lifted it. My father was responding to my text about tea: *How about now?*

Me: *Perfect. Hideaway Café on Lincoln.* I'd seen people entering earlier, so I knew it was open on a Monday.

Ten minutes, my father replied.

Quickly, I refreshed my makeup, assured Pixie and Fiona that I'd return soon, left a note for Joss, and made a beeline across the street.

Brady greeted me at the hostess's station. "Nice to see you again."

I toyed with the hair at the nape of my neck, suddenly aware that I was underdressed in a floral long-sleeved T-shirt and bib-and-brace denim overalls. Why dress up when I planned to do grunt work all day at the shop?

"You look nice," he said. "As fresh as a summer day."

My cheeks warmed at the compliment. "Thanks. I needed that."

"Only saying what's true." I liked the way his eyes sparkled, as if he were having the best day of his life.

"I'm meeting my father," I said.

"Great. Follow me." He guided me to a table on the rear patio. "Here you go." He handed me two menus. "Coffee or tea?"

"Tea, please. With raw sugar. Coffee for my father. Black."

"I'd expect nothing less." He walked away with a jaunty spring in his step.

A minute later, my father strode across the patio, admiring the flowers and vines and lights strung across the expanse. Like me, he had dressed casually—denim shirt, jeans, and work boots. He smoothed his thick hair before kissing me on the cheek, and then took a seat opposite me.

"I heard you fired Gus," he said. "Not cool."

"Not cool that you stationed him outside my door."

He flipped open his menu, doing his best to hide a smirk.

"I want to apologize," I said, leaning forward on my elbows. "Not for letting Gus go, but for being, well—"

"Sassy? Stubborn? Impertinent?"

"I'm independent, Dad." I cocked my head.

"Being independent is an asset. You get that from me." He closed his menu. "By the way, you never need to apologize. I love you, warts and all."

"I don't have warts," I joked.

"Me, either."

Over the years, my father and I had learned to talk in shorthand. We rarely yelled at each other, though we'd had a few battles. We owed it to my mother to love each other. Forever. I remembered pinky swears with him. And hot cocoa at two in the morning when I couldn't sleep. And his arms around me after Christopher dumped me. He didn't talk. He didn't ask any questions. He was simply *there*.

"Here you go." A waitress in a red skirt and white bodice set my tea and my father's coffee on the table and asked if we wanted anything else. She recommended the honey banana muffins, fresh from the oven. We ordered two, and she left.

My father blew on his coffee and took a sip. "So, are you still a suspect in Mick Watkins's murder?"

"I assume so. The police haven't exonerated me. Thank you for the attorney, by the way. She's nice."

"You don't need nice. You need good." Dad set his coffee cup on the white iron table. "You look worried."

"I think my landlord might be trying to undermine my business." I told him about the woman from the nursery claiming I'd broken a loan covenant.

"Why would Logan do such a thing?" Dad asked. "And why wouldn't you suspect a competing business of sabotage?"

"Because there is no competing business within a hundred miles. Plus, I've heard rumors that Logan might want to oust me and all the other lessees in Cypress and Ivy." I told my father about Logan's stealing into the shop. I didn't mention Fiona acting like a ghost.

"Is Summers following up on the break-in?"

"Not really. Logan didn't take anything. And he's the landlord. He has a right to be inside, even if he steals in through a secret door."

I spotted Brady standing at the entrance to the patio, looking our way.

My father gazed in that direction. "Does he expect a formal invitation?" He crooked his finger.

Brady moseyed over. "Sir, good to see you. It's been a while." He extended his hand. They shook. "I think the last time was when you redid my family's yard. You were one of the first in the area to use drought-tolerant plants. My mother was over the moon with the result."

"That's nice to hear."

Yes, even in a mild climate like Carmel's, drought-tolerant plants were of value. Like the rest of California, we'd endured plenty of low-rainfall years.

"Got time to sit?" Dad asked.

"Sure. I've got a minute." Brady settled into the chair closest to me.

"And call me Kip, son. You're over twenty-one."

"Yes, sir."

"I'd heard you'd redone this place," my father said. "Nice job. You've got a ton of five-star Yelp reviews already. Way to go. Your dad loves to talk about you."

"Blab about me all you want. Secrets are highly overrated. Just ask my ex."

I wondered what that meant.

Brady started to rise.

My father pinned his shoulder. "Stay a moment longer. I think my daughter could use your perspective." He quickly explained my situation with Logan Langford.

Brady said, "You want my two cents? I don't think you have anything to fear from him. He's had a run of bad luck. First, his wife died. Shortly thereafter, his brothers passed away. Suddenly, he was the go-to guy for the entire family. Not only for his boys and grandchildren, but for his nieces and nephews, as well."

"That's just it." I stabbed the table. "What if he's in debt because he's overcommitted and would do anything to get out of financial trouble? 'Langfords don't quit; Langfords don't fail,' a friend of mine said."

My father shifted in his chair. "Nah. I don't buy it. Logan wouldn't kill Mick to get lease rights back. He could have done that through the court system. And I doubt he'd break into your place with the intent of sabotaging it. What would that get him?"

"If he'd trashed the place, it might have scared me into quitting my lease."

"Shelve this for a minute"—Dad stabbed the table—"and let's go back to the murder investigation."

Fiona flew into view, clearly agitated. Her eyes were squinting and her forehead was pinched, although her wings glowed with vibrant energy as if she'd broken speed records to get to me. Had she sensed what we were discussing? Was she determined to stay up on every facet of the case?

"Who else do you suspect, Courtney?" my father asked.

"Emily Watkins. She inherits everything."

"Was Mick wealthy?"

"I'm not sure." I shared the exchange I'd had with Emily and the attorney, adding that the attorney's card had been on the patio by Mick's body. "You can't tell anyone I said that. And it might not even be important. According to Emily, Mick had a penchant for picking up business cards. Petra Pauli's card was in the mix, too."

"Petra." My father sniffed, his disdain evident. "Her father was salt of the earth, may he rest in peace. He gave her way too much free rein."

"She and Mick were having an affair."

My father whistled.

I added, "It's possible she killed Mick."

"Why?"

"Because he didn't want to leave his wife."

My father pushed his coffee cup to one side and folded his arms on the table. "I doubt Petra would kill the man she loved."

"I agree, Kip." Brady shot a finger at him. "She'd sooner have killed Emily and taken out the competition."

Fiona alit on my shoulder. "Oho! That's what you said."

I gave her teensy foot a pat to let her know I'd heard her.

Brady stared directly at her, a bemused expression in his eyes. Could he see her? Or was he simply enjoying my quirk of patting my shoulder with a fingertip.

I said, "I asked Oriana Gray about Petra's alibi. It's iffy. Petra was in a secret political meeting that no one can speak about. Even Oriana couldn't confirm it."

"What's Emily Watkins's motive?" my father asked.

"Money. Apparently, since Mick's death, her German shepherd is suffering PTSD. She has hired Gregory Darvell to help the dog. That'll cost a pretty penny. You know Gregory, right? The dog trainer."

Brady nodded.

"Plus, I think she might want to show the dog."

"Hmm." Brady folded his arms across his chest. "If it counts for anything, I asked Mick why he was against showing Shep. He said he didn't want his dog to start acting like a spoiled poodle."

"Not all show dogs are spoiled," I countered.

"You couldn't have convinced Mick of that."

My father said, "Is Darvell the guy I see in the park all the time, working with little dogs?"

I nodded. "One of the dog owners at the tea on Saturday was gossiping that Gregory had lost his mojo."

"Having a dog like Shep might make a difference," Brady said.

I cut him a look. "Interesting that you'd say that. Another of the dog owners said she thinks Gregory should be a suspect in Mick's murder because Mick and Gregory fought last week, although another owner dispelled that possibility saying Gregory had a pat alibi. He was training a dog in San Jose that night."

"Uh-oh." Brady bounded to his feet. "I'm getting the evil eye from my hostess." He turned to my father. "Kip, it's been nice catching up."

Dad stood to shake his hand. "By the way, if it makes you feel better, George Pitt bombed in his last movie. Doing a noir action adventure wasn't such a good career move."

"Ha! Music to my ears." Brady slapped my father on the back and eyed me. "Pitt is the actor who won the heart of my ex."

"The tabloids were not kind," my father added.

Maybe that explained why Brady had said secrets were overrated. Had his name been dragged through the mud during the divorce?

"Courtney," Brady turned to me. "Call me if you need anything. I live over on Camino Real near Twelfth and can be anywhere in town in a pinch."

"I live a couple blocks away, on Carmelo and Eleventh."

"Small world." He winked at me then continued into the main restaurant.

"You like him," Fiona whispered in my ear.

I felt my cheeks warm.

My father reached out to me. "Back to you and your case."

"Holly Hopewell said she's been canvassing the neighborhood on my behalf. If I can find one person who saw me in my house and can verify my alibi—"

"Courtney!" Joss ran onto the patio, no decorum, no inside voice, her face as red as her blouse. She made a beeline to our table.

"What's wrong?" I scrambled to my feet. Fiona leaped off my shoulder and fluttered frantically beside me. "Did the security companies cancel?"

"No, I've met with one already. The other is on the way. But you need to get to the city council meeting. STAT. Tish Waterman"—Joss slurped in air—"I heard she's speaking soon. During public appearances." Public appearances allowed members of the town to discuss matters that weren't on the agenda. "She intends to make another stink about the shop. She wants it closed ASAP."

I groaned. Had my encounter with Tish at the post office pushed her to the limit? Shoot! I glanced at my father. "Tish Waterman hates Open Your Imagination. Maybe she's the one who put me in hot water with the lender."

Dad clasped my hand. "I'll pay the check. Go."

Chapter 16

Fairy roses, fairy rings, turn out sometimes
troublesome things.
—William Makepeace Thackeray, *The Rose and the Ring*

As I hurried out, leaving my father to cover the bill, Joss told
me she was already handling the problem with the lender and
the nursery, and not to worry about the other security company. What would I do without her? I advised Fiona to go
with Joss—I didn't want the distraction—and proceeded to
Carmel City Hall.

It was located in a peaked-roof building on Monte Verde
Street. The city council met the first Monday and Tuesday of
each month at half past four in the council chambers. All
meetings were live-streamed and open to the public.

By the time I arrived, roll call and the pledge of allegiance
had concluded. The public appearances portion of the agenda
was in progress. I squeezed in at the back of the packed room,
with many of the attendees accompanied by their dogs, and
turned my attention to Tish Waterman, who was standing at
the lectern at the front of the room, addressing the crowd.

The council consisted of the mayor and four councilmem-bers. Usually the mayor presided, but Petra Pauli appeared to be in charge. She was sitting in the lead seat, holding a gavel. Be-side her sat Oriana Gray. Unlike Petra, there was nothing soft about Oriana. She had hard-edged cheekbones, stick-straight hair, and wore boxy black glasses. I'd bet dollars to donuts she thought they were chic.

"Open Your Imagination is a nuisance, I'm telling you." Tish was dressed in black, her narrow, scarred face twisted in a snarl. Add a pointy hat and she could easily be cast as a wicked witch.

Poor thing whisked through my mind. I shoved the notion aside. She wasn't poor. She was spiteful. So much for thinking we'd had a decent exchange at the post office, however one-sided it might have been.

"How long has she been speaking?" I asked the woman next to me, not realizing until I turned my head that it was Hedda Hopewell.

"Too long." She handed me an agenda. "Look at all we have to get through."

I studied the agenda. Most items were dealing with zoning or use permits.

"Get the hook," Hedda whispered.

"All this fantasy," Tish continued, her voice rising in hys-terical pitch. "All this hoo-ha about fairies. It lures riffraff to our town. People hopeful for a sighting. If Miss Kelly pur-ported to have Big Foot living in the shop, at least we'd be able to see him."

The crowd tittered. I spotted Isabella Acosta among the throng. Actually, I saw the back of her Mohawk hairstyle. She was sitting in an aisle chair. Her poodle, Cocoa, was on the floor beside her. As if she felt me staring at her, she swiveled. Her eyes narrowed. On a whim, I smiled and waved. She snapped her attention back to the front of the room. She and I needed to clear the air, too, but if she was anything like Tish, that might be impossible.

"And did I mention there was a murder in the shop? A murder. Of one of our own. We have not had a murder in Carmel in years. It's appalling." Tish thumped the lectern with her palm. "Courtney Kelly is ruining the neighborhood, I'm telling you."

Unwilling to let her go on, eager to defend my business, I raised a hand to offer a counterargument, but before Petra Pauli could acknowledge me, a man in the first row stood.

"Mrs. Waterman." Detective Summers turned slightly so that those behind him could see his face. I was surprised he was there. Usually the chief of police attended the meetings. "Can you describe how this has hurt your business?"

I gulped. The detective was willing to take a bullet for me? Heart be still.

"Foot traffic is down," Tish carped.

Officer Rodriguez, who was sitting next to Summers, rose to her feet, hand raised. She was dressed in a stylish green dress, her hair cascading down her back. "Actually, foot traffic is up, Mrs. Waterman. All over town." She waved a piece of paper and grinned at Summers. "We've done studies." Again I wondered if they were an item. They looked good together.

"Well, my foot traffic is down," Tish complained. She must have realized that stamping her foot would have been over the top, or no doubt she would have added the physical exclamation point.

"Perhaps your business needs a makeover, Mrs. Waterman," Rodriguez replied.

That earned a few more laughs from the crowd. Tish's spa, A Peaceful Solution, promised a total makeover if necessary. I didn't know what that entailed. Shock therapy following a facial?

Rodriguez tapped her watch. Summers nodded, and the two of them eased along the row and out of the meeting. I noticed their fingertips brushed, but they didn't out-and-out hold hands.

"It's your fault." Tish pointed at someone in the audience.

I saw her target. My landlord, Logan Langford. Sitting beside him was my other landlord, Holly Hopewell.

Tish wagged her fist. "You allowed her to open the business at Cypress and Ivy, Logan. She believes in fairies."

Logan bolted to his feet, his face bright red. "I have no right to deny a lease based on a person's beliefs or line of business."

I stifled a snort. Honestly? Hadn't he been ready to kick Mick Watkins out because the grooming business was too loud? Hedda muttered something that sounded like *poppycock*.

"You're spouting sour grapes, Tish," Logan went on, "because I didn't lease to you."

"That's not true."

"Sure it is. You were a day late and a dollar short. Paperwork has to be submitted in a timely manner. If you'd had your act together—"

"You Langfords, using your money like a sword," Tish spat. "You think Carmel is yours to run any darned way you'd like, and—"

"That's it. You will not take my family's name in vain." Logan's voice swelled to a fevered pitch. "My family has devoted itself to enhancing Carmel and making it a beautiful place for all who visit here. We are stewards—" He scrambled across the row, excusing himself for inconveniencing people.

"Logan, stop." Petra Pauli leaped off her chair and nudged Tish to one side. She pounded a gavel on the lectern. "Don't move, sir."

Logan halted. Tish's face had turned ash white.

"No more outbursts," Petra bellowed. "No slurs. Anyone." She smoothed the front of her white linen suit.

Tish didn't listen. She flailed her hands. "It's all because of your son, Logan."

"It is not my son's fault," he shouted.

"Yes, it is. He is a wayward man with the devil's silver tongue."

"Tish, calm down." Petra put a hand on Tish's shoulder. "And wrap it up. Stay on point. You're not here to battle the Langford family. You came here to discuss the fairy garden store." Petra stepped aside but did not resume her seat.

Tish scanned the crowd. Her gaze landed on me. "You." She aimed a finger. "Courtney Kelly. Fairy believer."

Fairy whisperer, I mentally corrected.

"I want you gone. I want this nonsense to stop. I—" Tish sobbed with emotion. The sobs turned into hiccups. "I want—"

"Time's up, Tish." Petra Pauli signaled Oriana, who deftly guided Tish away from the lectern to the far wall. Oriana remained beside Tish, standing like a sentry, as Petra moved behind the lectern. "Start a petition, Tish. That's the proper way to handle these things."

I shivered. If Tish gathered enough signatures, could she really oust Open Your Imagination from Carmel? No way. I'd fight her tooth and nail. I'd start my own petition and charge her with harassment.

"FYI, Tish," the councilwoman continued, "if you open your mind to new horizons, with a modicum of business savvy I'd bet you could pick up a few clients from the fairy garden shop."

"What do you mean?" Tish wrapped her arms around her

torso. Her face was tear-stained. She looked like she'd had the stuffing knocked out of her, what little stuffing there was.

"Why don't you solicit the fairy garden shop's clientele?"

"Are you kidding? Solicit people who see and hear things that don't exist?" Tish twirled her finger beside her head. "I don't want any woo-woo clients."

Hedda whispered to me, "That's because her daughter is woo-woo."

"What do you mean?"

"Her daughter joined a cult twenty years ago. Logan Langford's eldest son introduced her to it, though he didn't get sucked down the rabbit hole himself. Since that day, Tish has spouted realism above all else. Between you and me," Hedda continued, "I bet Tish wishes she could rescue her daughter, except she doesn't know where she is. She's gone. Vanished. Within a year, the cult relocated to Colorado, but no one has a clue of the location. Some say they zoomed off in a spaceship. As if." Chuckling, Hedda squeezed my arm and said, "Don't let her rile you. That would give her the upper hand."

My father would have said the same.

Hedda scooted past me and sat in a chair another attendee had vacated.

I stared at Tish as a notion occurred to me. What if Fiona could locate Tish's daughter? Would finding the young woman change Tish's mind about me and my business? There must be some kind of fairy network out there. Would the queen fairy allow Fiona to utilize it while on probation? As if drawn to make peace, I moved toward Tish. I stopped short when I spied Emily Watkins approaching the lectern.

She wriggled the hem of her brown sweater over the waist of her trousers, hiked the rope handles of her Michael Kors tote bag higher on her shoulder, and cleared her throat. "I want to speak, Councilwoman," Emily said formally.

Petra gawped. "You?"

"Yes, me."

Emily peered over her shoulder at Gregory Darvell, who was holding on to Shep not far from where Oriana and Tish were standing. Gregory's mouth twitched at the corners, like he was trying hard not to smile. He twirled a finger encouraging Emily to continue. What was up?

Emily closed in on Petra. "The microphone please."

Petra Pauli blanched, but as required during the public appearances, ceded the spot to Emily. "Proceed, Mrs. Watkins."

"Good afternoon, everyone. Give me a sec," Emily said to the crowd. She rummaged in her tote bag. "I've got it." With a tug, she pulled out a large, sealed baggie stuffed with something hot pink. "Here, Petra, for you, as requested." Emily shoved the package in the councilwoman's direction. "I believe this teddy is yours."

I bit back a giggle. Emily had brought Petra's lingerie to the meeting? Talk about gall. It was a shaming to beat any I'd ever witnessed.

"Wh-what?" Petra faltered. "Why you—"

"What better place to return your dainties?" Emily gloated. "You took me on in front of others. I decided to return the favor."

"Why you—" Petra charged Emily, who dodged her and raced to Gregory and the dog.

Gregory stood, a smug smile on his face.

"Let's get out of here," Emily rasped.

Petra squared her shoulders and stared at the crowd. All were watching her with rapt attention. She smoothed her hair, softened her brow, and offered a confident smile. A true professional. But I could tell Emily had rattled her. Even from the back of the room, I could see Petra's cheek was ticking with tension.

Ooh, how I wished Detective Summers had stayed around to see that exchange. Was another murder on the horizon? *Bad Courtney. Don't make light of the situation.*

Quickly, Petra adjourned the public appearances portion of the meeting and suggested a ten-minute recess. People started to rise.

"Courtney, dear." Holly Hopewell eased along the aisle, her navy blue artist's smock brushing against the dogs she skirted. When she reached me, she said, "Tish made a vicious attack against you. She had no right." She put a comforting hand on my shoulder. "How are you?"

"I'm fine, thanks to your sister."

Hedda, who was gathering her purse and sweater, waved to Holly. She mimed getting something to drink. Holly nodded.

"Mrs. Hopewell," I said, moving closer to avoid the hubbub of the crowd, "have you found any witnesses who saw me in my house yet?"

"No, dear. I'm still working the issue. And it's high time you call me Holly like your mother did."

I nodded. "Holly, what can you tell me about Isabella Acosta? I heard you have a couple of art pieces hanging in her gallery. Joss said they're gorgeous."

"Thank you."

"Is Isabella good to you?"

"To me, yes. Placement on the walls is premium, but I'm new to her. She aims to impress. Between you and me, I've seen her interact with other artists, and she can be"—Holly tapped her chin—"prickly. No smile. No warmth. As far as I know, she has no personal life. She's not married. She has a friend or two."

"How is she as a businesswoman?" I asked.

"She pays on time and gets top dollar. Our split is fair. I can't fault her there."

"Did she poach you from another gallery?"

"No, dear. All my works in other galleries have sold. I have no outstanding agreements. Why are you interested?"

"Thanks to Isabella Acosta, I'm a suspect in Mick Watkins's murder. She said she saw me arguing with him. She lied."

Chapter 17

*In the midst of our lives, we must find the magic that
makes our souls soar.*
—Anonymous

As Holly joined her sister, I wended through the crowd toward Tish Waterman, but a number of her friends had rallied around her. Had she seen me approaching? Were fairies as protective of their queen? Tomorrow, I would reach out to Tish via telephone and invite her to tea. Not at my shop, of course. She wouldn't step foot in there. The Tuck Box, a gingerbread-style tearoom, the house originally constructed by designer-builder Hugh Comstock in 1927, could be neutral territory.

Keyed up from the meeting, I hurried to Open Your Imagination. When I entered, Pixie scampered to me, thrilled that I hadn't forgotten her. Joss had gone home but had left the lights on. She had left me a note regarding security company quotes. Both were the same, and we could discuss tomorrow. In addition, she wrote a note that she had contacted the bank and had fixed our credit issue. She'd figured out it wasn't a loan covenant breach but a glitch with an auto-pay *thingie*—the technical term, I presumed—and was not something nefariously engineered by Logan or anyone else. Relieved, I would call the nursery in the morning and ask the company to follow through with our order.

With Pixie in my arms, I strode onto the patio and called out to Fiona.

She swooped to me, her eyes wide. "You're okay. I was worried. Joss told me not to be, but I was. So what happened?"

"Calm down."

"I'm calm." She sat on a wrought-iron table cross-legged, her elbows propped on her knees.

Quickly, I explained the situation with Tish Waterman— her fury at Logan and her distress with me. I explained that she might start a petition to get rid of the shop. I shared my idea that if we could find Tish's missing daughter, we might be able to mend fences. "Do you think you can do anything to help?"

Fiona hummed for a long moment. Finally she said, "I'm not sure, but I'll suggest the mission to my mentor."

Once again, I wasn't sure of fairy protocol. How did it work? Did the mentor report directly to the queen fairy, or was there another level to the hierarchy?

Fiona scrambled to her feet and soared into the air. "I'll see you tomorrow."

"Wait," I called, but she was gone.

Feeling slightly adrift, I turned off the lights, double-checked all the locks on the windows, made a mental note to add a bolt lock to the secret door, and went home. Dinner held no appeal. Talking online to my friends didn't, either. I wrote my father a text to let him know Joss had fixed my financial problem and assured him that the matter with Tish Waterman was under control. It wasn't, yet, but why worry him?

He replied instantly: *Good to hear. Sleep well.*

Unable to sleep well, if at all, I retreated to the greenhouse. For a long time, I worked on a new fairy garden. I chose two clay pots, one large and one small. I filled the larger with soil, and then, after cracking the smaller in half, I wedged one half into the dirt of the larger planter, which created a path along the right side. I interspersed baby tears and small wooden steps to create a staircase. At the top of the planter, I scattered small stones and nestled a boulder at the center. It looked dreary and cold. Beside the boulder, I placed a blond fairy that was reaching for the sky, as if beckoning for help. At the base of the staircase, I set a dark-haired fairy, ready to climb. In my mind, she represented Tish on the hunt for her daughter. Along the staircase, I inserted teensy lights, representing Fiona and her fairy world. Again I wondered if she might be able to help Tish reunite with her daughter and whether the queen fairy would or would not allow such a quest. Only time would tell.

I didn't go to bed until after midnight.

Tuesday morning arrived with a riot of noises: birds chirping, mowers mowing, doors slamming.

Groggily, I clambered out of bed and peeked out the window. A neighbor was moving out of her house across the street, which explained the slamming doors. I washed up while rehashing my last dream, which included Tish running up a grassy knoll, Logan juggling a flurry of dollar bills, and Shep playing tug-of-war with Gregory. Surprisingly, neither Emily nor Petra had made an appearance in the dream. Did that mean I thought they were innocent of Mick's murder?

After feeding Pixie and downing an easy breakfast consisting of hard-boiled egg mashed with mayonnaise, dill, and mustard on whole wheat toast, I threw on a blue-striped poplin jumpsuit, a cardigan to ward off the morning chill, and suede loafers.

I didn't race to work. I strolled. Even on a crush-rush kind of day, I enjoyed drinking in the soothing scent of salt-sea air and gazing at the many flowers planted along the walkways.

Joss had beaten me to the shop and had started a pot of coffee. The aroma caught my attention. My mouth started to water.

I chanted, "Coffee, coffee," like Meaghan had yesterday.

Joss patted my shoulder. "Ready and hot. By the way, Yvanna dropped off cookies. Double chocolate chip, if you're ready for sugar."

"Am I ever!" I liked to eat healthy, but I was always in the mood for a sweet treat when having a cup of coffee. I nabbed a cookie and bit into it. Delicious. I set Pixie on the ground and gave her a nudge. She tore onto the patio looking for her fairy pal. "Nice top, Joss. Is it new?"

"A Goodwill discovery. Three dollars and fifty cents." She pulled the hem of the red-and-green-checked shirt wide and did a twirl. "Hard to find one in such mint condition. You know me and bargains."

"A penny saved . . ."

"Is a penny to be spent elsewhere."

"There's something going on with you." I twirled a finger in front of her face. "Did you have a date last night?"

"*Moi?* Get out of here."

"You're glowing."

"That's because I signed up for a cruise at the end of summer."

"And you're going with . . ." I dragged out *with.*

"Nobody."

"Liar." I didn't know much about Joss's personal life, but I knew she wasn't celibate.

"Okay, I'm going with a man I met on a speed date."

I cracked up.

"Don't laugh." She swatted me. "It was fun. I meet lots of interesting guys. You should try it."

I shook my head. I'd never go on one of those. Lots of people enjoyed them. Me? I'd get tongue-tied and dry-mouthed. Not pretty. "I'd rather walk over hot coals."

"We've been dating a month. He's really nice."

"I'm happy for you."

For the next few minutes, we discussed the security company quotes. As Joss had said in her note, both were identical, so I told her it came down to which salesman she had liked best. The one from Ever Alert Security had reminded her of her father, so I agreed to use him.

"Don't forget we have the garden club coming in a half hour," she said. "And the bonsai shaping event is this afternoon. Busy, busy."

The telephone jangled. "Get that please," I said, having taken another bite of cookie.

Joss answered and held the receiver out to me. "It's Detective Summers."

I licked a crumb off my lower lip and answered. "Good morning, Detective. I saw you and Officer Rodriguez at the city council meeting yesterday. You left rather quickly."

"We stopped in for a moment. I like to see who's attending."

"Thank you for standing up to Tish Waterman."

"That woman can carp," he said. "She needs a bit of reining in."

"Ha! You don't know the half of it. You left before the fireworks began." I told him about the blowup between Logan and Tish and how Logan had displayed quite a temper. I concluded with the news about Tish's missing daughter. "I heard Logan Langford's son had something to do with the girl's joining a cult."

Summers grunted. "That's not entirely true. When he and

Tish's daughter were dating, they went to one meeting. A month after that, they broke up, and the girl hooked up with the cult."

"And hasn't been seen since."

Summers sighed. "We can't save them all. Now, as for you—"

My insides lurched. "What about me? Are you saving me?"

"Sorry, no. I'm afraid we can't pinpoint your whereabouts on the night Mr. Watkins was murdered, although, as you've already shown and your attorney has tried to peddle as evidence, the ISP address does prove that someone was using your computer for three hours."

"Yes. *Me.*" I moaned. "Look, Detective, I have no motive. I did not argue with Mick. I do not want to lease his space. You've got to believe me."

"If I believed everyone who claimed to be innocent, I'd never lock anyone up. But don't worry. I'm still working the issue." Summers ended the call.

An annoying knot took up residence in my stomach. How could I not be worried? How I wished Holly Hopewell would dredge up a witness to verify my whereabouts. If only the detective could see Fiona. She could vouch for me.

Joss put her arm around me. "Cheer up. Meaghan left a message on the machine saying she's working an angle."

"About Logan and the Church of the Wayfarer choir?"

"No. She said, 'Something else.' You know how vague she can be. She draws outside the lines." Joss released me and said, "Let's focus on our garden club event, okay?"

I nodded.

Thirty minutes later, Hattie Hopewell led the Happy Diggers garden group into the shop. Each of the nine was wearing a floral scarf. Harriet's featured a field of poppies. I was surprised to see Miss Reade, the librarian, among the group.

"This way, girls," Hattie chimed. For weeks, she had been dying to show her plant-loving friends the beauty of making and owning a fairy garden. "Hello-o-o, Courtney. Hello-o-o, Joss." Years ago, Hattie had performed as a singer in a band. Words trilled off her tongue. She sauntered through the shop, pointing out the wind chimes and various teapots and accessories. I couldn't have asked for a better ambassador. At the door leading to the patio, she said, "Look around, ladies, and then take a seat on one of the benches by the learning-the-craft area. I see we have treats."

On a nearby table, I'd put out vanilla bean scones as well as pots of tea, a tea caddy, and teacups.

The women streamed through the doorway and *ooh*ed and *aah*ed.

Miss Reade said to me, "I hope your fairy is well, Courtney."

"She's thriving."

She joined her friends to admire the array of fairy figurines. One in the group stopped beside the fountain and called to a friend to inspect it with her. An image of Mick lying dead at the foot of the fountain sprang to mind; an image of me going to jail followed.

"Excuse me." The last of the Happy Diggers, a cherub-faced beauty, stopped beside me. She was carrying a toddler with the most gorgeous blond ringlets. "Our sitter got sick," she said. "Hope it's okay."

"Children are always welcome. Is your daughter allergic to cats?" I asked, even though Ragdoll cats were more or less hypoallergenic. They didn't have an undercoat, although I'd heard dried saliva could cause allergies, too. And every cat had that.

"She adores cats."

When I pointed out Pixie, she set the child on her feet and said, "Go play."

The little girl dashed off, chasing after Pixie, who ducked beneath tables and chairs. When the girl neared the fountain, she reached overhead. "Ooh, Mommy, look."

Her mother peered in the direction her daughter was pointing. "What do you see?"

"A fairy."

"That's lovely, sweetheart. Play with the fairy." The mother gave me a wink.

I winked back. Fiona was having a blast doing cartwheels in the air. *Showoff,* I mused.

After the garden club ladies settled on the benches with their treats, I began the demonstration. As I gave my spiel about why a fairy garden was a good addition to anyone's home, I chose a sixteen-inch round pot, already filled with dirt. I set a ten-inch, red-and-white house on top. "In order to draw the focus to your location, place it in the middle, but somewhat back of center. Think of it like a 3-D image."

"I have that same house," Hattie said.

"Next, let's talk about scale," I continued. "I like to use a bonsai cypress when featuring houses because they appear to be the perfect size. The ratio for this particular design should be twelve to one. One inch equals one foot in real life. Therefore, a child of four feet would be four inches. A ten-foot tall house would be ten inches. Make sense?"

The garden ladies bobbed their heads, thoroughly understanding.

For an hour, I took them through the steps. With their input, we decided the red-and-white house was a schoolhouse. We added a set of swings and a volleyball net, as a playful touch, and finished it off with three fairy figurines. Hattie suggested adding a red-haired boy fairy figurine with a baseball and mitt.

An hour later, five of the club, including Miss Reade, had outfitted themselves with take-home assemblies.

The cherub-faced beauty gathered her daughter into her arms and approached me. "I've never seen her so occupied. Your cat is magical."

"So is the fairy," the girl said.

Her mother giggled. I laughed, too.

"I'll come back when the sitter is better," the mother added. "I can't wait to get started."

As the Happy Diggers streamed out, Hattie lingered by the Dutch door. "Dearest Courtney, have they cleared you of Mick's murder yet?

"No."

She swatted the air. "Why, it's nonsense of course. We all know that. Whatever you do, do not let the police bully you. Trust in the truth."

I followed her outside and drew in a deep breath. Across the way, Emily was shaking hands with her attorney. As he left, she caught sight of me and waved.

She strode toward me while retying the belt of her leather jacket. "I saw you at the city council meeting."

"I think everyone in town saw *you*."

She flipped her long mane over her shoulder. "Petra deserved it."

And she'd never forget it. I hitched my chin in Wright Youngman's direction. "Is everything okay?"

"Yes. I'm going to keep the grooming business up and running. Clients are ecstatic."

"What about the lease?"

"Logan has no legal ground to boot us out. As it turns out, we have a ten-year unbreakable lease."

"Ten years? Whew!"

"Mick was very good at making deals. Wright—Mr. Youngman—will sue Logan if he tries any funny stuff. I am, by right, the lessee. I'm entitled to continue on, under the law."

If Logan had known he couldn't force Mick or Mick's heirs out any time soon, then he had no apparent reason to kill him.

"Sonja is going to stay on, too," Emily continued. "She does all the work anyway. Mick didn't. He was the face." She whisked her hand beneath her chin like a television model and smiled. "I can be the face. Pretty doesn't matter in the pet world. A welcoming smile does. I'll have to hire a book-keeper. I'm not a numbers person. Would your assistant like a second job?"

"I think Joss is as busy as she'd like to be."

Emily tugged the hem of her jacket around her hips. "No matter. Wright is going to help me find someone." Suddenly, tears sprang into her eyes. She blinked in an attempt to stem the flow. "I don't know what I would do without him. After losing Mick—" She placed her fingertips on her lips.

"How's it going with your dog?" I asked. "I saw Gregory tending to him at the city council meeting."

"Gregory has been a dream. Between you and me, I think he might be in love with my dog." She tittered. "You can't believe all the dog toys he's bought for him. Shep is in lust with the crocodile that squeaks."

I smiled indulgently.

"Gregory is taking him for playtime at the park. Isn't that sweet? He thinks Shep would be great in competition, but I'm not sure I want Shep to be a show dog. Mick was . . . against it. He didn't want Shep to become a spoiled brat." A tear slipped down her cheek. She brushed it away. "I miss him, Courtney." If she was acting, she was doing a good job. "Mick said . . ." She shook her head. "He said I shouldn't . . ." She let out a deep sigh and studied the pavement near the toe of her shoe.

When she met my gaze, I felt she wanted to offer something more. About Mick? About what he thought she should or shouldn't do?

"Go on," I said gently. "I'm listening."

"Nothing. It's nothing." Deliberately, she glanced at her watch. "I've got to go."

Chapter 18

Any man can lose his hat in a fairy wind.
—Irish saying

Emily was a conundrum, often brusque and at other times vulnerable. I still couldn't get over how she'd brazenly brought lingerie to the council meeting to shame Petra Pauli. That required a killer instinct. Was Emily a killer?

I returned inside Open Your Imagination, deciding it was time to deal with the other brusque woman in my life—Tish. I settled in the office and called A Peaceful Solution. A receptionist with a sultry voice answered. I asked to speak to Tish. The guardian at the gate asked what I was calling about. I spelled out who I was. Not recognizing my name, she informed me that Tish didn't have any open appointments for a month. So much for my business spoiling hers—foot traffic or no foot traffic. I pressed on, admitting that I wasn't interested in an appointment. I wanted to take Tish to tea at the Tuck Box. When the woman asked why, I told her I wanted to talk with Tish. I didn't need to elaborate.

"I'll relay the message," the receptionist replied.

I got the feeling she wouldn't, but thanked her anyway and ended the call. Then I dialed Meaghan. She answered after one ring.

"ESP," she said. Over the years, she and I had often reached out to each other at the exact same moment.

"Joss said you have an angle that might help prove my innocence."

"I do, but I can't talk now." She sounded rushed. "How about this afternoon?"

"At three," I said. "After the bonsai-shaping class."

"Deal. We'll go to tea. Chin up."

I set my cell phone down and scrambled to my feet, too antsy to sit. I needed to take a walk. Macro photography would be good therapy, I decided. I grabbed my Nikon Coolpix and 105mm f/2.8G lens from the office, told Joss where I was headed—she handed me an energy bar so I wouldn't forget to eat—and, with Fiona riding on my shoulder, sauntered up 8th Avenue to Mission Street and made a left.

"Where are we off to?" Fiona asked.

"To take pictures of flowers and bugs."

"Bugs?"

"Closeup nature photography helps me concentrate and set the world's problems aside."

My mother had enjoyed long walks and taking photos. I'd learned the art from her. I remembered her guiding my gaze to the exact thing she was going to capture. A grasshopper on a leaf, a bee sniffing a flower, a dragonfly circling a rose. One of my favorite photos that she'd taken was of a frog hiding beneath a lily pad. Nature's camouflage at its best. I recalled her telling me how focusing on the minutest detail could open her mind so she could deal with life's ups and downs. I didn't know at the time that she'd been ill.

Devendorf Park, which was located between Junipero and Mission Street at Ocean Avenue, was home to the Carmel Art Festival. In a few weeks, the festival would take over the area. On Thursday and Friday, artists would paint in the park as well as many other locations throughout Carmel and Monterey. On the weekend, there would be Sculpture in the Park as well as live music and awards. The festival was a joy to attend.

Today, however, the park was fairly quiet. A dog owner was checking out the gigantic oak and its canopy. Across the way, near the fountain, I spotted Gregory Darvell with Shep. Against regulations, Shep was off leash. Gregory was using a ball tethered to a rope to teach the dog to fetch and catch.

"Shep!" Fiona cried. She sailed off my shoulder and hovered near him.

He spotted her, but Gregory depressed the clicker hanging on a red lanyard around his neck, which quickly drew the dog's gaze back to the matter at hand. Shep sat at attention waiting for a command.

Seeing the ball on the rope made me flash on Mick and the rope burn around his neck. Could the tethered toy have made the mark? No. It looked too thick and cumbersome. What about the red lanyard? It was flat, but was it textured? I removed the closeup lens from the camera and took a long-distance picture, and then replaced the lens.

Fiona flew back to me. "What are they doing?"

"Learning tricks," I said.

Shep didn't look like he was suffering an ounce of PTSD. He was reveling in the fun. Gregory clicked again, threw the ball, and Shep retrieved it. When Shep brought the ball back, Gregory fetched something from the leather pouch attached to his belt. A treat, no doubt.

"Aren't they wonderful together?" a woman behind me asked.

I turned and moaned. Ulani Kamaka, the reporter for the *Pine Cone*, smiled at me. She looked ready for an interview, dressed in a silk blouse, linen trousers, and espadrilles.

"Are you spying on me?" I asked. How long had she been standing there? I hadn't heard her approach.

"Don't be silly," Ulani said. "I like to walk on my lunch hour, too."

In espadrilles? Give me a break.

"You see?" She waved a hand between us. "We have something in common."

"Your offices are miles away in Pacific Grove."

"But I write about Carmel." She brandished a hand. "So here I am. Actually, I'm doing an article about shopping trends, citing which are the most popular stores in town and why. Yours happens to be one, by the way, which reminds me, your article will be coming out in a week. I'll drop off a copy. I say favorable things." She eyed Gregory and Shep. "Speaking of spying, are you spying on them?"

"What? No." I tapped the camera hanging on its strap. "I'm doing some macro photography. It helps me relax."

"And yet you've only taken one photograph, sans closeup lens."

She had been observing me. Why? Thinking I'd trip up somehow and prove myself guilty? Maybe she hoped to scoop my story so she could become an ace reporter for the *San Francisco Chronicle*.

I removed the lens cap from my camera and shot ten photos in succession. Of the oak tree. Its leaves. Of the grass.

Fiona stomped her foot on my shoulder. "I do not like her. Why is she staring at you?"

Quickly, I took a photograph of Ulani.

She covered her face. "Please don't."

"Why not? Hiding something?"

She blinked rapidly and glanced over her shoulder. No

one was near us. She turned back. "Yes," she whispered. "My
parents do not know where I am."

"Why not?"

"Not your concern. Let's just say, I'd like my whereabouts
to remain a secret. I write under a pseudonym, so they won't
find me that way, but a photo online or elsewhere could ruin
everything."

"Are you in danger?"

"As I said, not your concern. Please honor my request.
Thank you." She tucked her head and strode away.

Watching her retreat, I thought of Tish and her daughter.
What was it that made children abandon their parents and vice
versa? Cults? Abuse? Disagreements about lifestyles? How
horrible to live with that kind of estrangement. I made a mental note to touch base with my father more often. Not daily—
that would be overkill—but often.

Gregory caught sight of me and beckoned me to him. As I
drew near, he pressed the clicker and ordered Shep to sit. The
dog obeyed on cue.

"Looks like you're having fun," I said.

"We are. Shep is a natural."

"He doesn't seem to be suffering trauma as far as I can
see." I dangled my hand by Shep's nose to let him catch my
scent. He smelled and allowed me to scratch an ear. Fiona nestled on his other one.

"He's responding quite well," Gregory said. "Like humans, dogs need to be kept busy, otherwise they, like us, can
mope. It's a dark and dirty world down the rabbit hole of de-
pression. Believe me, I know."

I recalled the women at the tea talking about Gregory's
having lost his dog-show trainer mojo. Losing a number of
competitions in a row had to be disheartening. Would managing a dog like Shep—a *natural*—help rebuild Gregory's reputation and return him to glory? That could be a powerful

motive to want Mick dead. Mick had blocked Gregory from gaining access to the German shepherd.

"I'm sorry to hear that," I murmured. "Having lots of dogs to train must help you through those dark times. Planting fairy gardens helps me."

He nodded.

"Ladies at a tea the other day said you have quite a wide-spread clientele," I went on. "Dogs as far away as San Jose."

"Who said that?"

"Hattie Hopewell mentioned it."

"Hattie. That woman has a heart of gold."

"And a green thumb," I added.

"And the reddest hair in the world." He chortled, then grew silent and tilted his head. "You look as though you want to ask me something."

Yes, of course I wanted to ask him something. His alibi. "No-o," I stammered.

"Perhaps about San Jose? I'm guessing Hattie or one of her sisters mentioned that I drove there the night that Mick . . ." Gregory faltered. "The night he was killed. Am I warm?"

I didn't answer.

He smiled, but the smile didn't reach his eyes. "Shep, fetch." He hurled the tethered ball.

Shep tore after the toy. Fiona shot into the air. Playfully, she tried to keep up with Shep as he ran. She couldn't. Shep snatched the tethered toy after one bounce and trotted back with it. He dropped it at Gregory's feet. Slobber clung to the fabric.

Fiona settled on my shoulder and wrinkled her pretty nose. "Ew."

"Good boy." Gregory scratched the dog under the chin. "Sit. Paw, paw." Shep obliged by lifting his left paw. Gregory shook it. "All done." He clipped on Shep's leash, wound the rope with ball into a coil, fastened it with a small bungee cord, and hooked the coil over his shoulder. "Time to go back." Obeying a miniscule gesture by Gregory, Shep shuffled to the man's left side and paused. Gregory said to me, "Heading our way?"

"No, I'm going to take a few more photographs."

"Too bad. I thought we might talk a bit more."

Talk? He was about as chatty as a mime. He wasn't going to tell me about his client in San Jose, even if I point-blank asked.

"Enjoy the day," he added.

As he strolled off, an unnerving sensation snaked up my back. He'd been toying with me almost as much as he had the dog.

Chapter 19

❧❧❧

Raindrops are like fairy whispers.
—Anonymous

On the way back to the shop, I ate my energy bar and asked Fiona about magic, wondering what happened when a fairy lost it. I was trying to process how desperate Gregory Darvell might have been if he'd lost his dog show–winning talent.

"If a fairy loses her magic," she replied, "there are ways to find it again, but she'll need help from the queen fairy. She alone has the power to restore it. Way back when, a fairy lost her magic and begged the queen's favor. Punishment was involved. She is old now and keeps to herself."

"Losing her magic wasn't punishment enough?"

"You don't simply lose your magic." Fiona wrinkled her nose. "You have to have done something bad. Very bad. Bad enough that magic didn't want to remain a part of you."

Yipes.

"Luckily, I didn't do anything *that* bad."

I wadded up my energy bar wrapper, ready to stride into

the shop, when I spotted Isabella Acosta across the street—sans poodle. She was standing in front of her art gallery talking animatedly to Petra Pauli. Each wore a figure-slimming power suit. Petra was stabbing the readout on her cell phone as if proving a point to Isabella.

After checking traffic in both directions, I scooted across the street. Fiona kept pace. Petra caught sight of me, bid a hasty good-bye to Isabella, and darted into Hideaway Café. To, um, *hide?* I wondered.

Isabella spun around and frowned, but she didn't budge. She planted a fist on one hip. "What do you want?"

Until learning she'd supposedly witnessed me arguing with Mick, I'd never met the woman. Never been in her shop. And she'd never stepped foot in mine. Come to think of it, the day I'd seen her in front of Wizard of Paws was the first time I'd laid eyes on her. At the book club tea, she'd sat with the other dog owners. She and Petra seemed to know each other. Were they friends or acquaintances? Had the councilwoman pitted Isabella Acosta against me? Why would she do that?

"I'm Courtney Kelly." I jutted my hand and offered a friendly smile, one I used often when dealing with crusty clients. "I'd like to get something straight. You told Emily that you saw me arguing with Mick Watkins."

"I did."

"When?"

She smoothed the collar of her suit. "Hours before he was murdered. You were standing in front of Wizard of Paws."

"With Gregory Darvell, the dog trainer?"

"No, with Logan Langford."

"Aha. Logan and Mick were arguing. Not me."

"You were there."

"Not raising my voice."

Isabella pouted. "Mick was glowering at you. You swatted the air."

I tried to recall whether Fiona had come between Mick and me. Perhaps I'd shooed her away. My memory was blank. "Mick and I didn't argue. I liked him."

"That's not what Emily says."

"*Emily.*" Fiona circled my head and huffed. "That woman is poison."

I sighed. Emily could have been the one who'd set the lies in motion, in order to give the police a suspect other than herself. I offered another smile. Broader. Really working it. A door-to-door salesman couldn't have done a better job. "Mick and I weren't arguing."

"I must have been mistaken."

"Will you tell Detective Summers?"

"When I find time. He and I—" Isabella paused and cocked her head. "You're curious."

"So I hear."

"Curious, as in odd."

"Odd as in *different* can be a good thing. Who wants to be blah?" I forced a laugh.

She pursed her lips. "I enjoyed the tea the other day. Cocoa had fun, too. I didn't see any fairies, though."

I doubted she ever would. She was too aloof. She struck me as someone who had bottled herself into a perfect, tidy package, and that was all the world would ever see.

"Come visit the shop again," I said, "and I'll help you build a fairy garden. That might open you to their world."

"I'm not a gardener."

"You don't need to be. You only need inspiration and a bit of playfulness."

Fiona whizzed above Isabella's head and sprinkled her with fairy dust.

Isabella blinked and raised her chin. She inspected the sky, as if anticipating rain, and held out a hand, palm up. "Do you feel the mist?"

"The fog is rolling in," I lied. "Fairies enjoy the fog," I added.

"I can imagine them having fun in fog," she said dreamily. "Glowing as they dart back and forth."

"Exactly."

Isabella shook her head as if to clear the image. "No, no. I hate fog. It makes my hair curl."

"Longer hair doesn't curl as much," I said.

"This"—she pointed to her Mohawk hairstyle—"has a story behind it." Without adding more, she ended the conversation and strode away.

As I crossed the street, I said to Fiona, "What did you do to her?"

"Gave her a dose of imagination."

"Why would she need it? She owns an art gallery."

"That doesn't mean she dreams. Her artists do."

The moment I walked into the shop, Joss charged me and tapped her watch. "Where have you been? Are you ready to teach your class?"

"Sorry. I got waylaid." I tossed the energy bar wrapper in the garbage pail behind the sales counter.

"While you were gone, I prepped the craft area and fielded phone calls." Joss handed me a smock so I wouldn't soil my clothes. "Holly Hopewell is on her way. She's running a few minutes behind."

"I'm glad she didn't cancel."

"Her sister Hattie vowed to tease her mercilessly if she did," Joss said. "The others are already here."

I thanked her and fled to the restroom where I freshened my face and brushed my windblown hair. Then I filled a glass with water and strolled to the patio to teach the class.

The bonsai-shaping event was always one of my favorites. I offered it once a month. In the learning-the-craft corner, Joss had preset the table with trees the students would work on and the appropriate tools they would use. Three people were in attendance. Holly would make four. More were registered for next month's event. Word was getting around that the classes were fun and enlightening. I noticed a few customers who were browsing the shelves for fairy garden items pointing at us and whispering among themselves.

Seconds before the start of the class, Holly bustled in, looking hip in a semi-sheer Van Gogh–print cape over a denim jumpsuit, her curly hair secured in a fashionable silver clip. She said she had something to tell me, but I asked her to hold the thought as I guided her to the students' station.

"Welcome, everyone." I rounded my small presentation table, set up specifically for this occasion. It held a bonsai, a coil of 1.5mm copper wire, and six-inch stainless steel shears with a micro-tip.

After a brief introduction and sharing my affection for bonsai trees, I launched into the instruction. "Sitting before you are the same items that are on my table. Wiring is a crucial technique to shaping and training bonsai."

The word *training* gave me pause. I flashed on Gregory trying to *train* me in the park—okay, not train me, but definitely trying to manage me. Why? Maybe he treated humans the same way he treated animals. Was his alibi a lie?

I shook free of the notion and continued. "By wrapping wire around the branches, you are able to bend and reposition them. After a few months, when the branches are set, you can remove the wire. Try it with a branch. Like this." I demonstrated the technique. "One of the issues with wiring is that, during the growth season, branches can quickly become thick. The wire can create ugly scars. So you want to make sure you check your tree often and remove the wiring in time."

The owner of Carmel Collectibles, a cherry-cheeked man with twinkling eyes, mumbled that he couldn't quite get the hang of it. I moved to help him. He was holding his coil at an odd angle.

"Think of it like wrapping ribbon around a gift," I said to him.

That tip seemed to work. He was an expert with ribbon; he made gorgeous bows.

Returning to my presentation table, I said, "You want to wire all the branches you intend to shape before bending them. It's tricky."

For an hour, I instructed them. When all was said and done, I had four very happy customers.

As the class concluded, Holly approached me with a cup of tea in hand. Her cheeks were flushed with good energy. "How I wish I could train my garden as well as I can a bonsai."

"I could give you some tips on my day off," I said.

"I would love that."

"Now, what did you want to tell me? Did you find an eyewitness?" I asked hopefully.

"No, dear, I'm sorry. Not yet." She set her tea down. "However, I have something else to tell you. About Gregory Darvell." She clasped my hands. Hers were still damp from using soap and water following the bonsai session. "I found out that he entered Shep in a competition."

"Are you sure?"

"Positive."

"Emily has no clue."

"Aha!" Fiona hovered over Holly's shoulder. "I was right. He killed Mick to get control of the dog."

"Go on," I said to Holly.

"A friend of the family in San Jose has the inside scoop,"

Holly continued. "Hattie and Hedda know her. She shows her Dachshund. She's such a dear. And she never lies. She saw the paperwork." Holly hesitated. "Is it possible Gregory killed Mick to get his mitts on the dog?"

I gawked. Had Holly heard Fiona or had my fairy put the notion in Holly's head? I said, "You should tell the police."

"Oh, no, dear." Holly wagged a finger. "The police and I aren't cozy. They think I'm a bit of a crackpot."

"Why?"

"It's my secret." She grinned.

How I wanted to hear more. I imagined she'd lived a rebellious and colorful youth as an artist.

"Thank you for the class," she said. "I'm going home to set my bonsai in the proper window, after which I'll continue my search for a witness on your behalf. The Poms and I love to walk." She gathered her newly wired plant and bustled out of the shop.

At the same time, Meaghan trotted in. "Ready for tea?"

"Go," Joss said. She was sitting behind the register reviewing the days' receipts. "I've got this covered. This is our lull time, after lunch and before school's out."

Meaghan looped her arm through mine and steered me out of the shop and across the street to the café.

Brady seated us at a table on the patio. "Saw you taking a few photos at lunch," he said. "In the park."

"I didn't see you," I said, remembering how Ulani Kamaka had sneaked up on me.

"I was racing past and didn't stop to say hello. I was on a mission to pick up a few staples. We'd run out. Did you have fun?"

Even though I'd felt uncomfortable on the outing, thanks to conversations with Ulani as well as Gregory, I said, "I had a ball."

He handed us two menus and made a U-turn to greet more guests.

Meaghan leaned forward. "Am I sensing an attraction be-tween you two?"

"We're old friends."

"Old friends can be the best kind. You don't have to go through the craziness of getting to know each other."

"Stop. I'm happily single. Okay?"

"He's really handsome in an easygoing way."

He was that. I wouldn't disagree.

We ordered tea and chocolate caramel brownies from our waitress. Meaghan liked to try brownies wherever she went. She was intent on discovering the ingredients in any new flavor.

I closed the menu. "So, what's your angle about clearing my name?"

Meaghan chortled. "No preamble. No 'Hey, how are you doing? How's your love life?'"

"I didn't have to ask. I can see you're beaming," I said, "which means you must have seen *him* during lunch."

Her cheeks tinged cherry pink. "I did."

"Are you two getting serious?"

"I don't think we can be. I adore his passion, but his tem-per . . ." Meaghan traced a finger along the rim of the table. "My mother has warned me." Meaghan's father had had a temper, too. When Meaghan was five, her mother put a re-straining order on him. A year later, he moved to the East Coast. Meaghan received cards on her birthday, but she hadn't spoken to him in years. "So, for now, it's a lark. We'll have fun, but the moment he raises a hand, he's toast."

"Good to know you have limits," I said, and meant it. "Now, the angle that might clear me?"

"One of our artists is a techie. He said every Internet user has a digital footprint. We need to find yours."

"I'm not following."

"Let's see if I can get this straight. A digital footprint is a trail of data a user creates while using the Internet."

"But we already know the data is in my chat room."

"He can take it one step further. If you grant him access to your accounts, on Facebook and other social media, then he can track the way in which you communicate and be able to prove beyond a doubt that it was you in that chat room."

My breath caught in my chest. "Really?"

"Trust me, this guy is wicked smart. Are you open to the idea?"

"Absolutely."

"He'll need your ISP address."

"Joss wrote it down."

"Text her."

I did. Seconds later, Joss sent a reply. I copied it and sent it to Meaghan via text.

"How did we ever communicate before the digital age?" Meaghan quipped. "I'm forwarding this to my guy." She tapped instructions and set her cell phone to one side as our waitress brought our treats. "Oh, yum." Meaghan bit into her brownie and swooned. She hailed Brady who was chatting up a customer by the arched entrance.

He sauntered over. "Problem?"

"I think I've died and gone to heaven." Meaghan gestured to the second half of her brownie. "I love the caramel combined with the extra chocolate chips. I absolutely must have the recipe. Will you share?" She patted an extra chair at our table, inviting him to sit.

He didn't. He folded his arms, looking quite foreboding. "If I dole out trade secrets, what will make Hideaway Café special?"

"I'll take the recipe to my grave." Meaghan crossed her heart.

Brady turned to me. "What do you think?"

"You can trust her."

"I meant about the brownie."

"Delicious. The pecans are a nice touch."

He grinned. "It's a family recipe. Handed down from my grandmother."

"So you won't share?" Meaghan batted her eyelashes. Working it. She was incorrigible.

"I'll think about it." He turned to me. "By the way, what's going on with the investigation? Any news? I saw Logan Langford nosing around the Village Shops, asking my neighbors about their rents and such. I don't trust that guy."

Fiona appeared over Brady's shoulder. "You left without me." She alit on my arm and plumped her wings. "Of course, it was partly my fault. I was busy sleuthing. I wasn't around."

Sleuthing what? I wondered. At times, she was as elusive as the wind.

"And later," Brady said, drawing my attention back to the conversation, "Langford came in here to meet with that attorney." He snapped his fingers searching for a name. "Youngman."

"Wright Youngman?" I asked. "Emily Watkins's attorney?"

"Yes. He leases the unit in the Village Shops above Acosta Artworks."

I sucked in a breath. Could it have been Youngman, not Emily, who had sicced Isabella Acosta on me? Was the man in love with Emily or simply serving as her protector now that her husband was dead?

"You're frowning, Courtney," Brady said.

"Do you know Isabella Acosta?"

He nodded. "She comes in about once a week with a client. She's all business. Why?"

"She's one of the main reasons the police are interested in me as a suspect."

Brady smirked. "If you ask me, she ought to be a suspect. She was furious when she picked up her precious Cocoa the other day at the groomer. Mistakenly, someone had given the poodle a Mohawk. Not cool."

"But Isabella sports a Mohawk."

"She got her hair trimmed that night to match him so that he wouldn't feel self-conscious."

I bit back a laugh. "You're kidding."

"Poodle owners can be quirky." Brady's eyes sparkled with amusement.

Would a bad haircut on her dog have driven Isabella to murder? If the dog were a show dog, possibly. "Is she friends with Petra Pauli?"

"They have the occasional lunch. They're usually talking about city restrictions. Isabella would like a larger sign for the Village Shops."

Meaghan tapped the table. "Go on about Wright Youngman, Brady. Did you hear what he and Langford were talking about?"

"A lease perhaps?" I asked.

"Nope. They were discussing bank loans. If I heard correctly, Langford said he was being gouged."

"As in usury?"

Brady nodded.

Youngman's specialties were estate planning, trusts, and wills. Would he know how to rectify a debt?

"I've got to go." Brady brushed my shoulder with a fingertip. "Keep me in the loop."

A shiver—the good kind—shimmied up my neck.

"Brady." Meaghan grabbed the sleeve of his shirt and held fast. "Will you ask our waitress to bring me another brownie? Pretty please?"

He chuckled and said, "Sure. Are you planning to take it to a lab and dissect it?"

"Nope. I intend to devour every last morsel."

When he left, I said, "Go easy, girlfriend. You don't want to fight a sugar rush all afternoon."

"Yes, I do."

A short while later, after paying the bill, we left the restaurant and crossed the street. Dodging traffic, Meaghan promised to touch base the moment she heard from her techie artist. In front of Open Your Imagination, she bussed me on the cheek and said, "Keep your spirits up."

As she dashed away, I paused, captivated by a scenario that was playing out down the street.

"What's caught your attention?" Fiona asked.

I pointed at Logan Langford standing outside the driver's side of his Lexus SUV. He was tying an antique desk on top using nautical knots. A young, slender man with dark eyes and a hooded brow was standing on the far side of Logan. He said something. Logan glimpsed left and right as if trying to discern whether they were being watched.

Deftly, I pretended to be checking email on my phone. After a brief moment, I returned my focus to them, fascinated. What had the young man said? Did it have to do with Logan's usury issue? The young man jutted a hand at Logan. Pinning the desk with one hand, Logan used his other to execute what looked like a secret handshake. The men clasped wrists and slid their hands down to a grip. They then flipped their hands over, whacked the backs together, and gave a thumbs-up gesture.

"See you, sucker," the younger man bellowed.

He hopped into a green BMW and swerved onto the street, nearly striking Logan, who shouted a curse. The younger man cackled and waved a not-so-nice good-bye. The grinding sound the BMW made as it sped away was lethal.

Chapter 20

Nothing can be truer than fairy wisdom. It is as true as sunbeams.
—Douglas Jerrold, "Our Honeymoon:
An Apology and An Explanation"

The moment I walked into the shop, Joss darted to me. "Call Meaghan. Now."

My pal and I had only parted minutes before. What could be so urgent?

"Now," Joss repeated.

"Okay, okay." I skirted the sales counter and dialed Meaghan's cell phone.

She answered after one ring. "I've got good news. I'm coming right over."

Seconds later, Meaghan flew through the front door, breathless. "My guy has already accessed your chat room account and found your digital footprint."

"Her what?" Joss asked.

Meaghan recapped what she'd told me at the café. "He found digital proof that distinguishes Courtney's writing from anyone else's."

"Explain," I said.

Fiona flitted between Joss and me. "Is everything okay? What's going on?"

Meaghan opened the Notes app on her cell phone. "As it so happens, you always add a smile emoji after you write LOL."

"Big deal. Everyone does."

"No. Everyone does not. Most people use one or the other. In addition"—she referred to the Notes app—"you use the shortened version of *U* for you."

"My father hates that I do it. He doesn't like text shorthand."

"You also write *enuf* for enough and *LMK* for let me know. There are dozens of other abbreviations and repetitions that you use, making it unmistakable that it was you at the computer that night. My guy is writing up a report."

I grabbed Meaghan in a bear hug. "Who knew that being boringly predictable would prove I'm innocent?"

Joss said, "You should contact Detective Summers."

I tapped the detective's number into my cell phone. His phone rang three times. He didn't answer. I ended the call, dialed the precinct, and asked for him. He answered in less than a minute. Had he been monitoring his cell phone calls? Had he avoided mine on purpose? It didn't matter. I filled him in on Meaghan's friend's findings.

Summers sounded reasonably impressed. "Have him send his report to me. If our techs confirm . . ." He gave me his email.

I jotted the email on a notepad. "In the meantime, I have another bit of news."

Summers made a sucking sound, like he was enjoying a late lunch at his desk. "I'm all ears."

I told him that Isabella Acosta, the person willing to lay Mick's murder on me, had been upset about the haircut her poodle received at Wizard of Paws.

Summers snorted. "You think she'd kill Mick over a bad haircut?"

"If the dog's a show dog."

"It's not. I know Cocoa. The poor cur couldn't obey a hand signal if his life depended upon it. He walks and sits. That's the scope of his talent." Summers clucked his tongue. "For a poodle, he's not very bright."

"How do you know Isabella?" I asked as I sketched a fairy on the notepad.

"We dated for a nanosecond."

It was my turn to snort. "I can't see it."

"Nobody could. We'd met at the plein-air event last May and got to chatting about art. We went out for dinner. Our budding romance fizzled after one date. I learned more about her errant dog than I'd ever wanted to know." He wadded up something that crackled—the wrapping for his lunch, I imagined.

"Do you have any other leads?" I asked.

The silence was deafening.

After a long moment, Summers said, "Good-bye, Courtney."

I stared at my cell phone. Call ended. Shoot.

"Uh-oh," Joss said. "You're frowning."

"What did he say?" Meaghan asked.

"If his people confirm the evidence"—I twirled a hand—"I assume I'll be in the clear."

"That's great." Joss high-fived me.

Meaghan crushed me in a hug.

Fiona did backflips in the air. Fairy dust glimmered in her wake.

"*If*," I cautioned them. "In the meantime, I gave him another suspect to consider. Isabella Acosta. Although I'm not sure he took that suggestion seriously." Truth? I knew he hadn't.

"Hello-o-o, am I interrupting a celebration?" a woman called as she entered the shop.

Pastor Li, the silver-haired Asian leader of the congregational church near my house, limped toward us, her dog-
carved cane providing serious support.

"Please, come in." I hurried to her and offered my elbow.

The pastor didn't take it. She tilted her head back and
looked into my eyes. "I was speaking with Holly Hopewell a
bit ago. I've been in Chicago at a conference for a few days.
Holly told me the horrible news about the murder. She said
you're a suspect."

"Not any longer," Meaghan crowed.

"I'm so glad to hear that," Pastor Li said. "I told Holly it
couldn't be so. I saw you a number of times that night, Courtney, as I let my sweet pup out." Her dog wasn't a pup. He was
an aging shar-pei, more wrinkles and belly than legs at this
point. "Poor dear has to pee frequently. He didn't settle down
until nearly two a.m."

I clasped her hand. "That's wonderful. Not about your
dog. But that you saw me." I said to Meaghan and Joss,
"More corroboration of my innocence. Whee!"

They cheered.

"Pastor Li, would you go to the police precinct and tell
them?" I asked.

"Of course. I'll go there immediately, if'"—she smiled—
"you'll consider coming to church to celebrate."

"Will do." I kissed her cheek. I hadn't been to church in
months. Sundays were busy at the shop. Plus, I often considered nature my church. I did a lot of praying while walking.
"How about a set of wind chimes, ma'am, on the house?"

"No, thank you. We don't have boastful things at the
church."

"But angels love music," I countered.

She tittered. "Another time."

Meaghan said, "I'll walk with you to the precinct, ma'am."
She offered the pastor her arm.

At the same time, Petra Pauli rushed in, nearly steamrolling over Meaghan and the pastor as they were exiting the shop. Meaghan shot her a peeved look. Petra was oblivious.

"What's with all the hoopla, Courtney?" Petra asked. "I could hear you cheering from across the street." She ran her fingers though her tangled blond curls and shifted the Open Your Imagination shopping bag she was carrying to her other arm.

"Courtney is exonerated," Joss shouted.

"Of murdering Mick Watkins? How wonderful!" Petra exclaimed. "Of course, I never thought you were guilty." She gave me a hug that felt more like a chest bump. No squeeze. No hands on back.

I didn't judge. I sensed touchy-feely wasn't her thing. I eyed the shopping bag. "Do you have a return?"

"Yes. Actually, an exchange." She pulled down her red-cropped sweater—it had crept up on her dash inside—and smoothed one hip of her slim jeans. "Rather than the ones I purchased, I'd prefer to have teacups with fairies on them." She handed me the bag and roamed the shop. "I saw some the other day," she said over her shoulder. "How I would love to see a fairy."

Fiona popped into view and hovered by Petra's ear. The woman didn't have a clue. She didn't even feel the breeze.

Laughing, I hurried after her and steered her toward the Reutter Porcelain that featured a storybook tea set with flower fairies. "These are lovely." The sweet pea fairy was my favorite. "If you don't like them, we have Copeland Spode fairy dell teacups. They would be lovely for your project." I gestured to the nearby display table where the Spode cups were sitting. "By the way, if you're interested, I am offering a teacup fairy garden workshop in a few days. They're simple to make. You should join us."

"Maybe I will." Petra leaned in to me. "Speaking of Mick's murder . . ."

I gawped. We hadn't been.

"I asked around about Gregory Darvell," Petra continued. "I know he had it in for Mick. A few of us were talking the other day at the book club. One woman said Gregory wanted to get his hands on that dog. The German shepherd. Shep. You saw Gregory at the council meeting fawning over the dog, didn't you? While Emily—" Petra blew out a quick burst of air, obviously remembering how Emily had publicly shamed her with the hot pink lingerie. "This is pretty." She picked up the sweet pea fairy teacup and raised it to the light. "I love purple. It's such a regal color." She set it down and inspected another. "Back to Gregory."

Despite the fact that Gregory sneakily had entered the dog in competition, I said, "He can't have killed Mick. He was in San Jose on a training appointment when Mick died."

"That's just it," Petra said. "He wasn't. A fellow councilperson, Oriana Gray, saw him driving in Mick's neighborhood that night."

"That can't be true. I spoke with Miss Gray. She went to bed early, which was why she didn't attend your secret political meeting."

"Not that early. She thought he might have been stalking Mick."

"Stalking?"

"Following him to see when he could strike. She wondered if Gregory tailed Mick to your shop. She definitely saw—" Petra gasped. "Oh, no!" She pointed out the window. "There he is. Darvell." Her face turned ash white. "Is he following me? Has he figured out that I know his alibi is bogus?"

"Unless Oriana was mistaken."

"She never is. The woman has a steel-trap mind."

I wasn't sure a good mind substituted for decent eyesight. What kind of car did Gregory drive? Was it as unremarkable as Miranda Watkins's black Honda? Could Oriana have been misguided about who had been driving?

I peered out the window. Gregory was outside Wizard of Paws, taking Shep from Sonja. He wasn't looking in our direction, which suggested, to me anyway, that he wasn't coming after Petra. I presumed he was heading off to give the dog another training session.

"Big dogs," Petra muttered. "Too much work if you ask me."

"Your dogs aren't slouches in the size category."

"They're not lap dogs, but they're not the size of Shep." She splayed her hands, indicating a huge animal. "How Mick adored him."

I thought again of Gregory Darvell's motive. Would he have killed Mick for the opportunity to show the dog and revive his reputation as a premier trainer?

While Joss saw to Petra and her purchases, I grabbed my cell phone and headed outside. I caught a glance from Joss, but I ignored it. She didn't like Petra; I understood that. However, we didn't have the luxury of picking and choosing our customers.

Gregory was on one knee near the entrance to Wizard of Paws, slipping a leash over Shep's neck. Sonja stood nearby. "His teeth look good," he said.

Sonja nodded her agreement.

"His coat is glossy. You're doing well with whatever you're feeding him."

Sonja beamed. "Mick believed in a one-protein diet. No corn, wheat, or other fillers."

"Excellent." Gregory lumbered to his feet and asked Shep to sit. The dog obeyed, his gaze fixed on Gregory.

"Nicely done," I said as I joined them.

Fiona flitted past Sonja and behind Gregory. She hovered above Shep. The dog's eyes rolled upward, but he didn't move a muscle. That made Fiona giggle. "Should I tease him?" she asked with a trill.

I shook my head once, which made her giggle all the harder; she knew I wouldn't respond aloud.

"Hey, Gregory, I heard you've entered Shep in a competition," I said.

Sonja shot him a look. "You what? No, no, no. You cannot. Mick would forbid that."

Gregory's cheeks reddened. He tugged at the collar of his shirt. For air?

"Emily did not give you permission to do so, did she?" Sonja asked, acting as territorial as if she were the owner.

"She will. You've seen him, Sonja," Gregory countered. "He takes to training like a duck to water. I was going to tell Emily in time."

"When?" Sonja jammed a hand on one ample hip.

"After the funeral. After she's had time to grieve."

Sonja folded her arms and clicked her tongue, not believing him.

Fiona knuckled my forehead. "Ask him his alibi."

I licked my lips. "You know, Gregory, there are . . . rumors going around."

"I hate rumors," he shouted. Shep flinched. Gregory petted the dog's head to calm him. "Sorry, boy."

"I hate them, too," I said. "People were talking about Mick and me, saying I had reason to kill him. Thankfully, that rumor has been put to rest. A witness can verify my alibi." I offered a supportive smile. "What was your alibi again?"

He cut a sharp look at me. "I had no cause to kill Mick."

"As I said, there are rumors, one of which is that you want to own Shep for yourself." I was lying, but Gregory didn't know that, and he did adore the dog. "With Mick out of the picture . . ."

"No way," Sonja said. "Emily loves the dog. She will never give him up."

"Yes, of course," I said. "However, another way for Gregory to spend time with Shep is by training him. In addition, Gregory is hoping to win back his reputation. He can do that by making Shep a winner, right, Gregory?"

"I did not kill Mick Watkins," Gregory exclaimed. "I would never kill a dog's owner. That would bring grief to the dog. That would be against everything I am. Everything I stand for." His voice trembled with emotion.

"I heard you were driving to and from San Jose to see a client on the night Mick was killed."

Sonja edged closer, allying herself with me. "That means there are hours unaccounted for."

Gregory moaned.

"There's another pesky rumor," I went on. "Someone saw you driving in Mick's neighborhood on the night of the murder."

"That's not true. I don't even know where he lives . . . *lived*. I—" Gregory sucked in air. Shep mewled, sensing his distress. Gregory took a deep breath. "If you must know, in addition to seeing clients, I met with the head judge of the next regional competition. In San Jose. The lineup for the competition was full, so I . . . so I . . ." Gregory's cheeks burned red. "I convinced the man to give me a spot. For Shep."

"Convinced?" Sonja raised an eyebrow.

"I bribed him. Paid him off. Money talks. I'm not proud of it," Gregory mumbled, "but that's where I was. I took the judge for drinks. We talked well past midnight. He won't confirm it, of course, because that would compromise his reputation, but it's true."

"The police might get him to confess," I said. "That could help your case."

"If you were drinking, you should have a bar receipt," Sonja said.

I smiled at her. "Good thought. Do you?"

Gregory's eyes lit up. "Sonja, you're brilliant. I can pull up a list of credit card transactions online." He thrust a thankful hand at her, hoping to shake with her.

Sonja didn't. She said, "Bring the dog back the instant training is over," and marched inside Wizard of Paws. The screen door went *clack,* and then the front door slammed. Hard. Fortunately, the etched glass didn't shatter.

Gregory lowered his arm, clearly crestfallen.

"Sonja will tell Emily," I said.

"And Emily will never trust me again." He lifted his chin, his eyes moist. "I had to do it. I had to train Shep."

"Why?"

"A year ago, after I lost the last competition, I realized I needed to work with big dogs to win. I'm simply not a little dog guy anymore, which is why—"

"Your mojo left you."

He sighed. "My heart has to be in the training. I'm sure you understand, having changed careers and opened your shop."

"Don't you own two bichon frises?"

He nodded. "They're great companions, but they're not what I enjoy training. Shep is smart. Easygoing. Unspoiled. Little dogs can be . . . prima donnas. Emily has made sure that Shep—" He glanced over his shoulder and back at me. "Speaking of Emily, do you know where she is? I've been try-ing to reach her for the last hour so we could meet up for cof-fee after the training session, but she's not answering her cell phone."

Fiona flitted to me. "Courtney, something is off. I feel it here." She thumped her stomach.

A frisson of worry slinked up my neck. "Gregory, did you ask Sonja?"

"No, and I doubt she'd tell me anything now."

I stepped inside Wizard of Paws. Gregory, Shep, and Fiona followed. The noise inside was raucous. The aroma of shampoo and wet dog hair hung in the air. No one was at the front desk. Via the see-through window, I spied Sonja in the room beyond, blow-drying a white Pekinese that was perched on a table and tethered to a pole.

"Sonja," I yelled and waved.

She switched off the hair dryer. "Doesn't Shep want to go on his walk?"

"Shep's fine. Have you seen Emily?"

"About an hour ago, but it's weird because she said that she was going home to freshen up and then coming back in a half hour. She wanted to review the books. Have you tried calling her?"

"I have," Gregory said. "And I've texted her. She's not responding."

"Something is wrong." Fiona flapped fitfully. "Terribly, terribly wrong."

Chapter 21

The difference between fairies and you is that your wings are hidden in your heart.
—Anonymous

I asked Sonja for Emily's home address. She did me one better. She gave us a house key. Mick always kept a spare at the shop in case of emergencies.

Leaving Shep with Sonja, Gregory and I sprinted to the Watkins's house. As much as Fiona wanted to stay with the dog, she felt it was more important that she accompany me. She said her sleuthing senses were on high alert.

The Watkins's home, located on 6th Avenue near Carpenter, was a cream-colored, one-story house featuring fieldstone facing and an adobe-tiled roof. A sign by the path dubbed the house Copper-by-the-Sea.

I arrived at the door first. It was slightly ajar. I glanced at Gregory. "Maybe she forgot to close it all the way." I knocked. "Emily?" No one answered. I rang the doorbell. No response.

Fiona said, "We have to go in."

I pushed the door open. It creaked. "Emily? Are you here?

It's Courtney and Gregory." I stopped in the foyer and scanned the rooms on either side.

Gregory followed, inches behind me. "Emily?"

The kitchen on the left was done in a Tuscan style. The living room to the right held a small sofa, two easy chairs, and a huge dog pillow for Shep. The dark oak bookshelves were packed with books and small-scale statues. No sign of Emily.

Striding deeper into the house, I said, "Emily, we've been worried about you." I didn't hear water running. She wasn't taking a shower.

Someone moaned. Ahead. I dashed down the hall and veered into the bedroom on the right. Emily, dressed in a tawny bathrobe, was lying facedown on the floor. Her hair was wet and straggly. She moved her head and blinked at the sight of us. "Where am I?"

Gregory rushed to help her. "In your house. In your bedroom."

Emily let out a tiny *ooh* and touched the back of her head.

"Are you hurt?" he asked.

"Someone . . . hit . . . me."

I spotted a neutral-toned Himalayan salt lamp lying on the floor beyond her. "Gregory, be careful. I think she was struck with that. She might have a concussion." I called 911 using my cell phone, supplied the pertinent information, and ended the call.

"How long until they get here?" Gregory asked.

"Who knows? Soon, I hope."

With his help, Emily sat up. Her eyes were glassy. "What time is it?"

"Nearly five," I said.

Emily palpated the back of her head again.

Tenderly, Gregory rested his hand on her shoulder and inspected her wound. "Who would want to hurt you?"

"I have no idea. Maybe whoever murdered Mick?"

Unless she was the one to have killed him, I thought, though I doubted she'd have slammed herself on the back of the head to bolster her claim of innocence.

"Or a robber," she said.

"Has anything been stolen?" I asked.

"I don't know."

The honey-colored comforter on the bed was rumpled. Items of clothing, probably pieces Emily had planned to try on, were strewn on top. Stacks of books stood on each of the oak nightstands. Many of the drawers on the matching bureau hung open. The door to the closet was ajar, as was the door to the bathroom. Through the opening, I noticed a towel on the floor.

Emily glanced around. Slowly.

"I've been calling you," Gregory said. "I wanted to meet you for coffee. You didn't answer."

"Take photos," Fiona said.

I didn't. The police would do that. Instead, I crouched to Emily's eye level. "This morning, after you said good-bye to Mr. Youngman outside Wizard of Paws, I felt as though you wanted to tell me something."

"No." She shook her head and winced, as if the movement caused great pain.

"You said Mick told you something that you shouldn't do. Remember?"

She blinked rapidly. Then the blinking abated, and her cheeks turned crimson. "That night, the night Mick died, he said . . . he said I shouldn't be worried about the affair. It meant nothing to him. I was so dumb to believe him."

"No one would ever think you were dumb," Gregory said as he tucked a strand of wet hair behind her ear.

For a moment, I wondered whether, before picking up

Shep, Gregory had come here and knocked out Emily. Did he think he could win possession of the dog if Emily were dead? I nudged the notion from my mind. He genuinely seemed to like Emily.

"Go on," I prompted.

"I told Mick I didn't believe him. I said I needed time to think. So I went to the Equestrian Inn, like I said, but after a pre-dinner ride, I came home. I needed to talk to Mick. I wanted to work things out. I loved him. But he wasn't here." She drew in a sharp breath. "At first I was jealous, thinking he was with Petra, but then I saw the note he'd left about going to your place to meet fairies."

"Why did he want to meet fairies?" I asked.

"I don't know. Maybe he hoped, if he saw one, they'd help him tap into his creativity." She studied Gregory as if trying to figure out why he was there. "You wanted to take me to coffee?"

He smiled. "Yes."

"Keep going, Emily," I said. "You came home. Then what?"

"I saw the note, so I went to your shop. I thought if fairies were real, maybe they could help me, too. Help us. Rekindle our love."

Fiona flitted to Emily's shoulder and sat. "That explains the straw on the patio floor. She tracked it in from her trail ride."

I nodded. Exactly as we'd suggested to Detective Summers.

Oblivious to Fiona's presence, Emily said, "When I got there, the front door was open." Tears leaked from her eyes. She dabbed them with her fingertips. "I tiptoed in and—" She shot a hand out. "Mick was there. On the patio. By the fountain. Dead."

"Did you touch him?" I asked.

"No!" She pressed her knuckles to her mouth and stifled a sob. "It was so awful. He looked so pale."

"Why didn't you call the police?"

"I panicked. I realized my DNA would be there. They'd think I killed him."

I thought of the photos I'd taken of Mick and the surrounding area. "The business cards. Did you move them? Did you place Petra's at the top to implicate her?"

"I . . . I . . ." Emily swallowed hard. "My heart started pounding in my throat. I ran home."

"How did you hurt your hand?"

She glanced at her arm. "I didn't. I came up with the idiotic idea of bandaging it because I thought if I were injured, the police wouldn't think I'd killed him. My brother did something like that back in high school, to get out of taking a test." She reached across her body and gripped her shoulder, nearly catching Fiona with the sudden move.

Fiona flew to me. "Whew! That was close."

Maybe Emily was on the verge of sensing my sweet fairy's presence. Vulnerability could open the gateway.

"Who do you think broke into my house?" Emily asked, her voice as reedy as a frightened child's.

"It depends on what they wanted," I said. "Do you remember anything before you were struck? Did you hear anything?"

"The ice cream truck."

"The what?" Gregory asked.

"There's an ice cream truck that drives through the neighborhood twice a week. All the kids love it."

"Did you hear anything else?" I asked. "Did you smell anything unusual?"

"Vanilla."

"Vanilla ice cream?"

She shook her head.

"Vanilla, like the scent they spray on groomed dogs at your shop?" Gregory asked.

"It could have been."

The scent of vanilla would rule Gregory out as the perpetrator. He smelled like musk and dogs.

"Your house smells like vanilla, too," I said. "You use those air freshener plug-ins. Maybe that was your first memory upon awakening after being hit."

"Maybe."

"Do you feel up to a search to see if anything is missing?" I asked.

"Okay."

"If we figure out what is gone, we might determine who was here," I added.

"Can you stand, Emily?" Gregory asked.

"I think so."

He helped her to her feet. She didn't falter.

When she took in the room, she gasped. "I didn't pull out those drawers. Who put all these clothes on my bed?"

If she had suffered a concussion, she could have blocked out her movements prior to the injury, although she had recalled the details of our prior conversation.

With Gregory's arm as support, Emily roamed her bedroom. She found her jewelry box tucked at the back of her lingerie drawer. Everything was there, she said, even her grandmother's heirloom broach. She inspected her closet. The floor safe looked intact. Her passport and extra cash for a rainy day were inside. She scoured the cabinets in her bathroom. No drugs were missing. She added that she didn't use many— a sleeping pill on occasion and a low-dose aspirin for recurring headaches. Mick, she confided, hadn't used any medicine. Ever.

I orbited the house, noting a few expensive pieces of art.

Almost everyone in Carmel invested in something. "Any art-work missing?" I asked in the living room. There weren't any discolorations on the walls as if a frame had been removed.

"No," Emily said, trailing me, Gregory close at her heels. She traced her finger along the bronze statues and spines of books that lined the bookshelves. "Everything seems to be here. Mick liked to invest in first editions, like *Harry Potter and the Philosopher's Stone*, *The Hound of the Baskervilles*, and *The Hobbit*. I see them all."

She slogged back to the bedroom and turned in a circle. I followed her gaze. She paused, looking at the bed. "The books on my nightstand are in order."

"You organize your books?" I asked.

"Yes. I like to read books by season—books set at Christmas during Christmas and books set in summer during the summer. It's spring right now, so that's a spring-themed book on top."

Fiona soared to the books on Emily's side of the bed and perused the titles. "Mostly romances," she advised me.

"Are Mick's books in order, too?" I asked.

Emily took a closer look. "He didn't sort them like I did, al-though he was finicky about his first editions." She removed the topmost and set it on the bed. Then the next and the next. The fourth book flopped open. Three-by-five cards tumbled out.

Fiona flew above the book and its contents. "*The Artist's Way*," she said reading the title off one of the pages. "What's that?"

I asked Emily the same question.

"It's like a diary. The author encourages her readers to write daily. The program is a twelve-week journey to help her students discover a link between their creative selves and their spiritual selves. Writing their thoughts down gives them a benchmark for how far they've come." Emily shook her head. "I gave the book to Mick a year ago. I told you he wanted to be a writer. That's what the notecards are for. *Were* for." She bit back a sob. "They were the beginning of his outline for his thriller."

"Courtney," Fiona said, "read this."

I joined Fiona at the bedside and studied the cards. In the mix was Petra Pauli's business card. "It appears Mick was writing about a wealthy man harboring a secret," I said to Emily.

"I know." She nodded. "I've read the notes. Mick didn't know I took a peek." That meant she'd seen Petra's business card. How sad. One more knife to the heart. "His notes and musings were supposed to be private, but he had secrets, and I was afraid . . ." She chewed her lower lip. "I did something bad. I'm ashamed to admit it, but seeing his notes . . . and Petra's card . . . inspired me."

"How?" I asked.

"I wrote her anonymous letters saying I knew she had a terrible secret and telling her I'd reveal it to everyone if she didn't leave town."

"You lied?"

"I wanted to scare her away from my husband. It didn't work, of course, but I was desperate."

Gregory said, "Could Petra have been the one to knock you out?"

"I doubt she would have known I was the one who wrote to her. I disguised my handwriting and posted the letters from another town. Besides, she obviously didn't believe me. She didn't hightail it out of Carmel." Emily moaned. "I need to sit down."

Gregory wrapped his arm around her.

A siren wailed outside. The sound of footsteps pounding the cobblestoned path echoed into the house.

As the EMTs swept into the room and sped to Emily's aid, I eyed the three-by-five cards. Logan Langford was a wealthy man. His family had built a legacy. Did he or one of his relatives have a secret that could ruin that legacy? I knew a lot about the Langfords, but not everything. What if Mick had discovered something dire and told Logan what he'd learned? Killing Mick would have put that problem to rest, in Logan's mind, unless Mick, in his dying breath, had admitted to Logan that he'd kept notes.

I flashed on Logan meeting with the younger man in the BMW. Had Logan hired him to search for and destroy any evidence about the secret? I imagined the scenario: the young man showing up at the Watkins's house. Finding the door unlocked. Coming upon Emily fresh out of the shower. Panicking, he grabbed the first heavy thing he saw, the Himalayan salt lamp, and knocked her out. Then he searched the house. The drawers. The closets. Not realizing that *The Artist's Way* held notecards outlining Mick's book, the young man didn't consider leafing through it.

"Well, well," Detective Summers said, striding in with Officer Rodriguez moments after the EMTs. "Look who we have here." Both looked very official and judgmental.

"Emily wasn't responding to phone calls or texts," I said quickly. "Gregory—Mr. Darvell"—I thrust a hand in his direction—"was worried. Sonja, the assistant at Wizard of Paws, gave us a key. We didn't need it. When we arrived, the door was open."

As the EMTs carted Emily to the ambulance, Gregory asked if he could accompany her. Summers told him to stay put. Then he asked me to fill him in on the details. As expected, he fetched his notebook, removed the rubber band, and started taking notes.

My account came out in short bursts. Finding Emily on the floor. The salt lamp. The opened drawers. Nothing missing as far as Emily could see.

Neither Summers nor Rodriguez cut me off.

I suggested the possibility that Logan Langford might have a family secret, giving him ample motive to want Mick silenced. Then I mentioned the exchange I'd witnessed between Logan and the younger man, suggesting he might be the person dunning Logan for payment. I was about to offer more when I realized Fiona wasn't around. I scanned the room. Where had she gone?

"Did either you or Mr. Darvell touch the salt lamp?" Rodriguez pointed to it.

"No, ma'am," I replied.

"No," Gregory said.

"About this younger man that you saw meeting with Logan . . ." Summers clicked his pen once, twice. "Any idea who he might be?"

"No. He drove a green BMW. I didn't catch the license plate."

Summers made a note.

"Do you think we're on the right track?" I asked.

"*We* are not on anything," Rodriguez chided.

Summers held up a hand to her. "Chill." He eyed me. "FYI, my tech people have agreed with Meaghan Brownie's tech guy's assessment. Your digital footprint is verifiable. You were where you said you were when Mick Watkins was murdered."

I sighed with relief. "Can I assume Pastor Li stopped by the precinct and also confirmed my alibi?"

He nodded. "She did."

"May I tell my attorney I don't need further assistance?"

"Yes." Summers turned to Gregory, ready to grill him.

I tapped Summers's arm. "Hold on, Detective. Have you interviewed Isabella Acosta yet?"

"You no longer need to concern yourself with this case."

"I know, but have you?"

Summers squinted. "Yes, she has a solid alibi. She was

with a girlfriend drinking wine to douse her sorrow about her dog's haircut. And, yes, the girlfriend corroborates that. Miss Acosta spent the night. Now, Mr. Darvell . . ." Summers faced Gregory and asked for his account.

Gregory repeated everything I said, short of blaming Logan, seeing as he didn't know the man personally. Gregory also mentioned the ice cream truck that Emily had heard. Summers ruled out the truck's driver because Emily hadn't been robbed and the attack appeared to be personal.

When Summers completed his questioning, Gregory asked if he could now go to the hospital to be with Emily. Summers agreed. Gregory arranged for an Uber, and I returned to the shop, retrieved Pixie, and headed home.

During one of my favorite dinners of white fish with a beurre blanc sauce and a crisp green salad, I thought again about Emily. Had she faked the attack? Could she have struck herself with the salt lamp? Was she guilty of killing her husband? She'd lied about her whereabouts to the police, and she'd lied about her injured hand. How many lies did it take before a jury would find her guilty?

If Emily wasn't the killer and she really had been attacked, was she still in danger? Would her attacker steal into the hospital to finish the deed?

Seeing how tenderly Gregory had treated her, I was certain he wasn't the attacker. In fact, I was pretty sure he was falling for her . . . because of the dog. Would Emily be ready for a new relationship so soon after her husband's death? She had obviously loved Mick deeply, but his affair with Petra Pauli had created a rift in their marriage.

While I was washing dishes, Gregory called to say Emily was sleeping well. In addition, he was sending me a text with a PDF attachment of the receipt for the cocktails he'd had with the head judge of the dog show competition. He made me swear not to ask the competition's head judge for corroboration, for fear the man would give Shep's spot to another contestant. Explaining that it wasn't up to me, I made him promise he would share his alibi and the proof of it with the police. Reluctantly, he agreed.

After we ended the call, I thought about Fiona. She hadn't been at the shop and she wasn't flitting around my garden. Where was she?

Chapter 22

How to tell if a fairy is nearby: a strong scent of grass or violets.
—Anonymous

In the morning, feeling more rested than I had felt in days because I was no longer considered guilty of something I didn't do, I downed a protein-rich fruit shake and then dressed in a cheery green smock dress and sandals, gathered up Pixie, and headed to work. The sun was shining. The air was crisp. Hearing the distant pounding of waves as they hit the sand, I urged my breathing to match the steady pace of the tide. Heaven.

"You're late," Joss said as I strode into the shop.

"I'm early. You're earlier."

"We have the teacup fairy garden workshop coming up in a few days." Joss inserted the feather duster she'd been using into its bin and brushed dust off her shiny orange blouse. "And the security people are starting this afternoon. Best to get a jump on gathering your workshop items just in case they have to take over the patio for longer than expected and we're forced to hold the workshop inside. We have a lot of students for this one. Sixteen in all. I ordered an additional twenty teacups, in case there's breakage."

"Did Petra sign up?"

"Not so far."

As I gathered a bunch of teensy fairy figurines—we couldn't use the larger sort for a teacup garden; scale mattered—Pixie circled my ankles and mewed.

"I'm not sure where Fiona is," I said, worry taking hold. Why had she flown away? With no explanation? Nudging my concern aside, I scratched Pixie's head and said, "Help me come up with slogans for the teacup workshop." I headed to the sales counter. Pixie trotted behind me. "I'd like the younger attendees in the crowd to have a memorable saying to take with them."

"Talking to me?" Joss asked.

"No, to Pixie. Usually I work these things out with Fiona, but she's MIA. Have you seen her?"

Joss shook her head. "How about this saying? 'May you touch stars, weave new dreams, and dance with the fairies in the moonlight.'"

"I like it." I jotted it on a notepad.

"Or this? 'Close your eyes and listen closely. You may hear a fairy.'"

"Nice. Keep them coming." I headed to the office.

"Courtney!" Meaghan rushed in just as I rounded the desk. She skidded to a stop. Her hair was knotted in a messy bun. Her oversized silk blouse ballooned over her leggings. "I did what you asked."

"Which was?"

"I finally talked to one of my friends who's in the choir at Church of the Wayfarer. Guess what? Logan Langford was not there last Wednesday night."

"Are you sure?"

"Well, he was. For an hour. But then he left." She frowned. "Did he honestly think no one would remember?"

Huh. Detective Summers must have figured that out by now. Why wouldn't he have—

I balked. *Why wouldn't he have told me? Ha! As if.* I was not on the police force. I was not his confidante. Summers wanted me to butt out. On the other hand, he had listened to my theory about Logan Langford at Emily's house.

"Call him," Meaghan said.

"Who? Detective Summers?"

"Logan. Ask him to tea."

I glanced at Meaghan, expecting to see Fiona dousing her with fairy dust. No such luck. "Oh, sure. Ask him to tea and grill him about his alibi. Are you nuts?" Although I had done the same with Gregory Darvell. Not cool.

"Be bold," my pal said. "Isn't that on your ways-to-improve-myself list?" She knuckled my shoulder. "Contact him and ask him to discuss the lease. Tell him you've heard rumors about him selling the courtyard, and you want to put your mind at ease. That should make him sympathetic."

I plopped onto the desk chair, my happy mood fizzling. "Why me? Why not you? You're half owner of Flair."

"Ziggy makes all the business decisions. I supply the creative juices." She perched on the corner of the desk. "C'mon. You're strong and courageous."

"Flattery will get you nowhere. Go." I aimed a finger at the exit. "Get out of here."

In the doorway, she said, "Yvanna told me Logan will be at the bakery at noon to pick up a cake."

I arched an eyebrow. "So you've already spoken to Yvanna about this?"

She crossed her fingers. "We're like best buds."

"You mean you're both lily-livered chickens."

Meaghan cackled and breezed out the door.

★ ★ ★

Around noon, when there was a lull in customer traffic, I took a stroll through the courtyard and stopped in front of Sweet Treats. As promised, Logan Langford was inside by the register. The chimes above the door jangled as I entered.

There were no customers other than Logan in line, although all three of the retro-pink stools were occupied at the pink counter. Yvanna, dressed in her uniform of pink hat and apron over white dress, was behind the glass display case.

"Hey, Logan," I said, "fancy seeing you here."

"Hello, Courtney. What're you purchasing?"

"I have a hankering for something new to serve at the tea this weekend. Yvanna is our weekend baker. What are you buying?"

"That." He pointed to the three-tiered chocolate cream birthday cake Yvanna was setting in a white box. "It's for my nephew."

"How nice. How old is he?"

"Twenty-eight."

I gaped. "And he still celebrates?"

"The whole family does."

Silence fell between us. *Be bold,* I imagined Fiona and Meaghan chanting.

Drawing in a deep breath, I said, "Yvanna, will you please deliver a half dozen of your double chocolate chip cookies to the shop? And Logan, when you're done here, come over so we can talk about the lease. I've got a lot of tea selections. You're a tea guy, right?" I didn't wait for a response from him. My suggestion was direct, leaving little room for a *no.*

In the shop, I fetched some pretty floral napkins and set up a table on the patio. There were plenty of customers around. I could chat with a possible murderer and still be safe.

Logan strolled in moments later carrying a decorative

Sweet Treats bag, his cake box tucked inside. I asked Joss to bring in tea and showed Logan to our table.

He set the bag beside his chair and took a seat. "What's up?"

Joss arrived with a tea caddy and a teapot filled with hot water. She set both on the table and moved away. Logan selected chamomile tea. I chose Earl Grey.

As our teas steeped, I said, "I don't know much about your family other than that you have a number of children, eleven grandchildren, and a few nieces and nephews." Yes, I knew more. It was a small lie; I could sleep well at night. "Any deep dark secrets?"

Logan sat taller. His gaze narrowed. "I thought you wanted to talk about your lease."

"Here you go." Joss returned with a plate of the cookies I'd ordered from Yvanna. "Enjoy." She moseyed away.

I took a cookie. Logan didn't.

"Why are you prying, Courtney?" he asked.

"You haven't started one of the fairy gardens you promised to make, Logan. I thought if I knew more about you, I could help you come up with a few ideas." I bit into my cookie. "*Mmm.* These are great." I stirred my tea. "Did you hear Emily Watkins was attacked in her home last night?"

"No." Logan looked sincerely shocked. "Is she okay?"

"She's in the hospital."

"I'll send flowers. Do the police know who did it or why?"

"Not yet. It might have had something to do with Mick. It turns out he was writing a book—a thriller—about a wealthy man with a secret. It's possible whoever attacked Emily might have wanted to steal Mick's notes." I was flying by the seat of my pants. Summers hadn't bought that theory. "To keep the secret buried."

"It wasn't me." Logan stabbed the table with a fingertip. "The Langfords have a long, proud history in this town. No secrets. No skeletons in the closet."

"Good to know." I polished off the cookie. "But you are in debt, aren't you? Is a lender gouging you? Is that why you're thinking of selling this courtyard?"

Logan took a sip of his tea. "What have you heard?"

"Sources say you plan to oust all the tenants. You started with Mick, except he wouldn't budge."

"Now wait just a minute. I get what you're implying, but you're wrong. I wanted him out because I didn't—" Logan set his cup down with a *clack*. "I *don't* like his business. I'm not a pet person, unlike everyone else in Carmel."

"Why did you rent to him then?"

"Because I needed tenants, and he was the first to climb on board. Plus, his credit score was excellent."

I ran a finger around the rim of my teacup. "Who is the young man who drives a green BMW?"

He narrowed his gaze. "Why have you been spying on me?"

"Because you stole into my shop the other night."

"I did no such—"

"Don't deny it. I was there. In the dark." I sipped my tea. "Were you contemplating whether to trash it? Did you think you could intimidate me into canceling my lease?"

His face paled and shoulders slumped. "Yes, but I realized if I did, the developer might not buy the property, thinking it had bad karma. So I left."

"Uh-uh. You ran out. You got spooked."

"I didn't—"

"You yelled, 'Ghost!'"

His shoulders sagged. "I saw . . ." He jammed his lips together.

"You saw what?" I asked, goading him.

"Nothing."

"If you didn't kill Mick, why lie about your alibi?" I leaned forward. "And don't deny that, either. Oh, sure, you went to church. For one hour. Your time after that is unaccounted for."

"I lied because I was scared. You and others heard me arguing with Mick. I had motive." He heaved a sigh and smoothed his thinning hair. "As for my real alibi? I was walking. On the beach. Alone. Trying to figure out what to do." He folded his arms on the table. "Yes, I am in debt, big debt, because I made a promise to cover each of my grandchildren's college tuitions for a year. I never dreamed there would be eleven. My grandfather put my siblings and me through college. Knowing I would run low on funds, I tried day-trading to augment my income, but I stunk at it. I lost big time. I borrowed—"

"From a usurer."

Logan nodded. "He's the one who's gouging me. So, yes, I reached out to a developer. Selling one of the complexes would alleviate the problem. The developer is the one who wants all the tenants out. I started by pressing Mick, but—"

"The young man in the BMW," I said, cutting him off. "He's the developer? He was acting pretty shady. What was the secret handshake you shared?"

Logan smirked. "He's not the developer. He's my nephew. The one with the birthday. And the handshake was a fraternity handshake. He's a Theta Chi, like me." His eyes pooled with tears. "He's a Silicon Valley whiz kid worth a few million dollars. He has agreed to bail me out."

"'Langfords don't quit; Langfords don't fail,'" I quoted.

"That's our motto. Thanks to him, I can pay off my debt and won't need to sell to the developer, so I'm not kicking out any of the courtyard tenants." He sat taller, poised for another attack.

"You should talk to the police. I would imagine they know by now that your alibi is a sham."

"I will." Logan rose to his feet and picked up his bakery bag. "For the trouble I've caused you, I'll give you one month's rent free."

"I'd appreciate that."

As he trudged out of the shop, I wondered who had killed Mick. If not Logan and not Gregory Darvell . . .

Again I questioned whether Emily had whacked herself with the salt lamp to make it seem like she was a victim and not a killer. I considered Isabella Acosta, too. Would her friend have lied to provide an alibi? And what about Petra Pauli? Emily had written her saying she *knew her secret* in an effort to coerce her to leave town. Petra hadn't left. Did sticking around exonerate her of Mick's murder?

Chapter 23

For a fairy, as for humans, a book is worth more than gold.
—Daryl Wood Gerber

At two in the afternoon, a pair of middle-aged men from the security company showed up. One was nearly seven feet tall with Marine-trimmed hair. The other was shorter and scruffier. They had the specs for what they needed to accomplish and said they would start with the main showroom. I mentioned adding the bolt to the secret door on the patio.

No problem.

"It won't be messy," the taller one said. "You signed up for the wireless system. We'll be in and out of your hair by end of day."

Despite his assurances, I wanted to move some of our products from the showroom to the patio so customers could continue to browse. Joss was on board, but we needed more helpers. I called Meaghan. She showed up as the workmen were laying out their equipment.

Quickly, I circled the shop and apologized to customers

for the inconvenience. As everyone migrated to the patio, Joss, Meaghan, and I transferred items: tea sets and wind chimes, aprons and garden tools. When I grabbed a few of the macramé plant hangers, I balked. Holding the rough hemp in my hand made me flash on Mick. If only the police could figure out what had made the mark on his neck.

Due to the bustle, Pixie decided a safe spot was lying on one of the chairs on the patio. A customer with a calico set her cat on a nearby chair. Pixie raised her head, noting the intruder, and went back to sleep.

As I was organizing the learning-the-craft corner, Fiona whooshed into view. "Courtney, what's going on?"

Quietly, I told her about the disruption due to security installation. "Where have you been?"

"Were you worried? Did you think I'd abandoned you?"

"I wasn't sure. I don't know everything there is to know about fairies."

"Tosh." She flitted back and forth. "I won't leave you. You're mine, and I'm yours. Bonded for life. Soul mates." She stopped midair and folded her arms, nodding. "That has a good ring to it, doesn't it?"

"For a mushy romantic card," I joked.

Pixie stirred and scampered to my side. On her hind legs she reached for Fiona. The fairy swooped in front of Pixie's paws but didn't let her nab her. She giggled.

I held out a hand, inviting Fiona to light. She did. Pixie settled by my feet. "So, where were you?"

"At the library. Sleuthing."

"Again with the *sleuthing*."

"I was pursuing righteousness."

"Courtney." Miss Reade rushed through the doorway from the main showroom and hurried to me, pinning the tails of her aqua cashmere shawl to her chest so it wouldn't fly away. "Hello, love." She came to a stop and smoothed her skirt. Sotto voce, she said, "I've so enjoyed meeting Fiona and spending time with her. She is a breath of fresh air."

I gawped at Miss Reade. "You can see her?"

"As I hinted the other day, I am a visionary like my grandmother and I possess a childlike spirit." She beamed. "I particularly like Fiona's acrobatics. She's quite agile."

A flicker of something zoomed into view. Another fairy, larger and older than Fiona, drifted beside Miss Reade's head, her sizeable adult wings holding her aloft with ease. "May I introduce myself?" she asked in a lusty timber. "I'm Merryweather Rose of Song."

Miss Reade said, "Courtney, this is my library fairy. She's a guardian fairy and can be a bit of a rules follower."

"More of a rules enforcer," Fiona tittered. "She's my mentor."

"Rules create balance in the universe," the elder fairy said with all seriousness. She faced me and smiled an infectious grin. "You're just as Fiona described." Like Fiona, she had iridescent gossamer hair that glimmered in the light. Unlike Fiona, her cheeks were plump, her loose-fitting dress was a regal crimson, and one set of her wings sported matching polka dots.

Miss Reade said, "Readers need guidance. Cultivating the mind doesn't happen of its own accord. The young are particularly susceptible. Merryweather inspires writers of all ages."

Fiona did a somersault in the air. Was she trying to get my attention?

Merryweather tsked. "Did Fiona tell you I'm helping a local author do research for a new book?"

"We haven't gotten around to that, yet." I smiled.

"Eudora Cash," Fiona exclaimed.

I gazed at her. "Brady's mother?"

"Yes." Fiona batted her wings impatiently. "Merryweather, may I tell her the rest? Please?"

Merryweather nodded. "Go ahead."

"So I went to the library from Emily Watkins's house because, well, after seeing *The Artist's Way* and the cards that fell out of it, I had a feeling."

Customers were roving the patio. None appeared to notice our animated conversation. Meaghan and Joss were standing in the doorway, their backs to us. I presumed they were watching the security guys with an eagle eye even though the company was bonded.

Fiona went on. "When you said Mick's notes were about a wealthy guy having a secret, I knew who I needed to contact. Merryweather. Who better to dig up a hidden secret in Carmel? A guardian fairy is supersmart and very organized. At my suggestion, she and I started with Logan Langford because you mentioned his name."

Merryweather said, "His family has an extensive history in Carmel."

"But he's not the killer," I said. "I spoke with him. He was secretly in debt and worried about disgracing his family, but he had no reason to kill Mick. He's found someone to bail him out."

"You mean his nephew," Fiona said.

"Yes, how did you—"

"Many of his family are regulars at the library." Merryweather gestured to Miss Reade. "Your turn."

Miss Reade said, "Do you realize that some writers use special tools to write a story?"

"I'm sure they do. Outlines and such."

"Yes, well, I was chatting with Eudora—*Dory*; she comes in daily—and she mentioned that writers often write about someone they know, but"—Miss Reade held up a finger— "in order to disguise their inspiration, they change the sex of a character so the person will never guess whether he or she was the basis for it."

Fiona clapped. "What if the wealthy *man* was really a wealthy *woman?*"

Merryweather's eyes gleamed with delight. "And what if that woman had a sealed record from her teenage years?"

Fiona giggled with glee. "We checked. She does."

I said, "Who?"

"Wait for it," Fiona cried.

Miss Reade said, "We stumbled upon it because Eudora—*Dory*—is writing a story set thirty years ago. She's been poring over historical documents at the library, in paper as well as using our online archives, in an effort to create a few characters for her book. As I said, Dory and I were chatting earlier, and she mentioned a particular local woman, close to Mick Watkins, who has a sealed record."

"Who?" I asked.

"Petra Pauli."

I gasped. Had Mick tucked the business card into his workbook on purpose? As a clue? "Hold on." I shook my head. "A sealed document doesn't tell us much. Petra could have done something as benign as keying a high school rival's car."

Fiona snapped her fingers. "Remember Emily telling us that she sent notes to Petra saying she knew her secret?"

"If you'll recall, Petra didn't react," I countered. "She didn't leave town. It's a nothing burger."

Joss and Meaghan joined our little circle.

"What's a nothing burger?" Joss asked.

Meaghan said, "Is there a fairy here, Courtney? You and Miss Reade are doing a lot of listening." She gazed toward the skylight.

"Two," I said.

My pal blinked.

I clasped her hand and held a finger to my lips. "Go on, Miss Reade."

The librarian lowered her voice. "What if Petra did something truly horrible?"

I filled Meaghan and Joss in quickly about discovering Petra Pauli had a sealed record.

"If she did something horrible and the truth came out," Joss said, "it could ruin her political future."

"What if Mick knew the secret and threatened to expose it?" Fiona asked.

Meaghan echoed Fiona's question. Had she heard Fiona or intuited her?

"People confess to things when in love," Miss Reade said. "It happens all the time in novels."

"What if the letters Emily sent made Petra lash out at Mick?" I suggested.

"Which letters?" Meaghan asked.

I explained. "Emily didn't know Petra's secret, of course. She was vamping. She hoped the threat would scare Petra out of town."

"Does Petra have an alibi for the night of Mick's murder?" Joss asked.

"She claims she was at a political meeting that no one will corroborate because it was secret."

Fiona blew a raspberry.

"I spoke with Oriana Gray, who knew of the meeting, but she didn't attend." I turned to Miss Reade. "Could I see the files Eudora Cash was researching?"

"Of course."

"Eudora Cash?" Joss cried. "I love her books. Where is she? At the library? Right now?"

"She's gone home," Miss Reade said.

I asked Joss to watch the store and hurried off with Miss Reade, Fiona, and Merryweather. Meaghan, unable to see or hear either fairy but clearly intrigued, trailed us.

On the way, I received a text message. From Gregory

Darvell. Emily was being released from the hospital, which gave me pause. If she was being released so soon, perhaps, as I'd wondered before, her assault had been staged and she hadn't suffered a concussion.

Get real, Courtney.

Grasping that I had trust issues, I added seeing a therapist to my ways-to-improve-myself list.

Chapter 24

❧❦❧

No child but must remember laying his head in the grass,
staring into the infinitesimal forest and seeing it grow populous
with fairy armies.
—Robert Louis Stevenson, *Essays in the Art of Writing*

Harrison Memorial Library was located at Ocean Avenue and Lincoln Street and open Tuesday to Friday in the afternoons. It was a great place for people of all ages. For kids, they had story time, craft time, baby and toddler time, and preschool yoga. They even offered a drawing class for tweens. Busy minds were happy minds.

Though the library wasn't huge, it had a terrific collection of books, including fiction and nonfiction as well as a variety of cookbooks, e-books, audiobooks, and movies. In addition, it featured the history of Carmel through photographs, letters, diaries, maps, and yearbooks as well as works of art. Because the library couldn't house everything on site, it worked hard to provide links to television shows, movies, and magazines related to the area. *Play Misty for Me,* the Clint Eastwood thriller filmed in Carmel, was a popular search target.

As Miss Reade had forewarned, Eudora Cash was not present. She had wrapped up her research and headed home. But the documents she'd been browsing were stacked on a cart, ready to be returned to the appropriate locations—books, reels of microfiche featuring newspaper articles, and yearbooks ranging from the 1980s to the 1990s. Eudora had inserted the library's bookmarks into the books and yearbooks, and she had attached sticky notes with her notations on the microfiche reels.

"Aw, Dory," Miss Reade *tsk*ed. "Sometimes she's like the absent-minded professor. She never remembers to remove her memos. We have to do it for her."

Meaghan read from the sticky notes: "Petra at debate event. Petra cheerleading at football game. Petra on student council. She sure was busy excelling."

"Like her father," Miss Reade added. "The congressman was a go-getter. He died too young. Heart failure."

"So Petra became an overachiever to honor him," I said, understanding better than most how a daughter tried to please a parent.

"What does it take to open a sealed record if it hasn't been expunged?" Meaghan asked.

"A court order," Miss Reade said.

Merryweather and Fiona hovered above a yearbook. Their combined fluttering was creating a bit of a stir. With a shake of her wand, Merryweather doused the yearbook with fairy dust. The book opened.

Meaghan *eek*ed. "What the—"

I placed a hand on her arm. "Be cool."

"The book opened of its own accord, and"—she wiggled a finger—"I see something glimmering."

"Merryweather," Fiona cried. "Stop. Right there. Look."

Merryweather caused the pages to fall, landing on a picture of Petra in a cheerleading outfit. Her face was tear-stained, her mouth downturned.

"What do you think happened?" Meaghan asked.

"Maybe her team lost the game," I said.

"She looks like she's mourning," Fiona whispered.

"Mourning?" I asked. "You can read that on her face?"

"Notice her eyes." Fiona flicked her fingers beside her own. "They're vacant. The queen fairy told me that mourners often go away emotionally to a far place."

I must have looked the same when my mother died. I said, "Miss Reade, could we see correlating photographs and articles pertaining to this year, as well as obituaries?"

It took her about ten minutes to amass printed pieces of material. Meaghan and I laid them out on a rectangular table, side by side.

"Stop!" Fiona and I cried at the same time. "That one." She fluttered above the article in question.

"Is that a funeral?" Merryweather asked.

The child of a neighbor of Congressman Pauli's had died in a hit-and-run car crash.

"Oh, my." Miss Reade leaned in, scanning the article over our shoulders. "Look at the date."

"What about it?" I asked.

"Congressman Pauli died the next day."

"The sealed record," I said. "What if Petra drove the car that caused the crash?"

Meaghan nodded.

Had Petra's father disposed of the car and suffered a fatal heart attack after trying to hide his daughter's guilt? Was her mother able to seal Petra's record due to her age? Did Petra fear that if this information came out now her career would be destroyed?

"Courtney, look at this." Meaghan tapped another photograph.

I examined it and exhaled softly.

Three teenagers, arm in arm, dressed in matching T-shirts and jeans. Petra with her sweeping curls. Isabella Acosta, zaftig and happy, a complete one-eighty from the gaunt, uptight woman she was now. And Emily Watkins, her horsey face prettier in youth.

"And this." Fiona alit on another photograph.

All three girls. At the funeral. Clad in black and looking numb.

Miss Reade whispered, "Did you ever see that movie *I Know What You Did Last Summer*?"

"I did," Meaghan said solemnly. "It was so scary and sad. Dear friends bound by a tragic past."

Petra, Isabella, and Emily weren't friends now. This moment in time must have been the turning point.

Meaghan took notes, and I photographed the documents, after which I sent an email with attachments to Detective Summers, outlining what we'd learned. He probably wouldn't appreciate my help, but I didn't care. I was doing my citizenly duty.

Promising to keep Meaghan in the loop, I hurried with Fiona to the shop. The security workmen were leaving Open Your Imagination as we arrived.

"Courtney," a woman called. Petra Pauli, dressed to the nines, her hair in an updo with a few tendrils, trotted out of Wizard of Paws with her collies in tow and hurried toward me. "Sonja told me about Emily. I can't believe she's in the hospital."

I eyed the dogs' leashes and gulped. Hard. The other day, I'd noticed that they were slip-style, but it hadn't registered that they were made of rope.

Fiona must have sensed my discovery. "Ask her in for tea," she suggested.

My mouth went dry. I couldn't find the words.

"How horrible for her to be attacked in her home,"

Petra went on, looking truly concerned. "What is this world coming to?"

If I hadn't mistrusted Petra and if I hadn't seen her squabble with Emily at the council meeting, I'd have thought she was sincere. Boy, politicians could lie with ease.

Fiona orbited Petra, sprinkling her with fairy dust. "As you very well know, I can't make her tell the truth, but I can make her talk."

Petra blinked. A bit of dust caught her dogs. Zeus, the feisty one, looked up at Fiona and yipped.

"Hush, you brute," Petra said. "Courtney, how about a cup of tea? Let's chat. You must be shaken, having found Emily." She handed me the dogs' leashes and hurried ahead of me into Open Your Imagination. "Coming?" she asked over her shoulder.

I caught a whiff of her as she passed. "What is that scent you're wearing?"

"Thymes Vanilla Blanc. It's made with Madagascar vanilla and amber wood. Don't you love it? It's so subtle."

Not subtle enough, I mused. Before passing out, Emily must have caught of whiff of Petra's perfume.

As we entered the shop, Joss screwed up her mouth. She wanted to ask me something, but I gave her a silent warning to wait a few minutes. I handed off the dogs to her and filled two Wedgwood Hibiscus cups with hot water. I grabbed the tea caddy and led Petra to the patio. We chose a table close to the ficus trees. Fiona perched on the rim of the tea caddy, sitting cross-legged, her elbows braced on her knees. Joss brought the dogs out and ordered them to sit. They did. She released their leases, said, "Call me if you need me, Courtney," and returned inside.

A few customers passed our table, carrying their purchases into the shop. After they left, the patio was empty, save for us.

The dogs hunkered down on the slate floor and closed their eyes.

As our tea steeped, Petra said, "Tell me what happened. How did you find Emily? How did you know to look at her house?"

"Gregory was worried."

"Gregory Darvell?"

I nodded. "He'd called her repeatedly. He'd hoped to meet her for coffee after a training session. She didn't respond. Gregory and I hurried to her house. We found her on the floor. She'd been struck with a salt lamp."

Petra uttered a soft moan. "I think everyone has one of those nowadays. Supposedly they can clean the air in your home and help you sleep." She removed her tea bag and set it on the saucer. "Sonja said Emily's house had been torn apart."

"Not exactly torn apart, but definitely rummaged through. Whoever attacked her wanted to find something."

"And did they?" Petra added sugar to her tea and stirred with a spoon.

"I'm not sure. When we searched for what might be missing, we discovered a workbook that Mick had been using to inspire him to write a thriller."

"Aw, how nice. Mick told me he was going to try." Petra set her spoon on the china saucer. "He said he was keeping a diary with his notes. I told him I thought that was cute. Men don't usually keep diaries. Did you find that, too?"

"The workbook is a sort of diary."

"Really?" Petra blinked rapidly, a clear sign that she'd gone to the house to look for the diary. I'd bet she'd searched for the old-fashioned kind fitted with a lock and key.

"Busted," Fiona said sarcastically.

I said, "Mick's notes suggested he was writing a book about a wealthy man with a secret."

"How sad that he won't get the chance to finish it," Petra said.

"Did you know that an author will often change the sex of a character so the person the writer is basing the character on won't realize it's them?"

"Fascinating."

I folded my hands, hoping she'd blurt out her confession. She didn't. After a long moment, I said, "Do you have a secret, Petra?"

"Me? Heavens no."

"Try the tactic she used earlier," Fiona suggested.

I shook my head, not understanding.

"Frame her. Say someone saw her driving near Emily's house."

I cleared my throat. "By the way, a witness claims to have seen your Mercedes in Emily's neighborhood."

"That's not possible. I was—" Petra hesitated. "I was at a meeting."

"You sure do have a lot of meetings."

"Yes, I do."

"I repeat, do you have a secret, Petra?"

She nudged her teacup away. "What are you implying, Courtney?"

"Your business card was wedged into the workbook along with some notecards."

"Because he and I were paramours."

"I'm sure Mick had your phone number memorized. He didn't need to keep a card as a reminder."

She fanned the air. "I assure you he wasn't writing about me. I have no secrets."

I leaned forward and rested my elbows on the table. Zeus raised his head. Rather than upset him, I sat back. "Speaking of books, I was in the library earlier. The author Eudora Cash was doing research for her new manuscript."

"I'm not familiar with her writing."

"She's a very popular historical fiction author. For her current novel, she decided to focus on events that occurred thirty years ago in Carmel-by-the-Sea."

"Thirty years doesn't sound very historical."

"Anything that isn't set in the present falls into that category. Lo and behold, Eudora Cash discovered something about you."

"Me?" Petra propped an elbow on the table and rested her chin on her palm, the epitome of casual. "Do tell."

"When you were a teenager, you did something criminal. Your record was sealed."

Petra glanced at her watch. "Oh, my, I have an appointment. We'll chat later." She started to rise.

Fiona splashed her with more fairy dust. Petra sat down. Her mouth opened and closed. No words came out.

"A sealed record is a kind of secret," I said. "So I did a little digging."

"Why?"

"Because I'm curious. Isn't that how you described me to Isabella Acosta?"

"I never said—"

"Here's what I discovered," I continued. "I found a story about a child dying in a hit-and-run accident. She was your neighbor. There were photographs taken at the funeral. You were in one of them."

"I recall going to that. It was so tragic." Petra's eyes grew moist, but tears didn't fall. "She was such a sweet girl."

Wow, she was good.

"You were with two other girls in the photograph," I said. "Isabella and Emily. I had no idea you were contemporaries, let alone best buds."

"We *were* close. We aren't close anymore."

"You're still close to Isabella."

"Not true. We're acquaintances. We're not *close*." Her words had a bite to them.

"At the book club tea you looked pretty chummy."

"Dog owners unite," she said matter-of-factly, and raised her teacup to the light. Was she planning to crack it over my head and make a run for it?

I said, "Why was your record sealed?"

Petra set the teacup down and toyed with a tendril of hair.

"Did you accidentally kill the girl?" I asked. "Did Mick find out? Did he threaten to expose you? Did you kill him to keep it quiet?"

"I didn't kill him. I loved—"

"Petra!" a woman screamed.

Startled, Fiona catapulted into the air.

Emily burst onto the patio. Her face was hot pink and beaded with perspiration. She must have come straight from the hospital. She was still wearing the admission band on her wrist. She shook her fist at Petra. "Why did you attack me?"

Joss followed at Emily's heels. "I couldn't stop her, Courtney."

I hopped to my feet. "Emily, how are you feeling?" I peered past her to see if Gregory was nearby. He wasn't. She must have eluded him.

"Hold on, Em." Isabella Acosta charged onto the patio, out of breath. Via the window in her gallery, she must have spotted Emily entering the shop and hurried over. "I saw the text message you sent Petra. You were definitely out of line. How dare you call her a *slut*?"

Oho. That must have been what Petra and Isabella had been discussing the other day when I'd seen Petra stabbing her cell phone.

"Stay out of this, Bella," Emily hissed. Addressing Petra,

she said, "You hit me. You came into my house and cracked me over the head with a salt lamp, and then you rummaged through my things."

Petra frowned. "I don't know what you're talking about."

"Your vanilla scent. It's unmistakable."

Emily had known Petra was the culprit? She'd kept that tidbit from Gregory and me.

"Why did you attack me?" Emily persisted. "Why?"

"She wanted Mick's diary," I said. "*The Artist's Way*, to be specific, although she didn't realize that. She wanted whatever he'd written about her. As it turns out, she had a secret. When she received the anonymous letters you sent her, she must have thought *he* had sent the notes."

"You sent Petra anonymous letters?" Isabella exclaimed.

"You wrote them, Emily?" Petra squawked. "Why you—"

"Emily," I cut in. "Petra thought Mick was going to reveal her secret, so she killed him."

"No!" Petra pounded the table.

"You murdered my husband?" Tears sprang into Emily's eyes.

I said, "If her secret came out, it would hurt her chances for a future in politics."

"Why, Petra?" Emily asked. "Why did you choose him? You could have had anybody in town. You didn't love him."

"Yes, I did. We—"

"You should have kept your distance. We were happy until you came into his life." Emily sucked back a sob.

"Why did you send me letters?" Petra asked.

"To scare you. But you didn't take the bait. You didn't leave town. I didn't want to dredge up the memory, Petra, but I had to."

"The memory of the accident," I whispered.

"The accident," Isabella echoed.

Fiona fluttered over Isabella and sprinkled her with fairy dust.

Isabella sank into the chair beside Petra and shook her head. "Years ago, we were happy, the three of us," she intoned. "But the accident happened, and life turned dark."

"Bella, we vowed not to talk about it." Emily reached for her old friend.

Isabella wrapped her arms across her chest, wanting no part of Emily. "I devoted my life to honoring that poor girl. She loved to paint, so I put all my energy into providing more beauty to the world."

"What are you saying, Isabella?" I asked, slightly confused. "Were you the driver?"

"Yes."

"No, I was," Emily cried.

"Stop it, both of you." Petra shot to her feet. The dogs stirred. Fiona doused them with fairy dust and they settled down, but Petra didn't. She started to blink rapidly. "I was the driver," she cried. "I did it. Bella and Em were in the car, but it was my fault. I took my dad's car without asking. I was putting on makeup and looking in the rearview mirror at Emily. Not paying attention. The girl came out of nowhere. She was racing after a ball."

"The sound—" Emily's voice cracked.

"The *sound*," Isabella whispered.

Petra drew in a sharp breath. "I knew there was no saving her, so I sped away. I had to get my friends away from the scene. I confessed to my father that night. He was devastated. He . . ." She splayed her hands. "He drove the car to a dump and paid off the owner to demolish it. The next day . . . he died. His heart couldn't handle the pressure. I . . . I . . ." Her face pinched with pain. "A month later, the authorities found the compacted car, persuaded the dump's owner to confess to the bribe, and ultimately determined I was at fault. My mother held me responsible for my father's death and hated me for it, but she hired the best lawyer. My mother swore me to secrecy. If the truth got out about what I'd done, it would crush my sister's and brother's futures."

"And your own," Emily whispered.

"How did Mick play into this, Petra?" I asked gently.

"I divulged the truth to him one night in a moment of intimacy. A month later, Mick let slip that he was writing a thriller about a man with a secret. Soon after that, I started receiving threatening letters saying someone would expose my secret if I didn't leave town. I didn't want to believe it was Mick, but it had to be. I mean, I'd asked Isabella and Emily, and they both swore they hadn't uttered a word." She turned all her fury on Emily. "You lied."

"You stole my husband." Emily sank into a chair and tucked her hands between her knees.

Petra said, "When the third letter came, I lost it. Whether or not Mick ever finished his thriller, my secret was in his diary. If someone read it . . ." She shook her head. "I couldn't let that happen. I went to his house. He was climbing into his car. He didn't spot me, so I followed him. Here. I saw him enter through the secret door. I didn't know what he was up to, but I had to talk to him. I crawled in behind him."

"With your dogs," I repeated.

Fiona said, "That explains the dog hair at the crime scene."

"I couldn't leave them in my car," Petra said. "They'd yap. I caught Mick talking out loud, asking for a fairy to reveal itself. There were no fairies. He was nuts."

Fiona uttered, *"Pfft."*

"I confronted him about the letters," Petra continued. "He denied sending them. I called him a liar and shoved him. Hard. He fell back and . . ." She trembled.

"Hit his head on the fountain," I finished.

She nodded. "He collapsed to the ground. My dogs raced to him and mewled. He didn't rouse. He was dead."

"Why did you strangle him?"

"I . . . I needed it to look like someone else had killed him. Someone stronger."

"Like Gregory Darvell?" I asked. "Is that why you used one of your dog's leashes?"

"I'd seen Gregory earlier in the day. It seemed . . . reasonable. Mick and he . . . didn't get along."

"And then you lied and said Oriana Gray had seen Gregory in Mick's neighborhood, to make it seem that he was the one who had followed Mick here."

Petra didn't deny it.

"You opened the front door to confuse the police about how you got in," I went on, "and then fled through the secret door with the dogs. Nobody saw you."

Emily licked her lips. "Petra, I'm sorry I sent the letters. I never would have told anyone your secret. Ever. Mick, either. He did love you. He told me earlier that night that he was going to leave me. I went to the Equestrian Inn to ponder my options, but I couldn't stand it. I returned to have it out with him. Except he was gone. I think he hoped that a fairy might give him the blessing to leave me. He loved *you*."

Petra keened like a wounded animal. Isabella wept softly. Emily wrapped her arms around her body and rocked.

I regarded all three women, broken to the core. One mistake had led to another. Sadly, there was no way to turn back time.

Chapter 25

Every time a child says, "I don't believe in fairies," there is a fairy somewhere that falls down dead.
—J. M. Barrie, *Peter Pan*

While Isabella and Emily consoled Petra—yes, Emily comforted her, even knowing Petra had killed her husband—I called Detective Summers. He arrived within minutes. Officer Rodriguez didn't accompany him. Summers had received my email with attachments, so he was on board with Petra's history. I explained what had happened after we returned to the shop. He didn't say a word. He didn't even remove his notepad and take notes.

When I finished, he said, "Where is she?"

"On the patio."

He passed through the doorway. I didn't follow, although I listened in. He read Petra her rights. She nodded numbly. When Summers escorted her out of the shop, Isabella and Emily went with them.

Joss hurried up to me. "Well, that was dramatic."

"Tell me about it."

Fiona flew to my shoulder. "We did it. We figured out who killed Mick. So guess what?" She flipped up her wings and showed me. Her adult wing buds were growing. "It's just a matter of time before they're full-grown. Only two more sets to go." She kissed me on the cheek and flew back to the patio.

Pixie was there to greet her.

A week later, as Meaghan and I were dining on the rear patio of Hideaway Café, our new favorite go-to place, I spied Summers entering with Rodriguez, holding hands.

I set down my zesty burger smothered in cheese and mushrooms, blotted my mouth with a napkin, and whispered, "*Psst*. Look over there." I signaled with the tines of my fork.

Someone grabbed my shoulders. "Boo!"

I craned my neck and glowered at Brady. "You scared me." I eagle-eyed Meaghan. "You could have warned me he was sneaking up."

She laughed. "Not on a bet."

"What were you two staring at before I so rudely interrupted you?" Brady perched on one of the empty chairs.

I hitched my head in Summers's direction. "I had a hunch they were an item."

"Not officially until now," Brady said. "Rodriguez is quitting the force."

"Why?"

"She didn't like dealing with a homicide. Art theft was more her speed. She's joining the private sector. Now the two of them can freely date."

"Aren't you the gossip maven?" I joked. "Tell me, since you know everything about everyone in town, do you know why Summers and my landlord are at odds?"

Brady grinned. "As a matter of fact, I do, but only because my father clued me in. What's your guess?"

"I figure Summers's father tried to outbid Logan's father for a property or they vied for the same woman. Am I close?"

"You're warm." Brady leaned forward, propping both elbows on the table, and lowered his voice. "The two men went to school together. From kindergarten right through to business school."

"That's a lot of history."

"After graduation, Summers's father went into real estate like Logan's dad. And yes, they vied for the same properties—not the same woman. A couple of years later, Summers went behind old man Langford's back to negotiate a deal. He told lies about him, which poisoned the well. Langford accused him of stealing the property out from under him. As far as the elder Summers was concerned, it was a fair fight. The Langfords always got what they wanted, and dirty dealing was the only way to get what he wanted."

"No duel?" Meaghan asked.

"No duel, but plenty of animosity. Dylan Summers is nothing like his father. He believes honesty is the best policy, a boy scout is bound by his honor, and, at all times, he should do the right thing." Brady twirled a hand. "His father passed away years ago, but his father's reputation has been a sore spot for Dylan."

"Thanks for the insight."

Brady patted the table and stood. "I've got to get back to work. Courtney, remember you promised to find time to talk shop. I'm going to hold you to that promise. You've got my number."

"Actually, I don't."

He pulled a business card from his pocket and set it on the table. "Now you do."

As he strutted away, Meaghan flicked my arm with a finger. "*Talk shop?*"

"Photography."

She chuckled. "Don't blow this. Call him. Sooner rather than later. You two have chemistry."

Knowing she wouldn't let up if I didn't, I agreed.

"So fill me in on everyone else," she said. "I know Logan extended your lease, like he did for the rest of us, and I heard Emily Watkins is selling the grooming business to Sonja."

I nodded. "Emily doesn't want to run it. She wants to focus on her dog and horses. I think she's going to invest in a stable."

"Is it true she's dating Gregory Darvell?" Meaghan polished off her burger.

"We'll have to see how that works out. I think he's in love with her dog, not Emily. She's got baggage."

"Don't we all?"

When I returned to the shop, Joss was showing a thin, dark-haired woman around. The woman turned, and I gawped. Tish Waterman. In my shop. She wasn't throwing a fit, and she wasn't wearing black. In fact, she was dressed in a frilly pink dress and looking quite relaxed as she inspected a Villeroy & Boch teacup.

I strode to her. "How lovely to see you here, Tish."

She smiled. Radiantly. "It's nice to see you, too. I got your message about going to tea." Not only had she changed her appearance, but her voice was kinder and her gaze softer. "I would love to."

I jolted. Had I heard her right? What had happened to the old Tish? I glanced past her and spied a whirlwind of glittery energy. As the flurry settled, I made out Fiona dancing in a circle overhead.

"I adore the Tuck Box," Tish added. "I haven't been in years. It will be fun."

"Fun," I murmured.

Fiona whizzed to me and landed on my shoulder. "I worked a little magic."

Tish didn't acknowledge Fiona, but she gazed directly into my eyes. "I know you've heard what happened to my daughter. Hedda Hopewell is a client of mine. She said you and she talked at the council meeting. When my daughter joined the cult, I started drinking gin. A lot of gin. I went through a terrible bout of self-pity and self-recrimination. One night, I fell in my garden"—she dragged a finger along her abraded cheek—"I grazed the stone wall and . . ." She hesitated. "And a fairy came to help me."

"A fairy?"

"I didn't want to believe it. I thought I was hallucinating. I stopped drinking that instant and blocked the incident from my mind. My scar was my reminder of a life ruined, and I turned inward and grim. But your sweet fairy wouldn't give up on me. Or so I hear. I haven't met her. She came to my garden and encouraged my nurturer fairy to try again."

"She did what?" I gawped.

"I wasn't socializing," Fiona stated, and held up a pinky. "I asked for permission from Merryweather."

"You have a nurturer fairy?" I asked Tish.

"Yes. I saw Zephyr three nights ago for the first time in ages. She was playing a flute. I'm quite partial to flute music." Tish grabbed my hands. Her cheeks glowed with positive energy. "Thank you. For believing. And for being persistent. Let's do tea next week. How about Wednesday afternoon?"

"S-sure," I stammered, still absorbing her transformation.

She squeezed my hands and hurried out of the shop.

As she left, Ulani Kamaka sashayed in. "Miss Kelly, do you have a moment?" She held out a newspaper to me.

I stiffened. "Is this an article about the murder? If so, I don't want to—"

"It's not." She looked at me shrewdly. "Yes, I wrote something, but the piece was turned down. Sharing ordinary news about Carmel is what I do best. I will drive in the proper lane from now on." She waved the newspaper. "As promised, I've written a rave review of your shop. It should help business soar."

Fiona flew in front of Ulani and waved at her. Ulani didn't blink. "She still can't see me," Fiona said. "Maybe someday. I'm off to a seminar. See you."

As Fiona took flight, Ulani glanced in her direction. She couldn't see her yet, I mused, but she was on the verge.

If only my father would be open to the possibility.

Recipes

From Courtney:

These sandwiches are pretty, and delicious, and so easy to make. The trick is to make sure the Brie is at room temperature. If you don't like Brie cheese, substitute cream cheese.

Brie and Strawberry Tea Sandwiches

(Yield: 6 full sandwiches; 24 quarter sandwiches)

12 slices thin white bread
8 ounces Brie cheese, softened at room temperature, rind
    removed
⅓ cup mayonnaise
½ teaspoon sugar
2-4 tablespoons finely chopped fresh basil
12 fresh strawberries, hulled and sliced
more basil leaves for garnish

Trim the crusts from all the slices of bread.

In a bowl, mix the Brie cheese with the mayonnaise, sugar, and basil.

Spread the Brie mixture thinly on all of the slices of bread. Top half of the slices with strawberries. Set the remaining bread slices on top. Cut into rectangles or triangles. If necessary, cover the sandwiches with a damp paper towel or store in a sealed container until needed. You don't want them to dry out. Garnish with additional basil.

From Brady:

The biggest trick to baking with caramel, my grandmother says, is to let the baked goods cool completely after baking. Wait, wait, wait. Two hours at minimum. Also make sure you don't overbake these blondies. Dry blondies are no fun.

Caramel Blondies

(Yield: 9 blondies)

2 cups flour
2 teaspoons baking powder
½ teaspoon salt
1 cup butter (2 sticks), melted and cooled a tad
1½ cups packed brown sugar
2 eggs
1 tablespoon vanilla extract
½ cup salted caramel sauce, prepared ahead, kept warm (see recipe below)
½ cup chopped pecans or cashews
fleur de sel

Preheat oven to 350 degrees F. Butter a 9 x 9-inch baking pan or spray with nonstick cooking spray. Set aside.

In a small bowl, mix the flour, baking powder, and salt. Set aside.

In a large bowl, cream together butter and sugar until light and fluffy. Add in eggs, vanilla, and flour mixture. Mix until well combined. Spread half of the mixture in the prepared baking pan and smooth.

Spread salted caramel onto the blondie batter using a tablespoon, leaving a bit of space around the edges. Top with the chopped nuts. Drop the remaining batter in spoonfuls over the caramel and spread with a spatula. Using a knife, swirl the blondie batter with the caramel. If desired, sprinkle with fleur de sel.

Bake 28–32 minutes until set in the middle and golden brown; a toothpick should come out clean. Do not overbake. Make sure you cool completely, at least 2 hours, before cutting into squares. If necessary, place in refrigerator for 30 minutes to help the caramel set.

For the Salted Caramel Sauce:
1 cup granulated sugar
¼ cup water
6 tablespoons salted butter, cut into chunks
½ cup heavy cream, at room temperature
1 teaspoon coarse sea salt

In a 3-quart saucepan, add the sugar and water and cook at medium heat. Stir until combined. Do NOT stir again. Heat the mixture until a candy thermometer reads 350 degrees F. Remove thermometer.

Carefully add the butter and whisk until butter is melted. Remove the pan from heat and slowly pour in the cream, whisking all the time until the cream is incorporated. Whisk in the sea salt and set aside to cool.

Allow to cool about 5 minutes, then store in an airtight container until ready to use. Refrigerate.

Caramel Blondies—Gluten-Free Version

(Yield: 9 blondies)

2 cups gluten-free flour
½ teaspoon xanthan gum
1 tablespoon whey powder
2 teaspoons baking powder
½ teaspoon salt
1 cup butter (2 sticks), melted and cooled a tad
1½ cups packed brown sugar
2 eggs
1 tablespoon vanilla extract
½ cup salted caramel sauce, prepared ahead, kept warm (see
    recipe above)
½ cup chopped pecans or cashews
fleur de sel

Preheat oven to 350 degrees F. Butter a 9 x 9-inch baking
pan or spray with nonstick cooking spray. Set aside.

In a small bowl, mix the gluten-free flour, xanthan gum,
whey powder, baking powder, and salt. Set aside.

In a large bowl, cream together butter and sugar until light
and fluffy. Add in eggs, vanilla, and gluten-free flour mixture.
Mix until well combined. Spread half of the mixture in the
prepared baking pan and smooth.

Spread salted caramel onto the blondie batter using a tablespoon, leaving a bit of space around the edges. Top with the
chopped nuts. Drop the remaining batter in spoonfuls over
the caramel and spread with a spatula. Using a knife, swirl the
blondie batter with the caramel. If desired, sprinkle with fleur
de sel.

Bake 28-32 minutes until set in the middle and golden brown; a toothpick should come out clean. Do not overbake. Make sure you cool completely, at least 2 hours, before cutting into squares. If necessary, place in refrigerator for 30 minutes to help the caramel set.

From Meaghan:

I've been making brownies all my life. This is one of my favorites. I stole the recipe from Hideaway Café. Brady said it was his grandmother's secret recipe, but let's face it—I'm a brownie expert. I could figure it out. It's possible she added a dash of cinnamon. I did not. By the way, Yvanna tells me that baking brownies gluten-free is one of the easiest things to do. Chocolate really helps with structure. So I made this gluten-free, too, and voilà—she was right. Enjoy.

Chocolate Caramel Brownies

(Yield: 15-20 brownies)

2 cups sugar
¾ cup baking cocoa (choose the best available)
1 cup canola oil
4 large eggs
¼ cup milk
1½ cups flour
1 teaspoon salt
1 teaspoon baking powder
1 cup semisweet chocolate chips
½ cup chopped pecans, if desired

For the caramel sauce:
⅔ cup granulated sugar
3 tablespoons water
4 tablespoons salted butter, cut into chunks
⅓ cup heavy cream, at room temperature

Preheat oven to 350 degrees F. Butter a 9 x 13-inch baking pan or spray with nonstick cooking spray. Set aside.

In a large bowl, beat the sugar, cocoa, oil, eggs, and milk.

In another bowl, combine the flour, salt, and baking powder.

Gradually add the flour mixture to the egg mixture until well blended. Fold in the chocolate chips and add the chopped pecans, if desired.

Spoon two-thirds (⅔) of the batter into the 9 x 13-inch baking pan. Bake for 12 minutes.

Meanwhile, make the caramel sauce.

In a 3-quart saucepan, add the sugar and water and cook at medium heat. Stir until combined. Do NOT stir again. Bring to a boil and let boil until a candy thermometer reads 350 degrees F. It takes a few minutes. Remove the thermometer. Carefully add the butter and whisk until butter is melted. Remove the pan from heat and slowly pour in the cream, stirring constantly with a wooden spoon until the cream is incorporated. You want the caramel to thicken up. If necessary, return to low heat and stir until thick. Set aside to cool.

Remove the partially baked brownies from the oven. Pour the melted caramel sauce over the brownies and spread evenly.

Add the remaining one-third (⅓) of the batter by spoonfuls over the caramel layer. Using a knife, swirl the caramel with the batter.

(Note: If you didn't use enough of the batter in the bottom portion, don't worry. You just have more brownie on the top. However, it won't swirl as well. If you want to make it perfectly, this means you'll have to eat this entire batch and make another. Poor you.)

Bake 35-40 minutes or until a toothpick inserted in the center comes out semi-clean. You don't want to overbake brownies. Ever.

Cool completely on a wire rack before cutting into squares.

Chocolate Caramel Brownies—Gluten-Free Version

(Yield: 15-20 brownies)

2 cups sugar
¾ cup baking cocoa (choose the best available)
1 cup canola oil
4 large eggs
¼ cup milk
1½ cups gluten-free flour (I used a sweet rice/tapioca
     mixture)
½ teaspoon xanthan gum
1 teaspoon salt
1 teaspoon baking powder
1 cup semisweet chocolate chips
½ cup chopped pecans, if desired

For the caramel sauce:
⅔ cup granulated sugar
3 tablespoons water
4 tablespoons salted butter, cut into chunks
⅓ cup heavy cream, at room temperature

Preheat oven to 350 degrees F. Butter a 9 x 13-inch baking pan or spray with nonstick cooking spray. Set aside.

In a large bowl, beat the sugar, cocoa, oil, eggs, and milk.

In another bowl, combine the gluten-free flour, xanthan gum, salt, and baking powder.

Gradually add the GF flour mixture to the egg mixture until well blended. Fold in the chocolate chips and add the chopped pecans, if desired.

Spoon two-thirds (⅔) of the batter into the 9 x 13-inch baking pan. Bake for 12 minutes.

Meanwhile, make the caramel sauce.

In a 3-quart saucepan, add the sugar and water and cook at medium heat. Stir until combined. Do NOT stir again. Bring to a boil and let boil until a candy thermometer reads 350 degrees F. It takes a few minutes. Remove the thermometer. Carefully add the butter and whisk until butter is melted. Remove the pan from heat and slowly pour in the cream, stirring constantly with a wooden spoon until the cream is incorporated. You want the caramel to thicken up. If necessary, return to low heat and stir until thick. Set aside to cool.

Remove the partially baked brownies from the oven. Pour the melted caramel sauce over the brownies and spread evenly.

Add the remaining one-third ($\frac{1}{3}$) of the batter by spoonfuls over the caramel layer. Using a knife, swirl the caramel with the batter.

(Note: If you didn't use enough of the batter in the bottom portion, don't worry. You just have more brownie on the top. However, it won't swirl as well. If you want to make it perfectly, this means you'll have to eat this entire batch and make another. Poor you.)

Bake 35-40 minutes or until a toothpick inserted in the center comes out semi-clean. You don't want to overbake brownies. Ever.

Cool completely on a wire rack before cutting into squares.

From Yvanna:

Coriander, the plant, is widely used in my culture's cooking. It is also known as Chinese parsley, the stems and leaves of which are known as cilantro. Most people think the leaves have a tart, lemony taste, but some people think cilantro takes like bath soap. The dried fruits of the parsley are known as coriander seeds. They also have a citrusy, warm, nutty, spicy flavor.

Coriander Cookies with Vanilla Icing

(Yield: 24-30 cookies)

For the cookies:
1 cup butter, softened
⅔ cup packed brown sugar
⅓ cup granulated sugar
2 eggs
2 cups flour
1 teaspoon ground coriander
1 teaspoon baking soda
1 teaspoon salt
1 teaspoon ground cinnamon

For the icing:
1½ cups confectioners' sugar
2 tablespoons water
white sparkling sugar

In a large bowl, cream butter, brown sugar, and granulated sugar. Add the eggs and mix well.

In another bowl, combine the flour, coriander, baking soda, salt, and cinnamon. Stir the flour mixture into the butter mixture.

Wrap the dough in plastic wrap. Refrigerate for about 30 minutes to make the dough firm.

Preheat oven to 375 degrees F. Prepare a baking sheet by covering with parchment paper.

Remove the dough from the refrigerator. Break off small pieces of the dough and roll each piece into a walnut-sized ball. Place dough balls 2 inches apart on the baking sheet.

Bake for 5 to 7 minutes, until golden. Remove the cookies from the oven and set on a rack to cool.

Meanwhile, make the frosting.

In a small bowl, mix the confectioners' sugar with water until smooth. When the cookies are cool, frost the cookies with icing and sprinkle with the sparkling sugar.

Note: If you don't frost them, these make great freezer cookies. Store in an airtight container and enjoy whenever you want a cookie.

From Courtney:

I adore this custard. It's so easy to make, and it's perfect by itself or paired with fresh strawberries or added to a trifle. The thing I need to remember when I make custard is to take things slowly when the recipe says slowly and remove the custard from heat when the recipe says to remove from heat. Custard can take command if I'm not careful.

Custard

(Yield: serves 4–8)

4 egg yolks at room temperature
4 teaspoons cornstarch
2 tablespoons sugar
2 cups whole milk
1 teaspoon vanilla extract

Add the egg yolks to a bowl and whisk in the cornstarch and sugar.

Pour the milk into a small saucepan, add the vanilla extract, and heat on medium until it is warm but *not hot!* You should be able to douse your finger.

Remove the milk from heat and pour it slowly into the egg mixture, stirring the whole time. Pour the egg and milk mixture back into the saucepan and, using a whisk, whisk constantly until it comes to a boil.

Once it's boiling, remove from heat and keep whisking until the custard thickens.

Serve immediately or transfer to a container to let the custard cool. I prefer the cool version. If cooling, remember to press a layer of plastic wrap on it so a skin won't form on top.

From Yvanna:

I had these little gems when I took a trip to New York and told Courtney about them. They are delicious and beautiful. Courtney wanted to serve them for her Saturday teas. Lavender and lavender extract are not found in typical stores. We had to special order these items. Whatever lavender flowers (petals) you have left over, feel free to use in sachets and such. I'm sharing a regular version as well as a gluten-free version. My sister needs to eat gluten-free, so she tested that one and loved it.

Lemon Cupcakes with Lavender Frosting

(Yield: 12–18 regular or 24–36 miniature cupcakes)

For the cupcakes:
6 tablespoons unsalted butter, softened
¾ cup sugar
6 tablespoons sour cream
½ teaspoon vanilla extract
1 tablespoon grated lemon zest
3 large egg whites, room temperature
1¼ cup flour
2 teaspoons baking powder
¼ teaspoon salt
¼ cup milk
1 tablespoon water
3 tablespoons fresh lemon juice

For the frosting:
1 cup unsalted butter
4 cups powdered sugar, more if needed

2-3 tablespoons milk
½ teaspoon vanilla extract
1¼ teaspoon lavender extract, more if desired

For decoration:
Lavender flower petals, dried
Lemon slices

Preheat the oven to 350 degrees F.

Set 12 regular or 24 miniature cupcake liners in a cupcake pan.

In a large mixing bowl, cream the butter and sugar until the color is light, about 2 minutes. Add the sour cream, vanilla extract, and lemon zest, and mix 1 minute.

In a small bowl, beat the egg whites to a froth, about 2 minutes. Add the egg whites to the sugar mixture and mix well until incorporated.

Combine the dry ingredients in a small bowl.

In another small bowl combine the milk, water, and lemon juice.

Add half of the dry ingredients to the butter-egg mixture. Mix well. Then add half of the wet ingredients. Mix well and repeat, stirring until all the ingredients are incorporated. This is a very light, almost foamy cupcake mixture.

Fill cupcake liners about ⅔ full.

Bake mini cupcakes for 13-15 minutes and regular cupcakes for 15-17 minutes or until a toothpick comes out clean.

For the icing:

In a small bowl, beat the butter until smooth. Add in half of the confectioner's sugar and mix until smooth. Add 2 tablespoons milk and the vanilla and lavender extracts and beat until smooth. Add the remainder of the confectioner's sugar.

If necessary, add more sugar or the remaining tablespoon of milk. This should not be a runny frosting.

Using a piping bag fitted with a closed star tip, pipe the frosting onto the cooled cupcakes. If desired, decorate with dried lavender petals and a half slice of lemon.

Lemon Cupcakes with Lavender Frosting—
Gluten-Free Version

(Yield: 12–18 regular or 24–36 miniature cupcakes)

For the cupcakes:
6 tablespoons unsalted butter, softened
¾ cup sugar
6 tablespoons sour cream
½ teaspoon vanilla extract
1 tablespoon grated lemon zest
3 large egg whites, room temperature
1¼ cup gluten-free flour
2 teaspoons whey powder or flour
½ teaspoon xanthan gum
2 teaspoons baking powder
¼ teaspoon salt
¼ cup milk
1 tablespoon water
3 tablespoons fresh lemon juice

For the frosting:
1 cup unsalted butter
4 cups powdered sugar, more if needed
2–3 tablespoons milk
½ teaspoon vanilla extract
1¼ teaspoon lavender extract, more if desired

For decoration:
lavender flower petals, dried
lemon slices

Preheat the oven to 350 degrees F.

Set 12 regular or 24 miniature cupcake liners in a cupcake pan.

In a large mixing bowl, cream the butter and sugar until the color is light, about 2 minutes. Add the sour cream, vanilla extract, and lemon zest, and mix 1 minute.

In a small bowl, beat the egg whites to a froth, about 2 minutes. Add the egg whites to the sugar mixture and mix well until incorporated.

Combine the gluten-free flour, whey powder (which makes gluten-free baked goods more moist), xanthan gum, baking powder, and salt in a small bowl.

In another small bowl combine the milk, water, and lemon juice.

Add half of the dry ingredients to the butter-egg mixture. Mix well. Then add half of the wet ingredients. Mix well and repeat, stirring until all the ingredients are incorporated. This is a very light, almost foamy cupcake mixture.

Fill cupcake liners about ⅔ full.

Bake mini cupcakes for 13-15 minutes and regular cupcakes for 15-17 minutes or until a toothpick comes out clean.

For the frosting:

In a small bowl, beat the butter until smooth. Add in half of the confectioner's sugar and mix until smooth. Add 2 tablespoons milk and the vanilla and lavender extracts and beat until smooth. Add the remainder of the confectioner's sugar. If necessary, add more sugar or the remaining tablespoon of milk. This should not be a runny frosting.

Using a piping bag fitted with a closed star tip, pipe the frosting onto the cooled cupcakes. If desired, decorate with dried lavender petals and a half slice of lemon.

From Courtney:

I love a good, hearty soup. I can make a batch and eat it every night of the week. When I come home and want to work in the garden, an easy meal is the perfect solution. If desired, add chopped chicken to this recipe. It becomes a meal in a pot.

Minestrone Soup

(Yield: serves 8-12)

3 cloves garlic, minced
1 cup yellow onion, chopped
2 tablespoons olive oil
1 cup celery, chopped
1 cup carrots, peeled and chopped
1 package frozen chopped spinach, thawed and drained
1 package frozen peas
1 16-ounce can red kidney beans
1 pound mushrooms (may omit)
2 16-ounce cans whole peeled tomatoes, crushed
1 16-ounce can tomato puree
5 cans of water, using the puree can for measurement
2 cups chicken broth
½ cup rice, uncooked (may use pasta; if so, add 1 cup dry
    pasta, like elbow macaroni)
½ cup chopped parsley
½ teaspoon ground thyme
½ teaspoon dried oregano
2-3 bay leaves
salt and pepper to taste

In a large stockpot, brown garlic and onions in olive oil. Cook for about 3 to 5 minutes.

Add everything else—yes, it's that easy!—and bring to a boil. Turn to simmer and cook for 2 hours.

From Meaghan:

Brownie is my last name. Therefore, all my life, I've been baking brownies. I felt it was my duty to my family and to my friends. I never had the desire to be a professional baker, but I have to admit, my brownies are pretty darned good. Add the semisweet chocolate chips if you like the peanut butter-chocolate combo. If you want to be decadent, use dark chocolate chips.

Peanut Butter Brownies

(Yield: 9–16 brownies)

½ cup peanut butter
⅓ cup butter, softened
⅔ cup granulated sugar
½ cup packed brown sugar
2 eggs
½ teaspoon vanilla extract
1 cup all-purpose flour
½ teaspoon baking powder
¼ teaspoon salt
⅔ cup semisweet chocolate chips, if desired

Preheat oven to 350 degrees F. Grease a 9 x 9-inch baking pan or spray with nonstick cooking spray. Set aside.

In a medium bowl, mix the peanut butter, softened butter, granulated sugar, and brown sugar. Add the eggs and vanilla and stir well.

In a medium bowl, mix the flour with the baking powder and salt. Add the flour mixture to the peanut butter mixture and stir until well combined.

Pour the batter into the prepared pan. You might need your fingers to press down and make it even. Sprinkle the chocolate chips on top, if desired.

Bake in the preheated oven for 30-35 minutes, until a toothpick comes out clean.

From Courtney:

I love scones. Sweet or savory. They're so satisfying. And they're quick to make. You can use any of your favorite herbs in this recipe. I like rosemary. These would go beautifully with the minestrone soup. Just saying.

Savory Herb Scones

(Yield: 8 scones)

2 cups flour
2 tablespoons granulated sugar
1 tablespoon baking powder
¾ teaspoon salt
2 tablespoons finely chopped fresh rosemary
6 tablespoons cold unsalted butter, cut into cubes
¾ cup heavy cream
2 large egg yolks, lightly beaten

For the glaze:
1 large egg, lightly beaten
1 tablespoon milk
½ teaspoon kosher salt for sprinkling

Preheat oven to 400 degrees F. Line a baking sheet with parchment paper.

In a food processor, whisk together the flour, sugar, baking powder, salt, and rosemary. Add in the butter and pulse until the largest pieces of butter are about the size of peas.

In a small bowl, mix the cream and egg yolks. Add the flour mixture and combine, using your hands to knead the mixture until the ingredients can be gathered into a moist ball. *Don't over knead.* The dough is supposed to be sticky.

Set the ball in the center of the parchment paper and pat it gently into a 7-inch round, about 1 inch thick.

With a sharp knife (you might want to wet it), cut the round into eight wedges. Separate them.

Make the glaze by mixing the egg and milk in a small bowl. Brush the tops and sides of the scones with the egg-milk glaze. Sprinkle the scones with salt.

Bake in preheated oven until the scones are a deep golden brown and a toothpick comes out clean, about 18-20 minutes.

Cool the scones on a wire rack for 10 minutes before serving.

From Courtney:

One of my favorite dinners is white fish with beurre blanc sauce. I've used lots of different white fish for this recipe. One of my favorites is Chilean sea bass, which is a fish rich in omega-3 unsaturated oils. It's mild and sort of buttery in flavor, and it won't toughen up because of the extra oil.

White Fish with Beurre Blanc Sauce

(Yield: serves 4)

olive oil
4 Chilean sea bass filets (or other white fish, about 6 ounces
    each)
kosher salt, to taste
black pepper, to taste
¼ cup dry white wine
1½ tablespoons white wine vinegar
1½ tablespoons shallots, minced
1 tablespoon lemon juice
1 teaspoon lemon zest
1 tablespoon heavy cream
6 tablespoons butter, cold, cut into small pieces

For the garnish: lemon wedges

Heat oven to 425 degrees F.

Line a 9 x 13-inch baking pan with parchment paper. Brush parchment paper with olive oil. Set the filets on the paper and sprinkle lightly with kosher salt and black pepper. Place the pan in the oven and bake for 15-20 minutes. The fish should be cooked through, not pink.

While the fish is baking, prepare the lemon *beurre blanc* sauce. In a saucepan, combine the white wine, vinegar, and minced shallots. Bring the mixture to a simmer and cook until reduced by half, about 3 minutes.

Add the lemon juice, zest, and cream. Remove the pan from heat and whisk in a pat of butter. Set the pan back over low heat and continue whisking until the butter has melted. Add remaining pieces of butter until all are incorporated. Taste and add salt and pepper, as needed.

Note: If the sauce is too hot or too cold, it will separate, so keep it warm until serving time.

Arrange the fish on plates with lemon wedges as garnish. Drizzle with the *beurre blanc* sauce.

Read on for a preview of the next Fairy Garden Mystery
from Daryl Wood Gerber

A Glimmer of a Clue

Coming in Summer 2021 from Kensington Publishing Corp.

Chapter 1

*Come, fairies, take me out of this dull world, for I would ride with
you upon the wind and dance upon the mountains like a flame!*
—William Butler Yeats

"That woman is going to be the death of me, Courtney."
Didi Dubois bustled from Open Your Imagination's main
showroom onto the slate patio where I was designing a fairy
garden.

I was standing at the rectangular table in the learning-the-
craft corner at the far end of the patio creating a fairy garden
using a three-foot tall, wide-mouthed blue glazed pot. I loved
spending time on the patio, an outdoor garden space with a
skylight in its pyramid-shaped roof. Good vibes radiated
everywhere.

"I swear her tongue is a dagger and her fingernails are
talons," Didi carried on.

With long strides, she made a beeline past the wrought-
iron tables and ornate fountain carved with fairies and gnomes
to the verdigris bakers' racks. Recently, I'd doubled the stock

of fairy figurines and fairy equipment and accessories we carried at Open Your Imagination. Customers had been thrilled.

"If she morphed into the tigress that she is," Didi said, "she would eat me for breakfast, lunch, and dinner." Didi could be quite dramatic. When not working out or playing pickleball, like she obviously had today, judging by her outfit of spandex shorts and tank top, she dressed as dramatically as she came across, in colorful dresses and lacy shawls. "I need to make something that will calm my nerves," she said loudly.

A few of the customers who were communing near the vines and ficus trees that adorned the patio glanced in Didi's direction. She was oblivious.

"Any fairies about?" she asked.

The scuttlebutt in Carmel-by-the-Sea was that a number of fairies resided at my fairy garden and teashop. In fact, there was only one—Fiona, a fairy-in-training. I'd come to meet her a little over a year ago when I'd quit my job as a landscaper for my father's company and dared to open my own business. I'd lost my ability to see fairies after my mother died twenty years ago. Fiona said it was the leap of faith to start something new that had opened my heart to the unimaginable again.

Fiona should have been a full-fledged fairy by now, with three full sets of adult wings, but she'd messed up in fairy school, so the queen fairy had subjected her to probation. Fiona was working her way to earning her wings. As part of the probation, Fiona was not allowed to socialize with other fairies, although she could attend one-on-one classes with a mentor the queen fairy had assigned to her. Because Fiona was classified as a righteous fairy, which meant she needed to bring resolution to embattled souls, she could earn her way back into the queen fairy's good graces by helping a human. Only last year did I learn that there were classifications of fairies in addition to varieties of fairy types. Classifications included intuitive, guardian, nurturer, and righteous. Types were what most people understood about fairies; there were air fairies, water fairies, and woodland fairies.

"Help, Courtney," Didi wailed. "I need to rid my mind of these negative thoughts."

"Sure thing. Pick a pot first," I suggested.

The size of the planter determined the number of plants and figurines a fairy garden maker would need.

Didi wandered among the many selections the shop offered and stopped beside a hanging pot dressed with moss. "I like this one."

"Terrific. That's one of my favorites," I said. "Next, pick some plants. I like the Pink Splash hypoestes and baby tears, but if you're going to hang that in hot sun, you might want to consider succulents."

"What's that you're planting?" she asked, circling my work in progress.

"This is a bonsai. To be specific, a dwarf jade." It was one of the easiest to grow and recommended for beginners.

"I heard you're making a pot for the Beauty of Art Spectacular," Didi said.

"Yep. This is it."

The Spectacular, an annual fundraiser to raise money for community outreach programs in the arts, took place the first Saturday in September—two days from now. Wanda Brownie, the event chairwoman and mother of my best friend, had commissioned the garden that I was making. Because Wanda desperately wanted to meet a fairy, I'd encouraged her to help me. I'd reminded her that working on a garden might open her spiritual portals, but she'd pooh-poohed me. Her loss.

"It's quite pretty," Didi said.

"Thank you." For the theme, I'd decided to create an antique-style cityscape. As a focal point, I'd planted the twelve-inch bonsai at the rear of the pot and was currently creating a walkway to it using glass mirror chips. How they sparkled. "It's taking a bit—"

Didi was no longer listening. She had moved away and was swaying in a bell-like motion, her beaded salt-and-pepper cornrows swinging as she gathered items: a dancing fairy, a reading fairy, and a miniature pig in a pink tutu. She appeared to be humming. That pleased me. I wanted those who came into my shop to find a sense of peace and wellbeing. Making a fairy garden was an imaginative adventure.

She returned to me. "Okay, now what?"

"You're not very focused," I joked. To date, Didi had made four gardens. Not once had she needed me to hold her hand.

"Tell me about it."

"So, who has you wrapped around the axle?" Once a week, Didi and I played pickleball in a league. She was eons better than I was, but then she had been playing ten years longer than I had and worked out constantly at Sport Zone, the athletic club she'd inherited and managed since her husband passed away.

"Who do you think?" She smirked.

"Lana Lamar."

"Bingo." Didi rolled her eyes. "That woman thinks she is God's gift to mankind. Honestly, she has no sense of anyone else. She's a total narcissist. If only she were happily married like you, maybe she'd settle down."

"Actually, I'm not married."

"You're not? Where did I get that notion?"

"I almost was. Years ago." The day after our co-ed bridal shower, my fiancé announced he never wanted to be married. Ever. He did. He and his wife had three kids, last I knew.

"I'm sorry. My bad. I should have remembered that."

"No worries."

"Well, Lana is married, but not happily. She'll mess it up like every other relationship she's had."

Lana Lamar was an antique and art critic who wrote a column for a number of syndicated newspapers. She'd been married twice prior to marrying Elton, her third husband. They'd lasted fifteen years, so far. Lana believed she was beautiful beyond words. She wasn't. Nor was she objective and fair-minded, as she liked to claim. In truth, she was hypercritical of everything. Nothing cut the mustard. How did I know her so well? Whenever she wasn't working, she was at the athletic club using the StairMaster, which happened to be my machine of choice. Side by side, we would step for an hour. Lana was more than happy to talk about herself. The last time I'd run into her, she'd recited her latest review to me: *Without a doubt, Betsy Brahn's work adds up to a big ego trip. The last time I saw a painting as deluded as Miss Brahn's witless work, I was ten. Seriously, Miss Brahn, have you no one who will say this to you? Stop. Now. Quit painting. Spare us all. Find another career.* The harshness of her words had nearly knocked me off my machine. Lana had found it amusing.

"What did Lana do this time?" I asked, offering a darling set of miniature fairy signs to Didi. One read: *Fairies love to read.*

"Ooh, I adore this." She set it in her basket.

"Lana," I pressed.

"She bought a second home. In Lake Tahoe."

"Okay." I wasn't following why that upset Didi. The more Lana traveled to her second home, the less we would all see of her. Good riddance.

"Uh-uh, not okay. She thinks that because she won't be here as often, she deserves an exemption when it comes to the pickleball championship."

For eight years, Lana had been the reigning champion.

Years ago, she trained for the Olympics as a long distance run-
ner until a bout of mononucleosis benched her. Ever since,
she had striven harder at everything she does. Tennis. Rac-
quetball. Weightlifting.

"What kind of exemption?" I asked.

"You know Sport Zone has rules and regulations about
how many rounds one has to play in order to compete in any
competitive sport."

"Yes." I might have been a newbie, but I understood the
rules. Even though I never wanted to compete, if I were to do
so, I would have to wait an entire year before I'd qualify, and
in any given season, I would need to compete a minimum
amount of six times to maintain my competitive status.

"Well, she doesn't want to comply with the rules. She believes she should be able to compete no matter what. No min-
imums. No qualifications. End of story. 'Once a champion,
always a champion,' " Didi chimed, mimicking Lana's strident
voice. "No strings attached."

"Give me a break."

"I know, right? Did you know the name *Lana* means
child? That about sums it up." Didi picked up a ten-inch-tall
Schleich Griffin knight. He was clad in white-and-blue robes
and holding an ice bolt and awesome spear. "I love this guy."

"He's pretty incredible but too big in scale for what you're
planning."

"I could just buy him and put him on my bookshelf,
couldn't I? Next to my voodoo doll."

"Let me guess. The voodoo doll is for Lana?"

She let rip with a rollicking laugh. "I made it on my trip to
New Orleans. We went to a graveyard . . ."

As Didi reminisced, Fiona flew to me. "*Psst*. Courtney."
She hovered nearby, her green wings working hard, blue hair
shimmering, her silver tutu and silver shoes sparkling in the
sunlight that filtered through the overhead skylight. She whis-

pered, "Didi is really negative. She needs something to lighten her up."

Didi stopped talking and tilted her head. She was glancing in Fiona's direction, but I was certain she couldn't see her. Negativity made it difficult for anyone without innate ability to perceive other beings.

"So what are you going to do about Lana?" I asked Didi.

"Block her at every turn, which means she'll lash out."

"She wouldn't hit you—"

"There's no telling what she might do. I've seen her attack other women. It's not pretty. Don't worry. I'm prepared. I've got my weapons."

"The voodoo doll?"

"And other tools of the trade."

That sounded ominous.

"The pen is mightier than the sword." Didi raised a finger in the air to make her point.

"Oh, I see. A poem."

"A dastardly poem to strike fear in the hearts of enraged souls." In addition to running the athletic club, Didi did live readings of her poetry at Harrison Memorial Library.

"Will you read it aloud?"

"Perhaps I might." Didi cackled. "Plus I have a few more tricks up my sleeve." She kissed my cheek and hustled into the main showroom to buy her purchases. "Thanks for the help."

I wasn't sure I'd given her much. On the other hand, sometimes a receptive ear was all anyone needed to erase negativity.

Fiona plopped onto my shoulder and fluffed her first set of adult wings, which she'd acquired after helping me solve a crime. She was quite proud of them. They were striated with filaments of blue and green. "Didi needs a potion or a spell to cleanse her spirit."

"Can you do that?"

"My mentor is teaching me how."

"I mean, are you allowed to?"

"I'm allowed to practice." She mumbled a phrase that sounded like, "*By dee prood macaw.*"

I'd heard her utter words in her native language before, but I could never determine what she was saying. Back in college, I'd read *The Canterbury Tales* in Old English, which our professor said sounded like Erse and Gaelic. Fiona's language reminded me of that class. I'd figured out a few terms she used, like *ta* meaning thanks, *littlies* meaning *babies,* and *furries* meaning all small creatures like dogs and cats, but the rest sounded like gobbledygook.

"Courtney!" Meaghan Brownie, my best friend, beckoned me from just inside the French doors leading to the main showroom. "I'm so glad you're here." Her curly brown tresses bounced the more she waved. She, like Didi, loved wearing Bohemian-style clothing. Her white crocheted dress draped her lithe form nicely.

I joined her. "What's up?"

"My mother needs two fairy gardens, not one."

"Two?"

Meaghan and I had met in our sophomore year in college. When she visited me one summer in Carmel, she fell in love with the place, gave up her pursuit of becoming a professor, and decided to move here and devote herself to art and beauty. After Meaghan graduated, her mother, Wanda, moved to Carmel, too, and was now one of the premier artists' representatives.

"Can you make another fairy garden in time?" Meaghan asked as she toyed with the sleeve of her dress.

"Sure I can. No problem. Does she have a theme in mind?" I asked. "She wanted the first to be relevant to antiques, so I decided time should be the theme."

"*Time.* She'll love that. And how apropos for her."

In addition to managing the Beauty of Art Spectacular and

representing artists, Wanda brokered antique deals, played a mean game of pickleball, and was president of the women's association at Sport Zone. To help Didi Dubois, Wanda even offered assistance at the Zone. She always went a mile a minute. Meaghan worried that her mother's chakras were out of whack because she never slowed down. Wanda didn't give a hoot about chakras. After she kicked her abusive husband out of her life—Meaghan had been five at the time—Wanda had been determined to prove she didn't need him. She would live life to the fullest.

"Let me see what you've done so far," Meaghan said.

"It's about time gone by."

"Dinosaurs?"

"No, silly, dragons." I led her to the project. "I found a miniature castle called the Dragon's Keep."

"It's so big."

"Not every fairy garden has to be made with teensy fairies," I said. "This one is over-sized. I started with this ornate purple warrior dragon with a tooled letter opener as its sword." I lifted him from the setting. "Hold him."

"*Oof.* He's heavy. And ominous."

I replaced the dragon and said, "To combat him, I've added Eyela." She was a radiant Schleich fairy dressed in a turquoise gown and sitting atop a white unicorn.

"Awesome. I love the sign."

I'd set the stone-carved sign: *Warning: Dragon training site this way* prominently in the front of the design and had created a primordial ooze behind and around the castle using a glue gun, a plastic bag, and lots of pebbles. In addition, I'd added a fiddlehead fairy—not the prettiest of fairies, closer in likeness to a gnome with huge pointed ears and hooked nose—at the top of the keep. Who would mess with him?

"To contrast the first garden, why don't you make the second pot's theme beauty?" Meaghan said.

"Beauty it is. Pick out the fairies I'll need."

"Me? Shouldn't Mom have a say?"

"She gave me carte blanche."

Over the past few years, Wanda had become like a second mother to me.

"This will be fun," my pal said as she browsed the figurines.

Meaghan was the reason I'd risked investing in Open Your Imagination. She'd known how unfulfilled I was when I'd worked as a landscaper.

"Select a few accessories, too," I added, "like some twinkling lights and a lantern or two."

"Is she here?" Meaghan peered past me into the patio. Though she'd chanced upon Fiona a while back—she had felt her presence and seen a glimmering—she had yet to have a face-to-face with her. Up until then, Meaghan hadn't believed in fairies. The near encounter had changed her mind. How she wished Fiona would land on her shoulder and reveal every last wing of herself.

"She's by the fountain." I wiggled my fingers. "Playing with Pixie."

My creamy white Ragdoll cat was on her hind legs batting the air, the flame markings over her eyes squinting with focus.

Meaghan squinted like the cat and shook her head. No luck.

"I'll be right back," I said. "I've got to check on Joss. She looks swamped."

From the patio, I could see everything that went on in the main showroom. The French doors and beveled casement windows of the L-shaped space provided a full view. My assistant, Joss Timberlake, who was in charge of all financial dealings for the store as well as making sure we had enough change on a daily basis for cash transactions and guaranteeing that monies were deposited in the bank account, was a whiz when it came to dealing with customers. At least four of our regulars were waiting in line at the register and yet none appeared to be put out.

I moved into the shop and felt the lovely breeze floating through the open portion of the Dutch door. Carmel-by-the-Sea was blessed with Mediterranean-style temperatures. The Cape Cod feel of the Cypress and Ivy Courtyard, of which we were a part, had set the standard for the interior décor: white display tables, white shelving, and a stylish splash of blue and slate gray for color.

"Hey, Joss, need help?" I said, towering over her the way Meaghan towered over me.

"I'm good to go." She finished wrapping a set of fairy-themed wind chimes in silver tissue paper and then packed up a teapot and a pair of matching cups and saucers and placed everything in one of our white tote bags.

From the outset, we'd stocked the shop with an assortment of tea sets, garden knickknacks, wind chimes, and bells—fairies, Fiona informed me, loved anything that made an angelic sound. We also carried miniature plants, pots, toolsets, and aprons.

After Joss handed the tote bag to a customer and thanked her for her patronage, I said, "We've dressed alike again."

Joss was twenty years older than me, but we had similar taste in clothes. I didn't think either of us needed to dress *up* for work. We were gardeners. Today, we were each wearing a T-shirt with overalls. Hers was green; mine was red. I loved how powerful I felt whenever I wore the color. "You look elfin," I said.

Joss swept her pixie-style bangs to the right and rubbed her pointy ear. "What can I say? I'm partial to green. I'm surprised you're not, Miss Kelly, seeing as you're the one with Irish blood."

"My skin tone doesn't go with green."

"Good morning," a lean man in a serge suit—our book

rep—called as he entered rolling a dolly filled with boxes. A month ago, Joss had suggested that we start selling books about fairies, both children's literature as well as adult literature. We displayed them on a swivel stand by the Dutch door. I'd fallen in love with *The O'Brien Book of Irish Fairy Tales and Legends* and *Jamie O'Rourke and the Big Potato,* a beautifully illustrated Tomie DePaola folktale.

"I'll handle him," Joss said and hitched her chin. "I think those ladies could use some of your expert advice. Why don't you cozy up to them?"

Across the shop, by the antique white oak hutch that held a host of cups and saucers, stood a gaggle of ladies. As I drew near, I realized they were admiring a teacup fairy garden I'd set out last night. Although fairy gardens came in all sizes, from large pots to Radio Flyer wagons to four-, six-, and eight-inch pots that were perfect for a tight corner, teacup fairy gardens were the ideal fit for someone who didn't have much space or a green thumb. I had adorned the pink-themed cup they were admiring with a moss base, silk plants, and a crouching pink-and-purple fairy inspecting a snail.

"This is so cute, Courtney," one of the women said. "Promise me that you'll have a class so we can make one of our own."

"I do. Often. Pick up a schedule sheet at the register and check out the dates I've set for workshops for the remainder of the year. Don't miss the holiday one. We'll be making—"

Crash! Outside the shop, pottery hit the ground. Followed by raucous shouting.

Connect with Us

Visit us online at
KensingtonBooks.com
to read more from your favorite authors, see books
by series, view reading group guides, and more.

Join us on social media

for sneak peeks, chances to win books and prize packs,
and to share your thoughts with other readers.

facebook.com/kensingtonpublishing
twitter.com/kensingtonbooks

Tell us what you think!

To share your thoughts, submit a review,
or sign up for our eNewsletters, please visit:
KensingtonBooks.com/TellUs.